BOOKS BY

Carrie Carr

====================

Destiny's Bridge

Faith's Crossing

Hope's Path

Love's Journey

Strength of the Heart

The Way Things Should Be

To Hold Forever

Trust Our Tomorrows

Something to Be Thankful For

Diving Into the Turn

Piperton

Heart's Resolve

Carrie Carr

Yellow Rose Books
by Regal Crest

Nederland, Texas

ISBN 978-1-61929-051-8

First Printing 2012

9 8 7 6 5 4 3 2 1

Cover design by Donna Pawlowski

Published by:

Regal Crest Enterprises, LLC
3520 Avenue H
Nederland, Texas 77627

Find us on the World Wide Web at
http://www.regalcrest.biz

Printed in the United States of America

Acknowledgements:

I have to thank my fantastic beta reader, Kelly, who helped make this book much better than I could ever have expected. To my editor, Mary—thanks for putting up with me. You're awesome! Thank you to the cover artist extraordinaire, Donna, and last, but not least, Cathy, who has given me a chance to enjoy the little voices :-)

Dedication

To my mom, whose strength has always amazed me. And of course, most of all, to my Jan—you hold my heart. Forever and always, my love.

Chapter One

DARK AND SMOKY, the women's bar was doing a good business for a Sunday evening. At a small table in the corner, the heavy beat of the bass rumbled while a petite redhead watched the women on the dance floor. Delaney Kavanagh raised a sweating glass from the table and downed half of the rum and coke. Surrounded by shadows, she embraced the solitude until a slender body dropped into the chair beside her.

"Why are you here in the corner?" The butch woman had short, dark hair, with a cigarette dangling from her lips. She scooted her chair closer to Delaney. "Well?"

Delaney sighed and ran a hand through her hair. "I was just trying to enjoy a quiet drink, Chris. Is there a law against that?"

"When I called you today, you said you were too tired to come over." Chris' dark eyes narrowed. "You don't look tired to me." She took a long drag from the cigarette and casually blew the smoke toward Delaney, who coughed and fanned her hand in front of her face.

"I've asked you not to do that," the redhead growled.

Chris waved a server over. "Bring me another draft, will you? And whatever my girlfriend is having, too." Once the woman was out of range, the smile dropped from her face. "That second-hand smoke bullshit is getting old, Laney. You've been bitching at me over every little thing for months. What's the matter with you?"

Delaney stared at the woman she had been dating for a year. Christie Fannin had charmed her at one time, her butch swagger too much for the redhead to ignore. But what had started out as sweet attentions had changed to smothering once they'd slept together, and Delaney was beginning to have second thoughts about their relationship. "Maybe it's time for a change," Delaney muttered.

"You want something different to drink?" Chris questioned. "Damn it, Laney. I already ordered. If you want another drink, you'll have to pay for it yourself." Not seeing an ashtray on the table, she ground her cigarette out on the floor. "Unlike you, I'm not made of money. I still can't find a decent job around here."

"Have you even tried?"

"Of course I have! But no one's hiring right now." Chris dug a crumpled pack of cigarettes out of the breast pocket of her dark golf shirt. She bit down on the filter and flicked her lighter. "Get off my back. What about y'all? Do you need any extra workers? I'm sure I could figure out how to drive a dump truck, or something."

It was an old argument, one that Delaney had fended off before. "Chris, you'd need a special operator's license to drive our equipment.

Besides, shouldn't you be trying to get a job in a restaurant? Surely someone needs a line cook."

Chris stood quickly, which knocked her chair against the wall. "Fuck it! I'm tired of being in a hot kitchen. I want to do something different." She slapped her hands on the table. "I'm going home. Come by later if you're not too *tired*," she sneered.

The server returned with their drinks. "Excuse me."

"She'll pay," Chris snapped, grabbing her beer so quickly that the tray almost capsized. "Thanks." She drank half the glass before walking away into the crowd.

Delaney watched her girlfriend shove a few women out of her way as she left the club. She placed a twenty dollar bill on the server's tray. "I'm sorry about that. Could you bring me another rum and coke? I think I'll give her a chance to cool down." She sipped her drink, in no hurry to leave.

AS GIBSON PROCTOR stood on the bank of the lake, the warm sunrise striped her features. With her eyes closed, she took a deep breath and let the peace of the moment seep into her bones. Her head was bare and the light wind ruffled her short, blonde hair. She loved this time of day and was thankful the cabin she leased allowed her to be so close to her work. As a Park Police Officer with the Texas Parks & Wildlife Department, she felt lucky to be doing something she enjoyed. It had been four months since she'd transferred back to the area she had grown up in, and she had easily slipped into a daily routine.

The three-room cabin was on the less populated side of Lake Benton. It was accessible by either a long, winding dirt track or the narrow road that crossed the dam. There weren't many cabins on the lake, and those that were there were mostly owned and leased by the state to use for camping. The lake was surrounded by several small farming towns, where Gib had rushed to move away from when she graduated from high school. Over twenty years later, she returned, her reasons known only to her.

The solitude was interrupted by Gib's cell phone ringing. She grimaced and took the phone off her belt. "Proctor."

"Gibson, honey, do you have to answer your phone like that?" an older woman's voice chastised. Gib sighed and closed her eyes. "What can I do for you, Mom?"

"Well, I don't want to be a bother. Maybe I should call you later." Ida Proctor was well-versed in playing the martyr in order to get her way. She had nursed her daughter's guilt the moment Gib returned, and seemed determined to keep her under her thumb. She and the rest of Gib's family lived in Benton, a twenty minute drive north of the lake, with a population of almost seventy thousand—which was the biggest reason Gib leased a cabin at the lake. She loved her mother, but could only take so much of Ida and her histrionics at a time.

"Mom, I have to go into work soon. Just tell me what you need, please." Gib gave one final, wistful look at the sunrise before she turned to go into her cabin.

Ida took a deep breath. "I wanted to see if you're coming over for dinner this Sunday. Your father is planning on smoking a brisket, and you know he always buys too much for the two of us." She continued to bemoan the shortcomings of her husband, Eric, who could never do anything right in her opinion. The refrain was one Gib had heard all her life. Her father had no problem ignoring his wife's incessant nagging. Eric would open a beer and let her words float over him.

Gib buckled her duty belt and took a quick glance around the cabin to make sure she hadn't forgotten anything. Dark green slacks and a khaki shirt completed her uniform, which had a slimming effect on her stocky frame. She took her keys off the kitchen counter, detached her Bluetooth earpiece from the charger and stepped onto the covered porch. As her mother continued to complain, Gib switched to the Bluetooth and returned her phone to its holster. Once the door was locked, she got into her navy blue, four-door, Ford F-150 and started the engine. Due to budget cuts, they were allowed to drive their own vehicles, if they so chose. She removed the baseball cap with its Texas Parks & Wildlife emblem from its resting place on the dash and set it on her head.

"Have you heard anything that I've said?"

"Yes, Mom, I'm listening." Not wanting to take the long way around, Gib took the road across the dam, frowning at how rough it had become. She noticed a few places along the edge where the road had eroded away completely, and decided to remind her boss about its deterioration.

The park's office was across the two-lane highway from the lake. Gib parked in her usual space next to the new, white Ford truck her boss drove. Her older truck paled in comparison, but Gib didn't mind. She often teased him for polishing his vehicle on a daily basis, something her truck hadn't seen in years. "Mom, it's only Monday. I'll call you back later, all right?"

"I suppose. It's not like I have much choice, do I?"

"Love you, Mom." Gib disconnected the call and stepped into the one-story building that housed their offices as well as tourist information. Kind at heart, Gib knew she had to be sharp with her mother, or Ida would keep her on the phone all morning. The heavy responsibility of being the oldest child settled over her like a cloud, and her naturally sunny disposition was sorely tested by her mother's whining. Her peaceful mood was gone, replaced by the beginning of the headache that Ida tended to give her. She hung her cap on the coat tree in her office before going to the adjoining office.

Park Manager Clint Wright looked up when Gib tapped on his open door. "Come on in, Gib. You're early today." His round face and bald head were both already shiny with perspiration, despite it being seven forty-five in the morning.

"Only by fifteen minutes," Gib answered, looking at her watch. "Don't worry. I'm not trying to sneak in any overtime."

He laughed and leaned back in his chair. "I know. You never sign for over forty hours, even when you're out and about from dawn 'til dusk. Have a seat."

Gib settled into the guest chair and adjusted her duty belt. "The road across the dam is getting worse. I noticed a few places where the erosion is starting to compromise the integrity of the road."

"Yeah, I noticed it last week. Luckily, it won't be a problem for long." Clint leaned forward, propped his elbows on the desk and steepled his fingers together. "That's what I wanted to talk to you about. There's a construction company arriving sometime this morning. They'll be working on the road across the dam for the summer."

"The entire summer? Why are we just now hearing about this?"

He shrugged his shoulders. "Yes. I know it's not the best timing, but we're going to have to make due. And you know how the system works. Everything's on a need to know basis, and I guess we didn't need to know until right before they showed up. Hell, I only found out about it last night. I'd like you to be the liaison between them and our office."

Gib didn't like where this was heading. "Liaison?"

"That's right. I need someone out there I can trust, who will keep them in line and not allow them to ruin the summer for our guests. I know it's not really part of your duties, but since they'll be working on the dam, someone will need to keep an eye on the effect it has on the nearby wildlife. And the fire roads."

"Clint, with all due respect, is that really necessary?"

He sat up straight. "Yes, it is. Gib, I don't want them destroying anything they don't have to." He tapped on the desk. "Especially the fence across the road from the dam."

She nodded. "The buffalo and longhorns," Gib added. "One of the buffalo cows is due to give birth in the next few weeks."

"Another good reason to have you nearby. I know you think this amounts to a babysitting duty, but I think you're the best person for the job. I don't want any visitors getting in their way, either." They had two full-time rangers, as well as one part-time. But all were much younger, and not nearly as familiar with the lake and surrounding area as Gib. Her lifetime of growing up in the area gave her the most experience. "You don't have to spend every minute of every day with the crew. Just keep a close eye on them."

Gib gritted her teeth and stood. "Yes, sir. Is there anything else?"

"Be sure and give your phone number to the construction foreman, so they'll be able to reach you in case of emergency." He stood as well.

"Look at the bright side. While you're handling this for me, I'll make George do all your paperwork."

For the first time, Gib smiled. "All right. Tell him if he messes up the desk, I'll toss him into the lake." She tapped her forehead with her finger in a half salute. "Guess I'd better get out there before they do."

"Good luck," Clint called after her.

GIB CHECKED HER watch before she turned onto the dirt road not far from the lake entrance. The road ran along the east side of the lake. It bisected the lake property and the pastures where the small herd of longhorn cattle and bison grazed. Gib wanted to check the fire road and make certain the fence around the cattle was intact before the construction crew showed up.

The road curved around to the right with aged barbed wire fence on either side. Gib kept a close eye on the right-hand fence. She hoped to catch a glimpse of the pregnant buffalo cow, if only to ease her mind. Once she passed the empty holding pens, she slowed her truck. The fence appeared fine, which was one less thing to worry about. They never knew when one of the buffalo or longhorn would stubbornly break through, especially during the spring months. She was about to turn around when she saw a paper bag near the fence and stopped to investigate.

The bag appeared to be full, so Gib cautiously nudged it with her toe. It tipped over and several empty beer cans tumbled out. "Stupid kids," she grumbled. When she bent to pick up the bag, sunlight reflected off of something about twenty yards inside the fence. "Great." The nearest gate was at the holding pens. Time was short, so after getting a heavy garbage bag from her truck, she carefully slipped her body between two strands of wire, taking care to keep from snagging her uniform on the barbs.

As she got closer to the area where she had spotted the reflection, Gib saw a pile of beer cans around a hastily dug fire pit. "Looks like we're going to have to patrol this road at night." The warmer weather always brought out high school students looking for a place to congregate where they could drink and not get caught. Gib often spent the late evening hours writing tickets and calling parents. She picked up the cans and the scattered remains of cigarette butts. With the toe of her boot, she scuffed through the charred mess left behind.

The sound of heavy traffic on the road caused Gib to turn and look toward the main road. A heavy plume of dust announced the arrival of the construction company. She made one last sweep of the area and headed for her truck.

Ten minutes later, she was in the midst of several tractor trailers, parked on either side of the road. Four white pickup trucks mingled among the big rigs, and a handful of men climbed out and started milling around. The amount of construction vehicles caused Gib to curse under her breath.

Three flatbed trucks were offloading oversized equipment, while a pair of men began to cut down the fence that kept people away from the spillway.

"Damn it!" Gib parked a few feet from the men and jumped out of her truck before the dust settled. "Hey! What do you think you're doing?" she yelled.

One of the men raised his head, decided she wasn't a threat and went back to work.

Gib looked around and noticed a man wearing a white straw western hat. He had a roll of papers opened up on the hood of the truck, and was talking to two other men, both wearing hardhats. Gib walked over to them. "Excuse me, who's in charge here?"

The man in the western hat looked up into the officer's angry brown eyes. He was a couple of inches shorter than Gib's five feet, nine inches. "I am. At least right now. What can I do for you?"

"Why are you tearing down the fence?"

His green eyes twinkled. "Because it's impossible to work on the project with it in the way." He held out his hand. "Dylan Kavanagh. I'm the foreman for Kavanagh Construction."

Gib took his hand. "Gibson Proctor. I'm going to be your liaison this summer."

Dylan laughed. "Who did you piss off?"

"No one. It's my job to make sure everything goes as smoothly as possible. And to protect the wildlife and the people who will be coming to the lake." She pointed to the fence across the road. "Be careful around that fence. We have several head of longhorns and buffalo, and they're not pets."

"Gotcha. Say, is this road used for anything?"

Gib cocked her head. "What do you mean? It's a road. We drive up and down it."

"We need someplace to park our rigs. Is it used much?"

She shook her head. "No. Only by us. And the occasional kids, trying to find a place to make out. But we do our best to keep them out." She finally smiled. "While we patrol as often as possible, I'd suggest you don't leave anything out or unlocked." She handed him a card. "Keep this handy in case you need me."

"Thanks." Dylan took his wallet out of his back pocket and handed Gib one of his business cards. "My cell number is on there, in case you need *me*." He winked at her.

Gib laughed at his expression. "Sorry, buddy. You're not my type." But she took his card and tucked it into her shirt pocket. "Could you try to keep the fence destruction down to a minimum? I don't want people having access to the back of the dam."

"Sure, we'll do our best. We may have to shut down the road on the dam for a month or so, though. Oh, and don't worry. My wife doesn't let me out to play." He laughed at the expression on her face.

"A month? All right." She tugged her cap straight. "I'm going to do a quick check of the roads around here. Call me if you need anything."

He saluted her. "Ten-four, officer."

Gib couldn't help but laugh at his attitude. "Watch out for snakes. The copperheads love that thick brush." The shock on his face was priceless, and Gib returned the salute before heading back to her vehicle. She pulled up to the highway when a black, Lexus SUV turned onto the road, skidding on the loose dirt.

The driver was able to control the skid and gunned the engine. The SUV sprayed dirt and rocks onto Gib's truck as it took off toward the construction site.

"What the hell?" Gib made a U-turn, intent on finding out what kind of person would drive so recklessly.

DYLAN LOOKED UP as a petite redhead climbed out of the black SUV and stepped over to him. He grinned at the dark sunglasses that covered her face. "Rough night?"

"Bite me," the redhead grumbled.

"No thanks," he laughed and made a point to peruse her outfit. Tight, black jeans and a royal blue, long-sleeved silk shirt looked about as comfortable as her three inch heels. "You're not planning on working today dressed like that, are you, Del?"

She lowered the sunglasses and squinted against the bright sunlight. "I haven't been home yet, smartass." She stayed until the bar closed, and then somehow fell asleep in her SUV. She swore to herself not to get that tanked again, especially on a work day. "And as soon as I make sure your crew is doing what I need them to, I'm going to get a shower and take a nap. And quit calling me Del. You know I hate it." The glasses were returned to their previous position as Delaney turned to see a dark blue pickup with the state park's logo on the door. "What did you do?"

"I don't think it's me that's getting that look," Dylan waited until Gib was upon them. "Hi, officer. Miss me all ready?"

Gib nodded toward Dylan in acknowledgment. "Ma'am, you need to watch your speed on these roads," she addressed the redhead.

"Excuse me?" Delaney put her hands on her hips. "What?"

After taking a deep breath, Gib's voice was low and even. "I said you need to use more caution while driving on these roads. It doesn't take much to lose control, ma'am."

"Ma'am?" Delaney parroted. "Did you just call me ma'am?"

"Uh, yes, ma'am. I did." Gib glanced at Dylan, who appeared to be on the verge of losing his composure. "Is there a problem?"

Slightly shorter than her brother, Delaney stepped into Gib's space and looked up at her. "I'll have you know I'm not old enough to be called ma'am." She pointed a finger in Gib's face. "And I'm more than capable behind the wheel without some uptight park ranger telling me how to drive."

"Ma'am, I mean, um." Gib took a step back. "I'm sorry if I offended you, Miss. But, you were driving much too fast for the road, and I'd hate to see you ruin that nice SUV. And I'm not a ranger. I'm a commissioned park peace officer."

"My name's Delaney Kavanagh," Delaney ground out between gritted teeth. "and I'm *not* some bubble-headed little floozy that needs to be condescended to. I'm the architect for this project." She glared into Gib's eyes. "*Officer.*" At the snort from Dylan, she spun to glare at him. "Not one word out of you, Dylan." With a disgusted huff, Delaney headed across the road to speak to the men removing the fence.

Gib waited until the furious woman was out of earshot. "What's her problem?"

Dylan laughed and clapped her on the shoulder. "My sister just turned forty," he whispered. "And she's very touchy about it."

"Your sister?"

"Yeah." He fought off another burst of laughter as Delaney stumbled on the way to her Lexus. "I'd apologize for her temper, but she's pretty much always that way."

Gib shook her head. "Sorry to hear that." She took once last look at the redhead. "I'll check in with you later, Dylan." With a final tug on her cap, she headed for her truck.

"Sure thing. Take care." He noticed how Gib stared after his sister. "Interesting."

Chapter Two

IN THE LOW light of the sports bar, Gib blinked her eyes in an attempt to relieve the irritation from the smoke. She took another sip of her beer and placed the mug on the table. When a slender Hispanic woman set a fresh pitcher down, Gib looked up. "Took you long enough."

The woman poured herself a fresh mug before she sat. "Quit your complaining, Gibsy. Or I won't allow you to pay for the snacks."

"Maddy, you're too kind." Gib filled her mug and glanced around the bar. There were a handful of men scattered around, watching the different sporting events being played on several different televisions in the room. Gib and her friend were the only two women in the bar. "Why do we come here?"

Madina Ramirez's dark eyes squinted in the gloom in an attempt to see what her friend saw. "'Cause this one is the closest to my apartment." She studied her friend in an effort to see what was bothering her. They had graduated together from high school in Bison Ridge, a small town located fifteen minutes to the southeast of Benton. Madina had been surprised when Gib returned to Benton, but had no problem picking up their friendship where they had left off so many years previously. As the manager of her family's Mexican restaurant, Maddy had moved into the city of Benton right after graduation, and envied her friend's chance to leave the area for greener pastures. She still hadn't received the entire story as to why Gib had returned. "What's up? You seem out of sorts tonight."

"I don't know," Gib sighed. She stared into her beer mug, as if it were a crystal ball. "Have you ever heard of Kavanagh Construction?"

"Huh?"

"Forget it."

Maddy touched her friend's arm. "No, wait. What are you talking about?"

Gib shrugged. "I think I'm losing my mind." She took a healthy swig of the beer. "Nothing."

"Oh, no. You're not getting away with that one, my friend. Did you say Kavanagh Construction?"

"Yeah."

"I don't really know them, but I've seen their trucks around town. Why the interest?"

Gib drained her mug. "They're the ones working on the dam."

"And?"

"I was just curious, that's all." In an attempt to ignore her friend, Gib refilled her mug. "Want more?"

Maddy shook her head. "I'm okay, for now." She stared at Gib, until her friend cleared her throat and looked away. "Come on, hon. Out with it."

"I'm such a chickenshit," Gib whispered.

"What? What are you talking about, Gibsy?" Maddy had to lean closer to hear Gib.

"You wanna know why I transferred back here? 'Cause I'm too much of a damned coward to stay and see *her* every day." Gib raised her face and looked into Maddy's eyes. "Does that surprise you?"

Maddy's smile was gentle. "What? That you're gay? Come on, Gibsy. I've known you forever. I mean, we never talked about it, but I knew." She put her hand over Gib's. "It's not something you've just figured out, is it?"

Gib couldn't help but laugh. "Hell, no. I've always known." Her face sobered. "It doesn't bother you?"

"Why should it? This just means that we won't be fighting over the same guys. Not that there's that many to pick from around here." Maddy gestured around the room. "I mean, really. Not one of these guys is under sixty."

"I don't know why I was worried," Gib muttered.

Maddy patted Gib's hand before she picked up her mug. "So, a woman ran you off? What was she, stupid?"

Choking on her drink, Gib sputtered and wiped her mouth before she could speak. "Damn. I should know better than to drink around you. No, she wasn't stupid, and she didn't run me off. Not exactly." With a heavy sigh, she resigned herself to finishing the story. "She was one of the park rangers where I worked. Tall, blonde, and had the most gorgeous green eyes," she murmured.

"What was her name?"

"Gloria." Just saying the name brought a tightness to Gib's chest. "We were together for six years."

Maddy's eyes widened. "That long?"

"Yeah." Gib was silent for so long, it seemed as if she wasn't going to elaborate. But, after a few minutes, she exhaled heavily. "We had a place in Austin, and commuted together to the park. But she was always worried about how we looked to everyone else, you know?"

"How you looked? Oh, I see." Maddy lowered her voice to keep from being overheard. "She was in the closet?"

Gib shook her head. "No. She always liked to go to the bars and dance, and never seemed to mind telling anyone she was a lesbian." Her face flushed. "I finally had the guts to ask her. She had a problem with me."

"What do you mean?"

"She said I was too," Gib's voice trailed off, making her final words unintelligible.

Maddy leaned even closer. "What?"

"Manly. You know, too butch." Gib was unable to look at Maddy, instead concentrating on the water rings left by her beer mug.

"Oh, for god's sake, Gibsy. You've got to be shitting me." When Gib didn't answer her, Maddy tapped one bright red nail on the table top. "Hey." Once Gib's eyes were looking into hers, Maddy smiled. "So, I'm guessing when you first met this idiot, you were wearing a dress?"

"Huh?"

Maddy continued, as if Gib hadn't said a word. "I bet you were wearing something nice and frilly, with hair down to your waist." She put her index finger on her chin. "And once you snared her, you cut your hair and started to dress like you usually do, right?"

"Have you lost your mind? My hair's always been this short." Gib glared at her. "And I haven't worn a dress since I was six, remember?" When Gib kept destroying the nice dresses her mother made her wear, even Ida had given up on having a dainty daughter. She allowed Gib to wear jeans, if only to save money on replacing her clothes.

"Exactly my point." Maddy laughed at the look she received. "This woman knew who you were when you two hooked up. So it took her six years to decide she wanted a princess? Give me a damned break. She was just screwing with your head, my friend."

The thought had never crossed Gib's mind. She allowed Maddy's words to soak in. "I can't believe I let her get away with that. You know, all those years I let her dictate where we'd go, what we'd do. I always thought it was kind of fun, when she'd play hard to get when we went out. She'd act all shy and demure, not wanting to show any affection in public. I'm such a fool."

"No, you're not. You're a kind-hearted person, who tends to see the best in people. There's nothing wrong with that."

Gib snorted. "Yeah, right. More like a naive idiot." She hit herself in the head. "Geez."

Maddy grabbed Gib's hand before she could hit herself again. "Stop it. Don't let that bitch win, Gib. If you feel that way about yourself, it validates her opinion."

"Yeah, I guess." Instead of refilling her mug, Gib pushed it away. "I'd better stop now, or I won't be able to make it home." Her head was already spinning, and she realized belatedly that she drank the beer on an empty stomach.

"Come home with me," Maddy offered.

Gib raised her head. "You propositioning me, Ms. Ramirez?"

Maddy laughed. "I don't think you could handle me, honey. You know very well that my couch folds out into a bed and you're more than welcome to enjoy my hospitality, again. I'll even cook breakfast."

"I can't pass up an offer like that." Gib stood and tossed a handful of bills onto the table. She had to place her hand on the back of her chair as she swayed. "Good thing you're driving."

"Come on, Gibsy. Let's get you tucked in, so you can keep me awake all night with your snoring." Maddy tucked her arm under Gib's and led her out of the bar.

"I don't snore," Gib argued.

Maddy waved off the offer of help from one of the other patrons as she guided Gib through the front door. "Uh huh. Tell that to my cat, who always hides when you 'don't snore'. Poor Rudy's going to be scarred for life."

"That cat doesn't like me," Gib muttered. She leaned against Maddy's red Beetle. "When are you going to get a grownup's car?" She almost bumped her head when Maddy pushed her into the passenger's seat.

"Shut up, or I'll tie you to the top, like roadkill." Maddy walked around and got into the car. "You're just jealous because my car is at least a decade newer than that old truck you drive."

Gib leaned back and closed her eyes. "My truck's got character," she argued, right before she began to snore.

ON THE OTHER side of town, Delaney Kavanagh pushed herself away from her desk and ran her hands through her hair. Her stomach confirmed that the clock on the wall was correct, and that she had once again worked through dinner. She glanced guiltily at the blinking answering machine before she stood. "Later," she promised.

The drafting table was covered with papers, all in different stages of completion. After being read the riot act from her father, Delaney was glad she had started working at home. He wouldn't know how late she worked, and couldn't harass her about it. There were less interruptions, except for the phone, which she turned off and allowed the machine to get. She stood and stretched, wanting to raid the refrigerator before checking her messages.

There were no lights on in the rest of the apartment, which Delaney navigated by memory. Once in the kitchen, she flipped on the overhead light and opened the refrigerator door. Nothing appealed to her, so she closed the door and leaned against the counter, looking out the window over the sink. The view from her 3nd floor apartment wasn't anything special, but at least the park beyond her complex was better than staring at a parking lot. She grabbed the bag of cheese puffs and walked to the sliding glass door. The small patio was empty, and once again Delaney wished she had remembered to buy something so she could sit and enjoy the night air.

She stopped by the refrigerator once more and took a can of diet ginger ale from inside before heading toward her bedroom. Delaney closed and locked her bedroom door, then changed into an oversized nightshirt. She waited until she was comfortably ensconced under the covers before she turned on the television and started her dinner of cheese puffs and diet soda. The blinking light on her cell phone let her know that she had a message there as well, and with a resigned sigh she checked the log. There were seven calls from the same person, who had also left seven voice messages. Delaney deleted all the messages without bothering to listen to them. She had just placed the phone on her nightstand when it began to vibrate, startling her. "Damn it!" With a growl, she flipped it open and waited.

"Laney? Is that you?"

"Yes, it's me. Who else would be answering my phone?" Delaney snapped, right before she stuffed a cheese puff into her mouth.

"You don't have to be so damned nasty. I was worried about you."

Delaney closed her eyes and silently counted to five. "Chris, I'm sorry if you were worried, but you know I've got several projects going on right now, including the one we started today."

"Well, yeah. But you didn't come over." The whiny voice coming from such a butch woman should have been out of character, but Chris tried her best to make her girlfriend feel guilty. "I miss you," she added, softly.

It took everything Delaney had not to sigh out loud. "Not counting the bar, we had dinner on Thursday."

"Which you left early because you got a call from your father," Chris grumbled.

"I told you, it was business. We were about to start work on the dam at Lake Benton, and he had some questions about the blueprints. Which I explained to you then. And the last twelve times you've brought it up."

"Damn it, Laney. You act like everything else is more important than us. We've been seeing each other for a year. When are you going to let me move in?" She stopped griping long enough to light a cigarette, which could be heard over the line.

"I thought you were going to quit smoking?" Delaney asked.

After exhaling, Chris coughed. "Why bother? We're not living together yet. I can still do what I want."

"You know I don't like the smell of cigarette smoke on you. And you promised to quit months ago. At least that's what you said. And blowing it in my face at the bar was just rude."

"I don't smoke while you're here, do I? And I don't tell you what to do." Chris inhaled deeply. "As long as you're there and I'm here, I'm gonna smoke. I've got nothing better to do."

Delaney leaned back against the antique-gold finished wrought iron headboard. "Did you apply for that job at the burger place on Grant? The one I sent you a text message about?"

"No. I'm not going to even bother trying. Just because they have a sign up doesn't mean they're hiring. What do I know about cooking burgers, anyway?" The whining tone was back in Chris' voice. "I don't know how much longer I'll be able to live here."

Not rising to the bait, Delaney took a drink of her soda. "Didn't you say your parents still had room for you?"

"Yeah, right. I'm almost thirty years old. Should I really resort to living off my parents?"

"Yet you want to live off me?" Delaney asked without thinking. She felt guilty for avoiding Chris for as long as she had. Truth was, she'd much rather be alone. But Chris was safe, and comfortable. And she didn't have to keep going out on blind dates set up by friends and family.

A hurt silence came over the line.

Shit. "Chris, I didn't mean it like that." When there wasn't an answer, Delaney was half-tempted to hang up. Instead, she softened her voice. "Chris, honey, how about I cook you dinner on Friday?"

"Really?"

Hating herself for giving in, Delaney bit her bottom lip. "Uh-huh."

"Can I stay over?"

Damn. Damn. Damn. Why do I fall for this every time? "Let's see how it goes, okay?" Something told her that if she let Chris stay for one night, she might not ever get her to leave. *Time for a compromise.* "How about I come over to your place tomorrow night? We can rent a movie and order one of those pizzas you like so much."

"You'll spend the night?" Chris asked, hopefully.

"Sure. How about it?" Although the thought of spending an evening in Chris' smoke-logged apartment was about as appealing as a root canal, Delaney decided it was in the best interest of their relationship.

"All right. Guess I'll wash the sheets early this month. I'll see you tomorrow night, Laney. Love you."

"Me too," Delaney answered, already trying to figure out a way of getting out of tomorrow night. "Good night."

LOUD, ANNOYING TEJANO music woke Gib. She took her pillow and held it over her head in an effort to mute the sound. Unfortunately, that only made the music louder, as Maddy turned up the volume on the stereo.

"Rise and shine, Gibsy," Maddy sang. "You're going to be late for work." She never listened to Tejano, but knew it would be the best way to pester her houseguest.

"Only if you turn off that noise," Gib moaned. She sat up as the music disappeared. "Why are you torturing me this morning?"

Maddy sat on the edge of the sofa bed. "Because I can," she teased.

From the cool draft on her skin, Gib belatedly realized she was in her bra and underwear. She pulled the sheet up to cover herself. "Where are my clothes?"

"Hanging up in my laundry room." Maddy handed Gib a cup of coffee. "Do you remember last night?"

Gib tucked the sheet under her arms and held the mug as if it held a magic elixir. She leaned over it and inhaled, hoping to gather the caffeine by the steaming vapors. "I remember you driving, but after that, it gets a little hazy."

"So, you don't remember getting sick?"

"No." Gib looked frightened. "Oh, my god. Did I throw up in your car?"

Maddy laughed. "No, thank god. Otherwise, I would have awakened you earlier so you could clean." At her friend's confused look, she gently brushed Gib's hair away from her eyes. "You threw up on my neighbor's car."

Gib groaned and closed her eyes. "Which car?"

"The silver Volvo."

"Shit." Gib blinked and tried to clear her vision. "And my clothes?"

"You pretty much soaked them while you tried to wash the car off with a hose. I had to strip you so you wouldn't get sick."

Gib blushed and stared into her coffee mug. "I'm sorry."

"I'm not." Maddy grinned. "You know, if I wasn't so fond of men, I might switch teams for you, my friend. You've got a nice body, for an old woman."

The blush on Gib's face darkened. She finally worked up the nerve to look up at Maddy. "Who are you calling old? You're four months older than me."

"Yeah, well, I lie about my age. So that makes *you* older." Maddy nudged Gib with her shoulder. "Now run and get dressed, so you can get home and change into a clean uniform. I've still got to take you back to the bar for your truck."

"Oh, yeah." Gib sipped her coffee and placed it on the table beside the sofa. She looked around and then looked at her friend. "I guess I'll get up now."

Maddy leaned back and crossed her arms. "I'm not stopping you."

Gib glared at her. "I'm not getting up and parading around naked in front of you."

"For god's sake, Gibsy, you're not naked. And I saw you last night."

"That was different." Gib pulled the sheet up around herself tighter. "I thought you were going to make me breakfast."

Maddy rolled her eyes. "You're a weird lesbian."

"What?"

"Come on, Gibsy. Most lesbians would love to parade around half naked in a hot woman's apartment." Maddy stood and took Gib's coffee mug. "At least I think I'm hot. Do you?"

"Uh, well—"

Maddy laughed again at Gib's expression. "You are so easy to tease, girl. Now run and get dressed. Your uniform is wrinkled, but it's dry. Hurry up, and I'll buy you a breakfast sandwich on the way to the bar."

"I thought you were going to cook," Gib grumbled, as she climbed out of the sofa bed. She was almost to the utility room when she heard Maddy's answer.

"You'll have to do more than sleep on my couch to get me to cook for you, Chica," Maddy yelled after her.

"Damned tease," Gib yelled back, remembering too late about her hangover. "Ow."

BY MID-AFTERNOON, Gib's hangover had retreated to only a slight headache. The nausea that had plagued her throughout the morning had dissipated, leaving her grumpy and tired. She sipped on the canned cola she had gotten from the office and decided it was time to check in with the construction company.

Gib was pleased to see that the tractor trailers were gone, leaving only the heavy equipment and four white pickup trucks lined along the edge of the fire road. She parked in front of the first truck and got out, looking around for the foreman.

The high grasses that had been at the foot of the dam were gone, crushed flat by the heavy treads of the trucks. Gib could tell that they had taken great care in adding a temporary fence on either side of the construction area. She heard a loud voice and looked in the direction of the dam.

"Officer!" On the road across the dam, Dylan Kavanagh waved to Gib and turned to say something to the person next to him. He cautiously started down the path they had made on the slope.

Gib walked across the road and met Dylan as he hit the bottom of the grade. "Hey there. It already looks different."

"Yeah, we got a good start yesterday. How's everything going for you, officer?"

"Just call me Gib," she offered. "We had a guy patrol a couple of times last night. He said everything looked quiet out here."

Dylan nodded. "Thanks. I couldn't see that anything was bothered. I appreciate y'all keeping an eye out on our stuff."

"We'll do our best, but I can't promise anything. The closer to summer it gets, the busier it'll be. It's hard to keep the kids out of trouble all night, every night. There's too many little roads, and too many places for them to hide. But if you see anything out of the ordinary, just give me a call."

"All right. Do you think I'll need to post a guard?"

Gib shrugged. "It's hard to say. This is my first summer here in years, and all I have to go by is what other folks have said. But I have a place nearby, so I'm never too far away."

He grinned. "Either they pay you real well, Gib, or you're a workaholic, like my sister."

"Yeah, well." Gib appeared embarrassed. "I do what I have to do to keep the park safe." She glanced around, but didn't see the Lexus. "I take it your sister isn't here?"

"No, not right now. She was here bright and early, but after making sure we weren't going to screw up her plans, she went on to another site. Did you need her for something?"

Gib quickly shook her head. "No, not really." She gave him another card. "But pass this along, in case she needs anything from our office. I'll answer the cell twenty-four, seven."

"You will, huh?" Dylan's grin caused her to blush again.

"Uh, yeah. I've got to be going. Call if you need anything." Gib tugged the bill of her cap down and turned for her truck.

DELANEY STOOD IN front of her mirror and stared critically at her reflection. She was wearing jeans and a bra, but couldn't decide on a top. She didn't own many casual blouses, and only bought the jeans at Chris' request to see her in something besides expensive suits and slacks. "I really don't want to do this," she muttered, sorting through her wardrobe for something less dressy.

She had grown tired of the constant battles between her and Chris. They argued over every little thing, and Delaney wasn't sure if her heart was in it anymore. She found a navy blue, button-down, silk blouse and put it on. The thought of spending the night with Chris wasn't completely repulsive, and she struggled with her conscience. She had promised a sleepover, although she knew with Chris' appetite, very little sleep would be involved. "When did it become a chore?" Delaney asked herself. The image in front of her didn't answer, and she turned away to pack an overnight bag.

Half an hour later, Delaney had put off leaving as long as she could. She had folded all her laundry, and knew that if she wasn't at Chris' by six, her phone would start to ring nonstop until she arrived. She picked up her overnight bag and slung the strap over one shoulder, straightening her back as she stepped out of the apartment. Once she was downstairs, the redhead placed her bag in the back of her Lexus, noticing the slight coating of red dust all over the black finish. "I really should take it though the car wash. It won't take that long."

Another twenty minutes later, Delaney was on her way once again. She looked at the clock on the dash, hoping the time was wrong. When her cell phone rang, she grimaced. She was already fifteen minutes late. She decided to ignore the call, not in the mood to start their evening off with a fight.

Delaney parked next to Chris' beat up Celica and looked around the parking lot. The apartment complex was run-down, and she hoped that her car would still be in one piece the next morning. With a resigned air, she gathered her things and started up the two flights of stairs that led to Chris' apartment. Chris' door opened before Delaney made it up the last steps. Her lover stood in the doorway, a frown on her features. "Where have you been?" Chris' jeans were faded, and the gray button down shirt she wore held a pack of cigarettes in the front pocket.

"Nice to see you too," Delaney quipped, as she stood in front of the slender woman. An acrid smell permeated the air. "Just finish a cigarette, *darling*?"

"Don't start," Chris growled, opening the door wider and allowing the redhead to enter. "I was afraid you weren't going to come."

The living room smelled of stale beer and old cigarettes. A ratty, brown couch sat along one wall, and a broken-down entertainment center held a flat-screen television and DVD player. Delaney took her bag off her shoulder and placed it beside the cheap coffee table. "Give me a break. I'm not that late."

"I tried to call, where were you?" Chris slammed the door.

"I'm sorry. I ran my car through the car wash. I guess I didn't hear it ring." Delaney noticed the open pizza box on the sofa, with half the contents missing. There were also several empty beer cans scattered on the coffee table. "You've already eaten?"

Chris sat on the sofa and propped her socked feet on the coffee table. "I was starving. And you wouldn't answer the phone, so I assumed you had changed your mind."

"Pu-leez. You just wanted an excuse to eat without me." Delaney nudged the box and stared at the congealed leftovers. "You know I don't like sausage on my pizza."

"Well, you weren't here to ask, were you?" Chris yelled. She knocked the box onto the floor and stood. "I need a cigarette."

Delaney got up at the same time and gathered her things. "No, what you need is a lesson in manners, Christie Lou." She knew how Chris hated her middle name and used it to antagonize her.

Chris angrily pointed at her. "Don't call me that."

"Why? It's your name, isn't it?" Afraid she'd do or say something she'd regret, Delaney headed for the door. "That's it. I'm out of here."

"Oh, sure. You're too good to spend the night here, anyway," Chris yelled. She followed the redhead to the door. "If you leave, don't bother coming back."

Delaney paused and turned around slowly. "Are you threatening me?" She pulled the door open and gasped in surprise when Chris slammed it shut with one hand. "Don't you dare."

Chris leaned against the door and took the pack of cigarettes out of her pocket. "What's the matter, Laney? Afraid you'll catch something in my place?" She put a cigarette in her mouth and lit it, slowly blowing the smoke toward her girlfriend.

"You are so rude," Delaney yelled, waving her hand in front of her face. "Now let me out of here."

The look on Chris' face was one Delaney had never seen before.

Chris turned the deadbolt lock on the door and stepped closer to Delaney. "You know, we haven't been together in quite a while, Laney."

"I've been busy." Delaney refused to back away, instead holding her ground. She swallowed hard as Chris' hand touched her cheek. The cigarette smell was starting to make her sick to her stomach, and Delaney hoped she wouldn't embarrass herself by throwing up. "I'm going home."

"No, I don't think so." With the cigarette hanging out of her mouth, Chris lowered her hand and undid the top button on Delaney's shirt. "You promised you'd spend the night."

Delaney finally took a step back. "That was before you started acting like a complete asshole." The smell of stale beer on Chris' breath hit her and she frowned. "You're drunk."

"It's your fault for being late," Chris popped open another button, which showed off Delaney's pale blue, lace bra. "Nice."

Her anger finally getting the better of her, Delaney slapped Chris' hand away. "Stop it! I will not stand here and be pawed by a drunken animal!"

Chris held the hand that had been slapped. "You used to like when I undressed you." She stood still as her angry girlfriend stepped around her. "Don't go!"

"I didn't even want to come over tonight," Delaney admitted, as she unlocked the door. "But I came anyway, because I said I would." She re-buttoned her shirt. "Don't call me for a while, Chris. I need some space."

"Space? What the fuck do you think you've had for the last month or so?" Chris yelled, as Delaney started out the door. Her lit cigarette hit the floor, smoldering on the cracked linoleum. "Get back here, you frigid bitch!" She blinked as the door slammed.

Delaney ran down the stairs as quickly as she could, afraid that Chris would follow. Once she was in her car with the doors locked, she finally stopped to breathe. "Holy shit. What was that all about?"

Chapter Three

TWO DAYS LATER, Delaney paused inside the door and waited until her eyes adjusted to the dim light of the women's bar. Little Sisters had only been open a year, but soon found itself filled with not only lesbians, but women who wanted a place to get a drink and not be hounded by men. It took her a moment, but Delaney soon spotted her friends at a table near the bar. She weaved through the small, Thursday night crowd and dropped her purse into a spare chair. "Hi, guys."

"Glad you could make it," a stocky blonde replied. Kate Wilkins was slightly shorter than the redhead and always had a smile on her face. "I'm guessing you don't want to share our pitcher of beer with us, do you?"

The muscular brunette beside her laughed. "I don't ever remember Delaney touching a beer." Terri Reynolds pulled out the chair on the other side of her. "Take a seat, and I'll run get you a wine."

"That's all right. I'm in no hurry." Delaney sat and flipped her hair over her shoulders. "God, what a shitty week."

Kate patted her arm while Terri made a quick retreat to the bar. "Why don't you tell me what spooked you so. You sounded really upset the other night."

"Where do I start?"

"How about the beginning?" Kate gently prompted.

Delaney sighed. "Do you remember me telling you about the problems I've been having with Chris?"

"I really don't know what you see in her, hon. I mean, I know you like them butch, but." She laughed, remembering what brought them together. Ten years prior, Delaney had tried to pick up Terri at the supermarket, only to be told by Terri's diminutive partner that she was off limits. They had shared a laugh, and Kate invited Delaney over for dinner. They'd been friends ever since.

"It's not just that. As long as I have a girlfriend, I'm not being thrown to the wolves. My mother and father are almost as bad as you when it comes to setting me up on blind dates." Delaney smiled at Terri, who placed a glass of white wine in front of her. "Thanks."

"You're welcome." Terri sat and put her arm around Kate once again. "So, what did I miss?"

Kate poked her. "Not much, yet. We're about to find out why our friend here was so freaked out the other night."

Delaney glared at her. "I wasn't freaked out, per se. Just a little concerned."

"Uh-huh. Sure," Kate teased. "Go on, please."

"All right. Anyway, I had promised Chris that I would come over and spend the night at her place. But when I got there, she was drunk and surly." Delaney took a sip of wine to steady her nerves. "I decided to leave, but she slammed the door and locked it."

Terri sat up straight. "What?"

"I know. I told her to let me leave, and she started unbuttoning my shirt. It was like a flashback to Rachel."

Kate covered Delaney's hand with hers. "I still wish we could have put Rachel in jail," she snarled.

Delaney had spent three years with Rachel. Their parents were mutual friends and they all thought their daughters would hit it off. Unfortunately, Rachel was verbally and sometimes physically abusive, and only left Benton after Delaney's father threatened to have her "disappear" at a construction site.

"The police didn't think she was a threat, and pressing charges would have only made it worse. Besides, she left town years ago." Delaney never knew what had transpired, but she was thankful that particular nightmare was over. "I finally snapped out of it and got out of Chris' apartment. But now I'm wondering if I should just break things off with her for good."

"Hell, yeah, you should," Terri asserted. "Or I can take a few friends over to visit her. Maybe she needs lessons on how to treat a lady." Terri was a personal trainer and had plenty of gym-rat friends she could rely on.

Delaney shook her head. "No, Terri. I'll handle it." She ran her finger along the rim of her glass. "I should have broken it off with her a long time ago. It was just easier not to."

"Well, if you need any help, we're here for you," Kate offered. "Moral support," she reminded her partner.

Terri shrugged. "Take all my fun away," she joked. "But seriously, whatever you need, we're here."

"Thank you." Although she wasn't as fun-loving as her friends, Delaney still enjoyed spending time with them. They often tried to get her to cut loose, but she always held part of herself back. She couldn't imagine changing now.

BY FRIDAY MORNING, the construction crew had completely shut down the road that crossed the dam, much to Gib's displeasure. After being thrown around the cab of her truck, she seriously considered talking to Dylan to see if he could loan her a grader to repair her road. Once she was finally to the highway, she decided to see how the construction was coming along.

The dust and noise was unbelievable as she parked near Dylan's truck. Gib got out and put her hands on her hips as she looked around. She noticed a familiar black Lexus nearby and expanded her search to include a certain redhead. She spotted both people at the same time. It appeared as though they were having a heated discussion at the foot of the dam. Delaney was wearing a gray pantsuit, and to Gib's eyes, looked even lovelier than the last time she'd seen her.

Gib considered joining them, but didn't want to end up on the wrong end of Delaney Kavanagh's wrath. She couldn't help but grin at the thought. "That chili-pepper hair is a good warning," she muttered.

As if they'd heard her, both siblings turned and noticed the waiting officer at the same time. Dylan waved, while Delaney stood with one hand shading her eyes. Her mouth moved, but it was impossible to hear her from a distance.

When Dylan started toward her, Gib decided to meet him halfway. They met at the opposite edge of the road, and the foreman had a big grin on his face. "Have you finally come to take me away from all of this, officer?"

Not expecting the comment, Gib burst out laughing. "And what would your wife say about that?"

Delaney joined them. "She'd probably thank you for taking him off her hands," she teased, whacking her brother on the arm. "Good morning, officer. Have you harassed any innocent citizens today?"

"No, but the day's still young," Gib quipped. "Have you been speeding?"

The redhead flushed. "Wouldn't you like to know?" she playfully asked.

"Now that you mention it—" Gib's comment was cut off by Dylan.

"To what do we owe this pleasure, Gib?"

Gib shrugged. "I was on my way to check on the critters, and thought I'd see how things were going over here."

"Critters?" Delaney frowned. "Is 'critter watching' part of your job?"

"No, but we've got a bison cow ready to deliver any time now, and I want to make sure she's okay."

Dylan's laughter surprised them both. "Watch out, Gib. My sister is a sucker for any kind of baby animal. You may have to search her Lexus for contraband once the calf is born."

Gib stood up straight and put her hands on her hips. "Is that true, Miss? Would I have to search you?"

"I don't think that would be necessary, Officer Proctor." Delaney's face grew even redder and she automatically backhanded her brother in the stomach.

"Please, call me Gib." Seeing that the redhead had become uncomfortable, she took a card from her breast pocket. "I gave your brother one, but here's my card, in case you have trouble here at the site." She waited until Delaney accepted the card. "I live on the other side of the lake, so I can be here pretty quickly if something comes up."

Delaney glanced at the card before she slipped it into the pocket of her jacket. "You do? How are you able to get here after we blocked off the dam?"

"I take the long way around." At the pair's confused looks, Gib elaborated. "There's path that goes around the west side of the lake. It's not much of a road, but unless we get a lot of rain, I can make it okay in my truck."

"A path? Why isn't it a road?" Dylan asked.

"No money for it, I imagine. I'm surprised they authorized the repairs to the dam."

Delaney and Dylan exchanged looks, and she nodded. "Are you in any hurry this morning?" Dylan asked the officer.

"Not particularly. Things are pretty slow until next week when the school district lets out for spring break. Why?"

"Would you mind if I looked at your 'path'?" Delaney asked. "I feel bad about us taking away your usual route to your home."

A delighted grin covered Gib's face. "No, not at all. Sure beats me renting a grader." She gestured toward her truck. "Would you like the ten-cent tour now?"

"Sure." Delaney turned to her brother. "I'll be back in a little while."

He waved her away. "Take your time. We've got everything under control."

Delaney nodded and followed Gib to the truck. She was pleasantly surprised when the officer opened the passenger door for her. "Thank you."

"You're welcome. Watch your legs." Gib closed the door and walked around the front of the truck to climb in. She fastened her seatbelt and waited while her passenger did the same. "I appreciate you taking the time to look at the road for me."

"I think I should be the one thanking you. Five more minutes with my brother, and we would have probably started wrestling."

Gib laughed and turned the truck around. "Well, I may have paid to see that." Once they were at the highway, she turned right and headed for the lake entrance. "Do you always get physical in your discussions?"

"Not anymore," Delaney admitted. "But I'm the only girl out of four, so I learned early on how to defend myself." She braced her hand against the dash as they turned off the lake road to an overgrown trail to the west, and the truck tilted dangerously to the left. "Wow."

"Sorry," Gib apologized, downshifting and slowing to a crawl. She fought the steering wheel and grimaced as her head cracked against her window. "Damn."

Delaney held her breath until they finally broke through the worst of the path. She exhaled in relief when the truck parked beside a small cabin. "You weren't kidding, were you?"

"Nope." Gib put the truck in park and took off her cap to rub the knot on the side of her head. "That's why I always took the other road," she admitted ruefully.

"Are you all right?" Delaney asked when she saw Gib's actions.

Gib nodded, embarrassed at being caught. "Yeah. Hard head," she joked. But instead of putting her cap back on, she set it on the dash. "While we're here, would you like to look around?"

"Sure." Delaney reached for the door handle, shocked when Gib hurried around and opened her door for her. "Are you always so chivalrous?" she asked, accepting Gib's hand to help her from the truck.

"Sorry, it's a habit." Although Delaney's hand felt good in hers, Gib released it when the other woman was safely beside her.

Delaney touched Gib's arm. "Don't apologize. I'm not used to it. But I'm not complaining."

"Um, okay." Gib gestured toward the cabin. "Would you like the entire tour?" Although by nature a neat person, she privately worried if the place was fit for company. At Delaney's nod, she put her hand lightly on the redhead's back and escorted her to the covered porch. "I'm afraid it's not much, but the rent's cheap." She unlocked the door and motioned for Delaney to step inside.

At first glance, Delaney had to agree with Gib. The small cabin wasn't much, but what was there looked comfortable and clean. Next to the door was a dark oak side table, where a neat stack of mail lay. A red and yellow striped sofa faced a large picture window on the back wall. There was a matching red chair to one side, and a heavy oak coffee table in front of the sofa that looked right at home. Several bookshelves were on different walls, filled with all genres of books. The kitchen, open to the living room, was clean with off-white appliances. Two stools with red seats sat along the bar, which was the only eating area. There were three doors, and Delaney eyed them curiously.

"Um, that door is the bedroom, the one over there is the bathroom, and that's a coat closet," Gib explained, pointing out the different locations.

"It's lovely," Delaney honestly told her. "Was the furniture here, or—"

Gib jangled her keys nervously. "The appliances were here, but I had to furnish it. I'm not quite through, but honestly, I usually come home and crash. Not much use to adding more stuff if I'm not awake to enjoy it."

"I know what you mean. I usually work until I'm too tired to keep my eyes open, then fall into bed. I'm lucky if I even bother with a nightgown." Delaney blushed when she realized how personal the conversation had become. "Since we're here, do you mind if I wash up?"

"Sure. I think it's presentable," Gib teased. "Holler if you need anything. I'm going to check my fridge and see if I need to go shopping."

A few minutes later, Delaney stepped out of the bathroom and saw

Gib sitting on the sofa. "Thank you. I always hate using the portable johns on sites."

Gib stood as soon as Delaney came into the room. "No problem. There's also a clean restroom at the office, if you'd rather use it. Or, give me a call and you can use mine."

Delaney's genuine smile lit up the room. "You're too sweet. Especially after I went off on you the other day. I'm truly sorry about that."

"Don't worry about it. We all have bad days."

"Well, still, I'm sorry. But, since you've been so nice, I don't think it'll take much to even out your road."

"Really? That would be great. Are you sure it's no trouble?"

Delaney began to walk toward the front door. "Honestly, my brother tends to bring more men than he needs on a job, and they usually stand around waiting for something to do. This should keep them out of trouble for a few days. I'll make certain they know it has to stay passable while they work on it."

"Thank you." Gib followed her out and locked the door behind them. "My boss isn't going to get a bill for this later, is he?" she joked.

"Only if you pull me over and give me a ticket," Delaney countered. "Would you rather I do it myself?"

Gib almost stumbled down the steps. "You?"

Delaney turned and put her hands on her hips. "Don't you think I'm capable of running the equipment?"

Caught flatfooted, Gib took in the redhead's appearance. "Um, well," she stammered. At the glare she received, she tried to backpedal. "To tell you the truth, I do have a hard time picturing you driving one of those things. But not because you're a woman," she added quickly.

"Oh? Then why?"

Gib escorted her to the truck and helped her get seated. Once they were both inside, she answered truthfully. "While I'm sure that you could handle any piece of equipment you wanted to, you look much too refined to be in the cab of one of those things." She turned red. "I'm sorry, I know that sounded sexist."

"Actually, that's one of the nicest things someone's said to me in a long time." Delaney was mesmerized by Gib's strong hands as she turned the truck around and started toward the road. "I noticed that you didn't have a television in your living room."

"No, not much sense in it out here, unless I wanted to get a satellite dish. And I don't watch enough television to care. When I do have some spare time, I'd rather read and listen to music." She tried to avoid the worst of the potholes. "Or be out on the lake."

Delaney braced herself with both hands, one on the dash and the other on the door. "Lake rat, huh?"

"Used to be," Gib admitted. "Don't know how much I'll get to enjoy it, now that I'm working out here. But hopefully I can get in a little fishing." She narrowly avoided banging her head again. "Damn!" Realizing her language, she apologized.

"Please. I've heard, and used, bad language," Delaney laughed. "But I appreciate your consideration."

Gib tried to fight off the blush, but failed. She remained quiet until they were on the highway. "So. Do you spend a lot of time at the sites?"

"More than I should, at least that's what Dyl would say." Delaney turned and gave the other woman a sexy grin. "Are you planning on visiting me?"

"Well, I—"

The loud tones of a cell phone interrupted their conversation. "I knew I should have put this damned thing on silent." Delaney took her phone from her coat pocket and looked at the display while it continued to ring.

"Are you going to answer that?"

Delaney growled and answered her phone. "Yes?" She barely listened. "No! Listen Chris, I told you to quit calling me. Can you comprehend the definition of space?" She disconnected the call and slapped the phone. "God! I can't believe her."

"Problem?" Gib turned onto the fire road and slowed the truck. She was surprised at the amount of venom that came from the redhead. "Is everything okay?"

"Yes, it's fine." Delaney tucked her phone in her pocket. "Thank you for the grand tour. I'll try to get the guys started on your road either today or tomorrow."

Realizing their time had come to an end, Gib nodded. "I appreciate it." She parked close to the Lexus and stepped out, intent on opening Delaney's door. But the redhead was out of the truck before she could walk to the other side.

"I'm sure I'll see you around," Delaney offered awkwardly.

Gib leaned against the hood of the truck. "Yeah. Call if you need anything." She waited until the other woman stepped away from the truck before she climbed in and drove away.

ONCE GIB'S TRUCK was out of sight, Delaney stalked to her Lexus and unlocked it. She was about to put her phone in her purse when her anger got the best of her. She sat in the driver's seat and hit a speed dial on the phone.

Chris answered immediately. "Yeah?"

Delaney gritted her teeth. "Chris, I don't appreciate you calling me while I'm at work. I told you the other night that I would call you when I was ready to talk. Do you remember that conversation?"

"Don't get all pissy with me," Chris snapped. "I only called to see how you were doing, but you bit my head off. Besides, I drove past your place, and your car isn't there. I thought you worked at home."

"Sometimes, yes." Delaney spoke slowly, as if to a child. "Chris, I don't care for the way you've been acting, lately. We've been dating for a while, but—"

"Are you breaking up with me?"

The thought had crossed Delaney's mind, especially after their last argument. "I told you I needed some space to think."

"But, but, I need you, Laney! My landlord just posted another eviction notice on my door this morning. I have to be out in two days." Chris' voice became more panicked. "What am I going to do?"

"I'm sorry, Chris. But my place is barely big enough for me." The last thing Delaney wanted was to drag this out. "I've been thinking a lot about us this week, and—"

"No! Don't do this, please. Give me another chance, babe. Please," Chris whined. "Let me crash at your place for just a few days, until I can come up with something else."

The high-pitched tone grated on the redhead's nerves. "I can't, Chris. I wanted to do this face to face, but you're leaving me no choice." She gentled her voice. "It's not going to work out with us, and you know it. We're too different."

"Damn you, Laney. Is it because I can't find a job? Or maybe because you think you're so much better than me? Is that it?"

"No, that's not it at all. Chris, you know I care for you, but it's just not enough."

"Care for me?" Chris' laughter was harsh. "You never cared for me. All the times I told you I loved you, you never said it back to me. You're a cold bitch, Delaney Kavanagh. Fuck you!"

Delaney pulled her phone away from her ear and looked at it. "She hung up on me?" She thought about calling Chris back, but decided the other woman wasn't worth it. "There goes a year of hell down the drain." She tossed the phone onto her passenger seat, leaned back and closed her eyes. "Damn."

UNSETTLED FROM THE VISIT, Gib decided to try and find the bison cow and see how she was doing. But even though she kept her eyes scanning the pastures and scrub along the road, her thoughts kept going back to Delaney. The redhead was something of an enigma - one moment she was sweet, gentle and refined, and the next, her fiery temper would explode. Gib wondered which Delaney was the real one before laughing at herself. "After her phone call, at least I know she plays on my team. What am I saying? Stay far away from that one. She's trouble with a capital T."

She drove farther around the fire road until she came upon the area where the buffalo liked to graze. There were two bison and one longhorn, lazily munching on the fresh green grass that had recently come up. Gib parked her truck on the edge of the road and watched them.

The longhorn, colored rust and white, was usually not far from the pregnant cow. And since the cow was nowhere to be seen, Gib left her truck to walk around the field. She was unable to see very far, due to the amount of cedar and mesquite trees that littered the landscape, so it was necessary to explore the area on foot.

Once she squeezed through the fence, she made a wide trek around the grazing animals. One of the bison raised its head. Since she wasn't a threat, it went back to its lunch. Gib found a path the animals used and followed it through the brush.

After a fifteen minute hike, Gib had just about given up, when she saw the most beautiful sight. The bison cow, standing guard over an orangey-tan colored calf. Not wanting to spook the animal, Gib stayed silently by a cedar tree and stared for a few minutes. The calf looked strong and healthy, most likely born the previous day. She wished she had her camera, but was content to stand back and enjoy the view.

When the new mother started to snort, Gib slowly backed away from the clearing. Once she was far enough away, she took her cell phone from her belt and called her boss. "Hey, Clint."

"How's the construction going, Gib? I was going to go by and check, but got waylaid by paperwork."

Gib laughed. She knew as well as anyone that Clint would rather spend his day in the air-conditioned office than outdoors. He claimed an old football injury made it hard for him to do much in the way of field work, but few believed him. Why he worked for the Texas Department of Parks and Recreation, she'd never know. "Right. The crew is doing a good job, I guess. Not that I can tell what's going on from the road. But they're not destroying anything, and even took the time to put up a temp fence."

"Good, good. And you haven't shot anyone yet?"

"No. Probably won't, either. They seem like decent people." She paused. "I know something you don't know," she sang.

Clint sighed. "We're not going to play twenty questions again, are we? You know I suck at that."

"Nah, I'll give you a break. We have a new addition at the park."

"Really? I'm assuming you mean the four-legged variety, unless you've got something else to tell me," Clint teased.

Gib crawled through the fence and got into her truck. "That would definitely be news, but no. I saw the new little calf a few minutes ago. Looked like mom and baby were both doing fine."

"Excellent. Do you think they'll be safe? I'd hate for anyone to mess with them."

She started the truck, but only to roll down the windows. "They're pretty well hidden. But I'll patrol this area more often, just to be on the safe side."

"Good idea. Are you going to be around this weekend?"

The question was an unusual one, and it caught Gib off guard. "As far as I know. I'm supposed to have lunch with my folks on Sunday, but nothing else. Why?"

"Bud said he found some tracks this morning. Looks like someone may have parked off the highway and snuck into the lake area after dark last night."

Gib took her lake map off the dash and opened it on the seat beside her. "Where?"

"About a mile west of the gate. He said he wouldn't have even noticed, but he spotted something in the ditch, and went to investigate. Turns out it was part of a deer carcass, and it was fresh."

"Poachers?"

"Yeah, he thinks so. They were pretty careful with how they went in through the fence, so they may come back. Keep your eyes open, okay?"

"Sure will." Suddenly the fire pit she saw the other day took on an entirely new meaning. "Monday I found a fire pit not far from the holding pens. There were cigarettes and beer cans scattered around and I thought it was a bunch of kids. But now I'm not so sure."

Clint's voice sounded tired. "It might have been. Until we find these guys, I'm going to ask for extra patrolling around the park at night. We can work some split shifts, so I won't have to beg the brass to authorize overtime."

It was just the excuse Gib needed to cancel her Sunday meal. She loved her parents, but wasn't in the mood to listen to Ida's real and imaginary problems. "I'll take midnight until noon, starting tonight," she volunteered.

"Gib, I didn't mean," Clint's voice trailed off. He exhaled heavily. "All right. But take midday off and get some rest, please? I'll have the guys contact you for assignments."

"Okay. Guess I'll run home and get a nap. Call me if you need anything."

"Will do. Keep me updated, Gib."

Gib placed her phone on the seat and put the truck in gear. She'd wait until after her nap to call her mother and cancel her visit.

Chapter Four

IT HAD BEEN almost a week since she had seen Gib, even though Delaney had made it a point to be at the job site every day. By Thursday morning, she was completely discouraged. She parked her Lexus in front of Dylan's truck and checked her hair in the rearview mirror. "I'm being ridiculous. She's obviously got better things to do." Mad at herself, she left the SUV and stepped across the road to find her brother.

She passed a front-end loader and noticed several cigarette butts on the ground. "Dylan!"

Dylan came around the vehicle, carrying a rolled up set of plans. "What's up?"

"Who's been breaking the rules?" she asked, pointing to the ground.

He followed her finger and frowned. "No one. At least not from our crew."

"Obviously someone's been smoking, Dyl. Those weren't there yesterday."

Dylan squatted and used a stick to stir the butts around. "I'm telling you, no one on this crew smokes. At least not on the job. Maybe the park cop—"

"Gib doesn't smoke," she cut in.

His eyebrow rose. "And how would you know?"

"I rode in her truck, remember? The ashtray was full of change and there weren't any ashtrays at her cabin, either." Delaney snapped her mouth shut, hoping her brother missed that last part.

"Her cabin?" He stood and dusted off his hands. "Why, you dog! I thought you already had a girlfriend."

Delaney slapped his arm. "Shut up. And for your information, I broke it off with Chris." When her brother was quiet, she glared at him. "What?"

"Nothing." He mimed zipping his mouth shut. When she swatted him again, he covered the spot on his arm. "Bully."

"What are you going to do, tell mom?"

He shouldered past her. "I'm not the tattletale in the family," he tossed over his shoulder.

Delaney thought about chasing him down and making him take it back. If they were anywhere else, she wouldn't have thought twice. But, being at a job site, there was a certain decorum she knew they had to follow. "Paybacks, little brother," she yelled after him. Her mind went back to the mysterious cigarettes. Nothing at the job site had been disturbed, or she would have heard about it from Dylan. "Still, it's always good to take precautions." She took her cell phone from her pocket and hit the most recently added number.

The phone rang six times before a sleepy voice answered, "Proctor."

"Gib? Did I wake you?" Delaney asked. "Are you all right?"

"Hmm?" There was a rustling sound before Gib returned, sounding more awake. "Sorry about that. Delaney?"

"Yes, it's me. I didn't mean to disturb you."

Gib muffled a yawn. "No, that's all right. What's wrong?"

"Now I feel silly for bothering you. You were obviously asleep. You're not sick, are you?"

"What? No. I've been working at night, trying to catch poachers. So far, I haven't been able to find them."

The idea of Gib trying to catch poachers at night worried Delaney. "Isn't that dangerous?"

"It's most likely just some kids, but we're always extremely careful with everything that we do. I'm sorry I haven't been around to check the job site lately. How's it going over there?"

"That's sort of why I called. We found some cigarette butts near one of the loaders, and no one on our crew smokes."

Gib sounded even more alert. "When?"

"I found them a little while ago. They weren't there yesterday, and Dylan assures me it wasn't one of our guys." Delaney started walking toward her Lexus, so she could have some privacy.

More rustling sounds came over the phone as Gib got dressed. "Are you still at the site?"

"Yes. But I don't really think—"

"Would you mind waiting for me? I'll be there in five minutes."

As much as Delaney wanted to see Gib, she hated to disturb the other woman's sleep. "Are you certain? I mean, I'm sure it's probably nothing." She heard the obvious sound of a door slamming. "Gib?"

"Be right there." Gib disconnected the call.

Delaney stood beside her Lexus and waited. A few minutes later, she saw the familiar blue truck heading toward her. She was surprised to see Gib slow down, then realized why. The other woman obviously didn't want to bring a wave of dust from the road toward her. "You've got to be kidding me. Is she for real?"

Gib parked behind Delaney's SUV and got out of her truck. Dressed in jeans and a tan golf shirt with an embroidered badge over her left breast, she still exuded an air of authority. She wore a gun clipped to her belt on her right hip and a pair of scuffed black cowboy boots. "Sorry about hanging up on you, but I don't like to talk on the phone while I'm driving, and I forgot my Bluetooth."

"Uh, sure. No problem." Delaney had thought Gib looked sexy in her uniform, but nothing prepared her for the sight of the other woman in a pair of faded jeans. She tried to swallow, but her mouth was dry.

"Are you all right?" Gib asked.

Delaney nodded. "Butts," she blurted, then immediately turned a bright red. "I mean, I'll show you where we found the cigarette butts."

"Oookay." With a bemused look on her face, Gib followed her across the road.

AFTER INVESTIGATING THE scene and questioning several of the workers, Gib was no closer to an answer than when she arrived. She bagged several of the butts and planned on checking them against the ones she found in the grazing area the previous week. Blowing out a tired breath, she walked to where Delaney and Dylan were having a loud conversation.

"I'm not going to let someone vandalize our equipment," Delaney emphatically stated.

Dylan threw up his hands. "There's no way in hell I'm going to allow you to do that," he countered.

Gib stood nearby and cleared her throat. "Excuse me, I hate to interrupt."

Delaney turned around and smirked. "Don't feel bad, Gib. You just saved my brother from being wrong," she gave him a sweet smile, "again."

"Oh, yeah?" He pointed at Gib. "Why don't you tell her what you're planning on doing?"

Gib cocked her head. "And what's that?"

"Nothing you need to worry about." Delaney hooked her arm in Gib's and led her away. "You look exhausted, officer. Why don't you go home and try to get some rest? I'm sure you'll be up all night again."

"All right." Gib allowed herself to be escorted to her truck. "Promise to call me if you see anything else unusual around here?"

"Of course I will," Delaney guaranteed. She opened the driver's door and gently pushed Gib inside. "Sleep well, Gib."

Gib frowned, feeling she was missing something, but didn't know what it was. "Thanks." She drove away, occasionally glancing in the rear view mirror to see Delaney's wave goodbye.

IT WAS CLOSE to two o'clock in the morning when Gib took her first pass down the fire road. She was coming upon the construction site when she saw a tiny flicker of light coming from one of the track loaders. She turned off her truck lights and parked off the road, taking her flashlight with her.

Gib pulled her gun and began to creep up on the vehicle. She stepped on the rear of the track tread and cautiously peered inside. All she could see was the back of a shadowy figure, holding what appeared to be a cell phone. Gib turned on the flashlight and knocked sharply on the glass door. "Park Police! Let me see your hands!"

A high-pitched scream answered her, and the figure dropped the cell phone.

"Delaney?" Gib moved the beam of light out of Delaney's face. "What the hell are you doing here at this time of night?"

The redhead picked up her cell phone and unlocked the door. "Me? What are you doing, besides trying to give me a damned heart attack?"

Gib holstered her gun and held out her hand. "Let's go talk in my truck." She helped Delaney down and led her by the hand. Once they were inside her vehicle, Gib turned on the interior light. "Is there a reason you're sitting in one of your trucks at," she checked her watch, "two in the morning?"

"I wanted to see who was messing around our site and make sure they weren't there to steal or vandalize our stuff." Delaney turned to face her and crossed her arms over her chest. "You didn't have to scare me to death."

"What if I had been a vandal, or worse, a poacher?" Gib asked. "Just what were you going to do? Ask them to wait while you contacted the authorities?"

Delaney huffed. "Of course not. I was going to hide until they went away, and then call you."

"Have you lost your mind?" Exhausted from lack of sleep, Gib snapped, "That's the stupidest thing I've ever heard. If someone had caught you—"

"How dare you call me stupid! I have as much right as anyone to be here, protecting our equipment." Delaney angrily stuck a finger in Gib's face. "Lord knows we can't depend on you and your little ranger friends to keep things safe."

Gib glared at her. "Get your finger out of my face," she growled.

"What are you going to do about it?" Delaney taunted, wriggling her finger.

Her anger at a boiling point, Gib leaned forward and bit the offending digit gently with her teeth.

Both women froze. Delaney's skin almost matched her hair color as she felt Gib's tongue touch the tip of her finger. She yanked her hand away. "That was extremely childish," she admonished, her voice shaking.

"Yeah?" Gib's voice wasn't much stronger. "So was sticking your finger in my face," she countered. She stared at the other woman for a long moment. "Uh. Yeah." Gib rubbed her face. "Where's your car?"

"Huh?"

"Your vehicle. SUV. Whatever. Where is it?"

Delaney shook her head to clear it. "I, um, parked it in the brush. Why?"

"Because I'm going to take you to it and you're going home."

"Like hell I am! I'll go home when I'm damned good and ready."

Gib opened her door. "You're ready now. Come on." She turned out the overhead light. The moment she closed her door, she heard the snick of the lock. "You've got to be kidding me." She turned around and looked inside the truck, where Delaney gave her a victorious smirk. Gib tapped on the window. "Unlock the truck."

Delaney shook her head.

"Damn it, Delaney, unlock the door!"

Another head shake, punctuated by a larger grin.

Gib held up her metal-cased flashlight. "Unlock it, or I'll break out the damned window."

The grin faltered, but Delaney didn't move.

With a disgruntled sigh, Gib pulled the flashlight back and started to slam it into the window. Before she could make contact, the sound of the door unlocking clicked loudly in the dark. She jerked the door open and ripped the keys out of the ignition. "Speaking of childish."

"Look. You can't possibly be everywhere at once. What if I promise to call you the second I see anything?"

"Delaney—"

The redhead held up her hand. "Okay. How about if we hire a guard? A professional?"

Gib sighed. "I don't like the idea of *anyone* spending the night out here. It's too remote."

"But it's okay for you to be running all over the place at night? Do you realize how ridiculous you sound?"

Rubbing her eyes, Gib shook her head. "It's too damned late to be arguing about this. Can we talk about it later?"

Delaney finally noticed how exhausted the other woman appeared. "All right. But you haven't won."

"Believe me, I know." Gib put the keys in the ignition. "Can I take you to your car?"

"Thank you." Delaney leaned against the seat and watched Gib drive. "How about lunch on Saturday?"

Gib spun her head around. "Excuse me?"

"You know, to discuss the logistics of protecting our equipment."

"Oh." Gib took a moment to consider the proposition. "Yeah, sure. Give me a call Saturday morning and we'll figure out what time, if that's okay with you." She found where Delaney had hidden her Lexus, noting it was a decent hiding place. She parked so the truck lights would illuminate the dark vehicle.

Delaney opened her door before Gib could move. "Don't bother. I think I can get out okay." She tempered her tone with a smile. "I'll call you around eleven on Saturday, so you can get a little sleep first."

"All right, thanks." Gib waited until Delaney was safely inside the Lexus. Once it started, she backed her truck to the road and watched until the SUV had safely navigated to the highway.

THE SUN'S APPEARANCE was still hours away on Saturday morning when Gib's cell phone rang. She was driving along the outside road around the park, and pulled over to answer. "Proctor."

"This is Conroy. What's your twenty?" He was the newest member of their team, a Level I Park Ranger, fresh out of college and full of energy - and himself.

Gib glanced at the clock on the truck's dash. It was a few minutes after five, and Conroy wasn't scheduled to come on until seven. "I'm on the farm to market road south of the park, checking the fence. Why?"

"I think I found something." His voice cracked with excitement. "There's some dried blood on the north shore of the lake."

"What are you doing on the north shore? And how in the hell did you get over there?" Gib used her free hand to search the passenger seat for her Bluetooth. She tucked it over one ear and activated it, waiting for his answer. "Well?"

Conroy muttered something unintelligible.

"Speak up, Dan. I didn't get that." She drove onto the road and drove toward the lake.

"I said, I thought it would be a good idea to take the boat out and scour the shorelines. And I was right," he added defensively.

Although his eagerness was commendable, the idea of taking a boat out onto a totally dark lake was not. "Did Clint authorize your use of the boat?"

"Uh, no. Not exactly."

Gib turned onto the lake road. The only way she'd be able to reach him by vehicle was to take her private road. The construction crew still had a few days of work to complete the project, but it was already much easier to navigate. "What do you mean, not exactly?"

"I told him yesterday that I had an idea on how to check a large area and he said go ahead. He was busy so I didn't get to give him any details."

Once she passed her cabin, she could see his lights near the shore. "Dan, I'm coming up from the west. You should be able to see my headlights soon." She broke through the trees and parked as close as she dared, perhaps twenty yards away. "I'm heading the rest of the way on foot."

"Roger that," he answered.

Gib rolled her eyes and got out of the truck, armed with a handheld, battery-operated spotlight. "Can you see me?"

"That's a roger. I have visual confirmation."

She was going to have to talk to him about his use of radio lingo while using a cell phone. It was wearing on her nerves. Without another word, Gib disconnected the call. She trudged toward the young ranger, who was wet from the thighs down. "What happened to you?"

He turned his own spotlight toward her voice, instantly blinding her. "I didn't want to ground the boat so I walked up to the shore."

"Turn that light off," Gib ordered, shielding her eyes. Once the light was turned away, she had to blink several times to get rid of the bright spots in her vision.

"Sorry, Proctor." He shined the light on the shore. "See? Right there. Lots of blood."

Gib waited for her vision to clear before she stepped forward. It did appear to be dried blood, but she couldn't figure out how he had spotted it from the boat, especially in the dark.

"Should I gather some evidence for analysis?" he asked.

She shook her head. "And where would you send it for analysis? CSI?" She knelt and picked up some of the stained mud between her fingers, bringing it up to her nose. By the smell, it most likely was not left by a poacher. "Did you check it out?"

"No. I didn't want to disturb the evidence," he told her. "Should we tape off the area?"

Gib stood and dusted off her hands. "Are you serious?"

"Just because I'm young, it doesn't mean I can't do good work. You and Clint never give me any credit, and I'm always stuck doing the shit jobs." He stepped closer to her. "For your information, *Officer*, I have a college degree in Wildlife and Fisheries Sciences. Did you even go to college?"

She held up her hand to stop his rant. "Enough. If you would have checked the *evidence*, you would have realized that someone cleaned their catch here. It reeks of fish. And it was probably done sometime early this evening, *before sunset*. Most poachers don't operate in broad daylight."

"Yeah, but—"

"Here." Gib handed him her keys. "Take my truck to the dock and wait for me. I'll bring the boat back."

He snatched the keys out of her hand. "I can do it."

"But you're not going to. The boat is only supposed to be used during the day, and then only by authorized personnel. Or did you not read that part in the manual that Clint gave you?"

Conroy looked as if he wanted to argue, but he kept his mouth shut. He stalked away, grumbling under his breath.

Gib waited until he got to her truck before she looked at the boat, which was at least ten yards from shore. "I'm going to kick his ass for this one." She slowly walked out into the lake, gritting her teeth as the cold water quickly seeped through her jeans.

AFTER LEAVING DAN sulking in the office, Gib drove toward the construction area. As she turned onto the gravel road, her headlights shined on a light-colored Chevy pickup that was parked on the edge of the construction site. She slowed her truck and turned out the lights. When she came to a stop in front of the truck, she shut off the engine.

There didn't seem to be anyone in the cab of the Chevy. So, with her heavy flashlight in one hand and her other hand on the butt of her gun, Gib edged closer to the open bed of the truck.

"Henry," a young woman breathlessly exclaimed.

Gib dropped to one knee and listened. At the sound of heavy grunting, she rolled her eyes. The old truck bounced in rhythm to the grunts. With an evil grin, Gib stood and shined her Maglite into the bed of the truck. "Park Police!"

The bright light caught the teenage lovers off guard. The young woman screamed and, from her seated position, used her arms to cover her breasts.

"What the fuck?" The young man sat up and pushed the girl off of him. "What's going on here?"

"You're trespassing on park property," Gib explained. "How old are you?"

The girl, who had wrapped a blanket around herself, glared at Gib. "None of your fucking business." She picked up a pack of cigarettes and a lighter.

Gib shook her head and held out her hand. "I don't think so. Hand 'em here." She caught the items against her chest when they were thrown. "You two get dressed and climb out of there."

"We're not doing anything wrong," the girl argued.

"Yes, you are. Now get dressed, before I call for backup and have a whole slew of cops out here."

"Bitch," the girl snapped, as she searched for her clothes.

The young man had his hands over his crotch. "Um, ma'am? I've kinda got a little problem."

Gib forced herself to look him in the eye. "Cover up the best you can, son." She looked at the cigarettes in her hand. They were the same brand as the ones she'd found in the pasture, and at the construction site. "Is this where you two usually come to be alone?"

"Don't tell her nothin', Henry."

Henry shook his head. "No, ma'am. This is the first time I've been out here with Taylor."

"Shut up, you idiot!"

He struggled into his shorts. "I swear, officer. I've never done anything like this before."

Taylor slapped his leg. "Idiot. Shut the fuck up!" She stood in the bed of the truck and stepped into a pair of cutoffs. "We're both eighteen, so there's nothing you can do to us."

"Wanna bet?" Gib held out her hand to assist Taylor out of the truck. She grinned as her offer was ignored and Taylor dropped to the ground beside her. "I'm going to need to see some identification."

"Are you fucking kidding me?" Taylor snapped. "This is harassment."

Gib silently stared at her until Taylor gathered her purse from the cab of the truck. She shined her light on the license and laughed. "According to this, you're twenty-two, Taylor. And it's the worst fake ID I've seen."

"It's not fake," Taylor snarled as she snatched the ID away from Gib. "You obviously didn't notice that I'm from New Mexico."

"Uh-huh." With the sun coming up, Gib could see that both kids were nowhere near legal drinking age. Or eighteen, for that matter. "Henry, go sit in the truck for a minute. If you behave, I'll let you off with a warning."

Henry enthusiastically nodded. "Yes, ma'am. Thank you." He rushed to sit in his truck, not bothering to glance at his date.

"Idiot," Taylor grumbled. She crossed her arms over her chest. "Are you going to arrest me?"

"I could. You know as well as I do, that Henry's under age. And, if you're really twenty-two, there's a law against what you two were doing."

Taylor shook her head. "No. No fucking way. You're not pinning me with statutory. We both go to Benton High school," she finally admitted. "I'll be eighteen in a couple of months, and so will he."

"That wasn't so hard, was it?" Gib stepped closer to the young woman. "Now, if you answer my questions truthfully from here on out, maybe we can just chalk this up to being in the wrong place, at the wrong time."

"All right."

"Have you, or any of your friends, used this area to party recently?"

Taylor frowned. "Maybe."

Gib tightened her grip on the flashlight. She felt like shaking the girl to get the answers from her. "How about in a pasture, not far from here?"

"We might have. Why?"

Gib held up the crumpled pack of cigarettes. "Because I've found this brand in several places. Do you know how dangerous it is to toss out a lit cigarette? You could start a brush fire."

"I guess." Taylor shrugged and looked away. "Is that all?"

"No!" Gib tucked her flashlight in her back pocket and crowded the girl against the truck. "Listen to me. Not only is it against the law, it's very dangerous for you kids to be out here late at night. Some of the wild animals we have around here aren't friendly, and neither are the people who illegally hunt."

Taylor's eyes grew wide. "Wild animals?"

"Mountain lions, javalina's, poisonous snakes. Not to mention poachers. It would be easy to hide bodies out here, and no one would ever know what happened to you."

"W...what's a javalina?"

Gib stepped back. "Wild boar. They get as big as a sheep, with large tusks. I've heard they've killed quite a few people down south." Although Gib was exaggerating, she could tell she was finally getting through to Taylor. "They'll tear a person apart and leave them bleeding, so the wolves and wild cats have something to eat."

"Oh, my god." Taylor covered her mouth. "Really?"

"Yeah. And their hides are so tough, a bullet can't penetrate them. So, believe me, it's much safer not to be out here all alone."

Taylor nodded. "Right." She glanced at the cab of the truck. "Can I go?"

"Only if you promise not to be out here again."

"All right." Taylor started to step around the officer. "Can I have my cigarettes back?"

Gib laughed at her. "I don't think so. You might want to consider quitting. You'll live longer."

Taylor snorted. "Yeah, right." She got into the passenger side of the truck and began chewing out Henry.

Gib was unable to hear what was being said, but she couldn't help but laugh as the girl seemed to read the riot act to her date. "That takes care of one mystery, anyway." She checked her watch and sighed. "It's going to be a long day."

AWAKE LONG BEFORE her alarm sounded, Delaney spent the morning cleaning her apartment. She dusted, swept, vacuumed and removed a months' worth of old takeout from her refrigerator. Every time she checked the clock it seemed as if very little time had passed.

She dropped from exhaustion onto her living room sofa. "I've lost my mind. I should have just gone back to sleep this morning." She glanced at the display on the cable box and her eyes grew wide. "Shit." It was ten minutes until eleven, when she was supposed to call Gib. "And here I sit, covered in sweat and god knows what else."

Frantic, Delaney hopped off the couch and ran into her bedroom, stripping as she went.

Ten minutes later she stepped out of the shower. Tiny trails of blood mixed with the water dripping from her legs. The nicks from a dull razor burned along her shins and knees, but she ignored them as she wrapped a lavender body towel around herself. The search through her walk-in closet for something casual, yet classy, left her feeling anxious. Most of her clothes were to impress clients, not to have lunch with, what? "A friend? Something more? Oh, god. What am I doing?" She desperately flipped through her hangers. "I don't even know if she's interested."

She finally decided on a black, linen skirt with a gray, silk blouse. Her legs, now blood-free, were sleekly encased in nude-shaded pantyhose. She carefully applied the minimum amount of makeup, since she had a feeling Gib was the type to appreciate the "less is more" theory. At six minutes after eleven, she took her cell phone into the living room and sat on the sofa.

Gib answered on the second ring. "Hello?"

Delaney grinned at the anxious voice on the other end of the line. "Good morning, officer. I'm sorry I'm late. Were you able to get a nap?"

"Um, not exactly. But I'm looking forward to lunch."

"Are you sure? I don't want you falling asleep at a restaurant. It might be bad for your image," Delaney teased.

Gib laughed. "What image?" She stifled a cough and cleared her throat. "So, Ms. Kavanagh, what time and where?"

Several interesting ideas popped into Delaney's head at the question. "Well." Her smile turned devious. "Just what kind of tastes do you have, officer?"

A choked gasp came from Gib, who tried for several seconds to get herself under control. "My tastes run pretty simple. But I'm game for just about anything," she finally was able to get out.

"Oooh. You are? I'll have to remember that."

Gib laughed so hard she snorted, which immediately caused Delaney to start laughing as well. Embarrassed, Gib offered an apology. "I'm sorry," she chortled, not sounding very contrite. "I must be more tired than I thought."

"Are you up to having lunch? We can always reschedule," Delaney offered, although it was the last thing she wanted to do.

"No, I'm good. Do you want me to pick you up or should we meet somewhere?"

Delaney looked around. Her apartment was clean, and now she had a good reason for it to be. "Would you mind picking me up? We can decide where to go once you get here."

"Sure. Just give me your address, and I'll be there at," Gib paused.

"Is noon too soon?"

"Nope. Noon's perfect."

With a huge smile on her face, Delaney gave Gib her address, and the directions for the easiest route. Once they hung up, she double-checked the living room to make certain everything was in order.

GIB PLACED HER truck beneath the covered parking, two spaces away from Delaney's Lexus. The apartment complex appeared new, with perfectly manicured shrubbery and grass that looked like it had been taken from a golf course. Most of the cars in the lot were expensive, and she suddenly felt completely out of her element.

She took a calming breath and got out of the clean truck. Gib had blackmailed Dan into cleaning the truck, in exchange for her not telling their boss of his unauthorized use of the boat. With a quick glance down at herself, she hoped she was as presentable. "It's not a date, idiot. Calm down." She was wearing her newest jeans, a green golf shirt, and freshly polished boots. "Damn. I feel like a moron." Still nervous, Gib walked into the lobby. The shiny white marble floor was as clean as an operating room, and the small leather chairs looked as if they'd never been used. Tall, expensive live plants gave the room it's only warmth. The apartments were only accessible from the inside, and she nodded to the man sitting behind a nearby black granite desk.

"Good afternoon. May I assist you?" His young and clean-shaven face wore a distant yet polite expression.

"Uh, no. I'm here to see Delaney Kavanagh, in thirty-one-twelve."

He nodded. "She's expecting you. Take the elevator to the third floor, and turn to your right."

"Thanks." Gib followed his instructions, and was soon standing in front of Delaney's apartment. She wiped her sweaty palms on the front of her jeans before lightly knocking.

The door opened immediately, and Delaney greeted her with a friendly smile. "Hello, officer. Please, come in." She stepped aside and allowed Gib to enter.

Once she was inside the apartment, Gib relaxed. As fancy as the outside had been, the interior of Delaney's apartment was comfortable and homey. She especially liked the look of a pea green, worn recliner that sat at an angle to the sofa. "You have a very nice place."

"Thank you." Delaney gestured toward the furniture. "Would you like to sit down?"

"Sure." Gib chose one end of the tan sofa, encouraged by its softness.

Delaney sat at the opposite end and turned to face her guest. "You look nice."

Gib lightly blushed. "Thanks." She took a moment to scrutinize the redhead's appearance. "Wow." At Delaney's delighted grin, Gib's blush deepened. "I said that out loud, didn't I?"

"Yes, you did." Delaney patted Gib's shoulder. "Thank you. Did you have any trouble finding the place?"

"No, not really. Although I'm about half afraid they'll tow my truck," Gib joked.

The redhead laughed. "They wouldn't dare. It has emblems on the doors. They're probably worried that you're here in some official capacity."

Gib joined her in laughing at the absurdity. "Yeah. Poachers and park troublemakers are known to live in places like this."

"You'd be surprised at the clientele here. I know of one convicted felon, two judges, and I believe there's a topless dancer on the second floor."

"Oh, wow. That's awesome." Gib propped her left ankle on her right knee. "So, any ideas on where you want to go for lunch?"

Delaney shrugged her shoulders. "I was thinking, maybe Mexican? I know this fantastic little place, over off Fourteenth."

"Rodrigo's?" Gib's face lit up.

"That's it. Have you been there? I absolutely love their fajitas."

Gib stood. "One of my favorite places. Are you ready?" She held out her hand to Delaney.

"Ready as I'll ever be." Delaney took the offered hand and smiled as Gib helped her to her feet.

GIB HELD THE door of Rodrigo's open for the redhead, who nodded her thanks and passed by her. When they stepped in front of the hostess podium, a tall, slender Hispanic woman greeted them.

"Good afternoon. Welcome to Rodrigo's." Her gaze shifted from Delaney to Gib, and her mouth dropped open. "Gibsy?"

"Hi, Maddy. Have a table for two available?"

Madina Ramirez, granddaughter of the original Rodrigo, grinned at her friend. "I've got a very nice table for VIP's. If you two will follow me." She took them to a booth in the quietest part of the restaurant. Once they were seated, she leaned close to Gib. "You will so have to give the details later." To Delaney, she smiled. "Please, order whatever you'd like. It's on the house."

"You're very kind, but that's not necessary." Delaney looked at Gib. "Right?"

Gib shook her head. "I'm not going to cross either one of you." She gestured to Maddy. "Delaney, I'd like you to meet my oldest and dearest friend, Madina Ramirez. This is her family's restaurant."

Delaney held out her hand. "Very pleased to meet you. I'm Delaney Kavanagh."

"Delighted," Maddy assured her, giving the redhead a firm handshake. "Please call me Maddy. Would you two like to start with some guacamole and chips? Or maybe some queso?"

"I'd like some queso with a glass of iced tea, if you don't mind." Gib grinned at Delaney. "What about you?"

Delaney nodded. "Iced tea is good, but I would give my right arm for some of your guacamole." She lightly blushed. "I can probably eat my weight in that and your chicken fajitas," she admitted ruefully.

Maddy laughed. "Oh, Gibsy. I like her! I'll send someone with your drinks and appetizers, ladies. Enjoy your meal."

Once they were alone, Delaney leaned over the table. "She's very sweet."

"Don't say that too loud. I'll never hear the end of it." Gib nodded at the server who brought them tea and their appetizers. "Thank you."

They ate quietly until another server brought their fajitas. Once they each filled their plates, Delaney took a bite and moaned her approval. "Oh, my god!" She took her time finishing her fajita before taking a sip of tea. "Is Maddy married?"

"No, why?"

"Because I'm going to propose to her." Delaney quickly assembled another fajita.

Gib almost spewed her tea across the table. "I'm afraid you'd be fighting a losing battle."

"Why? Does she have something against Irish redheads?"

"No. Just ovaries. She's as straight as they come."

This time Delaney sputtered, and ended up spitting her tea all over Gib.

They were both laughing hard when Maddy returned. "I swear, Gibsy, you cause trouble every time you come in here."

Gib pointed to Delaney. "It's her fault!"

"You started it," Delaney countered.

"Whatever." Maddy waved her hand. "Listen, I have to take care of a few things in the office, so take your time and have fun." She poked Gib's shoulder. "Call me tomorrow."

"Okay, sure will." Gib stood and gave her friend a hug and kissed her on the cheek. "Thanks, Maddy."

Maddy returned the hug and then shoved Gib away. "Go on, now. You're going to make your new girl jealous."

"She's not—" Gib was stopped when Maddy covered her mouth with one finger.

"Tomorrow," Maddy whispered. She turned to Delaney. "It was nice to meet you, Delaney. Don't let Gibsy get away with anything."

Delaney grinned. "Don't worry, I won't. It was a pleasure to finally meet the person whose children I would gladly have," she joked. "I've been a huge fan of your restaurant for years."

"Then I'm glad I got to meet you." Maddy winked then patted Gib on the cheek. "Have fun." She wriggled her fingers at them as she walked away.

"You know, I like your friend a lot," Delaney told Gib, as the other woman sat across from her again.

Gib dipped a tortilla chip into her queso. "I'm glad. She's been my best friend for as long as I can remember. I spent a lot of years back in that kitchen, stealing bites of whatever I could get away with." She popped the chip into her mouth and happily chewed.

"Lucky you. I've always loved coming here, although I haven't been here in about a year. My girlfriend, make that ex-girlfriend, didn't like Mexican food."

"She doesn't know what she's missing." Gib eyed Delaney across the rim of her tea glass, her meaning clear.

The sentiment touched Delaney deeply, and she covered Gib's hand with hers. "Thank you."

Gib looked into Delaney's eyes. "There is something I'd like you to promise me."

"Yes?"

"No more late nights at the job site."

Delaney's smile faltered. "What?"

"At least not until we catch the poachers. Please?"

As much as she wanted to be angry at Gib, the redhead found herself agreeing, if only because those sincere brown eyes were asking her to. "All right."

Chapter Five

THE KAVANAGH CONSTRUCTION office was housed in an aged, industrial strip center. Surrounded by similar companies, it had been in the same space for close to thirty years. Colin Kavanagh, owner and self-proclaimed, "chief bottle washer," sat in his daughter's guest chair and glanced at his watch. He was supposed to meet with Delaney and discuss how she thought the work on the lake was going. He had already gotten an earful from his son, Dylan, and had a few tough questions for his chief architect.

Delaney's desk phone buzzed, and a voice came over the speaker. "Delaney, are you there?"

"Not yet," Colin answered out loud. He leaned forward and picked up the receiver. "She *is* supposed to be here this morning, isn't she? Or did I get the day wrong again?"

Maureen Kavanagh laughed at her husband's comment. As the office manager for the company, she had to keep everyone organized, especially Colin. "No, honey, you're not wrong. At least not this time. When she gets in, tell her that Chris called."

"I sure will. Did she say what she wanted?"

"No, she didn't. But knowing our daughter, they're probably fighting again."

Colin's snicker was all the agreement he needed to give. The sound of heels clicking on the tile floor announced their wayward child's arrival. "She's coming now. I'll give her the message." He hung up the phone and returned to his original position just as Delaney stepped into her office.

"Hi, Dad. What's up?" Delaney sat behind her desk and tossed her purse into the bottom right hand drawer.

"We had a meeting scheduled for nine," he reminded her. It was now close to ten.

She cocked her head at him. "We did?"

"Yes."

Delaney shrugged. "All right. What's this meeting supposed to be about?"

"The lake project. Don't you read your appointment calendar that your mother set up?"

"Of course I do." She opened the drawer, dug through her purse, and brought out her PDA. A few clicks later, the cocky expression fell from her face. "Oh, damn. I'm sorry, Dad."

He leaned back in his seat and grinned. "No harm done. How do you think the work out at the lake is going so far? Your brother seems to think we'll be finished ahead of schedule."

"I agree, as long as the weather holds out. This week we're putting in some concrete pillars to strengthen the dam. I can't believe it hasn't collapsed before now."

Colin scratched his chin. "I also heard from your brother that we've done some repair work on a road. What's that all about?"

Her face turned a light shade of pink. "The park police officer who's been keeping an eye on things lives on the far side of the lake. When we blocked off the dam, she had to take what looked like an old cattle trail to get from her cabin. I thought since some of our guys weren't busy, they could even it out for her."

"Is she cute?"

"What?"

He laughed at the look on his daughter's face. "I figure there's got to be another reason you're donating our services, besides the goodness in your heart. That's it, isn't it? You've got your eye on her?"

"No!" Delaney vehemently denied. The blush on her face darkened. "I mean, that's not the reason," she added quietly.

"Uh huh. Right. Oh, speaking of your women, your mother wanted me to pass along a message. Chris called for you this morning."

"Damn her." Delaney covered her face with her hands. "I'm sorry, Dad. I was talking about Chris, not Mom."

He nodded. It seemed his daughter fought more with her girlfriend than anything else. "Trouble in paradise?"

"I wouldn't exactly call it paradise. I broke up with her last week, and she hasn't given me a moment's peace."

Colin stretched out his legs and exhaled heavily. "I can't say I'm sad to hear the news."

"Oh? Well, I know you barely seemed to tolerate her when I'd bring her over for family dinners." She ignored the buzz of her cell phone. Even on vibrate, the noise was annoying.

"Aren't you going to get that?"

Delaney shook her head. "No. It's most likely Chris, whining again. She had the nerve to ask if she could move in with me."

"Was that before, or after you broke up?"

"Both. She's been out of work so long that she's being evicted from her apartment. I told her to move back in with her parents, and she got all pissy about it."

He laughed at the expression on her face. "How dare she? Thinking that after what, a year?"

"Don't start, Dad."

"I'm sorry honey, but I can't help it. Normally when people have been together for a while, they want to make their relationship more permanent. I was lucky your mother wanted a nice church wedding, or we would have eloped the first weekend we knew each other."

With her elbow on the desk, Delaney rested her chin on her upraised hand. "Not everyone's lucky enough to find the perfect mate. I honestly don't know what I ever saw in Chris to begin with."

"Well, maybe your luck is changing. Dylan said—"

She sat up and held up one hand. "Dad, please. Dylan is as gossipy as an old woman. Don't believe anything he says."

As much as Colin wanted to hear his daughter's thoughts on the mysterious park officer, he kept silent. There was confusion in Delaney's eyes which he suspected had little to do with her former girlfriend. Instead, he stood and stretched. "I reckon I'll go harass your mother for a while. Drop by her office before you leave, eh?"

"Sure."

IN HER CABIN, Gib adjusted the waterproof shoulder holster and looked at her reflection in the mirror. She was wearing charcoal colored cargo shorts, a tan golf shirt with the embroidered badge over her left breast and ankle-high work boots. She put on a belt that held handcuffs, a waterproof case for her cell phone, baton, pepper spray and her radio.

Since spring break had arrived for the local school district, Gib's main job was to help patrol the lake and surrounding area. As much as she looked forward to being out on the water, she knew it was all business. She would be in the park's twenty-three foot Mastercraft 230 Maristar Sport Ski and Wakeboard boat, while Dan was stuck in the fourteen-foot Angler boat closer to shore. Clint was going to stay in the office and handle the tourist's questions, while George would be the ranger driving around the park and keeping an eye on the campers. Bud had to take an emergency leave of absence due to a death in his family, and it wasn't known when he'd return.

She was on her way out the door when her cell phone rang. She tapped the Bluetooth on her ear. "Proctor."

"Gib, could you stop by the office before you hit the lake?" Clint asked. "I need to give you something."

"Sure thing, Clint. Give me five." She hung up, locked the cabin door and headed for her truck. "I wonder if Delaney will be at the work site today." She hadn't seen the other woman for a week, and wondered if perhaps she had been mistaken in how well they had gotten along. Unsure of herself, Gib shook off the thought and drove down the smooth road that the construction crew had repaired. It was still a narrow dirt road, but now the deep grooves and potholes were gone.

In less than five minutes, Gib parked at the main office and went inside. She saw Clint speaking to two women, both dressed in khaki pants and matching tee shirts. The three turned toward Gib.

Clint was the first to speak. "Officer Gibson Proctor, I'd like you to meet Jessica Middleton," he gestured to the shorter brunette, "and Kendall Wyatt," his hand touched the elbow of the blonde woman. "They're assigned to us for the summer as Level I Technicians. I thought you could take one and assign the other to Dan."

"Uh, sure." Gib shook hands with both women. "Nice to meet you, Middleton and Wyatt."

The brunette gave her a nod. "Same here. You can call me Jessica."

"All right. Everyone calls me Gib."

The blonde, who didn't appear old enough to drive, much less be a Level I Tech, gave Gib a shy smile. "My friends call me Kennie."

Gib looked over Kennie's head to Clint, who shrugged. "Okay, guess we'll head on out to the lake. Do you two have caps?"

Jessica frowned. "Do we have to wear them? They make me look like a—" she cut off her thought. "I don't like to wear hats."

"Believe me, you'll be glad to have it when the sun is right overhead. It gets especially warm on the water, and that's where we'll be."

Kennie removed the cap from her back pocket and tugged it onto her head. "I've never been out on the water at this lake. Is it really rough?"

Gib shook her head. "Not usually. There's little wind today, so it shouldn't be much of a problem. How about you, Jessica? Have you been out on the water?"

"Small craft, sure. After all, I am a Fish and Wildlife technician." She turned to Clint. "Is that all, sir?"

Clint conveyed his apologies to Gib through a slight smile. "Sure. Gib, why don't you take Kennie, and have Jessica help out Dan? Maybe tomorrow y'all can switch."

"Yes, sir." Gib gave him a half-hearted salute. "Come on, Techs. Let's go protect the lake."

WHEN GIB PULLED her truck up to the dock, Jessica groaned from the back seat. "Don't tell me I have to be on that little thing all day."

"Not all day. I'm sure you'll also have to patrol the beach, which is easier to do on foot." Gib got out of the truck and waited until they joined her. "I'll introduce you both to Dan." She took a bag from the back seat and walked down to the dock. "Hey, Dan."

He looked up from the craft and started to say something, but kept silent as the three women stood on the dock.

"Dan, this is Jessica Middleton and Kennie Wyatt. They'll be working with us this summer."

He held out his hand to Jessica. "Dan Conroy."

Jessica shook his hand. "Looks like you're stuck with me today, Dan." She tipped her head toward Gib and lowered her voice. "Lucky me."

Kennie nodded to Dan. "Nice to meet you, Dan."

"Same here." He glared at Gib. "You keeping the Maristar out all day?"

Gib put her hands on her hips and stared him down. She was at least two inches taller, and had probably thirty pounds on him. "Yeah.

Got a problem with that?"

"If I did, would it matter?"

"Nope." She made a point to look at his clothing. He was wearing dark green pants and a knit uniform shirt, along with a gray felt western hat. "You're going to burn up dressed like that today."

He shrugged. "I didn't want to look like a lifeguard. We're here in an official capacity, Proctor."

"Suit yourself." Gib bit back the nasty retort she wanted to say and led Kennie to the other end of the dock. She tossed her bag into the boat and climbed inside. "Do you need any help getting aboard?"

"Guess we'll find out," Kennie gamely responded. She followed Gib's lead and was soon standing next to her in the boat. "This is cool."

Gib was busy checking their gear. "There's some sunscreen in my bag. Feel free."

"Thanks." Kennie opened the bag and removed the sunscreen. Once she was properly covered, she settled into the seat across from Gib. "Do you need any?"

"I greased up earlier." Gib leaned over the edge and untied the boat from the dock. She lifted one of the rear padded cushions and brought out two life preservers, tossing one to her companion. "Can you swim?"

Kennie nodded. "Like a fish." She buckled the preserver with little trouble. "I'm guessing it's hard to make everyone else wear these if we're not?"

"You got it." So far, Gib was enjoying the newbie. She only hoped that Dan was able to get along with Jessica better than he was with her.

"WATCH WHAT YOU'RE doing!" Jessica yelled, as Dan swerved around the buoy near the dam. "Don't you know how to handle an outboard?"

"Of course I do," Dan snapped. He straightened out the tiller and grabbed his hat to keep it from blowing off. "Do you think you could do any better?"

Jessica kept a firm grip on the sides of the Angler. "A ten year-old could do better," she muttered. In a louder voice she added, "Do you want me to take over?"

"Hell, no." He maneuvered them away from the dam and headed toward the open water. "Let's cross to the west shore and check fishing licenses." Although it wasn't quite noon, the shores were full of people, and there were many boats and jet skis out on the water.

"You're kidding, right? I thought we were supposed to stay close to shore in this thing."

He frowned. "Just because that's what Proctor said, doesn't mean that's what we have to do. She's not our boss."

Jessica used her feet to brace herself, so she could retie her hair into a ponytail. She was regretting leaving her cap in Gib's truck. "This is a shallow-water boat, dumbass. If we hit a swell out in the middle of the lake, we're going to tip. And Clint told us to listen to what Gib had to say, since she has the most experience."

"She's a pushy dyke." He turned toward the center of the lake. "And it's her fault I'm out in this stupid little fishing dingy, anyway. I'm the one with the college degree, and should be in the bigger boat."

She looked at him like he'd lost his mind. "Are you serious?" Jessica and Kennie had both heard from Clint what Gib's qualifications were, as well as her two college degrees.

He opened up the small motor on the boat, intent of getting over to the other shore. The sound of fast-moving jet skis caused him to twist his head around. "Hey, watch it," he yelled.

AFTER SOME INSTRUCTION, Gib had relinquished the controls to Kennie. She stood nearby, in case of a problem. "How are you feeling, Kennie?"

"Fantastic," she replied, a huge smile on her face. "Thanks for letting me drive. I passed the written exam, but never got a chance to get out on the water on something this size."

"Always glad to gain another convert," Gib joked. She noticed a pair of jet skis zigzagging and racing each other across the lake. "Damn. Kennie, can you head toward those two jokers? They're going to hurt someone."

Kennie nodded and steered toward the center of the lake. "Hey, isn't that Dan and Jessica?"

Gib squinted against the glare on the water. "What the hell are they doing?" She took out her radio. "Conroy, do you read? Conroy?" Only hearing silence, Gib returned it to her belt. "Damn idiot." She stood directly behind Kennie and unclipped her phone's holster. She considered trying to call Dan on his cell, since he wouldn't answer the radio. "Let's go find out. But be careful."

"All right." Kennie turned the wheel. "It's getting crowded out here," she said over her shoulder.

"That's what I'm afraid of." When another boat started to cut them off, Gib braced one hand on the side of the boat. "Turn hard to starboard," she yelled.

UNABLE TO TALK her way out of it, Delaney joined her parents for lunch. The pizza parlor had a great lunch buffet and was her parents' favorite lunch time retreat. She took one slice of vegetarian pizza and placed it next to her salad.

"Is that all you're going to eat, honey?" Maureen asked. "It's not healthy to starve yourself to death."

"Mom, please. A plate full of salad and one slice of pizza is more than filling." Delaney followed her mother to the table where Colin was

already seated. His eyes were glued to a nearby television.

Maureen swatted him on the arm. "You can check out the sports when we get home tonight, love."

He shook his head. "They're showing the lake. Looks like there was some sort of accident out there."

Delaney's head whipped around and stared at the monitor. "What kind of accident?"

"I don't know. They've got the closed captioning on, but you know how garbled that can be." He tilted his head down so he could see over his glasses. "Ah. A boating accident."

With her heart in her throat, Delaney followed the words on the screen. *"Four park employees and three civilians were taken to Benton Memorial Hospital after a collision on Lake Benton. Their conditions are unknown. Park Manager Clinton Wright will be holding a press conference later this afternoon with more details."*

"Oh, my god." Delaney brought a shaky hand to her mouth as she stared at the television.

Colin touched her arm. "What's the matter, honey?"

Ignoring her father, Delaney took her cell phone from her purse and dialed Gib's number. It rang six times before going to voicemail. "Um, hi. This is Delaney. I just saw," her voice cracked, "Damn. Could you please call me when you get this message?" She set her phone on the table and bit her lower lip.

"Delaney?" Maureen scooted her chair closer to her daughter. "Are you all right?" She put her arm around Delaney's shoulder. "Honey?"

Shaking her head, Delaney didn't speak.

Colin looked first at Delaney, then at the television. Suddenly, his daughter's distress made sense. "You're worried about your park ranger, aren't you?"

"She's a park police officer," the redhead corrected automatically, nodding.

Maureen frowned. "What am I missing here?" she asked her husband.

"Delaney's become friends with a woman who works out at the park. Right?" Colin tried to draw their daughter into the conversation, if only to get her mind off the television news. "Since she's a police officer I'm sure she has to work the accident," he offered.

"Maybe." Delaney stared at her phone, as if she could will it to ring.

Colin wiped his mouth with a napkin and pushed his plate away. "Let's go to the house and see if we can get any more information. At least we'll be able to hear the news reports."

"Okay." Numb, Delaney silently followed them out of the pizza parlor.

THE GURNEY RATTLED down the tiled hallway as two nurses, a doctor and two paramedics worked feverishly on the unconscious woman. Orders were issued, accepted and followed out. The group burst through the doors, never slowing in their attempts to save the life that hung on by the narrowest thread.

Clint jogged to keep up, but ended up standing outside the door, peering in through the window. All he could see of the patient were a few strands of blonde hair. He had to step back when the paramedics came back through the door. "How is she?"

One of them shrugged. "Still alive." He rubbed his face and moved away. "Good luck."

"Thanks." Clint barely acknowledged the pair as he returned to his previous spot. The shrill sound of an alarm caused his eyes to widen.

Suddenly one of the nurses squeezed a bag over the patient's face.

"No," Clint whispered.

IN HER PARENT'S living room, Delaney paced the floor. "Maybe I should go to the hospital."

"I'm sure it's a circus there, honey. Why don't you try to relax?" Maureen patted the couch cushion next to her. "Your father is calling Dylan at the job site to see if he's heard anything."

Delaney sat for a moment, before jumping to her feet and resuming her pacing. "I should have thought of that." She picked up her purse from the coffee table and took out her phone. There had been no calls in the past hour. "Come on, Gib. Where the hell are you?" The uneasy feeling in her gut had grown, and she was only able to keep herself together by sheer will. "I can't stand this."

"Delaney, please. Sit. Working yourself into a lather isn't going to do anyone any good."

Unable to comply, Delaney picked up her purse. "I'm sorry, Mom. I think I'll go home. If Dad hears anything, could you call me?"

"All right. But are you sure you want to be alone right now?"

Delaney nodded. "No sense in all of us going crazy." She kissed her mother on the cheek. "I'll call you later, okay?"

"Of course, honey. And if you need anything—"

"I know. Thanks."

IT WAS CLOSE to ten in the evening, and Delaney knew no more than she had hours ago. Her brother had called around four, with only sketchy details. *"There were fire trucks, ambulances and at least four state trooper cars, Del. We stood on the dam and watched as they pulled at least half a dozen people out of the lake. It was wild."*

When she questioned him about Gib, he was apologetic, but couldn't give her any other details.

She had called the hospital to see if Gib had been admitted, but the

switchboard operator was unable to tell her one way or the other. The news reports were still not giving any names, but they did say that the authorities were keeping everyone away.

With her laptop on the coffee table, Delaney had the television on with the volume low. She would peer up from her computer and check the TV screen, then go back to web surfing. So far, she was unable to learn anything from either source.

A knock on her door startled her. Delaney frowned, but walked across the room and peered through the peephole. "Oh, god." She jerked open the door in surprise.

Gib gave her a weary smile. "Hi. I hope I'm not interrupting anything." Her eyes widened when Delaney grabbed a handful of her shirt and pulled her into the apartment. She was caught off guard when the redhead wrapped her arms around her. "Um, hi?"

"Hi." Delaney snuggled closer and placed her ear over Gib's heart. It was beating a little fast, but strong. She looked up into Gib's face, and noticed a white bandage across her forehead. Her shirt was filthy and wrinkled, and had dried patches of blood all over it. "Are you all right?"

"Yeah, pretty much. It's been a bitch of a day." Gib scratched at the holster that was still strapped to her body. There were scrapes and bruises along her bare legs, and her keys jangled on her belt when she moved.

Delaney could feel the other woman tremble and belatedly realized how exhausted she must be. "Come on." She led her to the sofa. "Are you hungry?"

"I, uh," Gib dropped onto the sofa and closed her eyes. "I don't know." She leaned into Delaney, who sat on the next cushion and put an arm around her shoulder.

"I've been going out of my mind. How'd you get here?"

Gib was silent for so long, Delaney thought she had fallen asleep.

Finally, she took a deep breath. "Uh, cab. I tried to get him to take me home, but he said he didn't go out of town. We weren't far from here, so—"

"Sssh. That's fine. Were you at the hospital?"

"Yeah. I tried to call Maddy, but I couldn't remember her number. It was such a madhouse I just wanted to get out of there."

Gib's clothes smelled like lake water and a patch of her hair over her left ear was matted with dried blood. Delaney lightly touched the bandage and could see a bruise that disappeared into Gib's hairline. "I think you need a hot bath."

"I'm sorry." Gib tried to get up, but was held back by Delaney. "I'm probably ruining your couch."

"No, it's all right. I just thought you'd be more comfortable if you were clean." Delaney pulled Gib close and put both arms around her. "Why don't you rest for a little while, then you can get cleaned up."

While Gib napped, Delaney held her. She wasn't quite sure where this protective streak had come from, but it was too late at night to try and make sense of it. They hadn't spent very much time together, and part of that was at each other's throats. But Gib felt good in her arms, so Delaney closed her own eyes and relaxed for the first time all day.

"NO!" GIB JERKED awake with a yell. She looked around in a panic, before remembering where she was. "Damn." She turned to Delaney, who looked just as startled. "I'm sorry."

Delaney touched Gib's cheek. "Don't worry about it. How are you feeling?"

"Like an idiot. I shouldn't have come here." Gib slowly stood. "I'm sorry to have bothered you so late."

"Hey, no. It's okay." Delaney got to her feet as well and took Gib by the arm. "I'm really glad you did. I've been worried sick about you."

"You have?"

The redhead nodded. "I was at lunch with my parents when we saw the news about the accident at the lake. All they said was that four park employees had been taken to the hospital. They never gave any names. And I couldn't reach you."

Gib lowered her eyes. "Yeah. I lost my phone in the lake." A heavy weariness settled over her. "I should go. If you could help me call Maddy, I'll get out of your hair." But she didn't move.

"Stay." Delaney tugged her toward the bedroom. "Let's get you into a bath, and I'll put your clothes in the wash. You don't need to be going anywhere tonight."

"I don't know—"

They stood together in the bathroom, so close they could breathe each other's air. Delaney tugged on Gib's holster. "Do you need help getting undressed?"

A shy grin crossed Gib's face. "Uh, no. I think I can handle it." She struggled with her holster while Delaney filled the tub. "I've got to clean my gun." She lowered the holster to the floor carefully, and started on her belt. Once the belt was loose, she bent over to untie her boots, but the strings were damp and knotted. "Crap."

Delaney turned. "Sit on the edge of the tub and I'll help."

"Thanks." Gib followed her orders and soon lost her boots. She tried to move her foot away when Delaney started to take off her socks. "I can do that."

"Probably. But I'm already down here." The socks were stripped off and dropped into a different corner of the tile floor, away from the gun and holster. "Do you need me to help with anything else?"

Gib shook her head. "No, thank you." She turned away and tugged her shirt over her head. Her white sports bra was stained a reddish brown and had several small tears.

"Oh, my god." Delaney stood behind Gib and lightly touched her back. There was a four-inch wide bruise that stretched from her left shoulder almost to her right hip. "What happened to you?"

"I'm not sure." Gib accepted Delaney's help removing the rest of her clothes before she lowered herself into the warm water. "Ahh. That feels fantastic." She closed her eyes and leaned back into the tub.

The redhead paused at the door. "I'll get your clothes into the washer."

"You don't have to do that. I have," Gib paused. "Crap. In my truck I have a bag of extra clothes. Not that they're doing me much good right now, are they?" Her truck was still parked at the lake dock.

"I'll find you something to wear." Delaney picked up the belt and holster. "These will go on the kitchen table, and I'll take everything out and lay them out on a towel, okay?"

"Yeah, that'll work. Thanks." Gib closed her eyes and relaxed again.

DELANEY HAD REMOVED everything from the belt and cleaned it to the best of her ability. She took the gun out of the holster, wrapped it in a hand towel and placed it carefully on the table. With that done, she scrambled a pan of eggs on the stove. She was so lost in her thoughts that she didn't hear Gib walk into the kitchen.

"That smells fantastic." Gib tugged on the sleep shirt Delaney had loaned her. It barely came to her waist, and was a little tight across the shoulders and chest. But at least she was covered. The cutoff sweat shorts were snug as well, and she hoped she didn't have to bend over for anything.

The spatula clattered as it fell onto the stovetop and Delaney sharply turned. "You startled me."

"Sorry." Gib stood at the bar, her damp hair in disarray. She had used supplies she found in the medicine cabinet to replace the bandage on her head. "Is there anything I can do to help?"

"Nope. If you'll have a seat, it'll be ready in a second." Delaney finished the eggs and split them between two plates. "Orange juice, milk, water or coffee?" she asked. She tried not to look at Gib's breasts, which were accentuated by the taut shirt.

Gib stood when Delaney came over. "I can get it. What would you like?"

"Sit." Delaney pushed on her shoulder. "I'm having milk, how about you?"

"Milk's fine."

They sat side by side at the bar and quietly ate. Once they were finished, Gib moaned and rubbed her stomach. "That was great."

"Just scrambled eggs, but I'm glad you liked them." Delaney put their dirty dishes in the dishwasher. She noticed a far-off look in Gib's eyes. "Are you all right?"

Gib shook her head, but didn't say anything. Her eyes filled with tears and she tried to blink them away.

"Gib, honey. What's wrong?"

"I can't— " Gib stood and held her hands in front of her, looking at them. "How can I sit here like this?" She started to rub her hands together. "I tried so hard," she whispered.

Delaney slowly moved closer. "It's okay."

"She wasn't breathing. I tried CPR, but we were in the water." Gib frowned. "Maybe if I had been piloting the boat, I don't know." She stepped backward until she hit the wall. "She's so damned young," her voice broke and she slid down the wall until she was on the floor. "Damned kid." All control gone, Gib started to cry.

Not knowing what else to do, Delaney joined Gib on the floor and put her arms around her. She held the sobbing woman's head to her chest and muttered words of comfort.

HOURS LATER, DELANEY sat in her recliner and watched as Gib slept on her sofa. She had tried to get Gib to sleep in her bed, but the stubborn woman had refused. So, instead of both of them being comfortable in the bedroom, Gib was lying on the sofa covered with a quilt, while Delaney tried to rest in the recliner.

It had taken quite a while for her to get Gib settled, especially after the other woman started telling her all the details of the lake incident.

Gib's trainee, Kennie, was piloting their boat to reach the other rangers when they saw that the smaller park craft was in the direct path of another speeding boat. In her haste to protect the other rangers, Kennie turned them toward the fast-moving craft. All three boats collided, and there Gib's recollection became hazy. Obviously suffering from her own injuries, Gib tried to keep Kennie floating right side up. She found out later that Dan and Jessica were also injured, although neither one seriously. Dan had a broken finger and Jessica a dislocated shoulder. Kennie, however, had received a skull fracture and almost died at the hospital. The last Gib had heard she was in the ICU but holding her own.

"I can't even begin to imagine what you're going through," Delaney whispered, as she watched Gib sleep. She blinked her own tears away. "You could have been killed today." She knew she had developed feelings for Gib, but wasn't sure if the other woman felt the same. "I hope to find out, though." After one final glance, Delaney closed her eyes and tried to get some sleep.

Chapter Six

THE RICH SMELL of coffee woke Gib. She attempted to roll into a sitting position, but her aching and bruised muscles protested, causing her to cry out.

Delaney rushed from the kitchen. "Gib? What's the matter?"

"Nothing," Gib gasped. "Just a little stiff." She finally made it up and carefully let out a shaky breath. "Wow." Since her original clothes had been cleaned, she was at least more comfortably dressed, although the bruise on her back didn't allow her to wear her bra.

"I hate to be the one to say I told you so, but you should have slept in the bed. It's one of those comfort air mattresses, and it's like sleeping on a cloud."

Gib took a few more cautious breaths before speaking. "I'll keep that in mind, next time."

"You do that." Delaney perched on the arm of the couch and lightly touched Gib's shoulder. "Can I get you anything? How about some breakfast?"

"What time is it?"

Delaney glanced at the cable box. "A little after nine."

"Crap! I need to get to work."

With her hand, Delaney easily kept Gib in place. "Actually, you don't."

"What do you mean?"

The redhead gave her a nervous smile. "I took the liberty of calling the park this morning and spoke to your boss. The main office number was on the card you gave me."

"Clint?" Exhausted from trying to get off the sofa, Gib slowly leaned back. "Did he say how Kennie was doing?"

"Her condition has been upgraded from critical to guarded. She still has swelling in her brain, but they're hopeful."

Gib appeared relieved. "That's better, right?"

"Yes." Delaney played with the end of Gib's hair, which had curled after it dried. "I hope you don't mind, but I told your boss that you'd be spending the day here. He said he looked all over the hospital for you last night, but figured a family member had taken you home."

"Yeah, I couldn't find him either. Wait. I'm staying here?"

Delaney laughed. "Yes, but on one condition."

"You're placing conditions on kidnapping me? I hope there's no ransom, 'cause I'm not as rich as you might think," Gib joked, privately enjoying the attention her hair was getting. A sharp tug let her know her joke wasn't appreciated. "Ow."

"Big baby. Okay, here's my condition. You're going to have a good breakfast then I'm tucking you into bed."

Gib slowly turned her head until she was looking directly into Delaney's face. They were close enough that she could see all the tiny flecks that made up her sky blue eyes. "You are?"

"Mmm-hmm." Delaney leaned closer and brushed her lips against Gib's.

The chaste kiss stirred something deep within Gib. Past caring what it would do to her sore body, she put her arm around Delaney and pulled her into her lap.

It was all the invitation Delaney needed. She cradled Gib's head in her hands and proceeded to kiss the other woman senseless. She moaned when she felt one of Gib's hands slip under her shirt and caress her back. Before the moment could become any more intense, Delaney broke off the kiss in order to catch her breath. "Whew."

"Yeah." Gib placed a few light nibbles on Delaney's throat. "I can't seem to get enough of you."

"Gib," Delaney gasped, "Honey, wait." Her resolve faltered when Gib's hands brushed against the underside of her breasts. "Oh, god."

Her hands shaking, Gib forced herself to slow down. The excitement was causing the knot and stitches on her head to throb, which made her queasy. She closed her eyes and leaned her head against Delaney's shoulder. "Sorry."

"I'm not. But I guess we should wait until you're in a little better shape." Delaney carefully brushed her hand through Gib's hair. "Are you okay?"

Gib nodded but didn't raise her head.

"Do you feel up to some breakfast?"

A head shake in the negative.

Delaney chuckled. "Honey, you need to eat something. How about some toast?"

Gib laughed and raised her head. "I could probably handle some toast." She kissed the tip of Delaney's nose. "Thanks."

"No problem." The redhead stood and held out her hand. "Come on. First food then right to bed with you."

"Propositioning me, Ms. Kavanagh? What happened to waiting?" Gib grimaced as she was helped off the sofa. "Damn, I'm getting old."

"Ha. Tell me another story, officer." Delaney kept her arm around Gib as she helped her to the kitchen. "And believe me, when I proposition you, you'll know it."

Gib gingerly sat on a barstool. "Sounds like fun."

"Trust me, it will be." Delaney kissed her on the temple. "Now behave while I amaze you with my culinary skills."

Sick to her stomach with a headache that would knock down an elephant, Gib had never been happier. She propped her elbow on the counter and rested her chin on her hand. "Amaze away, pretty lady."

GIB HAD JUST allowed Delaney to tuck her into bed when she remembered something important. "My mother's going to kill me. Not to mention what Maddy's going to say."

"What do you mean?"

"May I borrow your phone? I need to let everyone know where I am and that I'm all right." Gib sat up and looked around the room in a panic. "Knowing my mother, she's called out the National Guard."

"Sssh." Delaney kept her hand against Gib's chest. "I'll bring you the cordless phone from my office. Hold on." She stood and left the room, returning in a moment with the phone. "I'll close the door so you can have some privacy."

Gib accepted the phone. "You don't have to do that. You've met Maddy, and my mother, well, let's just say she's an acquired taste." She patted the mattress next to her leg while she dialed the number for her parent's home. Her friend took the hint and joined her.

"Hello?"

"Hi, Mom." Gib hit the speakerphone button so that Delaney could hear as well.

"Gibson Susanna Proctor! I'm been worried half out of my mind about you," Ida snapped. "Everyone keeps calling here asking me how you are, and do you know what I tell them?"

Gib gave Delaney a 'what can I do' look. "No, Mom. What do you tell them?"

"I tell them I have no idea, since my only daughter doesn't take the time to let me know anything." Ida covered the phone and yelled. "Eric! Your daughter finally called. Yes, I'm sure it's her." She uncovered the phone. "Well? Where are you? Are you all right? We saw on the news that some female park employee is still hospitalized. Your brother tried calling the hospital, but they wouldn't give him any information."

"Mom, if you'd stop for a minute, I'd tell you."

"Oh, sure. Now it's my fault." Ida sniffed.

Gib closed her eyes. "Mom. Listen, it was pretty late when they released me last night. I've got a few stitches and some bruises, but I'm okay. I'm staying at a friend's place right now."

"Madina's? You can stay with your friend but not with your family? We could have made up the futon in my sewing room for you."

The thought of the lumpy futon that was several inches too short caused Gib to grimace. "No, not Maddy's. As a matter of fact, I have to call her next. This was the first opportunity I had to call. I'm sorry I took so long."

Ida sighed. "That's all right. I know you've got more important things to do than keep me up to date with your life."

"Mom."

"No, no. Don't worry about us. After all, I haven't seen you for weeks. I barely hear from you at all, and when I do, you have to get off the phone."

Gib held out the phone while her mother continued to prattle on. She winked at Delaney, who had to cover her mouth to keep from laughing. Once Ida stopped, Gib brought the phone closer. "Mom, I've got to go. I'll call you tomorrow, okay?"

"Sure, sure."

"Love you, Mom. Tell Dad I love him, too."

"We love you too, Gibson. Tell your friend to take good care of you."

Gib smiled. "I will. Bye, Mom." She pushed the off button on the phone and dropped it onto the bed. "One down, one to go."

"Your mom sounded really upset."

"She tends to be a little melodramatic," Gib admitted. "But she'll be fine. Maddy's the one who'll chew me out for days." Her head was pounding and she closed her eyes to ward off the pain.

Delaney brushed the hair away from Gib's eyes. "I was going to go out and get us something for lunch. Why don't I stop by Rodrigo's and talk to Maddy for you?"

Gib's eyes slowly opened. "You're willing to face her Latina temper?"

"Honey, my Irish will outdo her Latina, anytime." Delaney stroked Gib's cheek with her fingertips. "Get some sleep. Is there anyone else I need to contact? Aunt, cousin or maybe girlfriend?"

"Subtle," Gib teased. "No, I'm single. And since I've already talked to my mother, everyone in the family will know pretty quickly. She's more reliable than a newspaper." When Delaney pushed on her chest, she took the hint and lay back against the pillows. "Thanks."

Delaney kissed her on the forehead. "Rest." She stroked Gib's face until it relaxed into sleep.

IT WAS AFTER the lunch rush when Delaney walked into Rodrigo's. There was a young man at the host podium who gave her a friendly smile.

"Good afternoon. How many for your party?"

"Actually, I need to talk to Maddy. Is she available?"

His smile faltered. "She only sees salespersons between three and five. If you'll leave your card, I'll make certain she gets it."

"No, wait. I'm not trying to sell anything. This is personal." Delaney stepped closer to the podium and lowered her voice. "It's about her friend, Gib."

"Gib?" He stepped around the podium. "Why didn't you say so? Please, follow me." He led her past the dining room, through the kitchen and stopped at a closed door. His soft tap was acknowledged by a gruff voice.

"Something better be on fire."

He turned to Delaney and grinned. "Have fun." He knocked again.

"Boss? Got a lady here to see you."

The door swung open and a furious Maddy glared at the young man. "Are you suicidal, Mike?"

"No. But I think you'll want to talk to her." He moved out of the way and showed the woman behind him with a flourish.

Maddy appeared confused for a moment, until she was finally able to remember where she'd seen the redhead. "Oh! Delaney, hi. Um – "

"Hi, Maddy. I've got some news about a mutual friend." Delaney came forward and took the other woman's hands in hers. "She's okay."

The bravado seemed to escape Madina at those two words. "Thank god. I've been half out of my mind. I can't get her to answer her phone, her family won't talk to me, and when I call the hospital they won't tell me a damned thing." She opened the door wider. "Please, come in." Once Delaney was inside, she closed the door and motioned to a nearby chair. "Have a seat."

"Thank you."

"So, tell me. Have you seen her?" Maddy sat almost knee to knee with Delaney. "I saw the coverage of the accident on the news. It scared the shit out of me."

Delaney nodded. "I know. I was going nuts until she arrived on my doorstep last night. She's got a pretty good-sized knot on her forehead that needed stitches and a nasty looking bruise across her back. But otherwise, she's all right."

"Your doorstep?" Maddy couldn't help but grin. "Really?"

"Not for the reasons you probably think." Delaney blushed. "Well, not completely, anyway." She checked her watch. "She'll be asleep for a couple more hours. Would you like to come by and see her?"

The grin on Maddy's face grew. "Come by? Sleeping? Just what have you two been doing?"

Delaney slapped her leg. "Stop it." She grew serious. "She was really in a bad way, between the injuries and her guilt over the accident. I didn't want her to go, so I talked her into staying with me."

"I'm glad you were there for her. Gibsy's always been a loner. I had to follow her around forever in grade school to get her to be my friend." She flipped her dark hair over one shoulder. "Of course, once you meet her family, you'll understand."

"I overheard her talking to her mother this morning on the phone. It wasn't pleasant."

Maddy shook her head. "Her mother has a big heart and loves her family dearly. But, she's always put all her expectations on Gib, and relied on her to fix every little problem for the entire family." She sighed. "And, no matter how hard Gib tries, she'll never quite measure up to her younger brother. At least in her mother's eyes."

"Why not?"

"He's the baby of the family, and he gave Ida the one thing she always wanted. Grandchildren. Even if Gib were to have a child now, it wouldn't matter. Ida thinks the sun rises and sets on Roger's kids." She leaned closer. "Even if they're spoiled brats."

Delaney cringed. "Ouch."

"Yeah. I don't blame Gib for getting out of Benton the moment she graduated from high school. Sure, she had a scholarship to Texas State University. But even after she graduated, she stayed away. I was completely surprised when she came back a few months ago."

"I had no idea." Delaney's stomach growled loudly. "Oh, lord." She covered her red face with her hand.

Maddy's laughter rang in the small office. "Sounds like it's time to feed you." She stood. "Come on. Let's get you some of that guacamole that makes you want to marry me."

MADDY NODDED HER admiration while Delaney unlocked her apartment door. "This is a great place. What's your rent like?"

"Not as much as you might think." With the door unlocked, Delaney gestured for Maddy to precede her inside. They both stopped and stared into the dining area, where Gib sat at the table. "What are you doing?" Delaney asked.

Gib looked up and shrugged. "Trying to save my gun and equipment. Hey, Maddy."

"Lord, you're impossible." Maddy bent over and gave Gib a one-armed hug. "How are you doing?"

"All right." Gib put the gun on the newspaper she had spread out on the table. "I hope you don't mind, but I found some WD-40 under your sink and some disposable rags."

Delaney shook her head and sat at the table. "No, I don't mind. I wasn't sure what to do with your gun, that's why I wrapped it in a towel."

"You did great." Gib stretched and gave the redhead a kiss on the cheek, which caused her to blush.

Maddy's eyebrow rose. "Nothing, huh?" she asked Delaney, whose face turned an even darker shade of red. She grinned and joined the pair at the table, placing a white bag close to Gib. "If you can quit playing with your toys, we brought you some lunch."

Gib opened the bag and sniffed. "Mmm. Chicken enchiladas?"

"Yup. There's a plastic fork in there too, so dig in."

Not needing to be told twice, Gib wiped her hands on a towel, unpacked the bag, and moaned in appreciation when the Styrofoam lid was raised. "When are you going to give up and let me move into the restaurant?" she asked, right before she stuffed a forkful of food into her mouth.

"Shut up and eat." Maddy stole a tortilla chip from the container. She watched her friend eat and exchanged amused glances with Delaney.

"Slow down," Delaney chastised. "Maddy's going to think I was starving you to death."

Gib did slow her fork, at least a little. "I can't help it. I didn't think I was that hungry, until I smelled the enchiladas." She shoveled another forkful into her mouth. "Mmm."

"Don't worry, I already know what a pig she is," Maddy assured the redhead. "What's next on your agenda, Gibsy?"

After swallowing and wiping her mouth with a paper napkin, Gib shrugged her shoulders. "I need to find a ride home, I guess. Or maybe a ride to my folk's house. If I don't go by and see my mom, she'll never let me hear the end of it."

"I can take you," Delaney offered quickly. "I mean, there's nothing for me to do this week at the site, and I'm caught up with all my other projects."

"Are you sure? I don't want to take advantage of you anymore than I already have."

Maddy laughed. "Pull your head out of your ass, Gibsy. The girl likes you."

Gib's head turned so fast it made her dizzy. "Maddy!" She glared at her friend. "Leave her alone."

"It's okay, Gib. Maybe she's jealous," Delaney teased. "After all, I did say I wanted to marry her. Now I'm letting you sleep in my bed."

Gib sputtered and started to choke on her food. She waved away their offers of assistance and took a moment to compose herself. "You're wicked," she gasped, patting herself on the chest. She pointed at Maddy. "Not one word."

"Hey, I'm being good," Maddy argued. "But, since I can see that you're all right, I need to get back to the restaurant. There's a supply order due in and I seem to be the only person who can count." She stood and kissed Gib lightly on top of the head. "Behave yourself and don't overdo it."

Delaney rose to her feet. "I'll walk you to the door." She patted Gib on the shoulder. "Be right back."

As they stood in the open door, Maddy cleared her throat. "Thanks for taking care of her. She's a pain in the ass, but she's the best friend I've ever had." She pulled the other woman into a firm embrace. "Don't let her get away with too much."

"I'll do my best. And now that you know where I live, don't be a stranger." Delaney felt Maddy take a deep breath, in an attempt to control her emotions. "It's okay."

"Thanks." Maddy stepped away and exhaled. "Don't let her go to her mom's house alone. She won't admit it, but I know it really gets to her."

"All right," Delaney answered quietly. In a louder voice, she said, "Thanks for coming by, Maddy."

Maddy winked. "Sure. I'll see you later."

Chapter Seven

THE BLACK LEXUS parked in front of a one story, ranch-style house. Delaney turned to Gib, who had a frown on her face. "What's the matter?"

"My brother's here."

"Is that a problem?"

Gib shook her head. "Probably not. I just wasn't in the mood to entertain him."

"Let me take you home, then. I know you said you felt better but you still look worn out."

"No, we're here. Come on, I'll introduce you to my family, although I'm going to apologize in advance for them." Gib paused to strengthen her resolve before she opened her door.

Delaney quickly exited the vehicle and joined her on the paved path to the front door. She stood quietly as Gib opened the door and poked her head in.

"Knock, knock," Gib called loudly, holding the door open wide and motioning for Delaney to go before her. They stood in the entry hall and listened. "Sounds like they're in the kitchen. Come on." Gib rested her hand against the small of Delaney's back and led her into cramped living room. Two mismatched sofas, a recliner, end tables and a coffee table filled the small space. A large flat-screen television was on, its animated program playing to the empty room.

Voices in the nearby kitchen were fighting for dominance. Two children, a man and a woman were all speaking over each other, each trying to be heard.

"Mom, I'm telling you. This is a once-in-a-lifetime deal. You could make a lot of money with just a small investment."

"Daddy, Daddy, Trevor won't let me watch my Disney movie."

"Grandma, tell Morgan to quit bothering me. You said I could watch SpongeBob."

"I don't know why you think I'm made of money, Roger. You'll have to talk to your father about your idea."

Gib stood in the doorway of the kitchen, while Delaney cautiously stayed behind her. The only person who noticed them was the two year old in the high chair, waving his hands wildly.

"Bib! Bib!"

"Hey, kiddo." Gib hurried to the table to keep her nephew from falling out of the chair. She ignored the gooey animal crackers he had squished between his fingers and pulled him into her arms. "How are you doing, buddy?"

"Bib, Bib," he continued to chatter.

Delaney stood beside her. "Wow, he's adorable."

"Isn't he? This is my nephew, Chase."

Ida finally noticed the new arrivals. "Gibson, it's good to see you." She walked to her daughter and gave her a stiff hug. Eyeing Delaney she asked, "And who's this?"

"Mom, this is my friend, Delaney Kavanagh. She's going to give me a ride back to the lake, so I can get my truck." Gib laughed as Chase tried to feed her some of his cookie. "Thanks."

"Yum, Bib. Eats." Chase pushed the goo toward his aunt's lips.

Delaney held out her hand. "It's nice to meet you, Mrs. Proctor."

"Nice to meet you, too." Slender and not quite five and a half feet tall, Ida pulled herself up to her full height. Her brown eyes were clear from behind the wire framed glasses she wore. Her gray, wavy hair was cut short in an easy to care for style. She brushed her hands down the front of her pale knit top and navy slacks. "I wish you would have called and told us you were bringing company, Gibson. I would have dressed better."

"You look fine, Mom." Gib nodded to her brother, who was leaning against the kitchen counter with a cup of coffee in his hand. "Roger."

"Gib." He raised his mug in salute. Roger was about the same height as Gib, but slender where she was stocky. His scruffy, blonde hair was thinning, and a pot belly showed his lack of physical activity. His teeth were crooked and stained from the cigarettes he thought no one knew he smoked. "From the way Mom talked, I thought you'd still be in the hospital. You were supposedly on death's door."

She shook her head. "I'm fine."

Ida stared at her. "Did you sleep in your clothes?"

"I may have napped in them." Gib moved her head away when Chase tried to touch the bandage on her forehead. "Chase, no."

"Aunt Gib," the blonde little girl tugged at Gib's shorts. "Make Trevor put in my movie."

Trevor left his father's side and started for the door. "It's my turn to watch TV, Morgan." He ignored his aunt and Delaney as he returned to the living room. Morgan trailed behind him.

"I wanna watch my movie," Morgan whined.

Delaney stared after the boy. With his imperial attitude, he looked and sounded like the man on the other side of the kitchen. The thought wasn't a compliment. Maddy's comments started to make more sense to her.

"You look horrible," Ida scolded her daughter. "You should lie down." She held out her hands. "Here, I'll take Chase."

"No, no, no. Wants Bib," Chase babbled. He hung onto Gib's shirt with both hands.

Gib kissed his sweaty hair. "Go to Grandma, handsome." She handed him off to Ida, who tsked and took him to the kitchen sink.

"I swear. You're wearing more of that cookie than you ate." She placed him on the counter and used a damp paper towel to wipe him clean.

There was one person missing, as far as Gib could tell. "Where's Ann?" she asked her brother.

His answer was the same as always. "She's got a migraine, so I brought the kids over here to visit Mom." His wife tended to get her headaches whenever the children were out of school. He tapped his head and looked at hers. "Concussion?"

"I don't think so. Just a bump." Gib put her hands in her pockets. "Um, Delaney? This is my brother, Roger. He's a teacher at Benton Junior High."

Roger winked at Delaney. "Assistant counselor and teacher of American History," he bragged. "Nice to meet you, Delaney. You're a friend of my sister's, huh?"

Delaney nodded. "I am. It's nice to meet you." She didn't offer to shake his hand, since he made no move to cross the kitchen. "And as her friend, I think I'll take her home. She needs her rest."

Gib turned to the redhead. "I do?"

Her brother placed his coffee cup on the counter and moved closer. "So, are you a friend like Maddy, or a *closer* friend?" He waggled his eyebrows.

"Shut up, Roger," Gib warned.

Not concerned with Roger, Delaney moved closer to Gib and wrapped her fingers around Gib's arm. "Let's get you home."

Roger grinned. "Ahh. I see." He pulled out a kitchen chair and sat. "I saw the news last night. You guys made a real mess at the lake. I hear they may close it to watercraft for the rest of the month."

Gib shrugged but didn't say anything.

"So, what happened? Did you see a hot babe in a bikini and lose track of where you were? There were plenty of them for the news cameras. Hell, I might have crashed, too."

Ida handed Chase to his father. "That's enough, Roger. Gibson, you're not leaving so soon, are you? Your father should be home from work in another hour or two."

Gib closed her eyes momentarily. "I'll try to get back over this weekend, okay?"

"I suppose. Are you coming to Trevor's baseball game Saturday morning? I believe it's at ten." Ida sat at the table with her son. "Isn't that right, Roger?"

"I think so."

"I'm not sure what my schedule looks like, Mom. I'll let you know after I go in to work tomorrow morning." Gib turned when she felt Delaney's fingers dig into her arm. "What?"

Delaney shook her head. "Nothing."

"Back to work?" Roger asked. "You can't be serious." Before he sounded too concerned for his sister's welfare, he continued, "You aren't being suspended for the accident?"

"Not that I'm aware of. But I haven't talked to Clint, yet." She took the second squeeze on her arm as a hint. "We've got to run. I'll call you tomorrow. Okay, Mom?"

Ida sighed. "Of course. But you're both invited to stay for dinner. I think we're ordering pizza, since that's what the kids like."

The thought of eating the cold cardboard that they got from a nearby pizza delivery place gave Gib a nauseous feeling. "Um, thanks, but no. I think I'll go on home and get some rest."

"If that's what you want to do." Ida allowed. "It was nice to meet you, Delaney."

"Thank you, Mrs. Proctor. It was nice to meet you, too."

Roger turned toward them and put one arm over the back of his chair. "Come over anytime, Delaney." The flirtatious tone in his voice belied the fact that he was married.

Before Delaney could tear into her brother, Gib turned to leave. "We'll be seeing you," she said, mainly to her mother. "Bye." She led Delaney out before the redhead could say anything to Roger.

Once they had closed the front door behind them, Delaney growled. "I know he's your brother, but—"

"Yeah, Roger's an ass. I'm sorry about that." Gib followed Delaney to the Lexus. "He thinks he's god's gift to women."

Delaney laughed. "With that pot belly and those stained teeth? Not hardly. Even if I wasn't a lesbian, I wouldn't give him the time of day." She turned her head and studied Gib. "Were you adopted? Because other than the hair and eye color, you don't look like either of them."

"I often wondered that myself," Gib admitted as they got into the SUV. Roger and Mom favor each other a lot. I'm more like my dad. Except his hair was darker when he was younger."

The car was started and Delaney pulled away from the curb. "Was it true what you told them? That you're planning on going back to work tomorrow?"

"I don't know. I do need to call my boss, but I don't know if he's going to want me there or not."

"What do you mean?"

Gib sighed and relaxed against the leather seat. "Maybe Roger was right. For all I know, he's going to suspend me or fire me. The accident was my fault."

"Like hell it was. I saw the news, and I read the report in the paper. Did you?"

"No."

"According to the paper, which got its information from 'Park Manager Clint Wright' it was an unfortunate accident, brought on by someone driving their recreational boat too fast. He said, and I quote, 'Only the quick actions of my staff kept it from being worse.'"

Gib turned her head. "He said that?"

"Yes."
"Huh."

IT WAS AFTER five in the afternoon when Delaney parked next to Gib's truck. She kept the engine running, hoping not to wake her passenger. But as soon as the SUV stopped moving, Gib moaned and opened her eyes.

"Damn. I'm sorry I fell asleep." She sat up and rubbed her face. "Thanks for the ride."

"Sure." Delaney watched Gib gather her things. "Do you mind if I follow you up to your cabin? It would make me feel better to see you get settled."

Gib gave her a tired smile. "Sure. I'll see you in a minute." She took her holster and belt with her and got out of the Lexus.

Delaney waited until Gib's truck was headed away from the dock before she backed up and followed. She smiled proudly as the Lexus easily navigated the narrow road that her crew had evened out.

The Ford pickup was parked not far from the front porch, and Delaney eased her vehicle behind it. She got out at the same time as Gib and hurried to catch up. "Nice road," she joked.

"It is, isn't it? I'm going to have to thank your brother," Gib returned, flinching as her arm was lightly slapped. "Kidding." There was an envelope taped to the door and she took it down and tucked it beneath her arm. She finally got the door unlocked and held it open. "After you."

"Thank you." Delaney walked in front of her.

Gib tossed her keys on the table by the door. She placed her holster on the kitchen bar. "Would you like something to drink?"

"No, thank you. I'm fine." Curious about the envelope, Delaney asked, "Are you going to open it?"

"Huh? Oh. Yeah." Gib carefully tore the envelope open and pulled out a note. She glanced over it, nodding.

Delaney waited as long as she could stand. "Well?"

"It's from Clint. He said they got me a new phone and it's at the office. I can pick it up tomorrow when I come in to work."

"So, you really are going back to work tomorrow?" She had hoped that Gib had changed her mind.

"Of course." Gib placed the note on the bar next to her holster. "Why wouldn't I?"

The redhead moved closer. "Maybe, just *maybe*, you should take another day or two off. You were almost killed yesterday."

"Nah. Besides, they're shorthanded right now and it's hectic."

Delaney sighed. "Hectic or not, I don't think you should rush back so soon."

"I'm fine."

"God! You are the most pig-headed, stubborn woman I've ever known! You're not the only person who can work. I'm sure there are enough people around here to give you another day off, if you ask."

Gib frowned. "But I'm the only licensed peace officer here. It's Spring Break, when all the kids seem to lose their minds. Underage drinking, sneaking into the park after hours, crazy pranks. And I still haven't found whoever is responsible for hunting out of season."

Delaney threw her hands up. "Aargh! You make me crazy!"

"Dee—"

"Don't 'Dee' me, Gib. Damn it!" Delaney felt like shaking Gib. She pointed to the bandage that stood out against the officer's tanned skin. "That could have been a lot worse. *You* could be the one in the hospital, or..." her voice choked and she stared at the floor.

Gib put her arms around Delaney. "Look at me."

Delaney struggled to break free. "No."

"Come on, Dee. Look at me, please." Gib's voice was soft. "Look."

Delaney raised her head and looked into Gib's eyes. They were clear, no longer full of pain.

"I'm really okay." Gib's hands moved up Delaney's arms until she was holding the redhead's face tenderly. "And I'll be extra careful, I promise." She lowered her face and covered Delaney's lips with her own.

When they finally broke apart to breathe, Delaney tightened her fist in Gib's shirt. "It's hard to stay mad at you when you can kiss like that."

Gib grinned. "All part of my plan, beautiful." She leaned her head against Delaney's and sighed. "Thanks for letting me crash at your place. And for taking care of me."

"I'm glad you came." Delaney raised her face. "Do me a favor?"

"What's that?"

The redhead lightly touched above the bandage. "No more of these for a while, please?"

"I'll do my best." Unable to fight it, Gib yawned. "Sorry. It's not the company."

"I know." After a short peck on the lips, Delaney backed away. "I'm going to leave so you can get some rest. Call me when you get your new phone?"

Gib nodded. "You'll be the first person I call," she guaranteed. "Maybe for a dinner date?"

"Sure." Delaney knew if she didn't leave now, she'd end up following Gib to bed. "Call me," she repeated, before she closed the door behind her.

THE DRIVE BACK to town was quiet. Delaney didn't bother with the radio, instead thinking over the events of the past few days. She barely knew Gib, yet couldn't get the woman out of her mind. Their time together was filled with so many emotions that she was partially afraid of what would happen if their relationship grew more serious. She had to laugh at that thought. "I think I'm already past the point of being able to stop."

Delaney considered her feelings. "Is it possible to fall so hard and so fast for someone?" she muttered. "And is Gib for real? Opening doors, being so considerate. Does anyone really do things like that anymore?" She stared ahead, where she could see the city of Benton take shape. "If she's so great, why hasn't someone snatched her up by now?"

Her thoughts were interrupted by the sound of her cell phone ringing. "I bet she left the minute I did, just to get her phone." With a big smile on her face, Delaney dug the phone out of her purse and answered. "Hey."

"Who was that woman?"

"Chris?"

The angry voice on the other end of the line got angrier. "I saw you with a woman."

"Are you following me?" Delaney looked in her rearview mirror as she asked the question. The road was deserted.

"No. Who was she? Is she the reason you broke up with me? Am I not good enough for you anymore?"

Delaney crossed into the city limits and tried to keep calm. "You know very well why I broke up with you, Chris."

"Yeah, right. 'Cause you thought you were such hot shit, and I was just some trash you felt sorry for."

"That's not true, Chris. When your cousin first introduced us, I thought we got along well. Didn't we?" Chris' cousin, Ray, worked for Kavanagh Construction, and when he found out Delaney was gay, Ray thought his cousin would be a good match. He introduced them at a company picnic, and they had hit it off. Delaney drove past the entrance to her apartment complex, on the off chance Chris was waiting for her.

Chris' voice broke. "Ray thought you'd be good for me." She cleared her throat. "You're not going to fire him, are you?"

"Of course not. My father hired Ray, and he's a great guy. Why would we fire him?"

"You used to think I was great, too," Chris whined. "And then you dumped me for no reason."

Delaney was quickly losing her temper. "I broke up with you because you were overly possessive and tried to control me."

"So, you picked up some Mexican? You really decided to slum, didn't you?"

"What in the hell are you babbling about, Chris? What Mex—" Delaney suddenly realized that Chris had seen Maddy, not Gib. "She's just a friend. *Not* that it's any of your business who I see. And for the record, she has more class in her little finger than you'll ever have." She hung up and tossed her phone onto the passenger seat. "Why on earth did I spend almost a year with that crazy woman? I need to have my head examined."

GIB WANDERED AROUND her cabin after Delaney left. Although tired, she couldn't seem to get her brain to stop. The fiery redhead was fun to tease and gave as good as she got. "She's a damned good kisser, too."

She walked into her bedroom and looked at the bed. "Nah." She went to the closet and removed a pair of jeans and a blue golf shirt. After quickly changing clothes, she left the cabin and headed for the park office.

In no time at all, Gib drove through the open gate that marked the entrance to the Benton State Park. She parked in the last available "official vehicles only" spot and stepped into the office. She waved to George, the ranger at the counter, who was busy explaining the park rules to a family of six. Coming to a closed door, she tapped lightly.

"Come in," Clint yelled.

Gib opened his door and stepped into his office, closing it quietly behind her. "Looks busy out there."

Clint looked up with something akin to relief in his eyes. "Boy, am I glad to see you. How are you doing?"

"I'm okay." Gib sat in one of the guest chairs. "I'm so damned sorry about that mess, Clint." She lowered her gaze, unable to look him in the eye.

"Hey, no. We've interviewed at least two dozen witnesses, and every one of them says that your boat saved the angler from being cut in half. Kennie did the best she could."

Gib raised her head. "How is she? I haven't had a chance to run up to the hospital to visit."

"She's awake, and mad as hell." Clint chuckled. "The doctors won't release her until Friday, at the earliest. I've been able to talk around it, but she's really going to be pissed when I have to tell her she's on extended leave until she gets complete medical clearance."

"How long will that be?"

Clint shrugged. "I've been told it could be as little as six weeks, or as long as four to six months. All depends on how well her head heals." He tapped his forehead. "How's yours?"

"I have a bit of a headache, but no other symptoms. That's one of the reasons I stopped by. I wanted to let you know I can be back at work in the morning, if that's okay."

"If it's okay? Are you kidding me?" Clint opened his desk drawer and took out a box. He tossed it to Gib, who caught it easily. "Poor George is going nuts, having to work the desk and cruise the park. We'd both be extremely grateful if you'd take the day shift."

Gib opened the box and took out a phone that was identical to the one she lost. "I'd be glad to. Eight to eight?"

He sat back in relief. "Oh, god. That would be fantastic. Are you up to it?"

"Sure. But I guess this will put the search for the poachers on the back burner."

"For now. I don't mind you keeping your eyes open for anything suspicious, but the safety of the park guests has to come first."

Gib stood. "Of course. What about Dan and Jessica? How are they?"

"Jessica has to wear a sling for the rest of the week, so I've assigned her to the office. Dan's out patrolling, but he's not happy about it." Clint got out of his chair and walked around to the front of his desk. "Don't overdo it your first day back, Gib. If you start feeling bad, let me know and I'll have someone cover for you." He held out his hand. "But I'm damned glad you're okay."

She shook his hand. "Thanks, Clint. I should be fine, though."

"All right." He clapped her on the shoulder. "Get some rest. You still look like hell."

"Thanks a lot." Gib laughed and left his office, ready to go home and call a certain redhead.

IT TOOK A lot of self-restraint, but Gib refrained from calling Delaney the moment she returned to the cabin. Instead, she took her gun cleaning kit from the coat closet and sat at the kitchen bar. She spread everything out and began to clean her weapon, a Glock Seventeen. In no time at all, she had disassembled, cleaned and reassembled the gun.

Gib put away her kit, washed her hands, and wandered around her cabin. She looked at her watch. "Almost eight. That's not too soon, is it?" Mad at herself, she decided to kill more time. With her new phone in hand, Gib grabbed her address book from the table beside the front door and sat on her sofa. She began the time-consuming task of entering all her phone numbers into the cell phone.

Forty minutes later, her task complete, Gib looked at her watch. "Close to nine. Hopefully she doesn't go to bed early." Unable to sit still, she stood and decided to go outside. After dialing Delaney's number, she paced restlessly along the front porch.

"Hello?"

Gib couldn't help but smile when she heard Delaney's voice. "Hi, this is Gib."

"Good evening, Officer. I take it you didn't go to bed after I left?"

"I was going to, really, but I wanted to talk to my boss about tomorrow." Gib sat on the front steps and watched the moonlight reflect off the lake. "I'll be working eight 'til eight, at least for the immediate future."

Delaney was silent for a moment. "Twelve hours a day? Are you up to that?"

"Sure. Most of it is driving around and being a visible presence. It's not difficult."

"I see."

Gib stretched out her legs and crossed them at the ankles. "Dee? Are you mad?"

The heavy sigh was its own answer. "No. Not mad, exactly. Why would I be?"

"I don't know. That's why I asked."

Delaney's voice softened. "Gib, I know you're an adult, and you have a job to do. But I can't help but worry."

"Oh." Gib stared out at the lake, thinking about what Delaney said. "You know, I've been doing this for over fifteen years, and the other night was the first time I've ever drawn my gun."

"Really?" Delaney giggled. "I thought I was going to wet my pants. You scared me to death."

Gib laughed. "To tell you the truth, I was a little nervous myself. All I could think about was how I was going to explain to you how I let someone get inside one of your trucks."

"Are you scared of me, officer?" Delaney asked in a breathy tone.

"Uh." Gib's mouth went dry. "I wouldn't say scared," she finally got out.

Delaney's mirth was contagious, and soon they were both laughing. The redhead was the first to recover. "So, about your work schedule. Is that every single day? Or do you get time off for good behavior?"

"That's what I was calling about. Are you doing anything on Friday evening?" Gib braced herself for the rejection she was expecting.

"It depends. Are you asking me on a date?"

Gib cleared her throat. "Let me try this again. Ms. Kavanagh, would you do me the honor of being my date on Friday evening?"

"Why, Officer Proctor. You do know how to turn a girl's head," Delaney answered, in an exaggerated southern drawl. "I would be delighted. What do you have in mind?"

"Dinner, for sure. I wish there was someplace we could go dancing." Gib liked the idea of having an excuse to hold Delaney in her arms. "If we were in Austin, I would know of several places. But, this being Benton—"

Delaney cut her off. "You like to dance?" It was another bone of contention with Chris. The woman refused to even attempt to go dancing. When they did go out, Chris ended up getting drunk, while Delaney fended off other offers.

"Oh, yeah. Love to dance. Always have."

"So do I. And I know of the perfect little place to go. So I hope you have a good pair of dancing shoes."

Gib grinned. "I'll see what I can do. Is eight-thirty on Friday too late?"

"It's perfect. I'll be waiting for you, officer. Now get some rest, so you'll be sharp for work."

"Yes, ma'am."

Delaney snorted. "And don't call me ma'am." She softened her voice. "Goodnight, Gib."

"Goodnight, Dee. Sleep well." Gib waited until Delaney hung up before she set her phone beside her. "Hurry up, Friday."

Chapter Eight

ALTHOUGH IT WAS after visiting hours, Gib had no trouble getting to Kennie's hospital room. She was still in uniform after her first day back to work and carried her authority well. After finding the correct room, she peeked inside the open door.

Kennie appeared to be sleeping. Her blonde hair was barely visible beneath a white bandage that covered most of her head. She must have sensed she wasn't alone, because she opened her eyes and looked around. "Gib?'

"Hey, there." Gib moved quietly to stand beside the bed. "How are you doing? Are you listening to the doctors?"

"I'm fine, Mama Bear," Kennie teased. Her voice was strong, belying her serious injury. There were dark circles beneath her eyes, but they were clear. "My parents said you saved my life."

Gib shrugged. "The news reports exaggerated. I hung onto you so we wouldn't sink." She picked up Kennie's hand and gently held it. "But you did some pretty fancy driving to keep from killing anyone. I'm proud of you, Kennie."

Her eyes welled with tears. "We could have all died."

"True, but we didn't." Gib sat on the side of the bed. "I'd be proud to ride with you any time. You make good decisions and you have a quick mind." She pulled the younger woman into a hug as Kennie began to cry. "It's going to be all right, I promise," she murmured softly.

A sound at the door caused Gib to look up. She saw a couple, who by their looks, were related to Kennie. "Hi."

The man was the first to speak. "Hi. I'm Pete Wyatt and this is my wife, Trisha. We're Kendall's parents."

Gib stood and accepted his hand. "It's a pleasure to meet you both. I'm Gibson Proctor." She had barely gotten her name out when she was hugged by Trisha.

"We can never repay you for what you've done for our daughter," Trisha whispered in Gib's ear.

The stocky woman blushed. "Kennie's the real hero. Without her fast reflexes, there would have been many more serious injuries."

Pete stood next to his daughter's bedside. "That's what Lt. Wright told us." He squeezed Kennie's hand. "Now if we can just keep her from breaking out of the hospital."

"Dad."

Gib laughed at the younger woman's expression. "Well, I need to get going. I just wanted to stop by and check on the hero." She walked to the bed and lightly tapped Kennie's nose. "Behave yourself and listen to your doctors, all right?"

"Yes, Mama Bear. I will." Kennie laughed at the blush her nickname caused. "Thanks for stopping by, Gib. I really appreciate it."

"I'll be back," Gib threatened in a bad accent. "Nice to meet y'all, Mr. and Mrs. Wyatt." She waved to Kennie as she left.

THE SPLATTER OF fat raindrops hitting her windshield caused Gib to frown. It was Friday night and she was on her way into Benton to pick up Delaney for their first real date. She didn't want anything to spoil their evening, but it appeared that Mother Nature had other ideas. Her truck had just crossed into the city limits when the sky opened and Gib was suddenly in the midst of a torrential downfall.

She cursed and clicked on the wipers, straining to see through the heavy rain. Visibility was poor, so Gib slowed the truck. She checked herself in the rearview mirror. The haircut she had received the evening before looked okay, although once the rain touched it, all bets were off. Her collar-length hair was usually straight, until it became damp. The way the ends curled made her wish she had remembered to bring a hat to protect it from the rain.

Soon, Gib parked beneath the covered parking at Delaney's apartment. She was three cars away from the front door. After she unbuckled her seatbelt, Gib leaned over the seat and searched for an umbrella. "Ah-ha!" It was small, but would be good enough to protect her date.

She jogged through the rain and almost slipped when she got inside the foyer. The same man was at the desk that she'd seen before, so she nodded her greeting and walked carefully across the marble in her boots.

Once she was in front of Delaney's door, Gib nervously wiped her free hand across her black shirt and matching jeans. She tapped lightly on the door, not surprised at all when it opened immediately. Her brain short-circuited at the vision in front of her. "Uh."

Delaney stood in the doorway with a very pleased look on her face. "Good evening, officer. You look nice."

"Wow," was all Gib could say. She blushed when she realized she had spoken aloud. "Um, hi. You look really fantastic."

"Thank you." Delaney stepped back. The navy blue silk dress accentuated all of her curves. Since it was sleeveless, her toned arms were highlighted as well. "Come on in."

Gib was so busy staring at Delaney that she almost ran into the door. "Thanks." She joined Delaney on the sofa, with only a cushion between them. She twisted the umbrella in her hand. "It's raining."

Delaney grinned and looked out through the sliding door to the patio. "Yes, it is." She leaned over and brushed her fingers through Gib's damp hair. "Did you not use the umbrella?"

"Oh, no. I brought it for you."

"Honey, you could have used it to come inside."

The thought hadn't even occurred to Gib. "Damn." She shook her head and laughed. "I think I've lost my mind."

"You're so cute." Delaney's hand drifted from Gib's hair, across her forehead and down her cheek. The stitches had been removed, and all that was left from the accident was a thin, red line. "I've missed seeing you this week."

Gib leaned into the touch. "I've missed you, too. Talking on the phone every night isn't quite the same." She closed her eyes when Delaney moved closer and kissed her. Gib's hands couldn't stay still and she moaned as they slid up and down along Delaney's sides.

"Gib," Delaney gasped, as she tipped her head back. Gib's lips soon began to blaze a path along her throat, and Delaney tangled her fingers in Gib's hair and pulled her closer. "Oh, baby, yes."

The whispered words urged Gib on. Her hands soon drifted lower and she started to raise the dress, when she realized what she was doing. She sat back and blinked. "Uh, I," she stammered. "Damn, Dee. I'm sorry." She carefully lowered the blue dress and tried to smooth it out with her hands. "I didn't mean to get so carried away."

Delaney's eyes, which were glazed with passion, slowly cleared. She used her thumb to wipe the lipstick away from Gib's mouth. "Honey, it takes two to tango. I wasn't exactly fighting you off, was I?"

"No, but—" Gib was stopped by Delaney's finger on her lips.

"As much as I'm enjoying this evening so far, you owe me a nice dinner and then an evening of dancing. And I plan to collect."

Gib grinned. "Yes, ma'am." She moved out of the way when Delaney tried to slap her arm.

"Don't call me ma'am," Delaney growled playfully.

"Whatever you say, beautiful lady." Gib stood and held out her hand. "If we're planning on dancing the night away, we'd better eat first." She helped Delaney to her feet and spun her around. "I hope those shoes are comfortable."

Delaney laughed as she was twirled around the room. "They are, don't worry. Take me dancing, Gibsy."

"You got it, Dee." Gib danced her toward the front door, laughing.

THE LIGHTING IN the Italian restaurant was dim, with candles on the tables for ambiance. Subtle instrumental music played in the background, reminiscent of Italy. Delaney looked across the table at her date. "You seem surprised that Benton has a place like this."

"I am. Before I left, I think the nicest place was Fran's Cafeteria. We all thought it was a big deal because a lady would come by and refill your drinks right at your table."

Delaney laughed. "We'll never be Dallas or Austin, but Benton's got a little bit of class, now." She held up her wine glass. "Here's to a classier Benton."

Gib touched her glass with Delaney's. "Amen." They both started laughing at the toast. "I don't think I've laughed this hard in ages," Gib admitted.

"Me, either." Delaney loved how the candlelight reflected in Gib's eyes. "I've been wondering something."

"What's that?"

"How'd you get your name?"

Gib continued to grin as she tore a breadstick in half. "The entire time my mom was pregnant with me, they thought I was a boy. Her father, Gibson Llewellyn Jameson the third, harped at them until they finally agreed to name the firstborn after him, at least partially. When I was born, I think my mother got back at him by still naming me Gibson." She shrugged. "He died before I turned one, so I don't remember him."

"Wow. Remind me never to piss off your mom." Delaney rolled her fettuccine on her fork before popping it into her mouth. "Mmm."

Gib cut into one of her lobster raviolis and took a bite. "I don't know what kind of sauce they use, but this is really good."

"It's a vodka sauce." With a devious smirk, Delaney tore off a piece of her breadstick and dipped it into Gib's plate. She moaned as she put it in her mouth. "Very good."

"You're a tease," Gib accused.

Delaney winked at her and slowly licked the sauce from her lips. "You think?"

It was Gib's turn to moan at the erotic display. "Behave." She took a deep breath and used her napkin to wipe her chin. "Watch out for paybacks."

"I can't wait." After slipping out of her shoe, she slid her foot along the inside of Gib's knee. The other woman jumped and sputtered. "Problem, officer?"

"Nothing I can't handle," Gib choked out. She reached beneath the table and caught the foot before it could travel any higher. "Look what I found."

Delaney tried to tug her foot away. "Gib," she warned.

"I wonder. Could you be ticklish?" Gib used her other hand to run a finger across the bottom of Delaney's foot.

"Aah!" Delaney kicked and almost knocked over the table. "Gibson Proctor," she drew out slowly.

Gib grinned evilly. "Yes?" Her finger took another pass along the nylon-clad foot, which kicked again. "Problem?"

"I'm going to," Delaney gasped as her foot was tickled again. "Stop! Please!" she begged.

"Ha." Gib caressed the top of the foot before releasing it. "There's your payback."

Delaney slid her foot back into the shoe. "Uh huh. Just wait."

LITTLE SISTERS WAS filled to near capacity by the time Delaney and Gib arrived. Delaney exchanged words with the brawny woman at the door, who gave her a hug and allowed them to enter. They were assailed by loud country music the moment they walked in.

Gib put her mouth close to Delaney's ear. "Come here much?"

"Maybe," Delaney answered coyly. She tugged on Gib's arm. "Come on. Let's grab something to drink and try to find a seat."

For her part, Gib was more than happy to tag along behind Delaney, her eyes rarely leaving the shapely behind that wriggled so enticingly in that slinky dress. She was surprised by the amount of women who waved and greeted her date, yet felt a little kernel of pride at being the one walking with her. She had to stop suddenly when Delaney paused and turned around.

The redhead grinned. "See anything interesting?" she asked.

"Definitely." Gib moved to stand beside her. "You look fantastic."

"Thank you." Delaney kissed her on the cheek before pointing to a group of tables near the bar. "If we sit over there, the music's not as deafening."

"Perfect." Gib put her hand on the small of Delaney's back and allowed her to lead the way. She held out a chair for the redhead, before taking the one closest to her. They had barely gotten seated when a heavily pierced woman with a tray stood at their table.

"Hey, ladies. What can I get for you?"

Delaney smiled at her. "I'd like a rum and coke." She turned to her date. "What about you?"

"Whatever beer you have on tap is fine, along with a glass of water," Gib ordered. She gave the woman a twenty dollar bill. "Keep the change."

The woman's eyes brightened and she gave Gib a sultry grin. "Thanks. Be right back."

When they were alone, Delaney couldn't help but laugh. "I think you made a new friend."

Gib shrugged. "They work hard and don't get much pay. I can afford it."

"You're just too sweet." Delaney scooted her chair closer until there were only a few inches between them. "Are you always like this?"

"Like what?"

Delaney waved her hand around. "So, I don't know...gallant?"

Gib stopped a moment to think. "I don't know about that. I just try to treat everyone with the same respect I'd like to get." She leaned forward when Delaney put a hand behind her head and pulled her closer. Her eyes closed when soft, moist lips touched hers.

After breaking from the kiss, Delaney brushed her thumb across

Gib's lip. "I've marked you again."

"Is it my shade?" Gib joked.

"It can be."

Gib grinned. "I'm beginning to like lipstick." She gave her date another light peck. "Do they always play country music here?"

"Some of the time. Saturday is Eighties Night, and Tuesday is rock. I know other nights are different types of music, but I can never remember them." She looked up when two women came to the table. "Hey!"

The taller of the two, a muscular brunette, had her arm around the shorter, stockier blonde at her side. "It's good to see you here again, Delaney."

"Terri and Kate! I'm so glad to see you." Delaney got up and immediately embraced each woman separately.

Kate, with her blonde hair cut in a bob, looked at Gib inquiringly. "I see you've traded up," she teased the redhead.

"What?" Delaney turned to Gib. "Oh, definitely. Guys, I want you to meet Gibson Proctor. She's a Police Officer for the State Park."

Gib stood and held out her hand. "Nice to meet y'all. You can call me Gib."

Terri shook her hand. "Pleasure's all ours, Gib. Have you known Delaney long?"

"A few weeks." Gib held out Delaney's chair, gently pushing her up to the table after she sat. "Would you like to join us?"

"Are you sure we won't be interrupting anything?" Terri asked.

Delaney shook her head. "Not at all. Right, Gib?"

"I wouldn't have offered if I didn't mean it." Gib stood until the other two women sat across from them. "I just recently moved back here, so it's nice to be able to socialize." She smiled as their server brought their drinks. "Thanks."

"You're very welcome," the woman told her. She noticed the two additions to the table. "What would you ladies like?" After she got their orders, she gave Gib one last flirty smile and left.

Terri whistled. "I can't believe you let her live, Delaney." She didn't think the woman would have been as lucky, if her attention had been on Kate.

The redhead laughed. "I'm not worried." She heard a slow song start playing and turned to her date. "Ready to dance?"

"Sure." Gib stood and pulled out Delaney's chair for her. "I'll try to be gentle on your toes."

They found an empty spot on the dance floor and Gib took Delaney in her arms. Gib released a content sigh as they fit together. As they slowly moved along the floor, she felt the redhead tuck her head against her chest. The feeling of contentment grew and Gib rested her cheek on Delaney's hair.

GIB STOOD AT the door while Delaney fought with her key in the lock. She couldn't keep her eyes off the smooth expanse of skin available, her hands nearly itching with the desire to touch those creamy shoulders.

Once the door was unlocked, Delaney stepped inside and tugged on Gib's hand. "Would you like to come in?"

"Sure." Gib grinned. The grip on her hand was so tight she didn't have much choice. "I had a great time tonight."

"Me too." Delaney staggered and kicked off her shoes, gently pushed Gib onto the sofa and climbed onto her lap. "You made me feel like a princess tonight."

"I did?"

Delaney nodded. "Mmm-hmm." She linked her hands together behind Gib's neck and brought her face close. "I don't think I've ever been treated so well before."

"You deserve it," Gib whispered, right before their lips met. She ran her hands along the redhead's shoulders and caressed the skin that had tantalized her all evening. The sudden feel of cool air against her chest caused her to pull away from the kiss. "Dee, wait."

"Why?" Delaney continued to unbutton the black shirt. She started to push the shirt off Gib's shoulders, nipping and kissing the exposed skin.

Lost in the haze, Gib struggled to remember why this was such a bad idea. "I, uh," she gasped when a warm hand found its way inside her bra. "Dee."

Delaney raised her head and captured Gib's mouth. She straddled her lap and couldn't seem to get enough of her.

Gib got a heavy taste of the tequila that Delaney had enjoyed earlier. The officer was the only one who refused the shots, saying she had to drive home. The heavy odor of alcohol on Delaney's breath reminded Gib what was more important. She pulled away. "Sweetheart, wait."

"Don't want to," Delaney muttered. She lowered her face to bite Gib lightly on the throat. "You taste good."

"Damn." She put her hands on Delaney's chest and gently pushed her back. "We can't, Dee."

Delaney glared at her through glassy eyes. "Why the hell not?"

"Because you've had too much to drink, and I don't want any regrets tomorrow." Gib adjusted her bra and buttoned her shirt. "Sweetheart, don't look at me like that."

"I'm not drunk," Delaney argued. She tried to climb off Gib's lap and ended up on the floor. "Fuck."

Trying not to laugh, Gib stood and held out her hand. "Here."

"Don't laugh at me," Delaney snarled. She crawled to her knees and tried to stand, but couldn't get her balance. After Gib put her hands under her arms and raised her to her feet, Delaney swatted her hands away. "I didn't need your help." She would have toppled over if Gib hadn't caught her. "Damn it."

Gib got tired of watching her struggle. She put her arm around Delaney's waist. "Come on. Let's get you ready for bed."

"Only if you're going to join me." Delaney leaned into Gib.

"Not tonight." Gib led her to the bedroom. "Can you get undressed while I get you some water?"

Delaney's sultry smile should have been a warning. She turned her back to Gib. "Unzip me?"

"Sure." Gib lowered the zipper. The more skin that appeared the harder it was to keep her resolve. Especially when she noticed Delaney wasn't wearing a bra. She backed away. "I'll just get that water now."

The dress dropped to the floor and the redhead stepped out of it. Clad only in a dark blue thong, stockings and shoes, Delaney turned around. "Oops."

"Ah, hell." Gib inhaled sharply. "You're not making this easy."

"Oh? What's the matter, officer?" Delaney started to move forward and got her feet tangled in the dress. She started to fall forward, when Gib lunged and caught her. She raised her head and grinned. "Looks like I fell for you."

Gib rolled her eyes. "Woman, you're trying my patience," she growled. Tired of fighting, she scooped Delaney into her arms and carried her to the bed. She dropped her onto the down comforter and leaned over her. "You are an incredibly beautiful woman."

"Kiss me," Delaney demanded. She grabbed Gib's head and drew it down. When their lips met, she wrapped her legs around Gib's waist. "Oh, god." Delaney pushed Gib away suddenly.

"What's wrong?"

Shaking her head, Delaney covered her mouth. She tried to sit up but wobbled.

Gib understood all too well. She picked her up and headed quickly for the bathroom. Arriving just in time, she placed Delaney in front of the toilet just as the redhead's stomach heaved. Gib held her hair away from her face and covered Delaney's shoulders with a clean towel to keep her from getting chilled.

Once her stomach was emptied, Delaney leaned back against Gib. "I don't believe this." She tugged the towel around her. "This is not how I planned on ending the evening." She began to tremble.

"Come on; let's get you off this cold floor." Gib helped her to her feet. She waited while Dee rinsed out her mouth and washed her face, then helped her back to the bed. As gentle as she could, she took off Delaney's shoes and tucked her into bed. "Are you going to be all right?"

"I think so."

"Okay. Let me get that water for you." Gib kissed her on the forehead and left the room. When she returned, Delaney was sound asleep, snoring softly. She placed the water on the nightstand and sat on the edge of the bed. "You're really going to feel this tomorrow, Dee." She considered her options. Since she'd only had the one beer, she was more than okay to drive home. On the other hand, Delaney had gotten sick, and Gib would worry about her all night if she left. She sighed. "I hope I don't regret this." She got up, walked to the other side of the bed, and took the extra pillow. "At least the sofa's comfortable."

THE HEAVY POUNDING in her head woke Delaney. She cracked open her eyes and groaned at the intense light. "Oh, god." Even the ragged whisper brought pain. She smacked her dry lips and almost gagged. "What crawled into my mouth and died?" she asked hoarsely. She raised her body into an upright position and swayed. "Ugh." She swung her legs over the bed and had to close her eyes as another wave of nausea hit. Once the room stopped spinning, Delaney slowly opened her eyes and looked down at her body. "What in the hell?"

After brushing her teeth, washing her face and taking care of other business, Delaney stopped at her dresser and put on a long tee shirt. She struggled to remove the nylons and thong, before leaving the bedroom in search of coffee. The sight on her sofa startled her and she let out a scream.

Gib sat up quickly and looked around. "What?"

"What are you doing here?" Delaney closed her eyes and grabbed her head. "Damn it."

"Are you okay?" Gib got up and put her arm around Delaney. "Why don't you sit down?"

Delaney slapped her hands away. "Stop it." She wobbled and slowly sat on the recliner. "Why are you on the couch?"

"I was worried about you." With her shirt tail out and her hair mussed, Gib looked unusually scruffy.

Delaney couldn't help but smile at the sight. "You can't be for real." She remembered all too well how Gib fended off her drunken passes the previous evening.

"What do you mean?" Gib tucked her hands in the front pockets of her jeans. "Um, would you like me to make you some breakfast?"

Just the thought of food caused her stomach to roll. Delaney shook her head. "Not today." She crossed her arms over her chest. "I guess I owe you an apology, huh?"

"For what?"

"Don't be coy with me, officer. I practically threw my drunken self at you last night." Delaney brushed her hand through her hair and grimaced. "God, I'm so embarrassed."

Gib sat on the end of the sofa nearest her. "Are you kidding? I was angry with myself for almost taking you up on it."

"Really?"

"Oh, yeah. When you," Gib blew out a breath, "um, stepped out of that dress, I almost had a heart attack."

Delaney sighed. "Yeah, bet I was real sexy when I was throwing up." She covered her face with her hands.

"Well, no, you weren't sexy," Gib admitted quietly. "All I wanted to do was hold you and make it all go away."

The heartfelt words touched Delaney's wounded spirit. "Oh, Gib. I don't deserve someone like you."

When Delaney began to cry, Gib dropped to her knees in front of her. "Don't say that, Dee." She put her hands on the other woman's knees and gently squeezed them. "You're a smart, beautiful, sexy-as-hell woman. I know I'm not the most sophisticated person in the world, but I really enjoy being around you."

Delaney sniffled and looked into Gib's eyes. The honest affection she saw was almost more than she could stand. "You must be a glutton for punishment."

"I've been called worse." Gib kissed the tip of her nose. "Look, I know you've got the hangover from hell and could probably use a lot more sleep. If you can hold down some dry toast, I'll get out of your hair for a while. Is there anything I can get you before I leave?"

"No, I don't think so." Delaney touched Gib's cheek. "Do you have any plans for today?"

Gib shrugged. "Not really. Got some laundry to do, and maybe run a broom around the cabin. Why?"

Lowering her gaze, Delaney stared at Gib's hands. "I swear I'm not usually like this, but," she stopped for a moment.

"What?"

So quietly that she could barely be heard, Delaney asked, "Could you stay here with me?" She damned herself for being so weak. "No. Never mind."

"Dee?" When she didn't look at her, Gib placed her fingers under her chin. "Hey." The unshed tears in those blue eyes caused a similar ache in her heart. "I could use some sleep myself." She gently kissed her. "Thanks for being brave enough to ask."

Delaney smiled at last. "You could be so dangerous," she mumbled, before she leaned forward and put her arms around Gib's shoulders. "Thank you."

After two pieces of toast, a cup of coffee and two bottles of water, Delaney felt much more human. She sat on the edge of her bed and waited for Gib to come out of the bathroom. When the door opened, she couldn't help but grin. "You look cute."

Gib stood in the doorway and put her hands on her hips. "Cute? I'm supposed to fill hearts with fear." She had gone to her truck for her clean workout clothes. The soft cotton shorts and matching gray tee shirt were slightly baggy. The shirt had small black letters over the left breast proclaiming Texas Peace Officer. She posed with her arms in a muscle pose. "Scared?"

Delaney giggled and fell back onto the bed. Her giggles turned to squeals when Gib raced across the room and tackled her. "Aaah!"

"Are you scared now?" Gib asked, straddling Delaney's hips. She leaned over the redhead and bent her fingers into claws. "Admit your fear," she threatened.

"Never!"

"Admit it, or pay the consequences." Gib lowered her hands and tickled Delaney's ribs.

The redhead squirmed and laughed. "Stop it," she yelled.

"Admit it!"

"No!" Delaney tried to avoid the fingers, but ended up rolling around the bed with Gib. "Evil woman!" Her screams silenced as she was wrapped up in Gib's strong arms. "Oh, god. I haven't laughed so much in a while," she sputtered, trying to catch her breath.

Gib rolled onto her back, allowing Delaney to rest on her chest. "Me, either." She looked into the other woman's eyes. "You are so damned beautiful."

Delaney cupped Gib's cheek. "So are you." She lowered her face and gently kissed her. They spent a few minutes enjoying the contact, neither one in a hurry to rush things. Delaney finally pulled back and laid her head on Gib's chest. "Am I squashing you?"

"Not hardly. Are you comfortable?"

"Very much."

Gib kissed the top of her head. "Good. Get some sleep, Dee."

"Okay." Delaney yawned and closed her eyes. "Goodnight."

Gib looked at the sunlight coming through the blinds. "Yeah. Sweet dreams."

Chapter Nine

MONDAY MORNING, GIB walked into the main office, whistling softly to herself. She noticed Clint at the counter with a sour look on his face. "Good morning."

"What are you so blasted happy about?"

She took off her hat and tried to wipe the grin off her face, without much success. "I had a good weekend. Why are you such a grump?"

"Well, let's see. Half my staff is either injured or gone, and I've got calls out all over the state, begging for help. How's that?"

"Where's George?"

Clint scratched at his neck. "Chicken pox."

"You're kidding."

"Do I look like I'm kidding?" He scratched at his arm.

Gib stared at him. "Do *you* have the chicken pox?"

"I had it when I was six. But ever since I heard, I keep itching like crazy." The phone rang and he grabbed it. "Benton State Park, Manager Clint Wright speaking. How may I help you today?" His face brightened as he listened. "Really? That would be fantastic. When? That soon? Thank you. Yes, I will. Good-bye." He hung up the phone and grinned. "Salvation!"

"Dare I ask?"

Clint laughed, almost maniacally. "That was one of the managers from Big Bend. He asked for volunteers to bail us out, and had a couple agree. He said he'll probably go by lack of seniority, since none of them seemed completely thrilled. Our extra body will be here next week."

"That's good. So, Bud is in Omaha with his family, George has the spots and Kennie is still in the hospital. What about Dan and Jessica?"

"Dan's patrolling the park and Jessica," Clint thought for a moment. "Honestly, I have no idea where she's at. Would you mind hunting her down? I'd like her to work the counter today."

Gib nodded. "Sure, no problem." She put her hat back on and saluted. "Reporting for duty, boss."

"Oh, shut up." Clint wadded up a piece of paper and threw it at her. "Go."

"Ten-four," Gib answered, catching the paper and tossing it in the trash on her way out.

She was still laughing when she climbed into her truck. She loved picking on her boss, and knew he enjoyed the banter as well. Her mind shifted to the past weekend.

Gib was awakened late Saturday afternoon by light kisses on her neck and throat. They spent the entire afternoon snuggled in bed, exchanging kisses and talking about anything and everything. Although they didn't go any further, Gib felt that the time was well spent, as they learned more about each other.

Her radio crackled to life, ending her pleasant daydreams. "This is Proctor, go ahead."

"There's a disturbance at the swimming pool," Clint informed her. "Could you please check it out?"

"On the way." Gib took the shortest route to the park's public swimming pool. Most of the time she was called in to sort out an altercation among the kids that congregated at the pool. Other times a belligerent parent had to be told that the pool was not a babysitting service. Any children under the age of twelve had to be accompanied by a parent or guardian.

The pool was surrounded by a tall chain-link fence. The main gate was set off by a large stone structure, which housed the restrooms, concession stand and showers. She parked in front of the entrance and hurried through the stone gates. "Great."

The sight that greeted the officer was a full-blown fight surrounded by at least twenty people, all yelling and cheering. Gib pushed her way through the crowd. Two teenage girls in swim suits were going after each other, wrestling and punching. Both had shoulder-length blonde hair and neither could have weighed more than one hundred ten pounds. They were cursing and slapping at each other and were covered in scratches and dirt. "Hey, stop it!" She reached for one but was unable to get a good grasp because of the girl's sweaty skin.

The crowd continued to egg them on, taunting Gib's presence.

"Ha! Stupid cop!"

"Get her, Meg!"

"Ooh, good one!"

Gib stepped in between the two girls and grimaced when a foot connected to her shin. "Cut it out," she yelled, wrapping her arms around the girl in a two-piece pink suit and turning away from the other.

"Bitch! I'm gonna kick your ass," the other girl screamed. Wearing a black one-piece suit, she charged and jumped on Gib's back.

"Damn it!" Gib released the girl in pink and started wrestling with the girl on her back. "Last chance. Get off or I will arrest you!"

"Fuck you, pig!" The girl put her slender arm around Gib's neck and tried to choke her. She knocked off the officer's baseball cap and started pulling on her hair.

Gib flipped her off her back and had her face down on the ground. She fended off the screaming and kicking from the other girl while she handcuffed the one on the ground. "Now stay put!" She stood and turned, holding her hands up around her face to keep from getting hit by the other girl. She kept one foot lightly on the other girl's back in order to keep her on the ground. In a loud voice she demanded, "Everyone break it up!"

"Aaah!" The free girl charged Gib, who caught her. "Damn you! Let me at her!"

"What the hell is your problem?" Gib wrestled with the girl and finally got her hands behind her back. "Stop it!"

"She stole my boyfriend! I'm going to kill her!" The girl on the ground yelled. "Bitch!"

"I did not, you ugly whore!"

"Enough!" As the crowd slowly dissipated, Gib used one hand to hold the girl's small wrists together behind her back. She carefully bent over and grabbed the other girl by the arm. "Stand up slowly."

"Stupid bitch," the girl on the ground spat as she was helped to her feet. She tried to kick her opponent but was jerked away by the officer.

"Cool it," Gib ordered.

"Looks like you have everything under control." Jessica stood a few feet away with a smirk on her face. "Sorry I got here too late."

Gib glared at her. "Yeah, right. Clint needs you at the office."

"I got his call earlier, but was having trouble with my Jeep. Later, Proctor." Jessica waved and walked away, laughing.

"Come on, ladies. Let's go have a chat in my truck." Gib led the girls out of the pool area, ignoring their curses and threats. She leaned the handcuffed one against the side of the truck while she opened the back door. "Sit down."

"Bitch."

Gib opened the front door and took her spare handcuffs out of the glove box. Once the girl in pink was cuffed she sat her in the front passenger seat. "Now. Who wants to tell me what's going on?"

"Fuck you."

"It's her fault, the bitch."

"How old are you?" she asked, not getting an answer from either one. Gib sighed and keyed her mike. "Clint, I need a police transport for two minors."

Clint immediately answered. "All right. I'll get them on their way."

"No!"

"Fuck that! My dad will kill me!" Backseat girl kicked at the open door.

Gib put her hands on her hips. "Too bad. Stop it!" When the girl in the front seat began to cry, Gib privately cursed her soft heart. "Hey."

"Stupid crybaby," the girl in black taunted from the backseat. "Whiny little bitch!"

"Shut up," Gib growled. She softened her voice for the other girl. "What's your name?"

"Megan." The girl sobbed and lowered her head.

The girl in the back kicked the seat in front of her. "I don't know what Justin sees in you. Baby!"

"Stop it, or I'll throw you in the back of my truck."

"Fuck you," the girl snarled as she kicked the seat again.

Gib took plastic restraints from the glove box. She grabbed one of the girl's legs, intent on tying her feet together. A well-placed heel against her cheek caused her to see stars for a moment.

"Suck it, pig!" the girl laughed victoriously. She cried out when her other leg was captured. "Fuck!"

Gib blinked to clear her vision. "One more word out of you and I'm going to wash your mouth out with soap."

The girl glared at her, but stayed silent.

Gib turned her attention to Megan. She held out her hand. "Step out of the truck so we can talk."

Megan sniffled and looked at her. Tears still tracked down her cheeks, but her sobbing had stopped.

"Come on."

After she helped Megan from the truck, Gib walked her far enough away so that the other girl couldn't overhear their conversation, but she could still keep an eye on her. "All right. Do you want to tell me what happened?"

"Lindsey thinks I stole her boyfriend," Megan explained quietly. "But we're just friends, honest."

"How old are you, Megan?"

"Sixteen." Megan wiped her face on her shoulder. "If I get arrested, my mother will have a fit."

Gib sighed. "If I free your hands, will you behave?"

"Yes, ma'am." Megan stood quietly while Gib removed her handcuffs. Once she was free, she rubbed her wrists. "I'm sorry for hitting you."

"Who started the fight?"

"Lindsey. I was walking out of the bathroom and she grabbed my hair and threw me down. You can ask anyone. That stupid bi-, I mean, *she* started it."

Gib stared into Megan's eyes. The girl never looked away. "How did you get here today?"

"I drove."

"All right. Get your stuff and go home. But if I ever catch you causing trouble again, I will let the Benton police take care of it, you hear me?"

Megan nodded vigorously. "Yes, ma'am. Thank you, officer." She jogged toward the entrance.

"Hey! Where's that bitch going?" Lindsey yelled. "Hey!"

Gib sighed and headed for her truck. Her good mood from the weekend was long gone and it wasn't even lunchtime. She stood beside the back door. "How did you get here today?"

"Bite me!"

"You know what? I can sit here all day while you curse and act like a little punk. Or, I can go inside and get your stuff so no one steals it. What will it be, Lindsey?"

Lindsey glared at her for almost a full minute before she decided to speak. "I came with my friends."

"All right." Gib leaned into the truck and fastened Lindsey's seat belt. "I'll be right back."

"Bitch," she growled.

Gib ignored her and went inside the pool facility. After speaking with the concessions employee who had called the office, she found Lindsey's friends and explained that Lindsey would have to go into police custody. They gave Gib the girl's tote bag, which held an oversized tee shirt and her wallet. It took less than fifteen minutes, and Gib was on her way back out front. She dusted off her hat and placed it on her head.

Once she closed the truck doors, Gib slid in behind the wheel. She placed Lindsey's bag on the passenger seat beside her.

"You stupid cow! I'm going to—" Lindsey shut up when Gib turned in her seat.

"Young lady, you need to shut your mouth and think about what you've done. We're going up to the office and waiting for the police. Maybe if you behave, they'll let you off with a warning." She started the truck and exhaled heavily.

AFTER HANDING OFF her charge to a pair of officers with the Benton Police Department, Gib walked into the office.

"Wow, Proctor. You look like crap," Jessica taunted from behind the counter.

Gib ignored her and continued to Clint's office. She tapped on his closed door.

"Come in."

She opened the door. "Benton's finest just left."

Clint raised his head from the paperwork he had been concentrating on. "Good grief. What the hell happened to you?"

"Two hormonal, teenage girls," Gib moaned, as she sat across from him. She took off her cap and rested it on her crossed knee. "Give me guys any day over girls."

"Amen," Clint agreed. "Now that Jessica's here, why don't you take a couple of hours off? Maybe get cleaned up?"

"Do I look that bad?"

He shrugged. "Well—"

"Gee, thanks." She put her hat on and stood. "If you're going to be that way, I'm going home and showering. Call me if you need me. I have to head into town later today to fill out the paperwork at the PD." She closed his door and tipped her cap at Jessica. "Have fun. There's a middle school tour group coming around one."

"I didn't hear anything about that."

Gib grinned. "Yep. They're coming for the camping safety lessons.

But don't worry, I don't think you'll have more than thirty second-graders."

"Shit." Jessica opened a lower cabinet and looked for the pamphlets they handed out on camping. "Where are you going?"

"Oh, didn't Clint tell you? I'm taking the afternoon off. Then I'm going into town to do the paperwork on today's scuffle. Bye." The cursing from Jessica was music to Gib's ears as she left the office.

BY THE TIME Gib left the police department, her stomach was growling. She checked her watch and saw that it was past six in the evening. "I wonder if Dee has had dinner yet." She hit the speed dial and waited with a smile on her face.

"Kavanagh Massage Parlor," a sultry voice answered.

Holding back her laughter, Gib lowered her voice and spoke in a thick Spanish accent. "This is Officer Sanchez from the Benton Police Department. We found this phone and are searching for the owner. Where are you located?" The dial tone that answered her caused Gib to laugh out loud. She drove toward Delaney's apartment.

Once she was in the parking lot, Gib dialed Delaney's cell phone again. It rang four times before it was answered.

"Hello?"

Gib started laughing as soon as she heard the tentative voice. "Hi, Dee. What's the matter?"

"Gib? I thought your phone—" Delaney grew quiet as she realized what had happened. "I'm going to kill you."

Still laughing, Gib got out of her truck. "Have you had dinner yet?"

"Dinner? Why? What time is it?" The curse from Delaney was anything but ladylike.

"I take that as a no." Gib waved to the concierge as she walked across the lobby. Once she was in the elevator, she had trouble hearing what Delaney was saying. "Hold on a second." She was soon standing in front of a familiar door. "What was that sound?"

"What sound?" Delaney asked.

Gib tried to keep from laughing. "I swear it sounded like someone was knocking on your door."

"Have you lost your mind? How in earth could you hear something over the phone that I didn't hear at my apartment?"

"There it is again."

Delaney growled. "I think you're imagining things, officer. But if it would make you happy," her voice trailed off and she opened the door. "I swear, I'm going to kill you," she said into the phone as she stared into Gib's face.

Gib couldn't hold in her laughter any longer. She took the phone out of Delaney's hand and turned it off. "Hi there."

"You are such a brat!" Delaney grabbed the front of Gib's shirt and pulled her into the apartment. Now that Gib was out of the dim hallway, Delaney got a better look at her. "What in the hell happened to you?"

"Had two women fighting over me," Gib answered, nonchalantly. "No big deal."

Delaney's eyes narrowed. "Excuse me?"

Gib dropped onto the sofa and patted the cushion beside her. "Come here."

"Are you through teasing me?"

"For now," Gib replied with a grin. She patted the cushion again.

With an air of indifference, Delaney took her time crossing the room. She sat primly beside Gib and turned her head away from her. "Hrumph."

"That's not going to do." Gib put her arm around the redhead and tugged her close. She pulled until Delaney sat on her lap. "Much better."

Delaney turned and rested her hands on Gib's shoulders. She could see a bruise on Gib's cheek, as well as several ugly scratches along her neck. "What really happened?"

"Two teenage girls got into a fight at the swimming pool and I had the honor of breaking it up."

"Girls? Were they wrestlers or something?" Delaney traced the bruise with her fingertip. "I can't see anyone getting the better of you."

Gib laughed. "Neither one was very big. I would have been fine, if one hadn't jumped on my back."

Seeing that Gib was amused, Delaney couldn't help but laugh as well. "I bet that was a sight. What were they fighting about?"

"What do girls usually fight about?"

They both answered at the same time. "Boys."

After their combined laughter had died down, Delaney lowered her face to Gib's and kissed her. She rested her forehead against a strong shoulder and sighed. "I'm glad you're okay."

"If I get kissed like that every time I break up a fight, I think I'll antagonize the children as often as possible." Gib flinched as she was poked in the stomach. "Careful, that's empty. Which is why I stopped by. Have you had dinner?"

Delaney raised her head and looked into Gib's face. "I was working on some new plans when you called."

"Time got away from you, did it?"

"It did."

"Well, good. That means I can take you out for dinner."

"Actually, I have what I need to make a decent meal, unless you've got your heart set on something in particular."

Gib pecked her lightly on the lips. "Home cooking? I'm sold. Would you like some help?"

"Sure." The redhead stood and held out her hand. "Come on,

officer. I'll show you how an Irishwoman makes an Italian dinner."

THE WEEK DRAGGED by for Gib, and by Thursday she seriously considered taking Jessica out in the brush and leaving her. The tech constantly made snarky comments to Gib, but never when anyone else could hear.

Gib was still seething over the thinly-veiled homophobic comment that Jessica had thrown at her as she was leaving the office for the morning. She was about to check out for lunch, when her radio crackled.

"Proctor, this is the office. We've had a report of a missing child near campsite twenty-three." Jessica sounded completely professional for a change.

Gib keyed her mike. "I'm on my way." She took the park map from between the seats and verified the location of the camp. She keyed the mike once again. "Base, I need verification. Did you say campsite twenty-three?"

"Yes. Is there a problem?"

"I wasn't aware that we were renting the space out, considering how far it is from the road. The only way to get there is by hiking, isn't that correct?"

Jessica sighed. "The family is a group of hippies. I wouldn't be surprised if they were all smoking something out there."

"Great." Gib clipped her mike onto her shirt and drove her truck to one of the most remote camping sites at the park. It took her ten minutes to get to the parking spot designated for the camp. There were no other vehicles around, which made Gib suspicious. She clicked her mike. "Base, I'm at the parking space. There isn't anyone here."

"Proctor, what part of hippies did you not understand?" Jessica snapped. "They hiked into the park and asked for the most remote campsite. Was that too hard to follow?"

"Middleton, all I did was ask for information. Cut out the attitude." Gib got out of her truck. "I'm heading toward the camp now. Will advise after I meet with the family." She walked down a path through the cedar trees listening carefully for any sign of trouble.

Fifteen minutes later, Gib stepped into an empty clearing. There was no sign that anyone had been there recently. When she knelt beside the rock-encircled fire pit, there were cobwebs in the stacked wood. She keyed her mike. "Base, this is Proctor. There's no one at campsite twenty-three."

The radio was silent for several minutes, before Jessica replied sweetly, "Oh, dear. It seems I made a mistake. That family was there *last* weekend. I must have read the note wrong. I'm terribly sorry."

"Damn it!" Gib picked up a rock and violently threw it into the trees. "Of all the asinine crap!" She took a few deep breaths before responding on the radio. "No harm done. I'm checking out for lunch. Call me if there are any *real* problems." Still seething, she picked up a large stick and broke it across her thigh. "Stupid brat."

AFTER BEING UNMERCIFULLY teased by her parents for actually showing up to the office, Delaney was able to buckle down and work without interruption. She reviewed several plans that had been accepted, and a couple of others that had been declined. "I don't know what's wrong with this one," she grumbled. "If we offered it for any less, we'd have to pay *them*." Disgusted with the idea, she pushed away from her desk. "Morons."

Delaney looked around at her office. At home she tended to have clutter, but here, everything had its place. Her drafting table was clean and her cherry desk only had a phone, inbox and blotter on it. She stood and walked around the desk, intent on getting a cup of coffee from the break room.

The intercom on the phone buzzed. "Delaney, there's someone here to see you," Maureen's voice was cool and professional.

"Damn." Delaney returned to her chair and hit the intercom. "Send them back, Mom. Thank you."

"Sure thing, sweetie."

While she waited, the redhead took out her PDA and checked her appointments. "Unless they forgot to tell me, I don't have anyone scheduled." She looked up at the knock on her open door. "Oh."

Christine stood at the door, wearing a pair of dark slacks and a white buttoned down shirt. In her hand was a small bouquet of wildflowers. "Hi."

"Hello, Chris. What brings you by?"

Chris looked down at the flowers in her hand. "Can I come in?"

"Uh, sure." Delaney indicated the chair across from her desk. "Please, sit down."

"Thanks." Chris stopped before she sat and held out the bouquet. "These are for you."

Not wanting to appear rude, Delaney took the flowers. "Thanks." She sniffed them. "What are you doing here?"

Chris shrugged. "We haven't talked for a while and I missed you."

"Um, Chris? When people break up, they generally don't talk. You do realize that we're no longer together, right?"

"I know you were mad that I was being a jerk. And I'm sorry about that."

Delaney put the flowers on her blotter and shook her head. "Chris—"

"No! I was. I totally get that." Chris stood and put her hands on the desk. "I love you, Laney. More than I ever thought possible. I mean, look. I got a job. I'm going to be a waitress, even though I hated doing it.

You know I'm a chef. But I want to be able to support us."

"There is no us, Chris! Can't you understand that?"

Chris stood up straight and blinked. "But there *can* be. Right?"

As much as she hated to hurt the other woman's feelings, Delaney knew she had to. "No, there can't. I'm sorry."

"But why?" Chris whined. "I *love* you!"

"Chris." Delaney stood. "I don't love you." She jumped when Chris slapped the desk.

"Bullshit!" Chris circled the desk and stood within a foot of her. "Did you ever love me?"

Delaney swallowed hard. "I...I don't think so."

Chris' eyes grew hard and she clinched her fists at her sides. "What about when we made love, Laney? Did you feel anything then?"

"Made love? You call what we did making love?" Delaney glared at her. "Making love isn't saying, 'let's get it on,' and then drunkenly groping the person you're with." She pushed Chris in the chest. "And it's certainly not guilting your partner into having sex. Yes, when we first got together, it was good. You were kind, considerate and loving. I enjoyed our time together."

"I still can be."

Delaney shook her head. "The last couple of months, I avoided you. I'm sorry. I should have broken it off. Not strung you along. That's my fault."

"But—"

"No. You've changed, Chris. And I don't like the person you've become." She backed away and held her hands up in front of her. "It's over between us. Please leave."

Chris frowned. "No. I won't accept that." She turned to walk away, but stopped at the door and pointed at Delaney. Her voice was strong as she declared, "You'll love me again. I know you will. And I won't give up on us."

The shaky breath that Delaney exhaled was the only indication she gave of her true feelings. Once Chris had left, she dropped into her chair. "How could I have read her so wrong?"

Chapter Ten

THE CLOUD COVER on Friday morning couldn't dampen Gib's mood. Although she hadn't spoken to Delaney in the past couple of days, the lovely woman was never far from her mind.

On the previous afternoon, Gib stopped by the construction site and spoke to Dylan. He let her know that his sister was at the office, but would most likely return to the site to check the week's work on Friday.

Gib tried to call Delaney the previous night, but was only able to reach her voice mail. She left a silly message and promised to contact her again soon. Now, as she left her cabin for the day, Gib hummed to herself.

The road to the construction site was filled with the usual equipment, and Gib maneuvered her truck around them with ease. Her grin widened when she came upon the familiar black SUV. She parked behind it and got out, adjusting her duty belt. When she spotted Delaney on top of the dam, she marched across the road. As she reached the bottom of the dam, she yelled, "Ma'am, you shouldn't be up there."

The redhead turned and glared at the voice, before a soft smile touched her face. "Gib! Give me a second, will you?"

Gib touched the brim of her baseball cap. "Certainly, ma'am." She laughed at the wagging finger she received and waited patiently for Delaney to finish what she was doing.

Dressed in jeans, sneakers and a turquoise, short-sleeved blouse, Delaney looked perfectly at ease as she took the path down the dam. She stopped a few feet away from Gib and put her hands on her hips. "And to what do we owe the pleasure of your visit, officer? Run out of innocent citizens to harass?"

"Not at all, ma'am. I'm only here to make certain you haven't strangled anyone today."

The redhead laughed. "Not yet, but the day's still young." Her expression turned serious. "I'm sorry I didn't return your call last night, but it was late and I—"

"Don't worry about it. I was just wondering how you were doing. Say, are you real busy at the moment?"

Delaney shook her head. "Not anymore. Why?"

"I was on my way to check on the new bison calf, and wondered if you'd like to tag along. If I can get your promise not to steal him."

"Oh, I don't know." Delaney linked her arm with Gib's and led her away from the dam. "What will you give me if I'm good?"

The sultry voice gave Gib the chills. "Uh, I, um," she stammered. It took her a moment to get her libido under control. She opened the passenger door for Delaney and helped her inside. "You are not playing fair."

"I never do," Delaney admitted with a grin. Too excited to sit still, she squirmed in her seat. "Thanks for thinking of me, Gib. I've never seen a baby bison."

Gib turned and gave her a gentle smile. "I'm always thinking of you," she said quietly. When Delaney didn't comment, she turned her attention back to the road. "Anyway, the last few times I've checked, Mama and baby were with the rest of the mixed herd. I'm hoping they'll be near the fence this morning."

"Do they always stay by the fence? And if they don't, what makes you think they will today?"

"I heard on the radio this morning that we have a pretty good chance of storms. The cattle tend to gather near the fence when that happens, although I don't know why." She slowed the truck as they passed the holding pens. "There they are."

Delaney turned and sat up higher. "Oh, wow. He's so ugly he's cute."

"Yeah." Gib parked and turned off the engine. "If we're quiet, we should be able to walk up to the fence for a closer look." She grinned when Delaney immediately opened her door and got out. It wasn't long before Gib stood beside the redhead. She kept her voice low so as to not startle the animals grazing nearby. "Brutus has already grown since the last time I'd seen him."

"Brutus?" Delaney questioned, just as quietly.

Gib chuckled. "Doesn't he look like a Brutus?"

"Well, I guess so," Delaney relented. She laughed when Brutus butted his mother's flank, before settling down for his breakfast. "Ouch!"

"I don't know why he does that. It seems like every time I've seen him eat he has to whack her first. If I were her, I'd whack him back." Gib moved closer to Delaney and put her arm around the other woman's waist. "Thanks for coming with me."

Delaney leaned into Gib's embrace. "I enjoy being with you, Gib."

"What are you plans tomorrow?"

"Just the usual weekend stuff. Laundry, housework, grocery shopping."

Gib kissed Delaney on the side of the head. "Would you like to go out to dinner with me? Maybe catch a movie or something?"

"I have a better idea." Delaney turned in Gib's arms and looked into her eyes. "Why don't you come over and I'll cook you dinner tonight?"

"Okay."

"Well, don't let me twist your arm, or anything," Delaney teased at Gib's immediate answer.

Gib laughed and shrugged. "Sorry. It's just that I don't usually cook for myself and getting a home-cooked meal is always a treat."

Delaney put her hands behind Gib's neck. "One more thing, officer."

"Hmm?"

Delaney kissed Gib tenderly. "Bring a toothbrush."

THAT EVENING, DELANEY moved around her apartment and double-checked each room. The floors had all been vacuumed or swept, the furniture was free of dust and the table was set for a romantic dinner. She straightened the linen tablecloth and carefully inspected each wine glass for spots. Once she was satisfied with the place settings, she went into the bedroom and looked at herself in the full-length mirror on the closet door.

Delaney studied her reflection carefully. The emerald, sleeveless dress she wore barely reached mid-thigh, and was cut low enough that she didn't even bother wearing a bra. Her hair had been pulled back into a chignon, with a few loose tendrils around her face. She nodded at herself and leaned closer to make certain her makeup wasn't too much.

When the doorbell rang, Delaney grinned at her reflection and hurried to open the door. "Well, hello there, officer. You sure clean up well."

Gib blushed. Her black slacks were pressed, and the light gray shirt went well with the black suit coat she wore. "Thanks." She made a point of slowly taking in all of Delaney. With a low whistle, she shook her head. "Wow. You look absolutely fantastic." She handed the redhead a single yellow rose. "For you."

"Thank you." Delaney took the flower and brought it to her nose. Its sweet fragrance brought a smile to her face. "Please, come in." She stepped back and allowed Gib to enter. "Have a seat while I get a vase for this."

Unable to take her eyes off the redhead, Gib lowered herself onto the sofa. She nervously jiggled her left leg and brushed her hands on her thighs. When Delaney returned, she jumped to her feet. "My god, you're gorgeous," she blurted, then blushed again.

Delaney stood in front of her and kissed her lightly on the lips. "Thank you. Now sit. We have a few minutes before dinner is ready."

Gib dropped onto the sofa again, grinning when Delaney sat almost on top of her. She put her arm around the other woman and sighed as Delaney snuggled closer. "This is nice."

"It certainly is," Delaney purred. She turned so that she could rest her head on Gib's shoulder. "How was the rest of your day?"

"Not too bad. Jessica had the day off, so at least I didn't go on any wild-goose chases."

Delaney raised her head. "Why do you let her get away with that? I'd kick her ass."

Gib laughed and gave the redhead a squeeze. "I wouldn't doubt it.

But right now, I can't really prove anything. It's only been twice, and she swears they were both mistakes. She'll slip up one of these days, don't worry." She kissed Delaney's hair. "You smell good."

"I hope so. I took a shower and everything." Delaney giggled when Gib started to tickle her. "Stop it!" she squealed, trying to move away. She fought off Gib's fingers and launched a counter-attack. "Ha!"

"Aaah," Gib yelled as she rolled away. So intent on escaping, she didn't realize she had ran out of couch space and found herself on the floor.

Delaney, forgetting how short her dress was, immediately straddled Gib. "Gotcha!"

Gib's eyes grew larger when she saw so much of Delaney's legs. The sight of the stockings being held up with black garters caused her to forget the game. She ran her hands up the outside of Delaney's thighs and groaned. "Dee, unless you want to skip dinner, I think you'd better get up," she begged.

"Give up?" Delaney loved how she affected Gib. She took a finger and traced a line from Gib's throat to her chest. "Are you sure?"

"Please," Gib whispered hoarsely.

Delaney slowly leaned over and kissed her, rocking her hips slightly. As much as she didn't want their first time together to be in the middle of the living room floor, she was almost past the point of caring. The buzz of the oven timer brought a smile to her face. "Saved by the bell," she murmured, leaving one final kiss before getting up. She adjusted her dress and winked. "Take off your coat, officer. You're not going anywhere tonight."

AFTER DELANEY WENT into the kitchen to check on dinner, Gib stood and brushed her fingers through her hair as she exhaled heavily. "Holy crap. She's going to kill me." She removed her jacket and folded it neatly over one arm of the couch. Once she was able to walk without embarrassing herself, she walked into the kitchen. "Do you need any help?"

Delaney turned away from the stove and grinned. "Probably not as much as you do," she teased.

"You are an evil woman, Delaney Kavanagh." Gib stood next to the bar and leaned against it. "Is there anything I can do to help with *dinner*?"

"No. I have everything under control. Unless you want to put that salad on the table," she nodded to the bowl on the bar.

Gib picked up the bowl. "Anything else?"

"Go ahead and sit down, and I'll bring the meatloaf in a second." Delaney went back to her preparations while Gib followed her instructions. Once she had moved the meatloaf to a serving dish, she brought it to the table.

Gib stood and held out a chair for Delaney. "Everything looks delicious," she said, as she kissed the back of Delaney's neck. "And the food looks good, too."

"Thank you." Delaney sat and shivered as Gib's hands went from the back of her chair, to stroke lightly across her shoulders. "Behave."

"I plan on it," Gib whispered in her ear, before taking her seat at the table, with Delaney to the left of her. "Thank you for cooking tonight. You're going to spoil me."

Delaney raised her wine glass. "All part of my master plan."

"And what plan is that?" Gib asked, raising her glass as well. "To a great evening."

"Oh, yes. A *great* evening," Delaney agreed with a smirk.

They watched each other over the candlelit table. The longer the meal went, the thicker the sexual tension became. Gib watched as Delaney used an index finger to wipe a smudge of mashed potatoes away from her luscious, red lips.

Delaney heard the groan. "Are you all right?"

"Yea," Gib cleared her throat. "Yes, I'm fine."

"Are you satisfied?"

Gib's eyes widened. "What?"

"Would you like more?" Delaney asked, pointing to the remaining meatloaf.

"Oh, no. I'm great," Gib squeaked.

Delaney leaned closer to her and lowered her voice. "Are you ready for dessert?"

"Uh, sure." Gib momentarily closed her eyes and silently prayed for strength. She heard the clatter of dishes, and opened her eyes to see Delaney clearing the food from the table. "Can I help?"

"No. I'm going to cover these dishes and put them in the refrigerator." In a couple of minutes, Delaney returned, with one large piece of cherry cheesecake and one fork. "Here we go."

Gib cocked her head when Delaney placed the plate between them. "Aren't you having any?"

"Yes. Scoot away from the table just a little."

Doing as she was told, Gib was surprised when Delaney sat in her lap. "Oh."

"I thought we could share."

Oh, god. She is *trying to kill me.* "Um, sure." Gib put her arm around the redhead's waist to help balance her.

Delaney took a forkful of the dessert and brought it up to Gib's mouth. "Open up."

Gib opened her mouth and took the bite into her mouth. She jumped when Delaney's free hand started playing with the back of her neck.

"Oops. Sorry."

After swallowing the cheesecake, Gib could stand it no longer. She kissed Delaney hungrily, groaning when her lover turned and straddled her lap. Her lips moved down across Delaney's throat, sucking on the rapidly beating pulse point.

"Gib, please," Delaney moaned, tilting her head back.

"I've had enough foreplay," Gib growled.

"Yes."

Gib stood and kicked the chair away, as Delaney wrapped her legs around her waist. They continued to kiss as she staggered toward the bedroom, refusing to let go of the woman in her arms. She got to the edge of the queen-sized bed and dropped Delaney, her own body following quickly behind.

Delaney tried to unbutton Gib's shirt, but her shaky hands weren't much help. "Damn it!"

"I got it." Gib sat up and tore open the top two buttons. She quickly pulled the shirt off over her head and grinned. "How fond of that dress are you?"

"Let me up for a second," Delaney answered. She stood and turned her back to Gib. "Unzip me, please."

Gib's hand trembled as more skin was slowly revealed. "You're gorgeous," she reverently whispered. When the dress hit the floor, she almost followed it. Delaney stood before her, wearing only shoes, a dark green thong, garters and stockings. "Oh, my lord."

Delaney sat on the edge of the bed and held out a foot. "Help me?"

"Yes." Gib swallowed heavily as she dropped to her knees. She watched Delaney unclip the garters on her left leg, while Gib removed her left shoe.

"Roll them down," Delaney ordered softly.

Gib slowly rolled the nylon down Delaney's leg. Unable to stop herself, her lips followed the same path. She felt hands in her hair, urging her on. "Dee—"

"Hurry," Delaney begged.

A triumphant grin broke out on Gib's face, as she slowed her pace. "Why, sweetheart? We have all night." The grip on her hair tightened.

"Now."

Gib took off the other shoe and make quick work of the stocking. Still on her knees, she looked up into Delaney's face. "You really are the most beautiful woman I've ever seen."

Delaney's face softened at the honesty in Gib's voice. She traced her hand across the other woman's cheek. "Gib?"

"Yes?"

"You're overdressed."

Gib looked down at herself, still only missing a shirt. Quickly her bra hit the floor. "Yeah, I guess maybe I am." She stood, kicked off her shoes and unbuckled her belt. Her eyes never left Delaney's as she lowered her slacks and stepped out of her underwear. "Now look who's overdressed."

Delaney grinned and scooted back on the bed, her satin thong shining in the light. "Come here and do something about it." She squealed when Gib leapt toward her on the bed. Her giggles disappeared as Gib's body covered hers.

GIB AWOKE IN a panic, unable to move. She blinked as the sunlight streamed through the cracks in the mini-blinds. Something tickled her nose and she looked down. A wall of red hair was all she could see of Delaney, who was lying completely on top of her. At some point during the evening, Gib had unpinned Delaney's hair, enjoying the feel of the silky strands against her skin. She used her hand to lightly brush the hair away from her face, which caused Delaney to groan. Gib smiled tenderly. "Good morning, beautiful."

"No. Can't be morning."

"Sorry, but I think the sun would disagree with you." Gib's hand trailed lower until it cupped a shapely behind. "Oooh. Look what I found."

Delaney grumbled and shifted, her knee finding its own interesting place. At Gib's grunt, she giggled. "Look what I found."

"Dee," Gib warned. Her voice went up an octave when Delaney moved her knee again. "Oh, lord. Dee, you need to behave before things get messy."

"Whatever do you mean, officer?"

Gib wrapped her arms around Delaney and rolled until she was on top. "I mean," she kissed the redhead, "that one more move like that," she kissed her again, turning up the heat, "and I'd pee the bed!" She tickled Delaney and jumped off the bed, racing for the bathroom.

"I'm gonna get you for that, Proctor!" Delaney laughed and stretched. "Oh, god. I'm so sore," she moaned. Her laughter turned into a wicked giggle. "It's a good sore, though."

"What's good?" Gib asked, as she came out of the bathroom. She stood by the bed, her nude body peppered by small hickeys.

Delaney put her hands behind her head. "Good? Did I say good?" She slowly stretched her legs out. "Oh, honey. I'd say you were more than good."

"Yeah?"

"Mmm-hmm."

Gib sat on the bed beside her. "I had a rather enjoyable time myself, Ms. Kavanagh." Her hand traveled across creamy skin, also adorned with a few new blemishes. "Have I told you how beautiful you are this morning, Dee?"

A flush traveled from Delaney's chest up to her face. Her eyes sparkled with emotion. "You don't have to say a word, Gib. I can see it all in your eyes." She reached for Gib. "Now come here and give me a proper good morning kiss."

"Yes, ma'am." Gib allowed herself to be pulled down.

"Don't call me ma'am," Delaney ordered, giggling when Gib fell on top of her.

BY EARLY AFTERNOON, both stomachs were growling so Gib volunteered to make breakfast. She padded to the kitchen, not bothering to dress. It didn't take long for her to find the eggs and bread, and was soon cooking enough to feed their ravenous appetites. She was so focused on what she was doing that she had no idea she wasn't alone, until a warm body curled up against her back.

"Smells good."

Gib looked over her shoulder. "You should have stayed in bed. I was going to bring it to you."

Delaney kissed between Gib's shoulder blades. "I was lonely," she pouted.

"Well, we can't have that, can we?" Gib switched the stove off and turned around. "If you'll set the table, I'll bring the food over."

"Aren't you forgetting something?"

Gib rolled her eyes toward the ceiling as she pretended to think. "Hmm. Eggs, toast, sausage, coffee." She tapped her chin. "No, I believe I've got everything."

Delaney pursed her lips and leaned forward. She cleared her throat.

"Oh!" Gib snapped her fingers. "Orange juice." She squeaked when Delaney pinched her. "All right, all right. You don't have to be such a grump." When Delaney closed her eyes and leaned forward again, Gib licked the tip of her nose.

"Eeeww, gross!" Delaney wiped her nose and glared at her lover.

Gib laughed and danced around her. "Come on, Dee. Time for brunch."

"I'll get you back for that, Proctor."

"Gripe, gripe, gripe." Gib swatted her on the rear. "Get with it, woman. I don't want our food to get cold."

The redhead scooted out of her way. "Hey, watch it!"

"I have been," Gib leered. "And I'm enjoying the heck out of it."

Delaney gathered plates and silverware, putting a little sway in her hips as she walked toward the table. "Sweet talker."

Gib joined her and placed the food on the table. "Keep teasing me like that and it'll be a while longer before you get lunch."

"Oh yeah?" Delaney turned and put her hands on the table behind her, which caused her breasts to come to Gib's attention.

"Um," Gib's eyes strayed below her lover's face. "Uh."

Delaney laughed. "My eyes are a bit higher, officer."

"Eyes?" Gib slowly raised her gaze. "Oh. Yeah." She gave her a bashful grin. "Sorry."

"I'm not." Delaney kissed her before moving to her chair. "Feed me. Then you can ravish me."

Gib laughed. "Ravish? I thought I already did that." She took her place at the table. "Or, maybe that's what was done to *me*."

"You haven't seen anything, yet, Officer Proctor. Now eat up. You're going to need all your strength."

"Yes, ma'am."

"Don't call me— " Delaney was cut off when Gib put a piece of toast in her mouth.

DAMP FROM THE shower, Gib fell back onto the bed. "You know, we aren't getting a lot accomplished today."

"Oh, I don't know. I think we've gotten quite a bit done," Delaney argued, sliding her nude body against her lover's. They had played in the shower until the lack of hot water ran them back to the bed.

Gib yawned, even as her hands continued to rub along the redhead's smooth skin. "If I don't go home sometime soon and work on my laundry, I'll be going commando to work next week."

"Although the thought has its merits, I understand." Delaney raised her head to look at the alarm clock. "It's almost six. Why not stay the night and go home tomorrow morning?" She propped her head up on one arm and stared into Gib's face. "Besides, you look too tired to drive."

"Why would I be tired?" Gib yawned again. "We've barely left the bedroom all day."

Delaney laughed and pulled the covers over them. "Uh-huh. That's the biggest reason. Are you hungry?"

They had breakfast around noon and lunch sometime after five. The last meal had turned into an impromptu painting session with chocolate syrup and cherry pie filling, which is why they had gone to the shower. Gib scratched at her damp hair. "Not really."

"Good. Then go to sleep. We can order a pizza later, if we need it." Delaney kissed Gib's jaw before pillowing her head on her lover's shoulder.

"Sounds great." Gib put her arm around Delaney. "G'night."

Delaney smiled as Gib's voice trailed off into sleep. "Sleep well, honey."

IT WAS AFTER eleven on Sunday morning by the time Gib was dressed. She stepped into the living room and laughed at her lover's posture. Delaney sat in the recliner, with her arms crossed over her chest. "Aww. Why are you pouting?"

"I'm not ready for you to go," the redhead admitted.

"I know what you mean. Part of me is scared to leave."

"Scared? Why?"

Gib sat on the sofa and sighed. "This weekend has been magical to me. I'm afraid that when I walk out that door the magic will go, too. And I don't know if I can handle that reality."

Delaney got out of the recliner and went to her favorite perch - Gib's lap. "Honey, as far as I'm concerned, *this* is our reality. You'll go home, get your weekend chores finished, and we'll make plans to see each other again this week."

"Yeah, I guess."

"Now look who's pouting." Delaney kissed those pouty lips. "You know, I don't care if you stay until you have to leave for work tomorrow morning."

Gib returned her kiss with fervor and then touched their foreheads together. "Yeah, but I hate going without underwear."

"It's actually not bad, once you get used to it."

"Excuse me?" Gib raised her head and looked her in the eyes.

Delaney grinned. "I usually skip it when I'm at home, especially if I'm relaxing in my sweats."

"I wish you hadn't told me that."

"Why?"

Gib kissed the tip of her nose. "Because now that's all I be able to think of when we talk on the phone at night."

"Good." Delaney couldn't hold back a wicked chuckle. "And I'll never think of cooking breakfast again without seeing you in your birthday suit in my kitchen. So I believe we're even." She kissed Gib again and slowly climbed off her lap. "Come on, officer. Laundry calls."

"All right." Gib wrapped her arms around Delaney and hugged her. "Want to come over to my place for dinner on Tuesday?"

Delaney nodded. "Sure. And since I'm not quite ready to say goodbye, let me walk you to your truck."

Gib stepped away, but hung on to her lover's hand. "That could be dangerous."

"Why?" Delaney grabbed her keys before following Gib out the door.

"Because, if you're with me, I might throw you into my truck and take you home."

Delaney tugged her into the elevator and pushed the button for the lobby. "Promises, promises." Once the doors closed, she pushed Gib against the wall and started kissing her.

They broke apart just as the doors opened. Delaney smacked her lips. "I've always wanted to make out in an elevator."

"Whoa." Gib stepped out on unsteady feet. "You are dangerous, woman."

"Heh." Delaney waved to the woman working the concierge desk. "Hi, Lauren. How are the boys?"

The heavyset blonde smiled. "They're doing great, Ms. Kavanagh.

Mikey's got the lead in his school play."

"That's wonderful! Please let me know when it is, so I can go." Delaney never released Gib's hand as she led her through the foyer. "This is my friend, Gibson Proctor. I'm sure you'll be seeing her from time to time."

"It's nice to meet you, Ms. Proctor," Lauren replied.

Gib stopped long enough to shake the concierge's hand. "Nice to meet you, too. Please call me Gib."

"Good luck with that one," Delaney muttered under her breath. "I've been trying to get her to call me by my first name for over two years, now."

Lauren blushed and shrugged. "Sorry, Ms. Kavanagh. Company rules, you know."

"I'll keep working on you," Delaney promised. "Come on, Gib. Your underwear awaits."

"Oh, lord." Gib blushed and waved at Lauren as Delaney dragged her from the building.

The noon sun was obscured by clouds, leaving the day humid but comfortable. Gib unlocked her truck and turned to Delaney. "Guess this is it."

"Hey, it's all right. You're not going out of state or anything. Just home."

Gib nodded, but was unable to speak.

"Oh, honey." Delaney moved into her space and put her arms around Gib's waist. "I'll probably be at the office tomorrow, and more than likely will go to my parent's for dinner. But I should be home by eight, at the latest. Call me?"

"Sure." Gib shook her head and grumbled under her breath. "Sorry that I'm being such an idiot about this."

Delaney kissed her on the chin. "I'm not. I'd be a lot more sorry if you had jumped out of bed Saturday morning and took off."

"I'm not built that way."

"I know." Delaney gave her a soft, slow kiss. "And I'm very glad. Now, run on home to your laundry, and I'll call you this evening before bed."

"Okay." Gib hugged her close for a long moment, before getting in the truck. "I," she stopped. "I had a great time, Dee."

"Me, too." Delaney stepped onto the sidewalk and watched as Gib started her truck and drove away.

GIB WAS HALFWAY home when her cell phone rang. She turned on the speaker function and let it rest in her cup holder. "Proctor."

"Hey, Gibsy! What are you up to?"

"Hi, Maddy. I'm about to get my laundry together. How's your weekend been?"

Maddy groaned. "Don't ask. Suffice it to say, I don't believe small children should be left to their own devices in the men's room."

"Ugh." Gib laughed as she imagined the language her friend had probably used. "Fun, was it?"

"It was for the plumber. For me, that's a few hundred dollars I could have spent on something else. Anyway, why don't you bring your laundry over here? We can argue over basketball while it runs. I'll even spring for the pizza."

Gib frowned. Her friend rarely paid for the food, usually getting out of it by claiming poverty. "What's the catch?"

"What?"

"I know you, Maddy. What are you plotting?"

Her friend sounded hurt. "You wound me, Gibsy. Maybe I've just missed your smiling face. How about it? It's not like you enjoy the Laundromat."

"True. All right. Give me half an hour."

"That long? Hey, wait. Are you in your truck?"

Gib winced. "Uh, yeah. I'm almost home. It shouldn't take me long to get my stuff." She waited patiently while Maddy put two and two together.

"Oooh, Gibsy. Were you not home last night?"

"No, I wasn't."

"Did we have a sleepover?" Maddy teased.

Gib sighed. "I don't know about you, but I didn't get much sleep."

"Ah-ha! Sounds like we have *lots* to talk about. Hurry up and get here. I wanna know *all* the details."

"Yes, dear. See you in a few." Gib disconnected the call and rolled her eyes. "Yippee."

Chapter Eleven

THE FIFTY-FIVE inch television's surround sound drowned out the rumble of the dryer, while the two women relaxed on the leather sofa. A loud explosion through the speakers caused them both to jump, knocking the bowl of popcorn over between them. Maddy turned the volume down. "I hate that none of our teams are in the finals. But, maybe a shoot 'em up wasn't the best movie idea today."

"Oh, I don't know. It's not like we haven't seen it dozens of times." Gib yawned and stretched. "What time is it?"

"After four. Tired of my company already?"

Gib tossed a piece of popcorn at her. "No. Just curious."

"Speaking of curious," Maddy turned in her seat to face her friend, "wanna tell me about your slumber party?" She had been after Gib to talk ever since the other woman had arrived, but so far, had no luck. "Come on, please?"

"God, you're nosy." Gib took a sip of beer. "I had dinner at Delaney's Friday night."

Maddy bounced up and down. "Dinner, huh? Wait. *Friday*?"

"Yes, damn it. Friday. We spent Saturday together, and I went home today to do some laundry. Satisfied?"

"Probably not as satisfied as you are, Gibsy." At her friend's groan, Maddy laughed. "Oh, come on. What good is sex if you can't talk about it?"

Gib shook her head. "I never ask you about your sex life."

"That's because it's mostly self-service these days," Maddy lamented.

"Ew. TMI, Maddy. I didn't need that visual." Gib fake-shivered.

Maddy tossed several pieces of popcorn at Gib. "Smart ass. You're just jealous 'cause I'm straight."

"I keep telling you, all you need to do is meet the right woman."

"Nah. There's only one you, and it seems like you're taken." Maddy scooted closer. "So, how was it?"

Gib looked offended. "I'm not going to tell you!" Her face flushed blood red. "I...I couldn't."

"Ooh. This sounds serious." Maddy leaned against her. "Is it?"

Staring hard at the bottle of beer in her hands, Gib nodded. "I think so. I mean, it is to me." Her voice became softer. "I think I love her, Maddy."

"You can't be serious." Maddy stared at her friend, who refused to look at her. "Oh, my god. You are."

Gib nodded.

"One weekend of hot sex, and you're in love? Really?" Maddy

poked her in the ribs. "I mean, sure, she seems like a nice person and all, but love? Hon, you haven't known her long enough for that."

The silent woman drained her beer and placed the bottle on the coffee table. Gib stood and stared into the fireplace. "I can't help the way I feel." She turned to face Maddy. "There's just something about her. I feel complete when I'm with her, and lost when I'm not."

Maddy closed her eyes and shook her head. "No, no, no. Don't do this to yourself. You could be setting up for a hard fall."

"I can't help it." Gib's face broke into a beautiful smile. "I really think she feels the same. Every time I look into her eyes, I can see it. The way she touches me and kisses me, shows me exactly how she feels." She sat down again. "I do love her, Maddy. I know I do."

"All right." Maddy squeezed Gib's knee. "Just try not to move too fast. Take your time and see where it goes."

DELANEY HAD PLANNED on spending her Sunday sleeping. But a phone call from her parents inviting her for dinner changed her plans. After a refreshing shower, she dressed in a pair of casual, gray slacks and a black, sleeveless top. In no time she was on her way to their house.

The Kavanagh house, where Delaney grew up, was in the older part of Benton. Well-cared for homes were set on half-acre lots, most of them occupied by the original owners. The outside of the two-story Colonial home was red brick, with white columns along the front. Tasteful landscaping completed the suburban package, and when Delaney parked in the circular driveway, the Lexus looked right at home.

She opened the front door and stood in the entryway, listening. The sounds of an auto race came from the den, so she headed in that direction. Her parents were in their usual places. Her father, stretched out in his recliner, "watched" the race while snoring. Her mother was doing a crossword puzzle while perched on her favorite end of a floral-print sofa. "Hi, Mom," Delaney whispered, joining her mother on the couch.

Maureen took the remote and lowered the volume. "Hello, sweetie. I'm so glad you could come over today." She marked her page in the puzzle magazine with her pen, and placed it on the end table. "I hope my call didn't ruin any plans."

"I was going to be lazy today, but I'd much rather spend it with you." Delaney leaned over and kissed her mother's cheek. After she returned to her previous spot, she turned so she could face Maureen. "Anything exciting going on?"

The older woman studied her daughter and her eyes sparkled. "Not a thing. I see you and Christine have made up."

"What? No." Delaney shook her head. "Actually, I broke up with her a couple of weeks ago. She just can't seem to get the hint." She began to feel uncomfortable with her mother's scrutiny, and glanced down at her shirt to see if it had a stain. "What?" she repeated.

"Gone out to sow your oats, have you? Not that I blame you. I always thought Christine was too possessive over you. Your father told me that you'd broken up, but after she came to the office with flowers, I wasn't too sure."

"Mom, what are you talking about? I haven't gone out," her voice trailed off when she saw where her mother's gaze zeroed in. "Oh, hell." She covered her throat. "Does it look bad?"

Maureen laughed. "Not at all, dear. If that shirt didn't have such a low neck, I would have never seen it." She touched the blemish, right above the neckline, not far from Delaney's right breast. "So, if Christine didn't do it and you haven't been out running around, have you been attacked by large mosquitoes?"

With a roll of her eyes, Delaney swatted her mother's leg. "You're nuts. No, I've, um, met someone else."

"Someone else? So soon?" Maureen lowered her head as if to peer over glasses. She had traded her eyewear for contacts years ago, but had never lost the habit. "Oh, I see. Your park ranger."

"Park police officer," Delaney automatically corrected. "Her name is Gibson Proctor, but she goes by Gib."

"That's an unusual name."

Delaney chuckled. "She's an unusual woman. Well, not really. But I don't think I've ever met anyone quite like her before."

"Tell me about her."

"I'm not sure what to say. She does things sometimes that totally surprise me. Opens my doors, holds out my chair, things like that." Delaney's smile grew. "And she makes me laugh. A lot. I don't think I've laughed so hard in years, as I do when I'm with her."

Maureen nodded. "I've noticed that you've been a lot less, shall we say, prickly, lately. If that's because of this Gib, I can't wait to meet her."

"Well, I don't know about that. We're pretty casual right now. Nothing serious."

"Really?" Maureen raised one eyebrow. "Seems like it's serious enough to let her do that," she said, pointing to her daughter's neck.

Delaney shrugged. "We're having fun, but no. I've just gotten out of a nasty relationship. I'm in no hurry to jump into another one," she argued, although she felt disloyal for saying so.

"Friends with benefits?"

"Mom! Where did you hear that?" Delaney asked, her face turning bright red.

"I wasn't born under a rock, you know. And your father and I have quite an active sex life."

Delaney covered her ears. "I don't need to hear about it. Nah, nah, nah, nah."

"Silly child." Maureen swatted her. "Don't wake your father. He'll want to cook on that nasty grill of his, when we have a perfectly lovely one in the kitchen." She stood and brushed the wrinkles from her slacks. "Follow me to the kitchen, and you can help with dinner."

"All right. But no more talk about," Delaney lowered her voice, "s-e-x. I don't think my fragile psyche could handle it."

Maureen had to cover her mouth to keep from laughing too loudly. "I don't know where I went wrong with you, girl. You're such a prude."

"I am not," Delaney argued, as they left the living room. "But there are some things I don't think I'll ever be comfortable talking to you about. I may be scarred for life as it is." She yelped as her mother swatted her on the rear. "Stop it."

BY NOON ON Monday, not even the thought of her girlfriend could brighten Gib's day. She had already gotten into a nasty argument with Jessica over dispatch procedures, and was now stuck driving the snotty woman around, per Clint's orders.

"Look, Middleton, I don't like it any more than you do. But Clint wants you to be familiar with the fire roads."

Jessica had her arms crossed over her chest. "I'm perfectly capable of checking them out on my own. I haven't needed an escort since I was ten."

"It's no picnic for me, either." Gib drove past the construction site. She didn't see Delaney's Lexus, but hadn't expected to. "Some of the roads around the lake can be a little confusing if you're not used to them."

"Yeah, right. Dirt roads out in the middle of nowhere are *so* scary. Total bullshit," Jessica added under her breath.

Gib turned onto another road. "This one goes behind the lake, but doesn't actually go to the lake. It's mostly a firebreak to protect the cabins on the north side. It dead ends at the top of that little hill," she pointed to the right. "Kids have a tendency to park up here and party. I try to check it at least once a night during the warm months."

"Why not in the winter?"

"Because we lock the gate to the road in the winter. Only the main park gate and the gate to the lake are open. We still have a few old guys who come out and fish in December or January, but not very often."

Jessica nodded. "Do we check their permits?"

"Nah. Most of them have been fishing here since before the state took it over, so we tend to leave them alone."

"But what about regulations?"

Gib counted silently to five, trying to calm down. Jessica had questioned every single thing she had told her all morning. "Sometimes to keep good relations with locals it's best to let some things slide. No one's being hurt by some old guy sitting on the shore, drinking a beer."

"Public intoxication? Come on, Proctor. Even you wouldn't allow that."

"What's that supposed to mean?"

The look Jessica gave her was one of mild contempt. "I figured you'd be a stickler for rules and regulations, that's all."

"Why?"

"Oh, come on. I've known women like you. They seem to thrive on being able to lord over everyone else."

Gib stopped the truck and turned to look at her co-worker. "Women like me? And what kind of woman am I?"

"Never mind."

"Oh, no. You started this. Go ahead."

Jessica opened her door and got out. "I need some air."

"Hey, wait." Gib got out and walked around to the other side of the truck. "Be careful. There are gopher holes in this area."

"For god's sake, Proctor. I'm not a child," Jessica snapped, walking across a grassy area.

"Sure act like one." Gib walked close by, keeping her own eyes toward the ground. "So, what kind of woman am I? Old? Tall? What?"

Jessica quickened her pace. "Just shut up. You know what I was talking about. It's like you're proud of it, or— " her foot went into a hole and she yelled. "Fuck!"

Gib took a step and put her arm around Jessica, to keep her from falling.

"Let go of me, you fucking dyke!" Jessica screamed. She pushed Gib away and fell to the ground. "God damn it!" Her hands went to her right ankle.

"I told you to be careful." Gib squatted next to her. "Let me see."

Jessica slapped at her. "No. Don't touch me!"

"Would you just settle down? I'm not going to attack you." Gib waited to see what Jessica would do. "We're out here alone, Middleton. You've got two choices: let me help you back to the truck, or sit here indefinitely. What'll it be?"

"Bitch." Jessica slowly stood, keeping all of her weight on her good leg. "I can make it back by myself."

"All right."

Jessica tried to stand on her injured ankle. "Fuck!" She immediately raised it off the ground as tears fell down her face.

"Jessica, please. Let me help you," Gib asked softly. As much as she disliked the other woman, she couldn't stand by and let her suffer.

"No! I can do it." Jessica took one hop, the motion bringing renewed agony to her injured ankle. "Oh, my god, it hurts." She dropped to the ground and rocked back and forth, crying.

Gib had seen enough. "That's it." She knelt beside Jessica and easily picked the smaller woman up into her arms.

"Don't touch me!" Jessica slapped Gib across the face. "Let go of me!"

"Just shut up," Gib puffed, as she carried Jessica back to the truck. She grunted as the woman continued to hit her, first in the chest and then a hard slap to the side of her head. "One more time and I'll leave you here," Gib growled.

Jessica pulled back her hand and made a fist. "I'm going to turn you in for sexual harassment!"

"Whatever." Gib set her down outside the passenger door. "Think you can get in by yourself?"

"Fuck off, Proctor!" Jessica opened her door and slammed it behind her.

"You're welcome." Gib rubbed her cheek as she walked around the truck. "Sexual harassment. Funny."

AFTER LEAVING JESSICA at the Benton Community Hospital, Gib returned to the park to write up a report. She ignored the sneer from Dan, who was working the counter, and went directly to Clint's office.

Clint looked up as Gib tapped on his open door. "How is she?"

"Sprained ankle. She'll be on crutches for a couple of days. Although the way she was carrying on, it may be more like a month."

He grimaced. "We're running out of people, Gib. Although George should be back by Wednesday."

"That's good." She stepped into the office and closed the door. "I want to give you a head's up, in case she follows through with her threat."

"Threat?" Clint sighed. "Now what?"

Gib sat in the chair across from him. "She said she'd turn me in for sexual harassment."

"What?"

"We were talking while we were driving around and she kept hinting around about 'your kind of woman' to me. I kept asking her what she meant. She got pissed and took off across the gopher field."

He nodded. "With you so far."

Gib blew out a breath. "After she fell, I offered to help her. She kept screaming for me to not touch her." She held out her hands. "I didn't know what to do, Clint. She obviously couldn't walk, and I didn't want to leave her for the snakes."

"Right."

"So, I picked her up. Then she started screaming and hitting me, threatening to turn me in." Her hands dropped to her lap. "What was I supposed to do?"

His chuckle surprised her. "That explains the scratch on your face. Seriously, Gib. I would have done the same thing. If she brings it to my attention, I'll take her report. But it won't go any further than my office. And if she goes over my head, I'll handle it."

"All right. Thanks, Clint. I didn't want you getting blindsided with this."

"If she's got any sense, she'll drop it completely. I'm one complaint away from having her transferred."

Gib grinned. "From your mouth to headquarters' ear," she teased.

DELANEY STRETCHED OUT on her bed and sighed. The lack of sleep during the weekend had caught up with her. The room seemed silent and lonely, and she cursed at her neediness. "This is ridiculous. We spent one weekend together. I've never needed anyone around before."

She fluffed her pillows and opened a book. "Once I get engrossed in my reading, I'll quit being so stupid."

Her cell phone rang. Delaney dropped the book to the floor and answered it immediately. "Hello?"

"Hi, Laney."

Delaney fell back against the headboard. "Chris. Hi."

"How are you doing? I've been thinking a lot about you."

"Chris, please don't do this."

"Why not? Can't I even think about you anymore?" Her voice turned soft. "I really miss you, Laney. My new job is going well, and I'm hoping to get a new place in a few weeks. I'm sleeping on my brother's couch for now."

Delaney closed her eyes and silently prayed for strength. "I'm glad things are going well for you."

"Are you?"

"Of course I am."

"Since I've got a job now, will you go out with me?" Chris begged.

"No, Chris. I won't. I'm sorry."

The sound of a lighter being flicked could be heard. Chris took a deep breath and exhaled. "Why not?"

"I broke up with you, remember? Now please quit calling me, Chris. Goodbye."

"No!"

Delaney hung up the phone. "Damn her. Why doesn't she get the hint?" She got off the bed and went into the kitchen for something to drink. She took a diet root beer out of the fridge, grabbed the bag of cheese puffs and headed for the recliner.

The sound of the television did nothing to stop her thoughts, as Delaney replayed her conversation with Chris in her head. It seemed that no matter what she said, her ex-girlfriend wouldn't take no for an answer. "She'll probably find someone else to latch onto, sooner or later. At least I hope so." She crammed a cheese puff into her mouth just as her phone rang. "lo?"

"Dee?"

Delaney chewed and swallowed as quickly as she could. "Hi, Gib."

"Is everything all right?"

"Mmm-hmm." Delaney popped the top on her soda and tried to

wash the stubborn cheese puff goo out of her mouth. "Sorry."

Gib started laughing. "Did I catch you enjoying a snack?" She had been introduced to what Delaney claimed was the 'world's greatest snack food' during their weekend together. "Are your fingers orange, yet?"

"No, smartass, my fingers aren't orange. I had just eaten one puff when you called." Delaney took another puff from the bag and daintily nibbled on the end.

"I hear you," Gib teased.

Delaney purposely crunched into the phone. "Did you hear that?"

"Uh-huh." Gib lowered her voice. "I miss you."

"Aww. That's so sweet." Delaney sighed. "I've missed you, too. This bed is a little lonely," she admitted.

"I know what you mean. I've had a hard time getting to sleep. Silly, huh?"

Delaney's laugh was gentle. "No, it's not silly at all. Are we still on for tomorrow evening?"

"I sure hope so. I've got a couple of steaks to grill if that's all right with you."

"Sounds good." Delaney took her soda and snack to the bedroom and stretched out on the bed. "Guess where I am now?"

Gib took a deep breath and released it slowly. "Why don't you describe it to me?" she asked softly.

"Well, I'm lying down in this big old bed, all by myself." Delaney looked down at her body. The long tee shirt had a cartoon cat on it, holding a cup of coffee.

"What are you wearing?"

"Um, well." Delaney smirked. "Remember that thong from Friday evening?"

Gib sputtered and choked. "Ahem. Yes, I do. Quite well, as a matter of fact."

"Less than that," Delaney teased.

The other end of the phone went silent.

"Gib?"

A sudden wheeze, then coughing. Gib hacked a few times before she was able to speak. "Are you trying to kill me?"

"What were you doing?"

Gib coughed twice more before her voice was clear. "I was trying to eat my dinner."

"This late? Gib, it's almost ten o'clock." The answer was unintelligible. "What was that?"

"I said, I wasn't that hungry. But I figured I might as well have something before I go to bed. Not all of us own stock in the cheese puff industry."

Delaney laughed. "And what great meal did you come up with?"

"Salisbury steak, mashed potatoes and corn."

"Wow, I'm impressed. I thought you said you didn't normally cook big meals for yourself." Delaney propped up against the headboard and nibbled on her cheese puffs, which paled in comparison to the meal Gib described.

"Uh, well, it wasn't too hard. All I had to do was cut a slit in the plastic covering and pop it in the microwave."

Delaney snorted and spit a half-chewed cheese puff onto her chest. "Ugh. Gross."

"Hey, they're not that bad."

"No, not that." Delaney used a tissue to pick up the gooey mess and tossed it in the trash. "So, do you eat a lot of frozen dinners?"

Gib paused. "Yeah, I guess I do. It's no fun cooking for myself, although I did have a great kitchen when I lived in Austin. I'm not a chef, but I do okay."

"I'm looking forward to having you cook for me. I usually run over to my parent's house when I want a decent meal. Like you said, it's no fun to cook for only one person." Delaney stared at the open bag and finally pushed it away. "Now you've got me wanting something besides my usual."

"Poor baby. I'll share my congealed steak and overcooked potatoes with you."

The thought made Delaney queasy. "No, thank you. I think I'll hold out until tomorrow night."

"Sounds good." Gib sounded like she wanted to say more, but instead she sighed. "I guess I'll see you tomorrow, then?"

"You sure will." Delaney softened her voice. "Sleep well, Gib."

"You too, beautiful. Pleasant dreams."

Once Delaney hung up the phone, she rolled onto her side and looked at the pillow that Gib had used during the weekend. Her hand caressed the smooth, cotton case. "I wonder what she'll dream about. Me, maybe?" She laughed at herself. "Yeah, right."

Chapter Twelve

ALL THE WINDOWS in the cabin were open, allowing a fresh, clean breeze to cool the interior. Gib darted from room to room, keeping an eye out for anything that looked out of place. She had swept the wood floors twice, scrubbed the bathroom until it gleamed and made then remade the bed. She peered out the front window, looked at her watch, then turned and searched the living room again. Nothing had changed. "Good grief. I've lost my mind."

Gib stepped away from the window and walked to the back door. She glanced through the screen and verified that her grill hadn't burst into flames. She would wait until Delaney arrived before she put the steaks on. The sound of tires on the graveled driveway caused her to sprint across the room and stand with her hand on the doorknob. "Calm down," she ordered herself. After taking a deep breath, she opened the door and stood on the porch.

Delaney got out of her Lexus and waved. She was wearing her office attire, a black pencil skirt with a cream colored sleeveless top. She opened the rear hatch and took out a small, overnight case. Before she could close the hatch, Gib jogged over and took the case from her. "Thank you."

"You're welcome." Gib put her free arm around Delaney's waist while they walked up the steps and into the cabin. "It's good to see you." She hadn't been able to stop thinking of the redhead all day.

"It's nice to be seen," Delaney teased, hip-checking Gib before they went through the door. She stopped and gazed around the room. With all the doors and windows open, everything appeared bright and airy. "Wow. This is such an amazing place, Gib."

Gib placed Delaney's bag near the bedroom door. "It really is. I wish I could afford to buy it, but I don't make that kind of money."

"Something like this is expensive?"

"Right on the lake? Oh, yeah. And I'll enjoy it as long as I'm allowed to rent." Gib opened the refrigerator. "Would you like something to drink? I found that white wine you like."

Delaney sat at the bar. "I'd love some, thank you." She watched Gib open the bottle and pour one glass. "Aren't you going to have any?"

Gib handed her the glass. "I'm not big on wine. I've got a Corona open by the grill."

"You drank wine at dinner the other night," Delaney pointed out.

Her bashful shrug spoke louder than any words. Gib turned and took the platter of steaks off the counter. "Since you're here, I'll get these started." As she stepped around the bar, Delaney stopped her by touching her arm.

"Hold on a minute, please?"

"Sure." Gib put the platter on the counter and gave the redhead her undivided attention.

"I know it's probably none of my business, but why did you drink wine the other night, if you don't care for it?"

Gib started to say something silly, but the serious look she received stopped her. "I guess I didn't want to embarrass you."

"How would ordering what you want embarrass me?" Delaney tugged on Gib's belt to bring her closer. She rested her hands on the other woman's hips. "You don't eat with your mouth open. I would have noticed that."

"Cute." Gib shrugged again. "It was a pretty classy restaurant, and they brought us a wine list. I figured if I asked for beer they would have laughed, and you would have gotten embarrassed. It's not a big deal. I'll have a glass of wine with a meal, but I prefer beer."

Delaney pulled her closer and locked her hands behind Gib's head. "You're sweet. Deluded, but sweet." She gave her a gentle kiss. "Gib, I like you just the way you are. Please don't try to be something you're not, just to please me."

"All right." Gib gave her a quick peck. "Now, let me get those steaks on, so we can eat."

"Do you need any help?"

"Nah. But you're welcome to come out and keep me company. I have a table and chairs out on the back deck. Since it's so nice, I thought we'd have dinner under the open sky." Gib led the way through the house, smiling her appreciation when Delaney opened the back door for her.

Delaney was impressed with the back deck, which opened out toward a grassy clearing. "This is great! Sure beats that little patio I have at the apartment." She stood at the round, glass table, which had been set for dinner. "Very nice."

"Thanks. I love it. I've even seen a few deer grazing back there. Truth is I'd like to have a place like this someday. One of my favorite things is to watch the sunrise come off the lake." Gib opened the gas grill and put the steaks down to cook.

"I bet it's beautiful."

Gib turned and smiled at her. "I'd love to show it to you tomorrow."

"You would, huh?" Delaney stepped to her and touched Gib's cheek. "I think I'd like that, officer."

"Yeah?" Gib turned her head and kissed her palm. "Good."

AFTER THEIR DINNER remnants had been cleared away, Gib talked Delaney into changing into something more casual to take a walk along the lake shore. The sun was beginning to set, so the colors on the water were something to see. Gib held her lover's hand as they walked. "So, tell me more about your family. I've met your brother. He seems like a pretty good guy."

"Dylan is actually my favorite. We're the closest in age, since he's three years older than me. I have two other brothers. Thomas, who's forty-six, and then Richard, the oldest, at forty-nine. Neither of them is in the business. Thomas is a sales rep for a pharmaceutical company in Dallas. Don't tell my folks, but I think he's gay. I can't remember him ever bringing a girl home." Delaney's grip on Gib's hand tightened as they stepped over a log.

"What about Richard?"

Delaney made a disgusted sound. "He's a jerk. After I came out, he kept telling me I was going to hell. He's a 'real' Catholic. Or at least that's what he tells us. He's married to some holier-than-thou woman he met online, if you can believe that."

"Any nieces or nephews?"

"Dylan and his wife, Marsha, have four kids."

Gib stopped. "Four? And she's let him live?"

"So far. I have three nephews: Alan, who's twelve, Brandon, who's nine and Charlie's seven. And one niece, Diana, who's four, going on twelve."

"Working their way through the alphabet, are they?"

Delaney laughed. "I've always teased them about that. They argued so much about naming Alan, they finally opened a baby-naming book and picked one. Since it worked so well, they continued the tradition."

Gib stopped. "Hold it. Look over there." She pointed about fifty yards ahead, where a raccoon was busy washing something at the edge of the lake.

"Oh, wow. Look at him go," Delaney whispered. "I wonder what he's got."

"There's no telling." Gib pulled Delaney closer and wrapped her arm around her. "The sun's about to set. Want to head back?"

Delaney nodded and linked her arm around Gib's waist. "Sure. Thanks for this evening, Gib. I never really took the time to enjoy the outdoors like this."

"Give me a chance, and I'll show you all sorts of things," Gib promised with a kiss to Delaney's neck.

"Oooh. Sounds good."

AFTER A SIMPLE dessert of vanilla ice cream with chocolate sauce, the couple sat together on the back patio, their reclining deck chairs side by side. Both were looking into the night sky.

Delaney was fascinated by the amount of stars they could see. "This is so strange."

"I'm sorry. If you'd like, we can go inside," Gib offered.

"No." Delaney squeezed the hand she held. "I mean the sky. I've looked up into it at night and never saw this before."

Gib returned the squeeze. "You've lived in town all of your life, haven't you?" At the redhead's nod, she explained. "That's the reason. The city lights always make it hard to see the stars."

"Well, of course. But what I mean is that even when I've been out where it's darker, I never took the time to appreciate the stars like this." Delaney turned her head to look into Gib's eyes. "Thank you for showing me." She leaned so that their lips could meet. Seconds later, Delaney found herself stretched across Gib's body. "I hope this chair can hold both of us."

"I'm sure it can. You don't weigh that much." Gib's eyes widened as the heavy plastic chair beneath her creaked. "On second thought, would you like to take this inside?"

Delaney giggled and started to get up. The chair crackled as she shifted. "Uh-oh."

"Careful," Gib warned. She had her hands on the redhead's hips. "I'll push while you sit up."

"All right." Delaney raised her leg to swing it over Gib's body. "Here I go."

Another creak, a loud pop, and the chair legs snapped. Gib grunted as Delaney landed directly on top of her. "Ugh."

"Oh, my god. Are you okay?" Delaney asked, her face inches from Gib's.

"Your knee," Gib managed to get out.

"What?" Delaney wriggled and moved closer. "I couldn't quite hear you."

Gib placed one hand between them and grabbed Delaney's leg. "Please move your knee."

Delaney looked down between their bodies and giggled. "Oops. Sorry." She moved her leg and rolled onto the deck, while Gib exhaled. The redhead knelt over her lover. "Are you going to live?"

"Probably," Gib admitted, finally stretching out. "Ow."

"Where does it hurt?"

Gib grinned. "If I tell you, will you kiss it and make it better?" She sat up, with her hands behind her to hold her up.

It took her a minute, but the redhead finally understood. She growled and pushed Gib down. "You are such a brat!"

Gib was laughing so hard she couldn't get up. She rolled and grabbed Delaney, ending up on top. "Who are you calling a brat?"

Delaney looked into her eyes. "You," she answered, her voice softening. "Has anyone ever told you that you have beautiful eyes?"

"Me?" Gib's voice was just as soft. "Not that I can ever remember. But thank you." She lowered her face and gently kissed Delaney. "Dee—"

Things had gotten too serious as far as Delaney was concerned. She raised her hands and tickled Gib along the ribs.

"Hey!" Gib tried to get away, but was pounced on immediately. "No fair!"

They rolled around the deck together, laughing, until Gib finally begged her to stop. Delaney sat straddled the other woman's hips. "Give up?"

With tears of mirth rolling down her face, Gib nodded.

"Now," Delaney asked, running a finger down Gib's shirtfront. "What should I get for winning?"

"Anything you want."

Delaney's smile widened. "Anything?" She unbuttoned the first two buttons on Gib's shirt.

Gib squirmed, but didn't say a word.

"Hmm." Delaney popped open two more buttons. "Ooh." She fingered the white, satin bra. "Nice." She wriggled her hips and moved down so that she could unbuckle Gib's belt. Once she had the belt loose, she opened the button on the jeans. "Still anything I want?"

"Y—," Gib had to close her mouth and swallow to be able to speak. "Yes."

"Good." Delaney slowly unzipped Gib's jeans, exposing the matching white, satin panties she wore. "Very nice."

Gib took a deep breath. "They're comfortable."

"Mmm-hmm." Once she completely unbuttoned the shirt, the redhead opened it to the night air. "Cold?"

Unable to speak as Delaney's hands traced a light pattern on her bare stomach, Gib could only shake her head.

"So," Delaney started, her finger skimming across the bra, "If I were to say," her hand cupped Gib's breast, "a certain something, what would you do?"

"Huh?"

Delaney jumped to her feet. "Last one in the bedroom is a rotten egg," she yelled, taking off across the deck and into the house.

Gib got up onto unsteady legs and took a single step, before her pants fell down. "Damn!" She pulled them up with one hand and headed after her lover. "You will pay for that!" The laughter from inside the house caused her to smile. "And I'm going to enjoy every damned minute of it."

WARM BREATH ON her neck woke Delaney. Lying on her side, she yawned and tried to stretch, but was hampered by the body tucked against her. Gib's arm was draped over her, and her hand was splayed across Delaney's stomach. She started to scoot away so she could get out of bed, and felt a light kiss on her back.

"Hey, it's early."

Delaney turned her head slightly. "Nature calls." She felt, more than heard, Gib's answering chuckle, but she was released so she could move. "Thanks. Be right back."

Gib watched her lover's mad dash out of the bedroom, enjoying the view immensely. She propped her head up with her hand and waited for Delaney to return. A quick glance at her alarm clock showed that they didn't have to be up for a couple more hours, which Gib hoped they could fill with more lovemaking. The evening before had been more intense than she had expected. Delaney's playful side slowly morphed into a woman who couldn't seem to get enough of Gib, much to the officer's delight. Gib stretched, feeling the ache of body parts that had been neglected until very recently.

The pitter patter of running feet announced Delaney's arrival into the bedroom. She hopped into bed and snuggled against Gib. "Brr. Wood floors are cold in the mornings."

"They can be." Gib enveloped her as best she could. "How's that?"

"Better." Delaney rubbed her freezing feet against Gib's legs.

"Aaah!" Gib tried to scoot away, but found herself running out of bed space. "You're evil."

Delaney mock growled. "I think I've heard that from you before." Her feet continued to chase Gib's legs.

"Watch it, woman," Gib growled, edging off the bed. She stood and tried to maintain her dignity, which wasn't easy, considering she was naked. "Just for that, I'm going to the bathroom." She strutted out of the bedroom, causing Delaney to break out into giggles.

When Gib returned, she saw the redhead reclining on her side, posing sexily. "Well, what do we have here?"

Delaney crooked a finger at her lover. "Why don't you come over here and find out?"

"Hmm. I guess I could. But maybe I should investigate before jumping to any conclusions." Gib walked around the bed, rubbing her chin and staring at Delaney from all angles.

"Have you figured it out, yet?"

Gib tsked. "I'm still deliberating." She ran her finger lightly across Delaney's hip, causing the other woman to jump and squeak. "Interesting."

"Proctor, you'd better join me soon, or I'll start without you." The redhead squealed when her comment was answered by a swat on her rear. "Gib—"

"Yeees?"

Delaney rolled onto her back. "I'm going to start counting. Don't let me get to three." She held up one hand. "One." Her index finger rose. "Two."

"Three!" Gib pounced on the bed. She effectively pinned Delaney, straddling her body. "How 'bout that. I can count, too."

"Ha. That's only because I got you started," Delaney teased. She wriggled, although didn't seem to be trying too hard to free herself.

Gib placed a quick kiss on the tip of her lover's nose. "Such insubordination! How should I deal with you?"

Unable to free her hands, Delaney used her knee, lifting it slowly until it made contact. She grinned triumphantly when Gib's eyes closed. "What was that, officer?"

"Uh, what?"

Delaney moved her knee back and forth. "Problem?"

Gib lowered her face and passionately kissed the redhead. "Not at all."

THE SHARED SHOWER took longer than Gib expected, but they were both dressed and sitting on the front porch steps just as the sky began to lighten. Delaney was on the step below Gib, who had her arms wrapped around the redhead and her chin resting on her shoulder.

"This is nice," Delaney commented, leaning into the strong embrace.

"Yeah, it is. I'm glad you came over last night." Gib nipped at her ear. "Although I'd better replace that lounge chair soon. If Maddy comes out and sees it broken, she's gonna give me hell."

"You've been friends a long time, haven't you?"

Gib nodded. "She's the best friend I've ever had. Crazy thing latched onto me in grade school, and demanded that I be her friend."

"How old were you when you came out to her?" The laughter behind her wasn't what Delaney was expecting. "What's so funny?"

"I guess I never really did. After graduation, I left town so fast that you'd have thought my rear end was on fire. I knew I was gay, but was terrified of anyone I knew finding out." Gib sighed. "Funny thing is, when I came back a few months ago, it was like I had never left. We picked up our friendship right where we left off. Maddy gave me hell because she said she had always known about me, but didn't think it was that big of a deal. But she was pissed because I never trusted her enough to talk about it."

Delaney kissed the only thing she could reach, which was Gib's arm. "I don't blame her. I'd be pissed off, too."

"I'm not real big on talking about stuff like that. With my family, it just wasn't done."

"How did you discuss family issues?"

Gib chuckled. "If my mother wanted my brother to know something, she'd whine to either me or my dad. Then we'd go talk to him. I don't think we ever spoke to the person that was actually involved. Lots of hinting around, but no real discussions."

"Wow. My family is big on talking." At Gib's laugh, Delaney poked her leg. "Hush. You know what I mean. We discuss everything."

"Sorry. I couldn't resist." Gib kissed her on the neck as an apology. The sun began to glint off the water. "Here comes the sunrise."

They watched in silence as the sun slowly rose into the morning sky, casting a beautiful glow onto the peaceful lake. The only sounds were bird calls and the occasional splash from the jump of a fish.

Once the sky was light, Delaney turned in Gib's arms. "You're right. That was absolutely beautiful."

"Not as beautiful as you." Gib kissed her tenderly. When she pulled away, her eyes shone with love. "I realize we haven't known each other very long, Dee, but I lo—"

Delaney felt a knot in her stomach as she covered Gib's mouth with her hand. "Gib, no. Please, don't." The sadness in Gib's eyes broke her heart, but she added, "I don't think I'm ready to hear that. Not yet. I'm sorry." She removed her hand and kissed Gib gently on the mouth. "I think I should go."

"No, don't. I'm sorry. I knew I shouldn't have said anything." Gib tried to keep her from getting up, but missed.

Delaney was unable to hold back her tears. "I'm sorry," she whispered, before going inside to get her purse and overnight bag.

Gib was motionless as she watched the redhead leave. As the taillights of the Lexus disappeared into the morning light, she lowered her head and cried.

AFTER CALLING CLINT and requesting the day off, Gib drove into town. At a loss as to what to do, she went to her parent's house. She parked behind her mother's old Buick and, because it was so early in the morning, rang the doorbell.

Ida opened the door and frowned. "Gibson? What are you doing here? Shouldn't you be at work?"

"I'm off today." Gib hid behind her sunglasses, not wanting to appear too vulnerable. It was an old habit. Their family tended to show their affection by teasing, and if someone had a weakness, it was like a bull's-eye on their back. "Are you busy?"

"No, not really. Your father has already left for work, and I'm watching my talk shows. Come on in." Ida stepped back and allowed her daughter to enter, then followed her to the living room. "Would you like some coffee?"

Gib shrugged. "Sure."

Ida sat on the sofa and held out her cup. "While you're in there, give me a refill, please."

"Okay." Gib took the cup and went into the kitchen. After she filled her mother's cup, she took a mug from the cabinet and filled it as well. She returned to the living room and handed Ida her coffee. "Here you go."

"Thank you, dear." Ida waited until Gib sat in the chair across from her. "To what do I owe this pleasure? Do you need money?"

Gib was offended by the remark. "Of course not. Why would you think that?"

"Well, it's usually the only reason I see your brother. Either that or he needs a babysitter. I'm sorry. I shouldn't assume you're like him."

"I'm nothing like Roger." Gib tightened her grip on the coffee mug in an attempt to keep her hands from shaking.

Ida nodded. "That's true. You've always been independent. Certainly nothing like your brother in that regard. Have you talked to him lately? He still owes me this month's car insurance."

"No, I haven't. You might want to call and remind him." Gib had long since quit trying to get her mother to stop paying most of Roger's bills for him. Ida had always taken care of Roger, even after he married. She claimed he was too busy to do things for himself, which always aggravated Gib to no end.

"Well, I would, but you know how busy he is right now. After all, he's an assistant coach for Trevor's baseball team. I'd hate to bother him."

Gib sighed. "Mom, whatever you do is between you and Roger. I'm not going to get into the middle of it." She could feel her blood pressure start to rise. "Look, I'm sorry I bothered you today. I'd better get going." She stood and took her untouched coffee into the kitchen and dumped it in the sink.

"Why did you come over?" Ida stood behind Gib as she poured out the coffee. "It wasn't to waste my coffee, was it?"

"Do you want me to pay for it?"

Ida shook her head. "Of course not. And why are you wearing your sunglasses inside?" She removed the dark eyewear from Gib's face. "Have you been crying?"

"No, it's just allergies. You know how it is this time of year." Gib took her sunglasses back and hung them in the neck of her golf shirt.

"Stay for a while. We don't get to talk much anymore." Ida gentled her voice and led Gib to the living room.

Gib sat next to her mother on the sofa. "All right. Are you busy for lunch? I thought we could run over to Rodrigo's."

"That sounds wonderful. I'll have to put on something more decent, though. I'm not dressed to go out." Ida stood, but the ringing of the telephone stopped her. She picked up the cordless receiver that sat on the end table beside her. "Hello? Oh, hi, Roger. No, I'm not doing anything." She covered the mouthpiece and looked at her daughter. "It's Roger."

Gib fought the urge to roll her eyes.

"What? No, not really. Hold on." Ida turned to Gib. "He may come over on his lunch break today. I'll need to stay home, just in case."

"Right." Gib stood and kissed her mother on the cheek. "I'll call you later." She left as her mother continued to talk to Roger, barely waving goodbye to Gib.

Back in her truck, Gib rested her forehead on the steering wheel. Her heart was broken and she didn't know what to do. "How could I have read Dee so wrong? I thought she felt the same as I did." She started the truck and drove away from her family's house.

The thought crossed her mind to stop at Rodrigo's, but she didn't feel like playing twenty-questions with Maddy. Her best friend could always read what was going on in her mind. "I might as well be working," Gib grumbled. She headed toward the highway out of town.

DELANEY SAT IN her home office, staring at the plans for the dam. Because of the mild weather, they were a full week ahead of schedule. She slapped her hand on the desk. "Why did she try to say that? She can't love me." Her vision blurred as tears filled her eyes. "Damn her!"

Unable to concentrate on work, Delaney left her office. She roamed around the quiet apartment. Everywhere she looked, something reminded her of Gib. "Why couldn't she leave things like they were? We were having fun."

The empty kitchen held no answers, and even the ever-present bag of cheese puffs didn't appeal to her. Delaney walked into the living room and stared at the old recliner. She remembered snuggling with Gib, who loved to tease her about the chair. Delaney picked up the maroon blanket off the arm of the sofa, curled up in the recliner and covered herself. She didn't try to stop the tears.

At the sound of her cell phone ringing, Delaney's heartbeat picked up. She struggled to pull the phone out of the pocket of her sweatpants. "Gib?"

"Who? Laney, is this you?" Chris asked.

"Chris? What do you want?" Delaney cursed at herself. *One of these days, I'm going to learn to look at the caller ID before I answer the damned phone.*

"Who's Bib?"

Delaney closed her eyes. "What do you want?" she repeated.

"I was hoping to leave a message on your voice mail. My boss gave me two free tickets to the Monster Truck Rally at the Coliseum on Friday, and I wondered if you'd like to go."

"I don't think so, Chris. We're no longer together. Haven't we had this conversation at least half a dozen times?"

Chris' tone grew angry. "Why do you have to be such a stuck up bitch? I thought we could be friends. You know what a friend is, don't you?"

"I know exactly what a friend is, Chris. And I also know that there's no way in hell that we could ever be real friends, not now."

"You are a cold bitch, you know that?"

Delaney's eyes were swimming in tears. "I know," she whispered. Gib's hurt expression flashed in her mind.

"I loved you, Laney. But you're not capable of that, are you?" When she didn't get an answer, Chris cursed. "Well, fuck you, Miss High and Mighty!" She slammed down the phone.

Delaney tossed her phone onto the sofa and pulled the blanket up under her chin. "Would Gib ever try to control me like that?" She sniffled. "Why am I so afraid to find out?" She lowered her face into the blanket. "Not like I'll ever get a chance to, now."

Chapter Thirteen

MADDY SLAMMED THE phone down so hard that a stack of papers beside it fluttered to the floor. "I'm going to kick her ass!" she growled. She bent to pick up the inventory sheets. "I'm sick and tired of her ignoring me." Once the papers were back where they belonged, she opened her office door. "Tomas!"

The head chef of Rodrigo's turned from what he was doing. "Sí, querida hermana?"

"Don't 'sister dear' me," Maddy grumbled. "I'm going to go kick Gib's ass. Can you keep things under control for the rest of the night?"

Tomas grinned. "Of course I can. It's Thursday evening. We should be fine. Where's Gib been lately, anyway?"

"That's why I'm going to kick her ass. Every time I call her, I get 'sorry, Maddy. I'm too busy right now' out of her. I'm tired of being brushed off, so I'm going out to her place."

"Good luck." Tomas kissed her on the cheek. "Tell her I still love her."

Maddy swatted him. "Like that's going to matter. You know you're not built right for Gib."

"I can dream."

"And I can tell your wife," Maddy tossed over her shoulder as she left through the back door.

Traffic was light, and in fifteen minutes, Maddy drove over the new road to Gib's cabin. "Wow. I wonder when this got done. And why didn't that rat tell me about it?" She parked behind Gib's truck and was surprised to see her friend standing on the porch. Maddy shielded her eyes from the setting sun as she walked toward the cabin. "Hey, Gibsy."

"Maddy? What are you doing here?" Gib was dressed in black jeans and a matching golf shirt with an embroidered badge over her left breast.

The dark-haired woman stomped up the stairs and stood directly in front of her friend. She punched Gib hard on the upper arm.

"What the hell was that for?" Gib asked, rubbing her shoulder.

"You're lucky I didn't punch you in the face, you big jerk." Maddy put her hands on her hips and glared at Gib. She noticed the dark circles beneath Gib's eyes. "What's the matter with you?"

"Nothing." Gib turned around and walked into the cabin. She held the door open for Maddy, then closed it once they were both inside. "Do you want something to drink? I'm going out after dark, but I've got some time."

Maddy sat at the bar. "Bottle of water if you have it." She watched Gib take two bottles from the fridge. "Where are you going?"

"I've been trying to catch the poachers. We keep finding the leftovers from their kills, but not where they're gutting them. I'm going to go out every night until I find those bastards." Gib opened a bottle and handed it to Maddy. "What are you doing here?"

"I've missed my friend. You won't return my calls, and when I do catch you, I get a lame excuse."

Gib slammed her bottle onto the bar. "Lame? These bastards are out there, probably every damned night, killing out of season. It's only a matter of time before they run out of wildlife and start killing cattle. And I'm not going to let that happen."

"Hey, calm down. You've obviously been working day and night for the past week. What does Delaney have to say about that?"

"Not a goddamned thing." Gib turned away and found something interesting to look at through the window over the sink.

Maddy took a sip of water and watched her friend. Gib's hands were on her hips, which usually only happened when she was really angry. "What's going on between you and Delaney? I thought you two were all hot and heavy."

"Drop it, Maddy."

"No, I won't. One day you're telling me you think she's the one you've been looking for, and the next time I see you, it looks like you haven't slept in a week." Maddy stood and stepped behind Gib. She softened her voice. "Come on, Gibsy. Talk to me."

Gib slowly turned around. "There's nothing worth talking about."

"Right. Like I believe that." Maddy moved closer, seeing the pain in her friend's eyes. "Hey, this is me. What's going on with you?"

"I think I blew it, Maddy."

"Blew what?" When Gib lowered her head, Maddy sighed. "Oh, no. You told her."

Gib blinked a few tears from her eyes. "I'm such an idiot. I should have listened to you. I guess I was nothing but a good time for her."

"Oh, Gibsy." Maddy pulled her friend into her arms. "Honey, maybe it was just too soon. Not everyone falls so hard, so fast. Give her some time."

"I haven't heard from her since that morning. She obviously didn't feel the same."

Maddy patted her back. "I don't know. I mean, the few times I've seen her, she can't seem to keep her eyes off of you."

Gib shook her head and moved away. "Yeah, right. You know, maybe this was a dumb idea, coming back here. My family has moved on just fine without me. My brother is the same self-absorbed jerk he always was, and my mother," she blew out a breath. "She's so busy with my brother and his kids it's like I don't even exist." She sat on a barstool. "I should just move on."

"Oh, no you don't!" Maddy grabbed her shirt and got into her face. "I ought to shake some sense into that thick skull of yours!" She growled and released her grip. "I like having my best friend around again, thank you very much. You're not going to run away again."

"I didn't run," Gib argued defensively.

"Like hell you didn't! The moment you graduated, you took off. Now I know why. You knew you were gay then, didn't you?"

Gib lowered her eyes. "Yeah."

"Why didn't you tell me?" Maddy's voice was full of hurt.

"I was afraid you wouldn't be my friend anymore."

Maddy threw up her hands and screamed. "Aaah! You make me so damned crazy, chica!" She jabbed her finger into Gib's chest. "I...have...*never*," she poked the hardest on the last word, "judged you, have I? No, of course not. You're just a big, fucking coward!"

"I am not!"

"Like hell you're not!" Maddy lowered her voice. "It's time you stopped running, Gibson Susanna Proctor. Or I'll start calling you Susie!"

Gib's eyes grew large. "You wouldn't!"

"Try me."

"All right. I'll stay." Gib pointed at her friend. "But don't ever bring up the S word again, got it?"

Maddy grinned in triumph. "We'll see."

AFTER SPENDING THE night at Gib's drinking more beer than she should, Maddy dragged herself into Rodrigo's. She stumbled through the kitchen and pointed a finger at Tomas, who was about to speak. "Not one word."

He laughed, but otherwise kept quiet.

Maddy ignored him and went into her office. She carefully closed the door. "One of these days I'm going to learn not to try and out-drink Gib." With a pained moan, Maddy lowered herself gingerly into her chair. She closed her eyes against the bright light and thought about the previous evening.

Once Gib had admitted the redhead's response to her near admission of love, it took all Maddy had not to call Delaney and curse her out. Instead, she held Gib while she cried, something Maddy had never seen her do before. When they were in fourth grade, Gib had fallen off her bike and broke her left wrist. Even then, the stoic child had only bitten her lip, never shedding a tear. But to see Gib completely fall apart, and over a woman, was almost more than Maddy could bear.

By early afternoon, Maddy felt more human. She stepped out of her office and poured a cola from the kitchen's soda dispenser. As she sipped she checked the kitchen and then headed for the dining room. Once she was assured that everything was going well, she returned to the kitchen and tapped Tomas on the back. "Hey, bro."

He turned and grinned. "You look a lot better."

"Thanks. I need to take off for about an hour or so. Think you can handle things?"

Tomas sniffed her drink. "No, you're not drinking. Two days in a row? You trust me to handle the restaurant twice in one week?"

She shoved him. "You are a jackass."

"Such love."

Maddy laughed and handed him her drink. "I'll be back later. Try not to burn the place down."

"Usted me había herida querida." Tomas clutched dramatically at his chest. "Wounded, I say."

"I'll do more than wound you, if you keep fooling around." She ducked around Tomas and left through the back door.

MADDY KNOCKED ON the apartment door and was taken aback at how disheveled the redhead appeared. "Hey. Are you all right?"

"Have you come to kick my ass?" Delaney asked sadly. She was dressed in an oversized black tee shirt that said Texas Peace Officer, and a pair of gray, stained sweatpants. "Because right now, I'd probably give you a hand, if I could." She walked away from the door and returned to her nest in the recliner.

"To tell the truth, yeah. That's exactly what I came over here to do. Gib's devastated, and I would like to know why." Maddy sat on the end of the sofa nearest her.

Delaney lowered her gaze and picked at the blanket. "God, I hate myself right now." She blinked tears from her eyes. "When I first met Gib, I was sorta in a relationship."

"Sort of?"

"Yeah. I'd been dating this woman for close to a year. But every time I'd think about getting more serious, she'd pull some crazy stunt, or start acting like she owned me. So I'd back away. I kept flashing back to a previous relationship and it scared the hell out of me."

Maddy nodded, but allowed Delaney to keep talking.

"About seven years ago, I was in a relationship with a woman." She wiped her face with the back of one hand. "Everything was going great, until we moved in together. Then she got really possessive and we started to fight all the time."

"Fight? You mean—"

"The first time she hit me, it was just a little slap across the face when I cursed her out. Then Rachel cried and apologized and we made up. Things were good for a long while, so I forgot about it." Delaney shook her head. "I should have realized then what a mess she was. But then we'd go out dancing with friends, and she'd start up again. We had it out in the parking lot of the club, and she slammed me against the car and started choking me."

Maddy held her hand and squeezed it. "That's horrible. What happened?"

"Our friends came out to see what was going on and had to pull her off of me. We were both screaming and cursing, and the cops came and took her away. While she sat in jail overnight I got all my stuff and moved out of her apartment. Once she got out, I told her that if she'd leave me alone, I wouldn't press charges. She moved to Memphis to live with her grandmother, and I got this place. Although I never quite understood why she gave up so easily, I was glad to be rid of her."

"Sounds like you've had some really bad experiences, hon but you can't think that Gib would be that way, can you?"

Delaney stared at their linked hands, unable to look Maddy in the eye. "I didn't think that Rachel or Chris would be crazy-assed freaks, but that's how they turned out." She wrapped the blanket around her shoulders.

"I've known Gib practically my entire life. I've seen her at probably her angriest, and even then, she never lost control. She'll yell, stomp her foot, and even cuss up a storm. But never, *ever*, has she gotten physical against someone. It's not in her nature."

"Really? Never?" Delaney finally looked Maddy in the face.

Maddy nodded. "That's right. And, if you've met her brother, you'd be surprised that she's allowed him to live this long."

"That's true. He seems like a real piece of work." Delaney let out a weak laugh. "I've only met him once, and I wanted to knock him into next week."

"Me, too." After hearing Delaney's story, Maddy couldn't stay angry with her. She knew in her heart that the redhead had deeper feelings for her friend, but right now needed a friend of her own. Maddy scooted forward on the sofa. "Now, tell me how you're doing."

Delaney gave a half-hearted shrug. "I'm okay."

"You're about as good a liar as Gibsy."

"Is she all right? I haven't heard from her since," Delaney paused. "Anyway, how is she?"

"She's about ready to request a transfer," Maddy answered truthfully.

Delaney sat up in a hurry. "No. She can't! I, I..." she looked around helplessly. "I can't let her do that."

"Why not? She's decided there's nothing for her here." She followed Delaney into the bedroom and stood by the bed as the redhead entered the walk in closet. "What are you doing?"

"I'm going to go talk some sense into that mule-headed idiot," Delaney growled from the closet. "Just because I wasn't ready to hear her say," her voice trailed off. "Well, anyway, I'm not letting her take off just because of me."

Maddy sat on the bed with a grin on her face. "Well, you can't really blame Gibsy. She's had her heart stomped on so many times, it's a wonder she even tries anymore."

Delaney stuck her head out of the closet while she pulled on her jeans. "What do you mean?"

"I probably shouldn't say anything." Maddy stared at the floor.

"Oh, no. You've got to tell me what you meant. I won't say anything." Maddy grabbed the first available blouse and buttoned it.

"The last woman Gib was with dumped her because she was too butch. Gib has always been very sensitive about how she looks. Her nickname in high school was Ox, although I never used it. Even her parents think she's a big lug and give her hell about it. You were the first woman in a long time to seem to like her for who she is. At least she thought so."

Delaney sat beside her and put on her sneakers. "I love who she is." She stopped and became completely still. "I do," she said quietly. "I love her," she added with more conviction.

"Do you really? Because this past week has almost killed her. If you go back to her now, you'd better be damned sure."

"I am, I promise. I just thought I blew it with her when she never called." Delaney kissed Maddy on the cheek. "Thanks for coming here, Maddy. Come on. I've got a woman to talk to."

THE SPEED LIMIT on the small, winding park road was posted at twenty miles per hour, but the blue pickup crawled along at half that speed. Gib's gaze roamed from side to side as she kept vigilant for anything out of place.

She raised her sunglasses and rubbed at her eyes, which burned from lack of sleep and the hangover she blamed on Maddy. They had stayed up past three in the morning, talking and drinking. "I'm too old to be doing that, especially on a work night." After the long conversation, Gib had promised to call Delaney and talk it out, but still hadn't worked up the nerve.

"You're such a lousy coward," Gib grumbled. She flinched as her radio buzzed.

"Proctor, what's your location?" George asked.

Gib clicked the mike on her lapel. "Southwest road, near campsite sixteen."

"Your presence is requested at the construction site."

"Did they say what was wrong?" Her heart rate picked up as Gib made a sloppy U-turn. "George?"

"Nope. Just that they needed to see you." The tone in his voice was one of confusion. "Do you think I need to dispatch BPD?"

Gib sped up, taking the hairpin turns of the park road at a faster speed than was safe. "Not yet. It might only a case of vandalism. I'll let you know if I need any kind of backup."

"Gotcha. Oh, hey, the boss wanted me to pass along that our new ranger should be here sometime next week. That should give you some relief, right?" Gib was pulling double shifts after Jessica had been suspended for a week. The surly woman had made the mistake of mouthing off at Gib within range of Clint. He wrote her up and sent her home without pay.

"Yeah." Gib's mind wasn't on the new ranger, but the fear that something was seriously wrong at the construction site. She sped past the office, not bothering to acknowledge George's wave from inside.

With no traffic on the highway, Gib was able to zip across quickly. Her truck slid when she turned onto the dirt road. She saw the usual vehicles near the construction site and skidded to a stop in the middle of the road. Out of the truck before the engine died, Gib jogged to where she saw Dylan talking with several other men. "Dylan!"

He looked up and said something to the men, who all nodded and left. "Gib. Thanks for coming."

"Sure." Gib looked around the site, but could see nothing amiss. "What's the problem?"

"Um," Dylan looked around to make sure no one else was listening, and then pointed north. "One of our people was taking a break and noticed something past those pens. I told them to stay there until you could check it out."

Gib nodded. "Great. Thanks for letting me know." She jogged to her truck and left as quickly as she came.

As she passed the holding pens, Gib could see a white pickup on the side of the road. She parked behind it and strolled to the passenger's side. When she looked through the open window, all thoughts left her head. "Dee? What are you...I mean, Dylan said—"

"Get in, Gib." Delaney took a deep breath as if to gather her strength. "Please?"

"Um, okay." Gib climbed in the truck and turned to look at her. "I take it there's no problem out here?"

Delaney held out her hand. "Actually, there is." She cleared her throat. "There's a huge problem, and I'm hoping to fix it." Her thumb rubbed across Gib's hand. "I'm so, *so* sorry for last week."

"No, I'm sorry. I should have never said that. It was too soon, and wasn't fair to you." Gib rested her other hand over Delaney's. "Can we just go back to how it was before?" When Delaney shook her head, Gib tried to pull her hands away. "I know. That was stupid."

The redhead scooted closer and took Gib's sunglasses off her face. "You're anything but stupid, darling. I want to see your eyes when I tell you this. It's something I should have said last week, but—" Her free hand caressed the officer's cheek. "I love you, Gib."

"What? But, I thought," Gib babbled. "You said—"

"I know what I said, and I was a cowardly fool. I wish I was half as brave as you." Delaney kissed her lightly on the lips. "I love you. Will you forgive me?"

Gib's answer was a half laugh, half sob. "Forgive? You?" She put her arms around Delaney. "God, Dee. I love you so damned much." She put all her love into the kiss they shared.

DELANEY SIGHED AGAINST Gib's chest. They had been sitting in the truck for the past half hour. "I know we still have a lot to talk about. Can you come over tonight after work?"

"Sure." Gib kissed the top of her head. "I can skip a night of searching for those blasted poachers. Not like I've had much success, anyway."

"You're still looking for them?" Delaney raised her head. "And you've had no luck at all?"

Gib brushed the hair away from Delaney's face. "Not really. I'll come across where they've entered the park, but by the time I get there, they're long gone. And I don't know how they're doing the hunting - I don't hear any weapons being discharged at night. It's damned frustrating."

"I'm sure it is. Are you the only one going out at night?"

"Yeah. We really don't have the manpower for anything else. And I'm not on the clock."

Delaney kissed Gib's jaw. "Please be careful." She sat up and brushed her hands through her hair. "I'd better get back to work."

"Me, too." Gib opened the passenger door and stepped out. "I guess I'll see you tonight."

"Come around to my side, officer," Delaney ordered gently.

Gib did as she was asked and was soon leaning on the open window. "What?"

The redhead hooked a finger into Gib's shirt and tugged. "I wanted to make sure you remembered something." She kissed Gib passionately, pouring her heart and soul into the kiss. When she finally pulled back to catch her breath, Delaney brushed her thumb over Gib's glistening lower lip. "I love you."

"I love you, too." Gib grinned at her bashfully. "It feels so good to say that."

"Yes, it does. What would you like for dinner tonight?"

Gib shrugged. "I dunno. Do you want me to pick up something on the way?"

"Sure. I don't mind cooking, but if we have take out, we can spend more time," she wriggled her eyebrows, "talking."

The officer's face turned pink. "Um. Chinese okay?"

Delaney giggled. "I'm sure whatever comes through my door tonight, I'll enjoy." She fell over in the seat, laughing hard at the look on Gib's face.

DRESSED IN FADED jeans and a white, button-down shirt, Gib juggled several bags of food as she knocked on the apartment door. It opened immediately. "Hey."

The wide grin Delaney wore lit up her face. She was barefoot, wearing only a tee shirt and gray sweat pants. "Hi. Can I help?"

"I think I can get it." Gib followed her into the apartment and placed the bags on the bar. "I got a little of everything because I forgot to ask you what you wanted."

Delaney kissed her on the cheek. "You're too sweet." She helped unpack the bags and placed all the containers on the table. "Would you mind getting the wine out of the fridge?"

"Sure thing." Gib opened the refrigerator. "How did you know what brand of beer I drink?" She took out red wine and a bottle of Corona.

"I remembered you drinking it at the cabin." Delaney put her hand on a chair. She smiled when Gib's hand covered hers.

"Let me."

"Thank you." She settled herself as the officer pushed the chair to the table. "You really do seem too good to be true, you know."

Gib sat to her right. "Trust me, I'm anything but that."

"You sure seem like it to me."

They filled their plates and began to eat, both seemingly comfortable with the lack of conversation. While she added a second helping to her plate, Gib noticed her lover appeared uncomfortable. "What's the matter?"

Delaney wiped her mouth with a napkin. "I have so much to tell you, but I'm not sure where to start."

"I don't need any explanations, Dee. We're here now, that's the important thing."

"I'd really like to try and explain why I freaked out on you."

Gib took Delaney's hand. "All right. But you can stop anytime."

The redhead smiled weakly and held onto Gib's hand as if her life depended on it. "I've had such rotten luck with the women I've become involved with," she kissed Gib's hand, "until now. I guess you could say I was a late bloomer. I never had any feelings for anyone, other than friendship, until college."

"College? You were a virgin going into college?"

Delaney nodded. "I had guy friends and girl friends throughout high school, but never clicked with anyone. I was more interested in my studies than dating. And when I got to college, my roommate was a lesbian. I'd never known anyone like her before."

"Did you, um, experiment with her?" Gib became puzzled when Delaney broke out into laughter.

"Sorry. No, Ranelle was a little too feminine for me. She was more like my big sister. Not to mention, her girlfriend would have kicked both our butts. But the first party I went to, a woman tried to pick me up. I was intrigued, and came back to the dorm to tell Ray all about it. She didn't laugh, but instead helped me work through my feelings." She finished her wine.

"Refill?" Gib asked.

Delaney shook her head. "No, thank you. Anyway, I dated off and on during college. I think my longest relationship was probably three or four months." She lowered her gaze and stared at her half-empty plate. "It seemed like I always picked the wrong kind of woman. They'd start out nice, but by the end, we'd fight over everything."

"Lots of couples get into arguments, Dee. Heck, we've had some good ones." Gib scooted her chair closer and put her arm around Delaney's shoulders. When she felt how stiff her lover was, Gib kissed the side of her head. "Did any of them ever physical with you?" The body she held grew even more rigid. "Sweetheart?"

"One of them did," Delaney whispered. "About ten years ago, my parents set me up with Rachel. She was the daughter of someone my dad had gone to school with. God, she was so strong and beautiful." She raised her head and looked into Gib's eyes. "A lot like you."

The blush on Gib's face made her blonde hair stand out even more. "Um, thanks."

Delaney patted her leg. "The first time I saw you in your uniform, I nearly swooned." She fanned herself. "Anyway, where was I? Oh, yeah. Rachel. We did really well for the first two and a half years. I thought we'd be together for life. But once I moved in with her, she got so possessive and controlling. A couple of times she slapped me or pushed me around, but I usually provoked her. She'd always apologize, and my parents liked her, so I kept trying." A few tears fell down her cheeks. "The final straw was when we went out dancing with our friends. She kept thinking I was flirting with other women. When we went outside to talk about it, and she started to strangle me."

"I rarely wish violence on anyone," Gib muttered. "But I would certainly like to meet her someday and teach her to pick on people her own size. No matter what you did or said, she had no right to touch you." She pulled Delaney into her arms and held her. "I promise you, Dee. I will shoot myself before I ever lay a hand on you. Or I'll give you my gun and *you* can shoot me."

"I'd never shoot you. Whack you with a softball bat, maybe. But I don't care for guns." The gentle stroking of her hair calmed her and Delaney found herself relaxing in Gib's embrace. "You really are too good for me."

"Nah. I think I'm just right. Have you had enough dinner?" The nod against her chest was all she needed. Gib stood, holding her lover in her arms. "Come on, beautiful. Let's go get more comfortable."

Delaney put her arms around Gib's neck. "Gib! You're going to hurt yourself, hauling me around. I can walk."

Gib laughed, but didn't put her down. "You're kidding, right?" She walked through the living room. "Here or the bedroom?"

"Bedroom." Her heart lighter than it had been in a week, Delaney giggled as Gib pretended to struggle, by walking with a wobble. "You're crazy, you know."

"Of course." Gib dropped her onto the bed. "Crazy about you." She tickled Delaney's bare feet before kicking off her own sneakers. "Mind if I join you?"

Delaney held out her hand. "Please." She pulled Gib down, laughing as the larger woman growled and wrapped her up in her arms. "God, I love you."

"I love you too, Dee." Gib lowered her head and kissed her tenderly.

WHEN DELANEY OPENED her eyes and saw the time as one-thirty, she had to take a moment to remember what had transpired before she dropped off. After they spent over an hour kissing and gently getting reacquainted, they curled up and fell asleep, still fully clothed. Now wide awake, she rolled over and watched her lover sleep.

Gib was lying on her back, one hand behind her head and the other resting on her hip. Her hair was mussed and her unbuttoned shirt was partially tucked into her jeans. The belt she usually wore had been removed by Delaney and tossed somewhere in the room.

Unable to resist, Delaney used her index finger to skim lightly across Gib's exposed stomach. She started to giggle when the other woman's breathing changed, but her eyes remained closed.

"Giii-b," Delaney sang softly.

A slight grin broke out on Gib's face, but there was no other movement.

Delaney took her lover's inaction as a challenge. "Oh, Giiiibsssy," she sang softly into Gib's ear. Her tongue traced along the outside of the ear before she bit down lightly on the lobe. "I loooooove you."

Gib opened her eyes and started laughing at the ticklish feeling. She rolled over to face her lover. "I love you, too. What time is it?"

"Oh! Did I wake you?" More giggles ensued when Gib's fingers found Delaney's most ticklish spots. "Aaack! I give, I give! It's around one-thirty in the morning."

Gib rolled until her body was over Delaney's. She put the majority of her weight on her hands. "Is there any particular reason you woke me?"

"There might be."

"Are you planning on telling me?" Gib lowered her face. Her lips hovered above Delaney's as their breath intermingled. "Well?"

Delaney licked her lips. "Kiss me."

"Hmm." Gib started to, but backed away. "I dunno. You wake me in the middle of the night and expect me to kiss you?"

"Please," she answered breathlessly.

Gib's face lowered and she barely touched her lips to Delaney's.

"How's that?" Her laughter was cut short when Delaney grabbed two handfuls of hair and pulled her down, crushing their lips together. Clothes were lost as the two lovers were enveloped in the passion that flared between them.

THE SUN WAS barely up when two laughing, wet women emerged from the bathroom. Gib tried to get her towel back from Delaney, who had whipped it off of her with a leer. "Come on, Dee. I need to get ready for work." They had spent the entire weekend together, only leaving the bedroom for food.

"Uh-uh. I like you just the way you are." Delaney danced away from her lover's hands. "What's the matter? Don't you believe in drip-dry?"

Gib held out her arms and stalked her. "Deeeee."

"Um," Delaney backed away. "Heh." She waved the towel around. "I'm guessing you want this?"

"Good guess."

The back of Delaney's legs hit the edge of the bed and she became nervous. "What are you thinking?"

"I'm thinking," Gib's voice trailed off right before she lunged at the redhead. At the last moment, Delaney moved out of the way, and Gib ended face down on the bed. A heavy weight landed on her back. "Ugh."

"Ha! Gotcha!" Delaney crowed. Her nude body was molded against Gib's. "Now what are you going to do?"

The officer laughed. "Guess I'm stuck here."

"You bet your," Delaney slapped her on the rear, "ass you are. I may keep you here indefinitely." She squealed as her lover rolled over and pinned her to the bed. "No fair!"

"All's fair in love and," Gib blew a raspberry on her throat, "war." The raspberry turned into a kiss. She indulged her libido for several minutes before raising her head. "Unfortunately, I've really got to go home and get ready for work."

Delaney groaned and put her arms around Gib's neck. "No."

"Dee—" Gib's voice was muffled as her face was pulled into Delaney's chest.

"Uh-uh. I'm going to keep you as my love slave. Aaack!" She pushed Gib away and wiped at her chest. "Did you lick me?"

Gib smacked her lips and grinned. "Yup."

"Gross." She smiled at the silly grin her lover wore. "I'm going to have to think of something equally disgusting to do to you, sometime." Delaney touched Gib's cheek. "You're beautiful when you smile."

The comment made Gib blush. "Thanks. Um, I guess I'd better get ready to go." She got off the bed and looked around for her clothes, which were scattered across the room. "Have you seen my bra?"

"Not since last night." Delaney rolled onto her stomach and propped her chin on her upraised hands. She kicked her legs back and forth as she watched her lover get dressed. "Do you have any plans for Wednesday evening?"

"I don't know. Do I?" Once her jeans were zipped and buttoned, Gib sat on the edge of the bed to put on her shoes and socks. She grunted as her rear was swatted. "What?"

"Smartass." Now on her knees, Delaney crawled to drape herself over Gib's shoulder. "Actually, if you're up for it, I'd love for you to meet my parents."

Gib turned to look at her. "Really? Are you sure?"

"Definitely."

"All right. Wednesday night sounds good." Gib tied her shoes and tried to stand, but was stopped by a firm grip around her shoulders. "Sweetheart, I need to go."

Delaney wrapped her legs around Gib's waist. "Nope." She giggled as the officer got to her feet, bringing Delaney with her. "Guess you'll just have to go to work like this."

"That could be fun. We're supposed to get a temporary transfer from Big Bend this week. I can always tell them that you're a perk." Gib jumped as her ribs were poked. "Careful. You wouldn't want me to drop you."

"I trust you," Delaney whispered in her ear. She climbed off of her lover and stood in front of her. In total seriousness she spoke from her heart. "I love you."

Gib's hands rested on the redhead's bare hips. "I love you, too." After sharing a tender kiss, she reluctantly stepped away. "Call me later?"

"You bet I will, officer. Be careful?"

"Always."

Chapter Fourteen

MONDAY AFTERNOON WAS going well for Gib, until her radio took her from her daydreams. "This is Proctor, go ahead."

"Proctor, return to the office at once," Jessica ordered.

"Is there a reason I'm needed there?" Gib asked, turning her truck around in the swimming pool parking lot. The radio crackled with an inaudible answer. "Repeat, please?"

"Just get here. That's per Clint," Jessica added snidely.

Gib grinned and made a silly face at the radio. "Sure. Be there in less than five." She laughed as she imagined the look on Jessica's face. The young woman had been more subdued since her suspension, but Gib knew it was only a matter of time before she lashed out again.

After she parked in front of the office, Gib got out of her truck whistling a tune. She walked in and her smile widened when she saw a familiar blonde sitting near the counter. "Kennie!"

The other woman stood and met Gib halfway. "Surprise."

"And a great one it is, too," Gib told her as she embraced her. "When will you be back at work?"

"Hopefully in a few weeks." Kennie led them to a sitting area, out of sight of the disgusted Jessica. "I'm still trying to get my strength back, but the doctors tell me I'm ahead of schedule." She held Gib's hand while they talked. "Thanks for all the flowers."

Gib squeezed her hand and smiled. "You're welcome. How is your family doing?"

"They're great. Mom's staying with me for another week or so, but my dad went home this past weekend."

"That's good. You still have my number if you need anything, don't you?"

Kennie laughed. "Yes, Mama Bear. I do." Her face turned serious. "I don't think I can ever thank you enough for saving me that day, Gib. Even though I was wearing a life vest, they said I would have died if you hadn't—" Tears welled up in her eyes.

Gib knelt beside her. "It's all right. I know you would have done the same for me." She was nearly knocked off her feet when Kennie lunged into her arms. Gib held her as she cried.

"Figures," Jessica snarled from the doorway. "Do you always entertain your little conquests while you're on duty?"

Gib released Kennie and stood. "What exactly is your problem with me, Middleton?"

"Oh, no. You're not going to get me suspended again." Jessica moved closer and lowered her voice. "But one of these days, I'll get a chance to tell you exactly what I think of you."

"No matter what you think, I had nothing to do with your suspension."

Jessica rolled her eyes. "Yeah, right. You and Clint are buddies, don't try and deny it. He wouldn't dare let anyone say a single thing against you."

"You're wrong. We're colleagues, Middleton. Nothing more. Your rotten attitude got you suspended."

"Bullshit." Jessica stepped as close to Gib as possible, without touching her. "Don't think I haven't seen you mooning over that slutty-looking redhead," she whispered.

Gib's hands curled into fists. "You can say whatever you want to about me, but don't you dare talk about her that way."

"What's the matter? Not used to being caught making out with your flavor-of-the-week?"

"Shut up," Gib growled.

Jessica gave Kennie a cruel smile. "You'd better watch out, Wyatt. Your cute little ass might be next."

Kennie laughed. "I should be so lucky."

Gib took Jessica by the arm. "Come on. We're going outside to talk where we won't be interrupted."

"Let go of me, or I'll scream," Jessica threatened.

"Shut up." Gib turned to Kennie. "How long will you be here?"

Kennie got out of the chair. "I'm on my way home. My mother's in the parking lot waiting for me." She gave Gib one final hug. "I'll call you later."

"All right." Gib blushed when she felt soft lips on her cheek. "Take care of yourself, Kennie." Once Kennie had left, Gib turned to Jessica. "Are you ready for our little chat?"

"You can't make me."

Gib led her through the office. "George, we'll be back in a few minutes. Let Clint know, will you?"

"Uh, sure. There's not much going on right now, anyway." He moved behind the desk and answered the phone.

Once they were outside, Jessica jerked her arm out of Gib's hand. "I don't appreciate you manhandling me."

"Then maybe you should start acting more like an adult." Gib gestured to the passenger side of her truck. "Go on, get in."

Jessica did as she was told, slamming her door as hard as she could. "What are you going to do, take me out in the boonies where no one will find my body?"

Gib ignored her and started the truck. She took the road toward the campgrounds. A few minutes later, she found a vacant campground and parked the truck. She unbuckled her seatbelt and turned to face the other woman. "All right. It's just you and me here. Would you like to tell me what your problem is?"

"I don't have a problem."

"Yeah, right. From day one, you've been antagonistic toward me. No matter what I do or say, you pop off with some smart-ass remark. Why?"

Jessica stared straight ahead, with her arms crossed over her chest. "Why did you choose Wyatt over me?"

"What?"

"You two seemed to hit it off right away. She got to go with you in the bigger boat, while I was stuck with Conroy." She looked at Gib. "He hates you."

Gib shrugged. "Tell me something I don't know." She considered what the other woman said. "Wait a minute. All this time, you've been pissed at me because I took Kennie over you? Clint's the one that made the assignment, not me."

"I don't remember that. And every time I'd go up to visit her at the hospital, you'd already been there." Jessica sniffled. "And then, not long ago, I saw you and that redhead that's with the construction company. She was looking at you like you were dessert."

The entire conversation was becoming too surreal for Gib. "You're *jealous?*"

"No! I'm not gay!" Jessica screamed. "I'm not!" She covered her face with her hands and began to cry. "I can't be."

Oh, shit. Now what? "Jessica?" Gib cautiously touched the younger woman's shoulder. "Hey."

Jessica jerked away. "Don't!" She wiped her eyes on her shoulder. "I'm not a dyke."

"I never said that you were. But even if you were, it doesn't matter." Gib removed a handkerchief from her back pocket and handed it to Jessica.

"Ha! Tell that to my father. He hates queers." She blew her nose. "Thanks." She started to hand the soiled cloth to Gib, but was waved off. ""He saw you on the news."

Gib tipped her baseball cap back. "What?"

"My dad. There was a report on the news about the accident, and they showed your photograph. He told me to stay away from you."

"You live with your folks?"

Jessica shook her head. "No, I have an apartment in Benton. But it's not far from my parents. Does your family know about you?"

"That I'm a lesbian?"

"Yeah."

Gib nodded. "They do. I think they figured it out before I did."

"Do they give you a lot of grief about it?" Jessica no longer sounded nasty, just curious.

"Not really. My mom thinks if she ignores it, it'll go away." Gib laughed at how Ida never really spoke of her sexual orientation, but danced around the subject. "Our family doesn't really talk about stuff like that. But my dad seems okay with it."

Jessica looked at her. "When did you know? I mean, was it a big epiphany, or what?"

"Um, well." Gib frowned as she tried to remember. "You know, I don't think I ever just looked in the mirror one day and said, 'Yeah, I'm gay.' It was like I always knew."

"Oh." Jessica started to bite at the nail on her right index finger. "Were you ever scared that someone would figure it out? And hate you? Or worse?"

Gib gave the question serious consideration. "Not really. I mean, I was kind of nervous when I moved back here. I had this entire life down in Austin that no one here knew about. And coming back to Benton, I felt like the teenager that left, not the grown woman I'd become." She softened her voice. "The one person I was worried about the most, didn't care. My best friend just chewed me out for worrying about it, and for not telling her sooner."

"Really?"

"Yeah. I'm not going to lie to you, Jessica. A lot of people feel like your dad. And some of them wouldn't think twice about hurting someone, just because of who they love. But when you find that special person, it's the most amazing feeling in the world. How old are you?"

Jessica lowered her face and stared at the floorboard of the truck. "Twenty-two. I'm sorry for being such a bitch to you, Proctor."

"Call me Gib. All my friends do. And don't worry. You've got a lot of time to figure out what you want. Don't rush it." Gib held out her hand. She smiled when Jessica took it.

DELANEY BREEZED INTO her father's office and sat on the edge of his desk. "Hi, Dad."

He looked up from his laptop. "Afternoon, honey. What's got you so chipper?"

"What? Can't I be in a good mood?"

"Of course you can. It's just that, no, never mind." Colin took off his glasses and rubbed them with a cloth. He scrutinized them carefully before returning them to his face. "It's nice to see you happy."

She laughed and messed up his thick, gray hair. "All right. I know I can be a cranky bitch every once in a while." At his snort, she shook her head. "Right. Most of the time."

"Not cranky, exactly. Just very focused and business-like. But lately, you've seemed almost giddy."

Delaney circled the desk and hugged him. "I am." She kissed her father's cheek. "I'm in love."

"Really?" Colin turned to look her in the eye. "This is rather sudden, isn't it? Or did you and Chris work things out?"

"Uh, no. Chris is history." She returned to her perch on the desk. "Remember the park police officer? Gib Proctor?"

He nodded. "Your friend, right? I should have realized it would turn into something more, especially after talking to your brother."

"What has Dylan been saying?"

Colin scooted his chair away from the desk and stood. "He may have mentioned a thing or two in passing."

The grin on her father's face should have warned Delaney off, but she asked anyway. "Like what?"

"Like how your face would light up whenever she was near, or the way you constantly talked about her."

Delaney blushed and nervously rubbed the back of her neck. "I'm going to kill him."

"Don't do that. I've finally gotten him trained to handle the on-site work," Colin teased. "So, when are we going to meet this woman?"

"That's actually the reason I came in here. I wanted to know if you two are busy Wednesday evening." She scooted off the desk and took his hand. "Let's go check with your better half, since she's the one who handles your social calendar."

Colin released her hand and put his arm around her shoulders. "I can't help being disorganized, you know. It's the main reason I married her."

"I'll be sure and tell her that," Delaney teased, as they walked out of the office.

LIGHT RAIN BEGAN to fall on the truck as Gib headed home for the day. It was the last thing she wanted to see, since she had decided to go out after dark and continue to search for the poachers. A camper had come across the dumped remains of a deer earlier in the day, making Gib more intent than ever to put a stop to the hunting.

She parked in her usual space and was halfway to the cabin when the skies opened and drenched her. "Crap!" Gib's walk turned into a run. She slipped when she hit the second wooden stair, but kept her balance and made it to the door.

Once inside, she dropped her keys on the side table and was removing her duty belt when her cell phone rang. "Proctor."

Maddy's happy voice came through the Bluetooth a little louder than necessary. "Is this the great Officer Proctor?"

"Good grief, Maddy. Please tell me you're not already wasted."

"Only on life, my friend. What are you doing?"

Gib hung her belt up and unbuttoned her shirt. "Changing clothes. You caught me as I was coming in the door. Why?"

"Have a hot date?"

"Not tonight."

Maddy laughed at the dejected tone. "Aw, poor baby. Well, perk up. You do now. Meet me at Tony's in half an hour." The pizza joint was near Maddy's apartment, promising cheap prices and big portions of pasta favorites.

"What?" Gib hung her wet shirt over the shower bar.

"You heard me. Get changed and get your butt into town. I'll see you there at six-thirty." Maddy hung up so Gib couldn't argue with her.

"Damn." Gib turned and looked into the bathroom mirror. "Why do I continue to let her do that to me?"

Twenty minutes later, Gib hit the city limits of Benton. The rain hadn't let up, making her wiper blades struggle to keep the windshield clear enough to see. She passed the road that led to Delaney's and had to struggle to keep from turning around. "Good lord. I need to give the poor woman some space." With a renewed determination, Gib found a parking space near the front door of Tony's.

She stood under the outside canopy and shook off the worst of the rain before going inside. The single dining room held about twenty round tables, with cheap plastic red-checkered tablecloths. Old, mismatched, pleather chairs didn't help the ambiance, but the smells coming from the kitchen were enough to make up for the décor. Faded posters of Italy dotted the ivy-patterned wallpaper that adorned the walls.

Gib headed toward a corner table, where she could see her best friend speaking animatedly with another person. When she arrived at the table, Maddy stood and gave her a hug.

"Hey, Gibsy. Thanks for coming."

"Like you gave me much choice," Gib grumbled good-naturedly. She released Maddy and looked up when the other occupant of the table stood. At six-feet tall, he was several inches taller than either woman. His dark hair and equally dark eyes sparkled in the bright light.

Maddy grinned. "Robert Winslow, this is my best friend, Gibson Proctor."

Gib shook the handsome man's hand. "Call me Gib."

"Rob," he answered. "Madina's told me a lot about you." He held out Maddy's chair and helped her get seated. The table had three glasses of iced tea, paper-napkin wrapped utensils and a basket of breadsticks.

"She has, has she?" Gib sat across from the pair. "I'm sorry I can't say the same."

He laughed. "No, I guess you couldn't. We only met a few days ago."

Maddy gave her friend a warning look. "This is our first night out together, Gib."

"Ah." Gib picked up a breadstick and took a bite. After she swallowed, she nodded. "So, Rob, how did you meet Maddy?"

"I dropped a case of wine at her feet."

Gib choked on the breadstick as she struggled not to laugh. She coughed a few times and took a drink of tea. "I bet that went over well."

"I don't think I've ever been cursed out quite that," Rob paused, "colorfully, before." He winked at Maddy, who blushed.

"Did she go directly to Spanish? 'Cause that's when it gets fun," Gib asked.

Rob laughed. "She started in English, but I think she ran out of words."

"Laugh it up, you two." Maddy shook her head. "And I still can't get the wine smell out of those shoes."

The look Maddy gave Rob was one of fondness, and it brought a smile to Gib's face. She had been waiting years to see such a look. She patted Maddy's hand and mouthed, *I like him.* Out loud, she said, "So, Rob, what is it that you do?"

"I'm the regional manager for Randolph's Liquor. One of my guys was out with the flu, so I was working his route." He exchanged looks with Maddy. "I'm going to have to give him a raise when he gets back."

Gib's eyebrow rose when she heard her best friend giggle. *Giggle? Oh, boy. She's a goner.* "I really appreciate you asking me to dinner, but I need to get going."

Maddy finally tore her eyes away from Rob. "What? But you just got here."

"Yeah, but," Gib paused when the couple returned to staring at each other. She pushed her chair out and stood. "It was great to meet you, Rob. You two have a great evening."

Rob began to get up, but Gib waved him down. "That's okay." She leaned to whisper in his ear. "Take care of her."

"You got it, Gib. I'm hoping to get to know you better." He shook her hand then went back to smiling at Maddy.

Gib shook her head. She stood outside under the awning and took out her phone.

"Hello, officer," Delaney answered softly. "I was hoping you'd call."

"You were? Did you know that the phone works both ways?" Gib teased, as she walked through the rain toward her truck.

Delaney laughed. "Really? I had no idea. What is that noise?"

"Rain." Gib opened her truck and got in, shaking her head to dispel the worst of the water in her hair.

"Where are you?"

"I *was* in the rain."

"My god, you're a bigger smartass than I am. Okay, I'll bite. *Why* were you in the rain?"

Gib grinned as she started the truck. "Because it's raining, of course."

"Gibson Proctor, you should be ashamed of yourself." Delaney continued to laugh. "Hey, what's your middle name?"

"Oh, no. I can't tell you that."

Delaney's growl would have been more menacing if she wasn't giggling through it. "Why not?"

"Because, well, just because. Are you busy?"

"Busy talking to you," Delaney shot back. "Ha! Two can play that game, officer."

Gib switched to her Bluetooth. "Other than picking on me, are you busy?"

"Not really."

"Have you eaten?"

Delaney's tone turned sultry. "Is that a proposition?"

"It could be. I find myself in Benton with nothing to do. Would you like for me to bring you some dinner?"

"I'll make you a deal," the redhead bargained, "you show up, and I'll throw together some pasta and frozen garlic bread."

Gib thought about the lasagna at Tony's, which she swore was heaven-made. Suddenly, it had lost all its appeal. "That's the best offer I've had all day. I'll be there in five."

"The door will be unlocked," Delaney promised.

EVEN OVER THE sound of the Norah Jones CD playing in the living room, Delaney heard the door open. "I'm in the kitchen," she called.

Moments later, a drenched Gib walked into the kitchen. "You know, leaving your door unlocked isn't very safe," she chastised.

Delaney turned away from the stove. "It is here. They don't let strangers come up, you know." She frowned at the drowned rat imitation from her lover. She took the dishtowel from the cabinet door and wiped the water from Gib's face. "Do you not know how to use an umbrella?"

"Um, well, yeah. I do." Gib stood still and allowed Delaney to towel her face and hair dry.

"Then why don't you?"

The towel wandered lower, getting the worst of the water from her clothes. Gib's mind went blank as she felt her shirt being unbuttoned. "Huh?"

"You're going to catch pneumonia if you keep running around soaking wet," Delaney continued, oblivious to the effect she was having on Gib. "I have one of your tee shirts you can change into, while I put this in the dry—" her words were cut off when Gib's mouth pressed against hers. The dishtowel dropped to the floor and Delaney's hands tangled into her lover's hair.

Gib backed her to the counter, as she continued to kiss her. She raised Delaney's tee shirt and groaned at the feel of silky skin beneath her hands. Her kisses trailed down to her lover's throat. "You make me so hot, Dee."

"Yes," Delaney cried, tipping her head back to give Gib better access. She pulled her closer.

The sound of water boiling over caused Gib to stop what she was doing. "Whoa." She took a single step back, breathing heavily. "Sorry about that."

"I'm not." Delaney took a shaky breath. She turned and gave the stove her attention, while Gib stood behind her and nibbled on her neck. "Baby, if you don't want me to ruin dinner, you-" she moaned, "Gib, please." She dropped the spoon into the sauce and moved Gib's hands from her hips to her breasts. "I need you."

Gib turned off the stove. "Dinner can wait, but I can't." She led Delaney to the bedroom, suddenly hungry for more than spaghetti.

Chapter Fifteen

GIB TIED HER shoes while Delaney stood in front of the mirror and brushed her hair. She moved behind the redhead and put her hands on her lover's hips. "Are you going to be out at the job site today?"

"No, I've got a ton of stuff to do at the office." Delaney put the brush down and turned. "What exciting things do you have planned?"

"Probably the usual. Patrol the park, ignore Dan and hope the temporary ranger comes in today."

Delaney put her arms around Gib's waist. "Is he still giving you a lot of trouble?"

"Not really. I haven't had much contact with him. Clint schedules him as far from me as possible." Gib lightly kissed her. "But I don't care about Dan."

"When you kiss me, I don't care about anyone or anything," Delaney admitted. "I'm really glad you came over last night." She snuggled closer and sighed. "Can we go back to bed?"

Gib chuckled and hugged her. "I wish. But we'll see each other tonight."

"Yeah, with my parents. Yippee."

"Hey, if you don't want—"

Delaney shook her head. "No, I really want them to meet you." She looked into Gib's eyes. "I love you, and I want to show you off."

"Show me off? You're kidding, right?"

"What do you mean?"

Gib backed away. "Come on, Dee. I'm definitely nothing to show off. I'm surprised you'll be seen in public with me."

"Hey." Delaney grabbed two handfuls of Gib's shirt and pulled her close. "I happen to think you're beautiful. My god, who wouldn't? You've got the most amazing eyes," her voice softened, "and the most beautiful soul I've ever known."

"Sorry. Old ghosts tend to jump up and bite me in the ass every now and then." Gib closed her eyes when she felt her lover wrap her in an embrace. She suddenly sounded very vulnerable. "Do you really feel that way about me?"

"Oh, sweetheart. Of course I do. And I'm so sorry I haven't told you before now." Delaney tightened her arms around Gib. "I love you so much, Gib. I keep thinking you're going to figure out that I'm not good enough for you and run."

Gib buried her face in Delaney's hair and sighed. "I love you, too. And I'm not going anywhere. Looks like we've both got some ghosts to fight."

"As long as we do it together," Delaney added.

"Yeah." After taking a cleansing breath, Gib gave one final squeeze and stepped back. "Have a good day at work."

Delaney found herself getting lost in Gib's eyes. "You, too." She caressed the officer's cheek. "Believe in me, Gib. Believe in us."

"I will." Gib lowered her face and kissed her.

IT HADN'T TAKEN Gib long to get home and change into her uniform. She was on her way to the office when the radio beckoned.

"Proctor, please report to the office," Jessica's voice was polite and professional.

"Sure thing. Is there a problem?"

"No, but the temporary ranger has arrived, and I believe Clint wants you to show her around."

As her truck drove over the muddy lake road, Gib was grateful for the construction company's work. The heavy rain from the previous evening would have made the old road impassable. Now she was able to drive from her cabin without much trouble. She stopped before turning onto the highway. "All right. I was on my way, so I should be there in about two minutes."

Once she parked beside a sparkling black Jeep Wrangler, Gib walked into the office, softly whistling a tune. She noticed the back of the new ranger, speaking to Clint and Jessica. "Hey, Clint. Didn't you explain to our newbie that getting here before eight wouldn't garner any overtime?"

The new ranger turned to face Gib, wearing a knowing smile on her face. Tall, blonde and more suited to be a model than a park ranger, Gloria Hoover gave Gib a visual once-over. "Hello, Gibson."

Gib stopped dead in her tracks and her good mood evaporated. She plastered what she hoped was a professional look on her face. "Hoover."

Clint, oblivious to the tension, patted his newest employee on the shoulder. "Gloria was just telling us that she worked with you in Austin, Gib. Small world, isn't it?"

"Yeah." Gib nodded to Jessica. "How's it going?"

"All right." Jessica glanced from Gib to the beautiful blonde. "I guess I'd better get on that paperwork. It was nice to meet you, Hoover."

Gloria barely glanced at Jessica as she continued to stare at Gib. "Same here. Call me Gloria."

Jessica rolled her eyes. "Sure. See you, Gib."

"Well, since we've all been introduced, Gib, why don't you show Gloria around?"

Gib swallowed hard. "Clint, can I speak to you for a moment?"

"Sure. Come into my office." Clint pointed to a far wall. "Gloria, there's a map over there so you can familiarize yourself with the area before Gib takes you out." He closed the door behind Gib. "All right. What's the problem?"

"Is there anyone else that can play tour guide? I'm still trying to find the base camp for the poachers."

Clint sat behind his desk. "Tour guide? Come on, Gib. Two pairs of eyes are better than one. Don't tell me you have a problem with Gloria. She spoke very highly of you."

"She's always had a selective memory," Gib muttered. She dropped into his guest chair. Not wanting to delve too deeply into her personal life, she tried to come up with a good reason. "Um, how long will she be here?"

"At least until Kennie comes back. With Bud gone for who knows how long, she could be here a while."

Gib sighed and closed her eyes. "Great."

"Are you going to have a problem?"

She stood. "No. I'll take her around, and then she can patrol on her own this afternoon. Is that all right?"

"Sure." Clint cocked his head as he studied her. "Are you sure there's nothing you want to tell me?"

"Nah. I'm probably grumpy because I didn't get much sleep." Gib adjusted her duty belt. "Buzz me if you need me." Her purposeful strides took her to where Gloria's stood. "You ready?"

Gloria turned and smiled. "Definitely. Your vehicle or mine?"

"Let's take mine. I'll bring you back later for yours." Gib led her outside to her truck. She waited until the other woman was buckled in before she backed up and started down the main road through the park. "We have mostly developed campsites, and each has to be signed in at the office. I go in every morning to see where we have campers."

"I've missed you."

Gib continued as if she hadn't heard. "We also have a swimming pool, hiking trails, and two screened shelters that are used primarily for family reunions. Another building, rented out for events, has air conditioning and heating, as well as a kitchen and bathrooms."

"Gibson, please. Can't we talk about this?" Gloria tried to touch her arm, but was shaken off.

"There's nothing to talk about." Gib slowed down and pointed. "Over there is the first of three emergency phone stations that go directly to the office. The emergency number is forwarded to an on-call ranger or officer after hours."

"I made a mistake." Gloria slapped the dash. "Damn it, Gibson. Won't you give me a chance to explain?"

Gib shook her head. "You have nothing to explain. I believe you made it perfectly clear when you broke up with me." She drove them past the public pool. "I'll show you a back road to the lake. It's off limits to the public. But it's faster than driving all the way around to the office. Let's try to keep our conversation on work, okay?"

"Why? From what little I've seen of this hole-in-the-wall, I'm light-years beyond what you're going to find here. I don't know how long I'll be here, but you couldn't do any better."

Gib snorted. "Still modest, aren't you?"

"Well, look at me. Homecoming Queen, debutante, college model. Do you honestly think there's any competition here?" Gloria sat back against the seat. "You should be thankful I'm here, offering you a second chance. Especially since it doesn't look like you've changed at all."

The laugh from Gib was bitter. "That's never going to happen. Let's get this 'tour' over with so I can go back to more important matters."

THE NORMALLY CLEAN desk was covered with blueprints, as Delaney tore through her pending projects with vigor. At the tap on her door, she raised her head. "Hi, Mom. What's up?"

Maureen leaned against the door jam. "I was going to ask you the same thing. You haven't stirred from here since you arrived this morning." At her daughter's wave, she slid into the guest chair.

"I haven't been doing much work on the weekends, so I was trying to catch up." Delaney sat up and brushed her hair away from her face.

"Do I want to know what you've been up to?" Maureen teased. "You know, I'm rather looking forward to dinner tonight."

The subject change was so abrupt it took Delaney a minute to process. "Uh, yeah. I know you're going to love Gib. She's just an amazing woman." She noticed the twinkle in her mother's eye. "Moooommm...don't you dare."

"What?"

"Please, please, *please*! Don't start tormenting Gib until she at least gets used to you. Promise me?"

Maureen grinned. "Torment? Whatever do you mean?"

Delaney covered her face with her hands. "Mom, please."

"You're such a spoil-sport. Don't tell me she's some sort of shy little flower? I can't imagine you dating such a woman."

"No, no." With a groan, she uncovered her face. "Gib's very open and honest, and a lot of fun to be around. But she's not used to a family like ours. So, if you don't mind, can you hold off on the teasing until she's more acclimated?"

"She must really mean something to you. I don't think I've ever heard you protect someone this much before." Maureen lowered her head and peered through her invisible glasses. "You are truly serious about her, aren't you?"

Delaney nodded. "More than anyone, ever."

"Then I'll try to behave myself. At least for tonight." Maureen stood and brushed off her slacks. "Oh, by the way. The reason I came back here was I have a message from Dylan. He wants you to call him whenever you get a chance."

"I wonder why?" Delaney shrugged. "You could have just buzzed me."

Her mother shook her head. "Your line was out."

"Really?" Delaney moved some of the blueprints off of her desk and found the phone receiver sitting awkwardly off the hook. "Oops."

"See? And here you acted as if I were lying." Maureen laughed and walked out of the office, making off-handed comments about silly children.

Delaney rolled her eyes and hit the speed dial for Dylan's phone. "Hey, Dyl? What's up?"

"Del, thank god. You need to get out to the site. The storm last night caused a shift in the dam and I'm afraid it might not hold if we get more rain."

"Calm down. You're overreacting, as usual. We didn't change the structure enough to have any major problems."

Dylan cursed. "You haven't seen it. Could you please get your butt out of that cushy desk chair and come see? It doesn't look good."

"All right. I'll be there in about half an hour, okay? Can you keep from coming unglued until then?" She opened the lower desk drawer and removed her purse. "Dyl?"

"Yeah, yeah. Just hurry, will ya?"

"HAVE YOU LOST your ever-lovin' mind, Dyl? It's just mud." Delaney kicked at the mud and glared at her brother.

He looked sheepish, but stood his ground. "How the hell was I supposed to know? It looked like half the blasted dam washed away during the night."

"Are you serious? This is nowhere near the amount of debris the dam would leave." She pointed to the top of the dam. "As you can see, the structural integrity is intact. I'll walk across it, if you want me to."

"No!" Dylan turned red. "Okay, so I panicked. But this job is so ahead of schedule that I figured we were due for a disaster." He tucked his hands into his pockets. "Sorry to have dragged you out here."

She shook her head and laughed. "That's all right. Maybe I can catch Gib while I'm here."

"No wonder you're not tearing me apart. This is a good excuse to see your sweetheart." Dylan ducked as Delaney halfheartedly threw a punch. "You're losing your touch."

Delaney narrowed her eyes. "If I wasn't wearing my good jeans, I'd show you," she threatened. When Gib had mentioned how much she liked seeing her in denim, Delaney bought several new pairs.

"Yeah, yeah. Talk tough. What are you gonna do? Get your girlfriend to beat me up?" He stuck out his tongue and danced backward.

"I don't need her to. I've always been able to kick your ass. Or did you forget your sophomore year in high school?"

Dylan frowned. "Hey, I slipped on the ice."

"Tell me another story, bro. I knocked you on your ass in front of your friends, *after* you teased me about my freckles. Or have you conveniently forgotten the bruise on your chest where I hit you?"

He shrugged. "Whatever." The very welcome sight of a blue pickup truck coming down the road made him smile. "Speaking of girlfriends, here she comes."

Delaney turned around so quickly that she almost fell. Her face broke out into a silly grin. "I bet she's going to go check on the buffalo calf." She playfully pushed her brother. "You can thank Gib later for saving you."

"Yeah, right," he called after her, as his sister traipsed through the mud toward her SUV.

GLORIA STARED AT the heavy thicket of mesquite trees as they turned onto a gravel road. Where are we going now?"

"This is the last of your tour," Gib muttered. "A fire road that goes beside the lake. I thought since we were out, I'd show you our small herd of buffalo and longhorns."

"Wow. You really lead an exciting life around here, Gibson." Gloria had always refused to use the diminutive for Gib's name, saying it sounded too butch. "However do you stand it?"

Gib sighed as they passed the construction site. She was so focused on her passenger, she didn't notice Delaney's Lexus parked by the other vehicles. "It's a nice place, Gloria. Of course, there's not much to keep you entertained out here in the 'boonies' as you call it. But I like it here."

"We used to keep ourselves entertained." Gloria tried to bring the conversation back to their previous relationship. "Remember our long weekends?"

"I don't want to talk about it." Gib slowed as they passed the empty pens. "I think we're up to maybe six or eight head of longhorn and around four buffalo. If you're lucky you'll get to see the newest member that was born a few weeks ago." She pulled off the road and turned off the engine. "Hop out, but don't slam your door. They're right over there."

Gloria looked in the direction Gib pointed, and saw two adult buffalo and one longhorn. "God, they're ugly." She stepped out of the truck and joined Gib at the fence, standing as close as she could. "Would you give me another chance?"

Gib turned, almost bumping the other woman. "No. I've found someone who loves me for who I am, not who they think they can make me. Even if I hadn't, my feelings for you are long gone. There's nothing you can do or say to change my mind." Her eyes grew wide as Gloria leaned in and kissed her.

IT DIDN'T TAKE Delaney long to get into her Lexus and follow the blue pickup. She saw it parked beside the road and came to a stop not far behind. It wasn't until she was out of the SUV that she realized Gib had someone with her.

Before Delaney could call out, she saw a striking blonde step forward and kiss Gib. *I should have known! Gib isn't any different, after all.* She was geared up to speak her mind, when she saw Gib shove the woman away.

"Damn it, Gloria. I told you no!" Gib wiped her mouth and crawled through the fence, away from the her.

"Gib!" Delaney yelled, startling the grazing animals. They turned away and lumbered into the brush. The redhead struggled to climb through the fence, ignoring the orders from Gloria.

"Lady, get back here. This isn't public property," Gloria shouted, but made no move to follow.

With her back to Gloria, Delaney held up both hands, with only her middle fingers extended. "Bite me," she tossed over her shoulder, never losing sight of her lover. "Gib, wait up."

Gib stopped not far from the brush, but didn't turn around. She stuffed her hands in the front pockets of her uniform pants and lowered her head. "Damn it."

"Honey?" Delaney stopped a few feet from Gib.

"If you're going to yell at me," Gib's voice was hoarse, "can it wait? I'm really not up for a fight right now."

Delaney moved closer until she could put her arm around Gib. "I'm not going to yell. I may kill that blonde bimbo, but I think you're safe."

"She's my ex," Gib explained. She leaned against Delaney and closed her eyes. "I had no idea she was the temporary ranger we were getting. I swear I didn't do anything to encourage her."

"I believe you."

Gib raised her head and looked into her lover's face. "You do?"

"Yes. Although I'll admit my first thought was that you were cheating on me."

"But, I wouldn't—"

Delaney kissed her lightly on the lips. "I know you wouldn't. You're not capable of something like that. But, if she touches you again, I'll kick her ass."

Gib laughed and hugged her. "I'll sell tickets. Come on. I'll introduce you." She kissed Delaney on the neck and whispered, "I love you, Dee."

"I love you, too." Delaney pulled her head down and gave her a passionate kiss. "All right. Now that I'm through marking my territory, let's go." She held her head high as they walked hand in hand to the fence.

"Here." Gib held two strands of wire apart so that Delaney could step through more easily. She followed, smiling when the redhead took a firm grasp on her hand.

Gloria angrily crossed her arms over her chest as the pair approached. "That's a new technique to capturing trespassers."

"Delaney, sweetheart, this grump is Gloria Hoover. She's here to help us while Kennie recovers." Gib never released her lover's hand, instead grinning at Gloria. "Oh, and she's my ex-girlfriend."

The redhead nodded. "Hello. I'm afraid Gib has told me nothing about you, Gloria. Welcome to Benton."

Gib was barely able to control the urge to giggle at the look on Gloria's face. She tossed her keys to Gloria. "Why don't you take my truck to the office, Gloria? I'm going to ride with Delaney."

"Whatever." Gloria caught the keys and stormed away.

Once she was out of range, Gib turned to Delaney. "Thank you."

"For what, darling?" Delaney released her hand and put her arms around Gib. "That was a lot more fun than kicking her ass."

"I love you so much," Gib proclaimed, right before she kissed her.

TWENTY MINUTES LATER, Delaney stopped her Lexus near the side door of the office. "I guess I'll see you around seven?"

"Yep." Gib unfastened her seatbelt and leaned across the vehicle. She grinned when Delaney mirrored her actions and met her halfway. "I'm looking forward to it." The quick kiss they shared enflamed her libido and made her want more. "I don't know how much work I'm going to get done between now and then, though."

Delaney fingered the layers of windblown hair around Gib's face. "Tell me about it. I have enough at the office to keep me busy for days, but I doubt I'll even look at it." She glanced over her lover's shoulder. "We've got a voyeur."

"Gee, I wonder who?"

An evil glint appeared in Delaney's eyes. "Wanna give her something to look at?"

"It's very tempting, sweetheart. But I do have to work with her for the time being." Gib kissed her again and grabbed the door handle. "See you in a few hours." She was about to close the door when Delaney called out to her. "What?"

"I love you."

Gib's smile lit up her entire face. "I love you, too. Be careful driving back." She closed the door and watched until the Lexus disappeared from view. Still wearing the grin, she went into the office and stepped past Gloria. "Enjoy the show?"

"You know, Gibson, I don't remember you being so rude before,"

Gloria whispered. She took a step back when Gib turned around and moved toward her.

"No, you remember me being your lap dog. But those days are over." She held out her hand. "Keys, please." With a wink, Gib walked away from her, twirling the key ring on her finger and whistling.

Behind the counter, Dan glared at the officer. "What are you so happy about?"

Gib stopped in front of him. "It's a beautiful day. Why wouldn't I be happy?"

"Well, we still have those poachers running around," Dan taunted. "You haven't found many clues about them, have you?"

"Not yet. But, I have a feeling my luck is changing." She tapped the counter. "Have fun working the desk today. I'm going out to enjoy the sunshine."

Dan glared at Gib's back. "Bitch," he grumbled.

Gloria overheard him and walked to the counter. "Problem?"

"Yeah. She thinks she's hot shit."

"Oh, I don't know. She has been with the department for over fifteen years and is a senior officer. Must know something."

He snorted. "Yeah, right. I'd think she was sleeping her way to the top, but she's a," Dan lowered his voice to a whisper, "dyke."

"Really?" Although not enamored with her ex-lover's newfound independence, Gloria still held hope for reconciliation. She decided to keep an eye on Dan. "Well, then I doubt she was able to get far that way." She drummed her manicured nails on the sign in clipboard. "You and I will have to stick together, won't we?"

"Sure." Dan's eyes lit up. "Hey, what are you doing after work? I know this great place in town."

Gloria cut him off. "Oh, sorry. I have to unpack. Maybe some other time." She winked at him and left the office.

Chapter Sixteen

GIB FOLLOWED HER lover into the steak house, surprised that the "family" dinner would be held in the moderately priced restaurant. She had expected the meal to be somewhere with dim lighting and linen tablecloths. The Wrangler had been a part of Benton's culinary scene for over forty years. Rough-hewn walls were decorated with burnt-on cattle brands while dim light flickered from the hanging wagon wheels. They were led to a large, round table in one of the semi-private rooms, where four others already were seated.

Gib held out Delaney's chair and helped her get settled. She took the final chair between Delaney and Dylan.

"Nice to see you could make it," Dylan teased his sister. "Hey, Gib. You look a lot different out of uniform." He flinched and glared at the dark-haired woman sitting next to him. "What?"

Delaney rolled her eyes. "Let me get the introductions out of the way. Gib, you know my brother, Dylan."

Gib nodded. "Hi, Dylan. You clean up pretty well, yourself," she joked.

"And his wife, Marsha, who should earn a medal for putting up with him."

Marsha looked surprised when Gib stood to shake her hand. Slightly overweight, with her dark hair cut stylishly short, Marsha was the epitome of a soccer mom. "It's nice to meet you, Gib."

"My pleasure, Marsha." Gib walked around the table. She held her hand out to Maureen. "Mrs. Kavanagh, I'm Gibson Proctor." She shook Colin's hand next. "Mr. Kavanagh, thank you both for coming tonight. Delaney has spoken very highly of you."

Colin got to his feet and looked Gib in the eye. "It's our pleasure, Gib. Our daughter raves about you constantly, so it's nice to finally meet you." He motioned to his wife. "And please, call us Colin and Maureen. I've left the shotgun in the car, so you're safe. For now." He grinned at the panicked look on her face.

"Dad," Delaney sighed. "You promised to behave tonight."

"A man has to protect his little girl, doesn't he?" He slapped Gib on the back. "Take it easy. We won't talk about the wedding plans until dessert."

"Wedd—" Gib choked. At the laughter from the entire table, she relaxed. "Now I see where Dee gets her sense of humor." She returned to her seat and exhaled in relief.

Delaney rubbed her shoulder. "I'm sorry, honey. My family takes a little getting used to."

Marsha nodded. "That's so true. Gib, when I first started dating

Dylan, I wasn't sure what I was getting into. But you'll never have to worry about what they're thinking, because they'll be more than happy to tell you."

A server brought three baskets of rolls to the table and took everyone's drink order. Once she left, Dylan smiled sweetly at his sister before turning his attention to her girlfriend. "So, Gib. What do you do besides harass contractors all day?"

"I mostly patrol the park. There's not a lot to do right now, but once summer comes, I figure to be pretty busy." Gib took a sip of her iced tea. "Although harassing contractors is a perk."

Colin laughed. "She's got you there, son. Say, Gib? What do you do for fun?"

"I like to fish when I get a chance. And since my cabin is within steps of the lake, it's something I can do whenever I want."

Maureen poked her husband. "Don't say it."

He tried to appear innocent. "What?"

At Gib's questioning gaze, she explained, "My husband is a huge fisherman. He'd be out on the lake every minute of every day, if we lived there."

Gib nodded. "You're welcome anytime, Colin. Just give me a call."

"You shouldn't have said that, honey," Delaney stage-whispered.

"Why not?"

Maureen was the one who answered. "Because you'll never get a moment's peace." She politely thanked the server who placed her iced tea in front of her.

Everyone laughed at the chagrined look on Colin's face. He shrugged. "If I can ever get my kids to take over the business, I can retire and fish full time."

"Yeah, right," Dylan snorted. "You'd last about a week before you begged to be back at work."

Everyone chimed in their agreement, while Colin shook his head.

Once all of their orders were taken, Marsha scooted her chair away from the table, giving Delaney a tip of her head. "If you'll excuse me, I need to freshen up before the food arrives."

"Um, yeah. Me, too." Delaney allowed Gib to pull her chair back. She touched her lover's hand and whispered, "Thanks."

After the two women left, Gib felt the weight of Dylan's stare. "What?"

"Are you trying to make me look bad?"

"I don't understand. What did I do?"

Dylan shook his head. "Gib, Gib, Gib. Isn't it enough that you've domesticated my sister? Do you have to try and steal my wife, too?"

The elder couple chuckled at Gib's apparent cluelessness. Colin tried to help. "Don't listen to him, Gib. He's just jealous because you're a better partner than him."

"I don't know about that, but thanks. But since we're talking about it, I want to thank you for this evening. It's been a lot of fun. Reminds me of when Dee and I are together."

"That's the funny thing," Dylan told her. "My sister is usually a very serious person. It's been years since we've seen her playful side come out, and we have you to thank for it."

Gib frowned. "Really? I find that hard to believe. We're always laughing or playing around, and she instigates it as much as I do."

"Don't misunderstand. Delaney is a wonderful woman, and we're all very proud of her. But she's been much too somber." Maureen raised her tea glass. "I hope you two continue to have fun, and enjoy all life gives you."

Gib raised her glass as well. "Thank you, Maureen."

IN THE RESTROOM, Marsha cornered Delaney. "Is she for real?"

Delaney couldn't help but grin. "Jealous?"

"Hell, yes. I don't think Dylan ever held out my chair for me, even when we were dating." Marsha washed her hands and looked at her reflection in the mirror. She fluffed her hair. "Looks like it's time to hide the old woman again. My hair grows too fast, and I spend most of your brother's money at the salon hiding the gray. Now, back to Gib. Does she do that sort of thing often?"

"Constantly." Delaney stood next to her and also looked in the mirror. "When I first met her, I kept thinking the same thing. There's no way a person in this day and age can be so gallant. But that's just how she is."

Marsha stuck her tongue out at their reflections. "I hate you." She giggled, causing Delaney to crack up as well. "Think she'll give your brother lessons?"

"Good luck with that one," Delaney laughed, bumping hips with her sister-in-law. "Do you think I'm crazy, to have fallen in love so quickly?"

"Honestly?" Marsha turned and looked into Delaney's eyes. "I've only just met her, and I'm a little in love, too." She embraced the redhead. "And if only a slight bit of her rubs off on Dylan, I'll be thrilled."

They were still giggling when they returned to the table, which was loaded with food. Delaney smiled her thanks to Gib, who once again helped her into her chair.

Marsha glared at Dylan, who quickly jumped to his feet and followed suit. "Thank you, honey."

"Uh, sure." Dylan frowned at Gib, who was trying hard not to laugh. "Shut up," he grumbled.

IN THE PARKING lot after dinner, Gib and Delaney waved to the family as everyone headed for their cars. They had agreed to a cookout at the lake the following weekend, much to Colin's delight. "I hope you know what you're getting into," Delaney teased, as Gib held open the driver's door on the Lexus.

"Come on, Dee. It'll be fun. Marsha wanted to go to the pool with the kids, and your dad is really looking forward to fishing." Gib glanced around, and seeing no one, gave her a quick kiss. She jogged around to the other side and got in. "It's still pretty early. What would you like to do?"

Delaney gave her a saucy wink. "I know of several things I'd like to do. But, since I don't want to waste us both being so dolled up, how about we go dancing?"

"Sure." Gib glanced down at her clothes. Her neatly-pressed black jeans and a starched gray shirt were dressier than usual, along with polished black boots. "What kind of music does the club play tonight?"

"I'm not sure." Delaney started the SUV and backed out of the parking space. "I think it's country. Is that all right?"

Gib laughed. "Sweetheart, as long as I can hold you in my arms, it's all good."

"Keep talking like that, and we're skipping the dancing."

"And that's a bad thing?"

Delaney giggled. "Hardly. But I do enjoy going out with you."

"I like that." Gib brought their hands up and kissed Delaney's knuckles. "Take me dancing, pretty lady."

THE CLUB WASN'T very crowded so they were able to find a table next to the dance floor. Gib helped Delaney sit, and then headed for the bar to get their drinks.

The bartender, a woman with multiple tattoos, gave her a friendly nod. "What can I get for you?"

"White wine and a bottle of water, please." Gib placed a ten dollar bill on the bar.

"There's no charge for the water," the bartender told her.

Gib grinned. "Keep the change, then."

"Thanks." The woman nodded toward the dance floor. "Are you with Delaney?"

"I am." Gib leaned closer and lowered her voice. "Is there a problem?"

"Not at all. I'm Lisa, Kate's ex." Lisa held out her hand. "You know, Terri and Kate?"

Gib shook her hand. "Nice to meet you. I met Terri and Kate a while back. Dee's really fond of them."

"So am I," Lisa admitted. "Kate and I dated during college, but decided we'd be better friends than partners. A year later, she met Terri, and the rest is history. Anyway, tell Delaney I said hi."

"I sure will. Thanks." Gib took their drinks to their table and sat next to her lover. "Lisa says hi."

Delaney turned and waved toward the bar. "She didn't give you the third degree, did she?"

"Nah. Just a little history." Gib sipped her water. "Ready to get your toes bruised?"

"I thought you'd never ask." Delaney stood and took Gib's hand. There were only four other couples on the dance floor. She snuggled close to Gib and sighed happily as the officer's arms snaked around her body. "I've needed this all evening."

Gib kissed the side of her head. "Me, too." She shuffled her feet and guided them slowly around the floor.

They danced to three songs before a fast beat chased them away. Gib took a seat at their table, surprised when someone tapped her on the shoulder. She turned her head. "Yes?"

"Didn't expect to see you here this evening," the muscled woman replied.

Delaney ran around the table and happily embraced the woman. "Hey, Terri!" She was lifted off her feet and swung around. "Where's Kate?"

"At the bar, picking on Lisa." Terri kissed Delaney on the cheek and shook hands with Gib. "Nice to see you again, Gib."

"Same here. Would you like to join us?"

Terri considered the offer. She smiled as Delaney sat as close as possible to Gib. "Are you sure you two wouldn't rather be alone?"

Gib put her arm around her lover, who leaned into her embrace. "We can be alone later. Have a seat."

"All right." Terri pulled out a chair, which was instantly occupied by her partner. "You're welcome," she teased.

"Hush." Kate placed their beers on the table and slapped Terri on the leg. "Hi guys."

Delaney laughed at the playfulness of her two friends. "How's work?"

"Busy, as usual. Not that I'm complaining. I know it's only going to get worse as it gets hotter." Kate was an administrative assistant for a landscape and sprinkler company. "How's the work at the lake going?"

"We're ahead of schedule. As a matter of fact, if the weather continues to cooperate, we should be done almost a month early." Delaney sipped her wine and watched as Gib drained the bottle of water. "Would you like me to get you another one, honey?"

Gib shook her head. "Nah. I need to run to the restroom, so I'll pick one up on the way back." She stood. "Anyone else need a refill?" When Terri and Kate responded negatively, she headed for the hallway off the dance floor.

She passed a slender woman in the dark hall and pushed open the ladies' room door. Just as Gib stepped over the threshold, she felt a pair of hands slam hard into her back. Knocked to her knees, Gib turned and was barely able to ward off a kick toward her head. "What the hell?"

"You fucking bitch!" the woman spat, as she jumped onto Gib. "You stole my girlfriend!"'

Gib rolled until she had the dark-haired woman face down on the floor. "What are you talking about?"

"She's mine! Laney's mine!" Chris blubbered as she tried to squirm out of Gib's hold.

"I didn't steal anyone." Gib pulled her up and pushed her back against the wall.

Chris continued to cry. "I had her first, you know."

"I don't care. She's with me now, and that's all the matters to me. Why don't you go home and sleep it off?"

"Fuck you!" Chris powered her head forward, slamming into Gib's face. "I love her, and she's mine, you fucking bitch!" She blinked as her vision swam from the force of the hit. A drunken smile covered her face when blood began to drip from Gib's nose and mouth. "Ha."

Gib twisted Chris' arm and forced her face into the wall, just as another woman stepped into the restroom.

"What's going on here?"

"She stole my woman," Chris bellowed, as she tried to break free of Gib's hold.

Gib turned to the woman and identified herself. "I'm a Texas Peace Officer. Would you please have Lisa at the bar call the police?"

The woman's eyes were wide. "Uh, sure." She hurried out of the room.

"You're a cop?" Chris asked, still struggling.

"I am. And you're under arrest for assault." Gib tightened her hold on Chris' bent arm, raising her hand higher against her back. "So just shut up and be still."

"Ow! Police brutality!" Chris slammed her head into the wall. "Help!"

Gib kept one hand holding Chris' wrist, while she brought her other arm around the woman's neck to pull her away from the wall. "You idiot! Stop that."'

"Bitch."

The door swung open again, allowing Terri and Delaney access. "Police are on their way," Terri advised. "Need any help, Gib?" She was pushed out of the way by a fuming redhead.

"Goddamn it, Chris. What the hell have you done?" Delaney wet a few paper towels and tried to clean Gib's face. "Are you all right, honey?"

"No! This fucking bitch attacked me," Chris screamed. "Laney, I love you!"

Delaney clenched her fists. "I wasn't talking to you, jackass."

"Want me to take her so you can get cleaned up?" Terri asked Gib.

"Fucking bitch," Chris kicked at Terri. "I never liked you."

Terri laughed and stepped back. "The feeling's mutual, asshole."

Two uniformed men stood in the open doorway. One kept his hand on the butt of his gun, while the other came into the room. "Could everyone clear out, please?" the one at the door asked politely.

Delaney looked as if she was about to argue, but she sighed and nodded. "I'll be right outside," she whispered to Gib.

Ten minutes later, a bawling and handcuffed Chris was led through the club by the officers. She tried to stop at the table where Delaney sat with Terri and Kate. "I love you, Laney. Please don't hate me." She stopped crying when Delaney stood and walked toward her, but had to be dragged away as the redhead passed and went directly into Gib's arms. "No!"

"Shut up," one of the officers ordered, as they pulled her to the front door. "Remember those rights we explained to you? Now would be a good time to exercise the silent one." His partner opened the door and the three of them stepped out into the night.

Gib held a damp paper towel to her lower face as she and Delaney joined their friends. "That was fun." She pulled the towel away and looked at it, grimacing at the new blood. "Damn."

"I can't believe Chris would do something so stupid," Delaney growled. She took over the towel and began to clean Gib's face.

"She kept telling me that you were hers." Gib watched her lover's face, which darkened with fury.

"Like hell I am. As soon as she gets out on bail, I'm going to kick her ass."

Terri nodded. "I'll help."

"No, you won't," Kate asserted. "That sorry waste of skin isn't worth you or Delaney getting into trouble over. Right, Gib?"

"Right." Gib moved away from Delaney's attempt to wipe the blood from her shirt. "Don't worry about it."

Delaney's chin quivered as she tried to control her emotions. "I'm sorry, Gib. She's been acting a little weird lately, but I never figured her for that."

"What do you mean? Acting weird, how?"

"She just wouldn't take no for an answer. She kept calling me and calling me, even after I told her to leave me alone. I don't know why she got so fixated on me. It's not like we were very close at the end of our relationship."

Kate patted Delaney's hand. "You never did seem very happy with her. Even when you first got together, I don't remember ever seeing you laugh." She smiled at Gib. "Not like you do now."

Gib pulled Delaney's hand into her lap. "Why didn't you tell me you were having trouble with her?"

"Honestly? I didn't think it was that big of a deal. She'd call and whine for a while, then I'd tell her off."

"All right. But do me a favor, next time?"

Delaney touched Gib's face. "I'll tell you, I promise."

Terri blew out a breath. "Well, I think it's time we got going. You guys going to be okay?"

"Sure." Gib stood and fished one of her business cards out of her wallet. "Give me a call, and we'll all get together. Maybe y'all can come out to the lake some weekend."

"We'd like that," Kate answered. She hugged a surprised Gib, and then moved on to Delaney. "Take care of this one," she whispered in the redhead's ear. "She's a keeper."

Delaney nodded. "I know. And I plan on it." She hugged Terri. "See you later." Once their friends left, she turned to her lover. "Can I interest you in a long soak in a hot bath?"

"Are you going to be there?" Gib asked with a grin.

"Perhaps." Delaney looked closely at Gib's face, which was beginning to bruise above her lip. "I'm so sorry."

Gib took her into her arms, careful to keep Delaney away from the blood on her shirt. "I'd rather she go after me than you. And you have nothing to apologize for. It's not your fault the woman is unbalanced."

"Still—"

"No. Do you blame me for Gloria's behavior?"

Delaney shook her head. "Of course not. But that's not the same."

"It's exactly the same. We can't take credit when others do great, so why should we take the blame when they get stupid?" Gib waved to Lisa as she and Delaney left the bar. "Would it upset you if I pressed charges against her?"

"Hell, no. If there were any extra charges I could get added on, I would," Delaney snapped. "I still want to kick her ass." She sighed as Gib chuckled. "I could do it, you know."

Gib held her close. "Of that, I have no doubts."

A COOL DRAFT woke Gib. She blinked in the gloom and tried to get her bearings. The soft breath on the back of her neck, along with the arm wrapped around her stomach, brought a smile to her face. The emotion was short-lived when her lip broke open again. "Damn."

"Whassa' matter?" Delaney mumbled, tightening her grip.

Gib patted the hand on her stomach. "Nothing. Go back to sleep."

"Mmm." Delaney snuggled close, her bare thighs brushing against Gib's. "What time is it?"

"After three."

Delaney lightly bit the back of Gib's neck. "Wanna fool around?"

Gib rolled over and wrapped her arms around the redhead. "Again?"

"Always." Delaney gave her a slow kiss, while her hands mapped out the contours of Gib's body. She pulled back and licked her lips, grimacing. "Your lip is bleeding again. Let me go get a washcloth."

"It's okay," Gib assured her, hanging onto Delaney's hips so she couldn't leave the bed. "It'll stop in a while."

With a heavy sigh, Delaney broke away and got out of bed. A minute later she returned to sit beside Gib. "Come here."

"Dee—"

"Please, don't argue with me." Delaney switched on the bedside lamp. "Honey, maybe you should get that stitched." She carefully dabbed at the cut.

Gib caught her hand. "Give it a couple of days and you won't even be able to tell, I promise." She frowned as tears welled in Delaney's eyes. "Hey, what's wrong?"

Delaney pulled her hand back and used a shaky finger to trace along Gib's mouth. "It's my fault you got hurt."

"No." Gib kissed the finger. "She did it all on her own. Even when she found out I was a peace officer, she didn't settle down. The woman has some issues, and they have nothing to do with you. Don't give her that power."

"My head says that, but my heart," Delaney sadly shook her head, "my heart tells me otherwise. How could I have been in a relationship with her for a year and not know what a nutcase she was? Am I that bad at judging character?"

Gib smiled. "I sure hope not. Or are you trying to tell me something?"

Delaney swatted her. "No, you loon." She caressed the arm she had slapped. "Do you think she'll go to jail?"

"Has she been into any trouble before?"

"Not that I'm aware of. But then again, I really don't know that much about her." Delaney felt Gib's hands cover hers in her lap. "I think I know more about you than I do her. I've never met her family, and she's only met mine because she's been to my office."

Gib cocked her head and looked directly into her lover's eyes. "Really? Even after a year?"

"Sounds odd, doesn't it? The more I think about it, the more I realize how wrong it was to be with her for so long. She didn't deserve to be treated that way."

"You're kidding, right?"

Lowering her head, Delaney looked at their joined hands. "At first, she seemed so sweet. We dated for a couple of months before we got serious. Once we became," she lowered her voice, "intimate, everything changed."

Gib's voice was almost as quiet. "Changed, how?"

"She became more...focused on me, I guess. Always wanting to know where I was, what I was doing. At first, I thought it was kind of sweet, like she missed me and couldn't wait to see me again. But when she would sit outside my office and wait for me to come out, it made me uncomfortable."

"And yet, you stayed together?"

Delaney shrugged. "Honestly? I didn't want to go back to blind dates or meeting someone at a bar."

"Did you love her?"

The answer was immediate. "No. Maybe that was the problem. She would tell me she loved me, and I'd never reciprocate. I cared for her, at first. But later, I kept making excuses to keep away from her. I think I was afraid of being alone. I'm such a selfish bitch."

Gib leaned back against the headboard and tugged Delaney with her. "Come here." She held her lover in her arms and stroked her hair. "It would have been worse if you had lied to her. A relationship takes two people, sweetheart."

"Maybe so, but I should have stopped it sooner. She wanted more and I kept backing away." Delaney raised her head and looked into Gib's eyes. "Don't let me do that to you, please. You mean too much to me, Gib."

"Don't worry, Dee. I'm not going anywhere, and I won't let you go, either."

THE ENTICING SMELLS of breakfast woke Delaney. She rolled over and snuggled into Gib's cold pillow, her mind warring between trying to get a few more minutes of sleep or seeing her lover in the kitchen. A smile crossed her face when she remembered how Gib usually cooked breakfast. Delaney scooted out of bed and put on the nearest shirt, which happened to belong to Gib.

She stopped in the doorway, content in watching Gib work in the kitchen. She couldn't help but smile at the woman wearing only a pair of cotton briefs. For someone who claimed to be a novice cook, the officer did a fine job on anything she decided to prepare. Delaney leaned against the doorframe and crossed her arms under her breasts.

Gib looked up from the stove and smiled at her lover. "Good morning, beautiful."

"It certainly is," Delaney agreed, pushing off the door and joining Gib by the stove. She put her arms on Gib's shoulders and linked her hands behind her neck. A gentle tug brought Gib's lips close, and Delaney gave her a heartfelt kiss. "Now it's even better."

"I've got to agree with you on that one. Are you about ready to eat?"

Delaney grinned. "Is that a proposition?" She laughed at the look on her lover's face. "Okay, okay. Would you like me to set the table?"

"That would be great." Gib swatted the redhead on the rear when she turned away.

"Hey!" Delaney spun and glared at Gib. "What did you do that for?"

Gib grinned. "Cause it was there, of course." She dodged the slap headed for her arm. "No beating on the cook."

"Why do you get to make all the rules?" Delaney gathered the plates and silverware. Then she poured two cups of coffee, all the while keeping her eye on Gib.

Once the omelet was done, Gib took the pan to the table and doled out equal portions. She returned the pan to the stovetop and took a seat beside her lover. "What are your plans for the next couple of days?"

"I've got a client meeting at ten on Friday morning, so I have quite a bit to do in order to prepare for it." Delaney took a bite of the omelet and moaned. "How do you manage to find something edible in my apartment, when I can't?" She frowned. "I know I didn't have mushrooms."

Gib shrugged. "I ran to the store earlier." She had her fork almost to her mouth when Delaney's arm swat knocked it away.

"But you're not dressed!"

"I was. But I like the look on your face when you see me cook, so I undressed when I got back." Gib switched hands and started to eat.

"Think you're pretty clever, don't you, officer?"

Gib nodded.

Delaney leaned closer and whispered in her ear. "I think you are, too." She kissed Gib's neck and returned to her breakfast.

After they cleaned the kitchen, they took a quick shower together. Delaney could feel Gib watching her as she pulled on her pantyhose. "See something you like?" she asked over her shoulder.

"Always." Gib buckled her belt and sat on the end of the bed to put on her socks and boots. "Would you like to come out on Friday night and stay for the weekend?"

"Sure." Delaney chose an electric blue blouse to go with her black skirt. She fluffed her hair out of the collar and added small earrings to finish the look. While she put a minimal amount of makeup on, she watched her lover's reflection in the mirror. "Gib?"

Gib looked up from her boots. "Hmm?"

"Are you all right? You seem kind of quiet."

"I'm fine. Just being stupid." Gib stood and joined Delaney at the dressing table. "You look beautiful."

Delaney turned to find herself in Gib's arms. "Thank you. Did you know that you're one of the few people that tell me that, whom I believe?"

"Really?"

"Yeah. Usually when someone would say something like that, it was always a precursor to getting me into bed with them." As Gib's arms tightened around her, Delaney snuggled closer. "But with you, I know it's not like that."

Gib kissed the side of Delaney's head. "As much as I enjoy our time in bed, I enjoy being with you like this, more."

"You do?"

"Definitely. I'm enjoying learning all about you. And to me, this intimacy is much more important than sex." Gib paused. "Not that the sex hasn't been amazing, but—"

Delaney laughed and squeezed the breath out of Gib. "I know exactly what you mean." She sighed and released her stranglehold. "Come on, officer. This isn't getting either of us to work."

"I know." Gib lowered her face and kissed Delaney, pouring all her love into the connection. When they finally broke apart, she felt her lover's finger on her lips. "Got me again, did you?"

"Uh-huh. Although I think it's a good shade for you." Delaney squealed when Gib started tickling her. "No fair!"

"All's fair in love and horseshoes," Gib stated, as she stalked her prey across the bedroom. "Come here."

"Oh, no. You're not going to get me this time." Delaney raced out of the bedroom, with Gib close on her heels. They ended up in the kitchen, where the redhead took the sprayer from the sink and aimed it at her lover. "Not another step, officer."

Gib stopped a few feet away. "You wouldn't dare." At the grin from her lover, she held out her hands. "Dee, you wouldn't want to make me late for work, would you?"

"Only if you're foolish enough to come closer." Delaney held the sprayer in front of her like a gun. "Don't do it."

Gib took a step. She sputtered as her face was hit with a blast of cold water. "Aarrgghh!" She rushed Delaney and flipped the screaming redhead over her shoulder.

"My clothes!" Delaney whined, ineffectually kicking her feet.

"I can't believe you sprayed me." Gib carried her prisoner into the living room and dumped her onto the sofa. She leaned over Delaney, water dripping from her hair onto the redhead's face. "Now you will pay!"

Delaney's giggles quickly turned into moans, as their wet clothes were peeled away.

Chapter Seventeen

GIB ARRIVED ONLY fifteen minutes late to the office, her hair damp from the shower she took at the cabin. She walked into the office and paused at the duty board.

"Well, well well. Look who finally decided to show up," Gloria teased in a whisper. "I've never known you to be late before."

"First time for everything," Gib muttered. "Looks like you're on call from tonight through Sunday. If you need a break, let me know."

Gloria shrugged. "Thanks, but I doubt anything's going to happen." Her glance lingered across Gib's face and around her neck. She traced a small hickey near Gib's collar with one finger. "She must be pretty special."

Gib slapped her hand away and put a few feet between them. "She is. Extremely special."

Gloria held up her hands and shook her head. "All right. I get it. I'll back off."

"Good." Gib adjusted her collar and lowered her voice. "Does it look bad?"

"Nah. I only noticed because I was standing right next to you. Don't worry about it. That's a nice bruise over your lip. She like it rough?"

Gib glared at her. "Delaney didn't do it. I had to subdue a drunk last night."

"Okay, I'm sorry. I didn't mean anything by it." Gloria held out her hand. "Friends?"

"Sure." Gib shook her hand, relieved to not feel the old pain of losing what they once had. "Do you know how long you'll be here?"

Gloria followed Gib outside. "I'm not sure. At first, it was supposed to be until some guy returned from having the chicken pox. But, now, Clint mentioned that I'm here until Wyatt returns. So I guess whenever the big dogs decide I'm not needed here anymore."

"Good luck with that. Getting headquarters to commit to anything is a joke." Gib stopped at her truck. "Are you settling in okay? I mean, do you need any help with anything?"

"I'm good, thanks. What would your girlfriend think about you offering to help me?"

Gib laughed. "She'd think I was being nice to someone I work with. Dee trusts me completely, and I never plan on giving her reason not to."

"God, you've got it bad." Gloria opened the door to her Jeep. "Thanks for the offer, though. See you later."

"Yeah." Gib waved and got into her truck, the smile never leaving her face as she thought about her lover, and the impromptu water fight that escalated into her being late for work.

AFTER SPENDING THE morning at the office, Delaney took the rest of her work home. As much as she enjoyed working with her family, sometimes all she wanted was to be left alone so she could get things done.

She placed the rolls of blueprints on her drafting table and went to the bedroom to change into something more comfortable. It was one of the many perks of working at home, probably her favorite. She shed the skirt, silk top and undergarments, trading them for baggy sweat pants and a tee shirt.

A short detour through the kitchen yielded cheese puffs and a diet root beer. It wasn't that she was addicted to the puffs, but needed something to crunch on while she thought. A bag would last her almost two weeks, if she didn't share. She sat at her desk and opened the bag, smiling. The memory of Gib showing her how well you could body paint with wet cheese puffs was a lesson she'd never forget.

She was soon totally engrossed in the upcoming project, her focus only on the work in front of her. A new builder planned a master community with houses, condos, apartments and shopping - all surrounding a man-made lake. He wanted Kavanagh Construction to join his efforts, and Delaney's vision for the waterfront would be their contribution. She wasn't sure if the area would be able to hold a lake, and feared that it would ruin the ecosystem.

The long hours of research made her eyes blur, and only the grumble from her stomach caused Delaney to look at the clock. "You're kidding me." The digital readout continued to glare at her. "Five-thirty?" Her stomach rumbled again to punctuate the point. "Crap." She shut down her laptop and pushed away from the desk. There were several more hours of work to do, but she didn't feel like doing it.

A walk to the kitchen didn't reveal anything interesting. She wandered through the living room, disheartened by the silence of the apartment. It wasn't something she had noticed before, but what once was her sanctuary had become her prison. "This is ridiculous."

An idea formed, and before she could talk herself out of it, she was in her bedroom, changing into jeans and a soft cotton top. She enjoyed the way Gib looked at her when she was wearing jeans, and besides, they were more comfortable than sliding into pantyhose every day. "She has changed me," Delaney told her reflection in a mirror. "And I like who I've become."

THE CALL ON Gib's radio came in right after four o'clock. "Proctor, meet Dan at the back of campsite seven, please," George requested.

"All right. ETA six minutes." Gib was on the fire road past the dam. She swung the truck wide on the gravel road and turned around. "What's going on, George?"

His answer came back hesitant. "I really can't get into it on the radio. Be advised there are also civilians on the scene."

"Are there injuries? Has city services been called?"

"Negative. No injuries and no one else was contacted."

Frustrated with the lack of information, Gib's hands tightened on the steering wheel. She soon crossed the highway and into the main park. Minutes later, she slowed as she came within sight of number seven. The campsite was somewhat secluded, a small wooden structure with a concrete floor and screens on all four sides. There were two men gesturing wildly as they tried to convey something to Dan.

Gib parked beside Dan's vehicle and got out. She adjusted her baseball cap to block the lowering sun. "Conroy," she greeted.

He turned to her, his face pale and covered in sweat. "Proctor. These guys called it in."

"Called what in?" She nodded to the middle-aged men. "I'm Park Police Officer Gibson Proctor. What seems to be the problem?"

The heavier of the two men stepped forward. "I was throwing away our garbage. Not very much, you know?" At her nod, he continued, "and I opened that dumpster. It smelled awful, and there were so many flies."

Gib cut him off. "Hold it." She turned to Dan. "Conroy?"

"Don't ask me to go over there again," he choked, covering his mouth and gagging. "I can't."

"All right. Let me check it out. Then," she tipped her head to the men, "I'll take your statements." Not quite knowing what to expect, she warily moved toward the dumpster. The smell of death assailed her senses before she could see inside. She peered over the edge and grimaced.

At first glance the gory remains were hard to distinguish. As she studied them, Gib was finally able to make out several slender legs mixed among a rather large pile of bloody entrails. She took a disposable glove from her back pocket and slipped it on. With her gloved hand, she sifted through the remains. "It appears to be at least two deer," she called over her shoulder to Dan, who turned away and vomited on a cedar bush.

The heavyset man danced away from him. "Hey, watch it!" His companion, short and slender, laughed.

Dan wiped his chin with the back of his hand. "Sorry."

"Conroy," Gib called. "Could you get a few trash bags and more gloves from my truck? We're going to have to take these back to the garage to get a closer look."

He nodded and rushed away, apparently eager to be away from the odor.

Gib snapped her glove off and rejoined the two men. "I appreciate you calling us about this."

"Freaked out Scott, that's for sure," the smaller man snickered. "I don't think your ranger enjoyed it too much, either."

"He's just young." Gib tipped her cap back. "I'm afraid I didn't catch your names."

The smaller man stepped forward. "Forgive me for not shaking your hand," he joked nervously. "I'm Lawrence Madding and this is my, um, friend, Scott Bueten. We've rented this campsite for the next couple of days and plan on fishing the creek back there."

Gib shook her head. "That creek only runs in the spring, sir. There's no fish."

"Oh."

She took in his appearance. Ironed khaki slacks and a pressed yellow polo shirt, along with expensive loafers weren't the usual camping attire. His Rolex watch and accompanying gold jewelry stood out as well. "Mr. Madding, if you really want to fish, you can set up during the day at the lake." As Dan came closer with the requested items, she took one of her cards from her breast pocket. "That's my cell, if you or your *friend* need anything." She lowered her voice. "I look out for *family*," she stressed.

Lawrence's relief was evident as his posture relaxed. "Thank you, Officer Proctor. If you're ever in need of an orthopedic surgeon, look me up in town."

"I'm hoping I never will, Doc. But thanks." She accepted the bags and gloves from Dan. "You ready to get busy, Conroy?"

He blanched, but gritted his teeth and nodded.

"Great. Why don't you take these gentlemen back to the office and help them pick out a better campsite? I'll take care of things here."

"Uh, yeah. That's a good idea." He straightened his duty belt. "If you guys will follow me, we'll get a new campsite signed out immediately." He continued to bluster as they walked away from Gib, who finally lost the battle and started laughing.

Once she got her mirth under control, Gib took the bags to the dumpster. She put on the gloves and methodically removed all the animal remains. She silently counted the limbs. After tying off the bags, she coughed and stepped away from the dumpster. "Damn, that was nasty."

She loaded the two bags into the back of the truck. The stripped off gloves landed next to the bags and she used antibacterial gel to disinfect her hands before climbing in behind the wheel.

It didn't take Gib long to drive to the park's maintenance garage. She backed her truck to the garage overhead door. Then she walked around to the main door, tapping a six-digit code into the nearby keypad.

Once inside, Gib turned on the lights and walked across the

concrete floor. She opened the garage door and gingerly removed the two bags from the truck bed. Even with the bags tied closed, she could smell the putrid remains. "I should have made Dan do this." She looked around the garage and snapped her fingers. "Drop cloths." As she searched for the drop cloths, she came across a pair of overalls. "Perfect. Now my clothes won't reek."

After sliding the overalls on over her uniform, Gib spread out several heavy, plastic drop cloths near the open garage door. She took a deep breath through her mouth and dumped the contents of the two garbage bags on the floor. The stench caused her to gag, but she donned rubber gloves and began to examine the remains.

Forty-five minutes later, the remains and drop cloths were bagged and disposed of properly. Gib scrubbed the concrete floor with a heavy duty solution, which made the entire garage smell like industrial-strength lemons. She swore she could still smell the deer carcasses and was almost tempted to snort several drops of the same cleaner. After she changed out of the overalls and washed her hands for five minutes, she closed the garage and headed for her truck.

She found a quiet place to call her boss. The daytime campsite had a concrete picnic table beneath a canopy of trees, and she sat on the table and watched a squirrel play with an imaginary friend not too far away. She dialed her phone and kept her voice low. "Hi, Jessica. Is Clint busy?"

"No, I don't think so. Let me buzz you through."

"Thanks." Gib kept taking deep breaths of the fresh spring air.

"This is Clint. What's up, Gib?"

She chuckled as the squirrel argued with no one in particular. "I checked out the remains found at camp seven. Two deer, with what looks like trap marks on their legs."

"Damn. So these poachers are trapping the animals now? Whatever happened to good, ol' fashioned hunting out of season?"

Gib's laugh wasn't a happy one. "Hell if I know. The problem is, if they're resorting to traps, we can't guarantee the safety of people out hiking, or our cattle."

Clint's usage of some particularly nasty curse words was out of character. "We'll have to post warnings for people going off the beaten path, I suppose. I want these assholes caught, Gib. Yesterday!"

"Yes, sir. We'll get them."

"Damn it." Clint hung up the phone.

Gib put the phone on the picnic table next to her leg and closed her eyes. "I couldn't have said it better myself."

THE LONG DAY, and the prospect of a lonely night, made the drive to the cabin more of a chore than a need for Gib. As her truck rounded the last turn, she blinked in surprise.

Parked in front of the cabin was a familiar Lexus. But the most welcoming sight was the smiling redhead perched on the front steps. Gib parked her truck in its usual spot and jumped out. She headed for her lover, who stood to greet her.

"You've ruined me, Gibson Proctor," Delaney chastised.

"I have? How?" Gib put her arms around Delaney and kissed her.

Once Delaney was able to breathe again, she leaned her head against her lover's chest and sighed. "I used to be able to work on a project for days at a time, only breaking for sleep or food. But the thought of not seeing you before tomorrow night was more than I could handle."

Gib smiled against the red hair. "And here I was, feeling sorry for myself because I couldn't see you tonight." She pulled back just far enough to look into her lover's eyes. "Thanks for coming out here, Dee. I know you have a lot of work to do, but—"

"Sssh. I can't stay all night, but I thought we could at least enjoy dinner together. I brought Chinese."

"I'll take whatever I can," Gib assured her. She handed her the keys. "Why don't you go on in, and I'll grab the food from your car."

Delaney took the keys, but waited for Gib before she went inside. "Did I happen to tell you that my sister-in-law wants you to give my brother lessons?"

After Gib put the bag of food on the counter, she removed her duty belt and had to try twice to hang it on the coat tree after hearing the comment. "What?"

"Yeah." Delaney came up behind her in the kitchen and watched over her shoulder as Gib unpacked their meal. "She said she totally understands how I can be in love with you, because she is, too."

The small box of rice dropped from Gib's hands and bounced off the counter. Only Delaney's fast reflexes kept it from hitting the floor. The officer turned to look at her. "She's what?"

Delaney put the rice down and patted Gib on the rear. "Not like I blame her. You are quite a catch."

"Buh...but—" Gib shook her head. "Never mind. I don't want to know." She took the filled plates to the living room and set them on the coffee table. "Give me a couple of minutes to shower and change. I feel particularly grungy tonight."

"All right. But hurry back." Delaney grinned as Gib hustled out of the room. She laughed as moments later a very naked Gib sped from the bedroom to the bathroom, with an armful of clothes. "You big tease," she yelled.

A short time later, Gib stepped out of the bathroom, dressed in faded jeans and a black tee shirt. "Sorry. I had a really disgusting day." She joined her lover on the sofa. "Thanks for bringing dinner."

"Purely selfish." Delaney took her fork and speared a shrimp. "Open up."

Gib did as she was told, grinning. Once she swallowed, she asked,

"Are you planning on feeding me the whole meal?"

"Maybe." When a forkful of food came toward her, Delaney obediently opened her mouth. "Mmm."

They fed each other for the next half hour, until both were full and relaxed. After she cleared the dishes away, Delaney returned to the sofa and patted her lap. "Come here, honey. You look exhausted."

For a moment, Gib appeared as if she would refuse. Then, appearing embarrassed, did as she was asked. She rested her head carefully on Delaney's thighs. "Is this okay?"

Delaney ran her fingers across her lover's brow. "It's very okay. Are you comfortable?"

"Any more comfortable and I'll fall asleep," Gib joked.

"Good." She could still see a slight frown on Gib's face. "Would you like to talk about it?"

Gib blinked. "Um, about what?"

"About whatever is causing this," Delaney traced the line across Gib's forehead. "What's bothering you?"

"It's nothing, really. Just work."

The stroking stopped. "Is your ex giving you a hard time?"

Gib couldn't help but smile at the angry set of her lover's body. "Sssh. No, Gloria's okay. We kind of called a truce."

"That's good. I'd hate to have to stop what I was doing, just to hunt her down and kick her ass." Delaney resumed her attentions. "Truce?"

"Yeah. She saw this," Gib touched the blemish on her neck, "and was giving me a hard time about it. I made sure she knew that she could joke about me all she wanted, but you were off-limits."

Delaney's expression softened. "My hero." She touched Gib's lips to stop the argument. "You're my hero, so hush."

"Yes, ma'am." Gib kissed the fingertip.

"Now, you were saying?"

"Huh?" The light thump on her nose caused Gib to smile. "Ah. Yeah. Those damned poachers are driving me nuts. A camper found some animal remains in one of the remote dumpsters. But we can't figure out where the hell their base camp is located." She started to rise, but a firm hand on her shoulder kept Gib lying flat. With a heavy sigh, she continued, "It's like they sneak in during the middle of the night, trap and gut their kills and disappear without a trace. The park is too big to search every square mile. We don't have the manpower for it."

Delaney began to comb her fingers through Gib's damp hair, the gentle motion soothing them both. "You'll get them."

"I sure hope so." Gib closed her eyes as her whole body relaxed. The furrow across her brow eased as she drifted off to sleep.

DELANEY JERKED AWAKE and looked around the darkened room. "Oh, shit!"

"What?" Startled, Gib almost toppled out of her lap and would have landed in the floor, if not for the firm hand holding her in place. She blinked in the gloom. "How late is it?"

"Two-fifteen," Delaney answered after pressing a button on her watch. Her head dropped against the back of the sofa. "I can't believe I fell asleep."

Gib rolled to a sitting position and ran her fingers through her hair. "Tell me about it. I was out like a light." She turned on the lamp beside the couch. "Why don't we go to bed?"

"I've still got a lot of work to do before my meeting. I really should head home."

"Dee, please. It's too late to be out on the road. Come to bed and I'll set the alarm to go off early."

Delaney stood and stretched. "That's not necessary. There's no sense in both of us having a short night." She held out her hand. "Come on. Walk me to my car."

"Damn, you're stubborn," Gib grumbled, as she was tugged to her feet. She put her arm around her lover and walked with her to the table by the door, where Delaney had left her purse. "Are you sure I can't talk you into staying? I'll make breakfast."

"I can't." Delaney stopped digging in her purse and looked into Gib's eyes. "I wish I could. But if I don't get a few hours of work done on this bid, we won't have a chance."

Gib sighed and rested her forehead against Delaney's. "All right. But I hate you being out on the road so late."

"I'll call you as soon as I get home, I promise." Delaney gave her a gentle kiss. "I love you."

"I love you, too." With a growl, Gib wrapped her arms around the redhead and held her tight. "Be really careful, okay?"

Delaney nodded and returned the squeeze with equal force. "Come on, officer. The sooner I get going, the sooner we'll both be able to get some sleep."

"Says you," Gib grumbled. She opened the door and led them to the SUV. After the doors unlocked, she helped Delaney into the driver's seat. "Last chance for breakfast."

"Behave." Delaney cupped Gib's cheek and kissed her. "I'll call you as soon as I get into my apartment."

"Thanks." Gib backed away and carefully closed the door. She tucked her hands into the front pockets of her jeans as she watched the Lexus disappear into the night.

Chapter Eighteen

DELANEY KEPT HER eyes on the rearview mirror until she could no longer see her lover in the glare of the taillights. Her duty to the company warred with her aching need to be in Gib's arms. "This is ridiculous. I think I'm old enough to spend a night away from the poor woman. She'll probably enjoy a good night's sleep for a change."

Stopped at the entrance to the lake, she exhaled heavily and shook her head. "Get it together. You'll see her soon enough." Less than a mile down the highway, a rabbit darted in front of the Lexus and caused Delaney to slam on the brakes.

She watched as it hopped off the road and toward the tree-lined fence. Tucked into the trees was a dark pickup truck with a matching dark camper. Although it was well hidden, Delaney knew she hadn't passed it earlier in the evening. Her natural curiosity made her want to pull over and check it out, but her more sensible side disagreed. She checked her rearview mirror. Satisfied the road was clear, she backed her SUV until she was on the shoulder a safe distance away. After she turned off her lights, she fished her cell phone from her purse and dialed her lover.

Gib answered on the second ring. "That was quick."

"I'm not home, yet," Delaney shared quietly.

"What's wrong? And why are you whispering?"

"I think I may have found the poachers."

"What?" A rustling could be heard. "Damn it. Where are my boots? The hell with it." Now the slam of a door. "Where are you?" When she didn't get an answer, Gib became frantic. "Dee?"

Delaney kept her eyes on the area where the truck was hidden. "I'm okay, honey. I'm off on the shoulder of the road, not far from the lake. But I saw a dark truck parked close to the fence, and called you."

"I'll be there in a few minutes. Don't move," Gib ordered brusquely.

"I hadn't planned on it," Delaney snapped.

Gib's tone softened. "I'm sorry, sweetheart." The sound of her truck's engine was unusually loud through the connection. "Just please be careful. If you see anything unusual, get the hell out of there."

"I'm perfectly safe." But even as she said it, Delaney checked the darkness around her with wide eyes. The glare of headlights in her mirrors temporarily blinded her, but she blinked and smiled fondly as Gib turned off her lights and parked directly behind her. The sight of her lover's confident stride caused a delicious thrill to Delaney, and she unlocked her doors as Gib came around to the passenger side of the Lexus.

"Thanks." Gib got into the SUV. She adjusted her duty belt, which she had put on over her jeans. Her badge was on a chain around her neck. "Okay, so tell me everything."

Delaney leaned across the console and kissed her on the cheek. "Well, officer, I was driving along, minding my own business, when a rabbit jumped out and scared me to death."

"A rabbit?"

"Mmm-hmm. I noticed a truck hidden there," she pointed off into the darkness, "when I watched the rabbit leave the road."

Gib squinted and tried to see. "You've got some great night vision."

"Thank you. So, what are we going to do?"

"We?"

Delaney frowned. "Well, I found it. So yes, we."

"Oh, no. You just get that thought out of your head this instant." Gib held up her hand to stop the argument before it got started. "I'm going over there and see what I can find out, and you're going to go back to my cabin, where it's safe."

"Like hell I am!"

In an attempt to calm her lover, Gib put her hand on Delaney's arm. "Dee, please. Listen to me. We have no idea if that truck belongs to the poachers. But I'm not about to jeopardize your safety."

"I'm not a child, Officer Proctor," Delaney snapped.

"I never said you were. But you're not trained to handle something like this, and I am. Please, Dee. I'd never forgive myself if anything happened to you."

Delaney's anger dissipated at the tortured look on Gib's face. "You don't play fair."

"Not where you're involved, no. I don't." Gib's hand traveled down Delaney's arm until their hands were tightly linked. "I love you, Dee. And I will do anything in my power to protect you. Even if it pisses you off."

"Damn. You almost had me crying, until you added that last bit." The redhead kissed the back of her lover's hand. "Can we compromise? I'll stay here if you'll keep me on the phone with you."

Gib sighed. "Dee—"

"No, wait. What if you run into trouble? I can at least call for help. But I'll go nuts if I don't know what's going on."

Against her better judgment, Gib removed her radio from her duty belt. She changed the channel before handing it to Delaney. "Okay. Gloria's on call, so she should answer on this channel if you need her." She stopped and gave her a serious look. "But, and this is a big one, you have to make me a promise."

"What?"

"Promise me, if you see anything, you high-tail it out of here. And under no circumstances, are you to leave this vehicle."

Delaney shook her head. "Don't ask that of me."

"I am. Please, Dee. Don't make me divide my attention between you and whatever is going on out there."

"Damn it, Proctor. All right. I promise." Delaney grabbed two handfuls of Gib's tee shirt and tugged her forward. Before their lips met, she whispered, "I love you."

Gib finally broke away from the kiss. "I love you, too." She took her Bluetooth from her jeans pocket and fastened it over her ear. "You know, with all this drama, it's probably just a couple of teenagers looking for a place to make out."

"I hope so." Delaney dialed Gib's number and nodded when Gib touched her earpiece. "See you soon."

GIB STEPPED OUT of the Lexus and closed the door gently. She crossed the road and unsnapped the holster on her gun. "I won't talk much, but I'll hear you," she whispered.

"That's fine," Delaney answered just as softly. "I wish the moon was out tonight, so I could see you."

Gib chuckled. "I'm glad it's not. If you could see me, so could they."

"Oh. Yeah. Never mind."

The green grass muted Gib's footsteps as she walked to the truck from the rear. Since she was wearing sneakers without socks, she could feel the long grass tickle her ankles. Gib removed her gun and snapped off the safety. The camper's back window was tinted, so she stood beside it and listened for any sound. The handle on the window was locked. Not hearing anything, she moved slowly around the side of the truck and cautiously peeked through the driver's window. "Truck's all clear," she whispered.

"Good. Now come back."

Gib used her small penlight to check around the fence. "I see where they tied open the fence. I'm going to check it out."

"Gib, no." When she didn't get an answer, Delaney slapped the steering wheel. "Damn it, Proctor. I'm going to kick your ass."

Ignoring the cursing coming through her earbud, Gib kept the light trained on the ground. "Doesn't look like they bother covering their trail until they come back. I may be able to find more clues."

"Gib—"

"Sssh." The officer picked her way through the brush, following the slight trail the truck's owners left. She kept her light close to the ground so it couldn't be seen by anyone else.

Fifteen minutes passed while Gib continued to follow the trail, which had turned into a well-used animal path. She stopped and turned off her flashlight when she thought she heard voices. Now moving by feel only, she could make out two men arguing in a secluded clearing. Both were dressed in hunting camouflage, their faces obscured by matching ski masks.

"Can't we just bury the guts out here? Why do we have to dump them inside the park?" the heavier one asked.

The answer was impossible to hear, so Gib edged closer to the clearing. The soft grass gave way and she had only a split second to realize what happened, before a blinding pain encompassed her right leg above her ankle. She bit off a scream and fell, reaching for her leg.

The larger man turned a battery-operated camping light toward the sound. "Did you hear that?" He picked up a nearby rifle. "I'm going to check it out."

"Not with a gun, you idiot. Sound carries like crazy out here, and someone might hear. Take the bow. Besides, it was probably another damned possum. And don't go too far. We're almost done. You have to bag up the shit this time. It makes me sick."

"I know. I'll be right back." He waved the lantern toward the trail they had come in on.

BACK AT THE SUV, Delaney was so startled by the noise that her head almost hit the roof. "Gib!" Her hand was on the door handle. "Gib, can you hear me? Forget the fucking promise, Gib. I'm coming after you." She stopped when she heard heavy breathing on the other end of the phone. "Gib? Honey?"

"...Call...Gloria," Gib whispered roughly. "Two—" her voice broke off.

"Gib? Goddamn it, Proctor!" Delaney's hands shook as she fumbled with the radio. "H...hello? Gloria? Can you hear me?"

The sleepy voice yawned before it spoke. "Who the hell are you? And how did you get on this channel?"

Delaney's nerves were on edge. "Shut up! I'm Gib Proctor's girlfriend, Delaney. We met the other day. She's out there and I think she ran into the poachers."

"What?" Gloria sounded more awake. "Slow down, and tell me what's going on."

"I was leaving her place when I saw a truck near the trees. I called Gib. She came out and went looking for whoever left it there." Delaney took a deep breath and released it slowly. "I had her on the phone with me and I think she's hurt. All she said was to contact you, and then, 'two.'"

Gloria snorted. "Figures she'd go all John Wayne like that. Okay, listen. Where are you, exactly?" She could be heard slamming a door.

"Not quite a mile east of the lake entrance, on the eastbound side of the road. How long will it take you?"

"Less than fifteen minutes," Gloria promised. "Stay put, and let me know if you hear anything else."

Delaney frowned. "Fifteen minutes? But—"

"Look. Gibson's a professional. She knows what she's doing. Hang tight, and don't do anything stupid, okay?"

"Now wait just a damned minute," Delaney snapped.

Gloria's tone softened. "I'm sorry, but please. Stay where you are. I'll need you to show me where she went in, all right?"

Slightly mollified, Delaney sighed. "All right. Besides, I promised Gib."

ALTHOUGH SHE WAS in excruciating pain, Gib listened to the conversation between the two men. She was lying in the middle of the trail and knew she was at an extreme disadvantage. The toothed leg-hold trap she had stepped in was made of iron and chained to a tree. Had she been wearing her boots, it might not have been as painful. She'd have to remove the trap from her leg in order to get away. And at the moment, she didn't know if she could do that without throwing up or passing out.

Instead, she gritted her teeth and dragged herself to a position behind the tree. Every movement brought renewed agony to the injury, but soon she was more or less hidden from view. She choked on the bile that rose in her throat and tried to stay conscious.

A bright light shined where she had been lying as the poacher checked the area. He stumbled a few steps down the trail, cursing under his breath. "I don't see nothin'," he yelled over his shoulder.

The other poacher came to the edge of the clearing. "Shut up, you idiot," he ordered quietly.

Even though she was fighting to stay alert, Gib thought the voice sounded familiar. She peeked around the tree and stared at the dark figure. "Gib?" Delaney's voice in her ear almost made her yell out, and she quickly slapped the Bluetooth to turn it off before the poachers could hear.

"GIB?" DELANEY PANICKED when all she heard was a dial tone. "No!" She immediately redialed her lover's phone number, only to have it go directly to voice mail. "Damn it!"

She dropped her phone into the passenger seat and started beating her fists against the steering wheel. "Damn! Damn! Damn!"

Headlights coming toward her stopped Delaney's temper tantrum. She flicked her headlights on and off, relieved when the other vehicle crossed the yellow stripes and parked in front of the Lexus. "Thank god."

Gloria got out of her Wrangler and came to Delaney's door. With her blonde hair down around her face, she looked softer and more approachable. The park-issued green polo shirt and faded jeans make her appear younger, but the no-nonsense look in her eyes was that of a seasoned professional. She leaned against the SUV as the window rolled down. "What's the matter? Have you heard anything else?"

"No. I lost contact with her and I can't get her back." Delaney wiped a tear of frustration from her cheek. She pointed out the window. "The truck is over there, and she went into the trees right beside it."

"All right. Hang tight and I'll see what she's up to."

ONCE THE POACHERS had returned to the clearing, Gib shifted so that she could work on getting out of the trap. The movement brought a new, more intense pain. She waited until the spots disappeared from her vision before she got a firm grip on the steel trap. She pried the jaws apart, her fingers slipping from the blood. Before she could get her foot free, the trap slammed shut again.

Gib dropped back against the ground, her head swimming. She fought the urge to throw up.

The sound of something coming down the trail brought Gib out of her pain-induced fog. She looked up in time to see blonde hair flash a few feet away from her. "Gloria?" she whispered.

"Gibson?" Gloria squatted beside Gib. "What happened?"

"Sssh." Gib pointed toward the clearing. "Poachers. Two of them."

Gloria nodded. "And you're sitting here, because?"

"Trap." Gib gestured to her captured right leg. "I can't—"

The tiny penlight Gloria held tracked down Gib's body. "Damn. That's not good." She handed the light to Gib. "Hold this."

Gib had to wipe her bloody hand on her jeans so that she could hold the light.

"Ready?"

Gritting her teeth, Gib nodded. She braced herself against the tree to keep from crying out as the trap was removed from her lower leg. The relief was short-lived when she felt another pressure on her injury. She tried to move it away, but Gloria kept a firm hand on her knee.

"It's okay, baby. I had to wrap it to stem the bleeding." Gloria tried to soothe Gib by rubbing her thigh. "Let's get you out of here."

"Not yet." Gib pointed toward the clearing. "I want those bastards."

Gloria shook her head. "Have you lost your mind? We need to get you to the hospital."

"No." Gib slapped Gloria's hand away from her leg. The endearment that slipped from Gloria's lips hadn't escaped her. "Help me up. There are two of them and two of us."

Grumbling under her breath, Gloria pulled Gib to her feet. "You and that redhead make a good match." She held up a hand to forestall Gib's defense. "Come on, Duke. You can back me up."

"Duke?" Gib put her arm around her shoulders and tried to take a step. The pain from her ankle radiated all the way up her right leg. She didn't know if it was broken or not. "Damn!" She would have fallen if not for Gloria's arm around her waist. "I'm not going to be a lot of help."

"Don't worry about it." Gloria leaned her against the tree. "Just speak up when I ask you to."

Gib nodded and waited while the ranger pulled her weapon and stepped to the edge of the clearing.

"Park Ranger," Gloria shouted. "Put your hands in the air and don't move!"

Both men turned at the sound of her voice. The heavier one dropped the skinned deer he had just slung over his shoulder, while the smaller one took a step toward the rifle propped against a tree.

"I wouldn't do that," Gloria warned, pointing her weapon at the man. "Proctor? Stay back in the shadows," she ordered behind her.

"You got it," Gib yelled as loud as she could.

The smaller poacher cursed and held up his hands.

Gloria grinned. "Cover me, Proctor." To the men, she said, "On your knees and link your fingers behind your head." As they followed her instructions, she used her handcuffs on the smaller one and plastic cuffs for the other. Once the men were restrained, she raised her radio to her lips. "Red? You there?"

"Red?" Delaney squawked indignantly. "Did you—"

"I need you to contact Benton P.D. and let them know we have two suspects for transport."

Delaney would not be deterred. "Is Gib..."

"She's with me. Contact the police, please. We're bringing the suspects out."

"All right." The redhead did not sound pleased with the turn of events.

Gloria backed away from the men. "On your feet."

The smaller one tried to step back when she grabbed his mask. "I'm going to see you anyway, buddy."

"No," he growled. He lowered his head and charged Gloria.

She stepped out of the way and slapped the back of his head, causing him to fall face first on the ground. "Jackass."

He rolled onto his knees. "Fuck you, dyke."

Gloria cocked her head at the tone. "Oh, yeah?" She stalked over and ripped the mask away. "I thought that was you, Dan. Nice seeing you again."

Dan spit at her feet. "Bitch."

"My, my, my. Aren't you the eloquent one? On your feet, loser." Gloria turned to the other man. "Are you going to give me any trouble?"

He shook his head. "Not much sense in it. Could you take mine off, too? I'm burnin' up."

Gloria laughed and did as he asked. "How's that?"

"Better, thanks." He struggled and needed her help standing. "All this was his idea, you know."

"Would you shut the fuck up?" Dan snarled.

The big man looked at Gloria. "We've been selling the venison to a fancy restaurant in Dallas." He glared at Dan. "I wanted to bow hunt, but he said we'd get more if we set out traps."

"What's your name?"

"Martin Conroy. Think I can get a deal if I testify against my cousin?"

Gloria shrugged. "That's up to the lawyers. Why don't you lead the way out of here, and we'll follow?"

Martin peered into the darkness. "If you'll cuff my hands in front of me, I'll carry the lantern. We've got traps set along the trail, and I don't want to find one by accident."

"For god's sake, Marty. Shut up!"

"Screw you, Dan." When he saw that he wasn't getting a light, Martin slowly headed for the trail. He stopped when he saw Gib. "Uh—"

Gib held up her flashlight. "I'll make you a deal. Let me lean on you, and I'll light the way."

He turned and looked at Gloria. "Look, I know I'm in a boatload of trouble. But I also know it'll go better for me if I cooperate. Cut me loose and I'll help her."

Gloria glanced at Gib, who appeared ready to collapse. "All right. But one wrong move and I'll shoot you." She used her pocketknife to cut the restraints. When he started toward Gib, Gloria stopped him. "Hold it." She stepped around Martin and lowered her voice to Gib. "Give me your weapon. Just to be safe."

"Good idea." Gib flicked the safety on and handed the gun butt first to her. "Hope I don't embarrass myself and faint."

"Don't worry if you do. I won't tell anyone," Gloria teased. She turned to Martin. "Be careful."

He nodded. "What happened to you?" he asked Gib, as she put her arm around his shoulder.

"Stepped in one of your damned traps."

Dan laughed. "Good. I hope your fucking leg falls off."

Gloria roughly grabbed his arm and shoved him forward. "I wonder if you'd change your tune if you *accidentally* found one, too."

"I'm not that stupid," Dan countered.

"That remains to be seen. Let's go." She picked up the rifle and slung it over her shoulder.

THE SKY HAD changed from black to muted pink before the two police cruisers drove off with Dan and Martin. Delaney stood by her SUV while Gloria, Clint, and an obviously exhausted and hurting Gib talked. The trio continued to rehash the early morning's events as Gib sat in the bed of her truck. Her injured leg was stretched across the open tailgate. The ambulance that Gloria had requested during their trek back to the highway had tried to take her to the hospital, but Gib refused, citing the need to give her boss a full report. They bandaged and splinted the injury, and made her promise to have it checked by a doctor as soon as possible.

When she saw Gib close her eyes for the third time in as many minutes, Delaney couldn't stand it any longer. She stomped to where Clint was verifying the story from Gloria. "Excuse me, Mr. Wright?"

Clint turned. "Yes, Ms. Kavanagh? What can I do for you?"

"You can tell Gib to get her ass to the hospital. Or have you forgotten her injury?"

Gib opened her eyes and tried to sit up straighter. "Dee, it's okay. We need to make sure we've got everything—"

"Shut up." Delaney glared at her lover. "You're already on my shit list. Don't make it worse by arguing with me."

Gloria chuckled until that same glare turned to her. "What?"

"She's right," Clint wisely agreed. "Gib, you're dismissed. I think Gloria and I can handle things from here."

Too tired to argue, Gib nodded. "All right. I'll call you after—"

"I don't want to hear from you until Monday, is that clear?" Clint interrupted. He turned to Gloria. "Let's help her to Ms. Kavanagh's car."

With Gloria on one side and Clint on the other, Gib was easily carried to the Lexus and settled across the back seat. "What about my truck? I don't want to leave it on the side of the road."

Clint held out his hand. "Give me your keys. We'll take it to your cabin. You can get these later at the office."

"Thanks." She leaned her head against the seat and closed her eyes.

Gloria carefully closed the door. "Do you need any more help with her, Red?"

"I think I've got it, thanks." Delaney was too tired to fight about the nickname Gloria had continued to use. She looked at her resting lover for a long moment. "Thank you for getting her out of there."

The ranger appeared embarrassed by the praise. "It wasn't that big of a deal."

"It was to me, and I know it was to Gib." Although she still didn't trust her, Delaney realized without Gloria, what happened to her lover could have been much worse.

"Yeah, okay." Gloria blew out a breath and flipped her hair over her shoulder. "Are you sure you don't need any help getting her to the hospital?"

Delaney shook her head. "No. But would you like me to call you when we find out anything?"

"Sure. Um, Gibson has my number. Good luck." She ducked her head and went to her vehicle.

It was hard for Delaney to take her eyes off of Gib, but she gathered herself and got into the Lexus.

As she drove toward town, she wondered if she should call Gib's family. From what little she knew of the rest of the Proctor clan, they didn't seem too concerned about the officer's welfare. With a glance in the mirror, she picked up her cell and called her own mother for advice.

The phone rang three times before Maureen answered. "Hello?"

"Hi, Mom."

"My goodness, honey. What are you doing up so early? Are you worried about the presentation today?"

Delaney's mind went blank for a moment before she understood what her mother meant. "Damn. I forgot about the presentation."

"What? But you've been working on it for weeks."

"I know, but—"

Maureen covered the mouthpiece and muttered something to her husband. "Your father wants to know if you need help."

"Mom, I—"

"I thought you were about finished with everything. Did something unexpected come up?"

"Dammit, Mom. Would you please shut up for a minute?" Delaney yelled. At the silence on the other end of the line, she realized too late she went too far. "I'm so sorry, Mom. I didn't mean it."

The older woman's voice was subdued. "May I speak, now?"

"I'm sorry," Delaney repeated. "It's been a really rough night."

"Are the plans not going well? I'm sure your father can get an extension."

Tears of frustration burned the redhead's eyes. "Momma, I'm on my way to the hospital. Gib's been hurt."

Maureen was silent for a moment. "Is it serious? What can we do to help?"

"I don't know. Her leg was caught in an old, nasty bear trap. The kind with the teeth. Or whatever they call those damned things. I'm taking her to the hospital now."

"I'm a little confused. What was she doing to run into one of those things? Are they even legal anymore?"

Delaney sighed. "I don't know, Mom. All I know is she was out chasing poachers and stepped on the trap. Can you meet me at the hospital?"

"Of course. Is there anything else we can do?"

"Tell Dad that I tried everything, but there's no way to safely add a lake to that area."

Maureen became exasperated. "Don't worry about that. Just take care of Gib, and we'll see you soon, all right? I'll have your father take care of the presentation."

"Thanks, Mom. Love you."

"We love you too, honey. See you soon."

BENTON GENERAL HOSPITAL, a five-story, red brick building that dated to the late nineteen fifties, handled all the medical needs for Benton and the surrounding farm communities. The emergency room waiting area was usually full. This early Friday morning was an exception. Four people were scattered about the plain room. One man, older and wearing a mechanic's work shirt, dozed in the far corner. Another man, young and wild-eyed, stared at the muted television as if it were speaking directly to him.

Nearest the entrance to the emergency room were Delaney and her mother. The plastic chair Delaney was perched on had been white at one time, but years of use had stained it to a grungy gray. She sat on the edge and stared at the closed doors.

"You can't will them to work any faster," Maureen commented quietly. They had been sitting for over two hours with no word from the staff. Her husband was taking Delaney's place at the presentation. "You said earlier that you called her family?"

Delaney nodded. "I spoke with her mother right after I got here. She was baking cookies for her granddaughter's troop and said I could call her back later. And Gib's father was at work."

"Lovely people," Maureen huffed.

"I've met her mother and brother. They seem a little," Delaney paused as she tried to come up with the right word, "self-involved."

Maureen's undignified snort echoed loudly in the quiet room. "I can't believe her mother thinks that baking cookies is more important than being with her daughter in the hospital. That's more than self-involved, that's nonsense."

"Mom."

"No, seriously." Maureen put her magazine down and turned to her daughter. "They'd have to lock me up to keep me away if anything happened to you or one of your brothers. For a mother not to drop everything for her child is inconceivable to me."

"You're a different kind of mother. Just from the few conversations we've had, I don't think Gib has ever felt much love from her family. They don't seem like the demonstrative type."

The door opened and a middle aged woman looked around the room. She wore pale green scrubs covered by a white lab coat, and consulted her clipboard before speaking. "Is there anyone here for Gibson Proctor?"

Delaney jumped to her feet. "Here." She hurried to where the woman stood. "How is she?"

"Are you family?"

Maureen, who had followed her daughter, spoke up. "Yes."

The woman didn't appear to believe her, but continued anyway. "I'm Dr. Branch. Ms. Proctor will be prepped for surgery shortly to repair the lower tibial compound fracture."

"Surgery?" Delaney's voice trembled. "Wait. Fracture? Her leg is broken?"

"Yes. The surgeon will be available later to discuss the procedure." Dr. Branch tucked the clipboard under her arm. "Now if you'll excuse me, I have to get back."

Delaney touched her arm. "Can we see her?"

"I'm afraid she's already been sedated."

"Just for a moment? Please?"

Dr. Branch sighed. "All right. But one at a time. And not for long."

"Thank you, Doctor." Delaney turned to her mother. "Um."

"Give me her phone, and I'll make the calls."

Delaney dug Gib's phone from her back pocket and handed it Maureen. "Thanks, Mom." She followed the doctor through the double doors and tried to calm her racing heart. The stark hallway had several doors on either side.

Dr. Branch stepped into the third door on their left. "Remember, just a few minutes."

"All right." Delaney peered around the physician. Her lover's eyes were closed and she was dressed in a hospital gown, with a sheet up to her waist. Delaney purposely ignored the exposed right leg. "Can she hear me?"

"Probably not. But I'll give you a couple of minutes alone."

Once the doctor left, Delaney moved closer to the bed and grasped a slack hand. "Hi, honey. I don't know if you can hear me, but they're going to take really good care of you." Her thumb rubbed across the back of Gib's hand as she leaned closer to whisper, "Don't think this gets you out of trouble, officer. You're still on my shit list."

Gib's eyes fluttered open and she gazed blearily at the redhead. "Love you, too," she muttered.

"I swear, I'm going to kick your ass when you get out of here," Delaney threatened tearfully. She gave her a light peck on the lips. "And for the record, I *do* love you. Oh, I called your mother."

It took quite an effort, but Gib turned her head and looked toward the door. "Yeah?"

"She's, um, on her way."

Even as incapacitated as she was, Gib knew her mother too well. "Liar." She squeezed Delaney's hand. "S'okay. Not a big deal." Her eyes started to close. "Maddy?"

"I'm sorry, honey. I totally forgot. I'll call her as soon as I can." She stroked Gib's cheek. "Don't worry about a thing."

Gib tried to see her leg. "Is it bad?" she slurred, her eyes half-open.

"All I know for sure is that it's broken, and they're going to take you to surgery to repair it. I'll find out more when we talk to the surgeon."

"Stupid."

Delaney played with Gib's hair. "Well, stepping into an animal trap wasn't the brightest thing you've ever done," she teased. "But don't worry. I won't pick on you too much about it."

Her half grin made Gib look drunk. "Yes, you will."

"Probably," her lover agreed. "But not until you're back on your feet." Delaney heard the doctor's voice in the hallway. "I'm going to have to go, honey. But I'll see you as soon as you're out of surgery, all right?" She pressed her lips to Gib's. "I love you," she whispered.

Gib's eyes closed. "You, too," she mumbled, before falling asleep.

Dr. Branch stepped into the room. "I'm afraid you'll have to leave. But she'll get our finest care," she gently assured Delaney. "Dr. Madding is one of the best orthopedic surgeons in the area."

Delaney reluctantly lowered Gib's hand and released it. "Thank you." She backed away from the bed. "Please, take care of her. She means everything to me."

"I promise." The doctor put her arm around the redhead's shoulders and escorted her from the room.

Chapter Nineteen

THERE WAS ONE lone person in the surgical waiting room. After hearing Delaney's stomach growl for the third time, her mother had left to find food. Tired of the waiting, Delaney rested her elbows on her knees and cradled her head in her hands.

She didn't bother to look up when the doors opened and footsteps came near. It was too soon for Gib to be out of surgery, so she assumed it was her mother.

"Delaney?" Maddy cried, swiftly crossing the room. "Thanks for calling me." She hugged the redhead who had jumped to her feet. "Sorry about the voicemail thing. That damned phone only rings when it wants to. How's Gib? Have you heard anything? Did you call her family?"

"Calm down and I'll tell you everything." Delaney sat and patted the plastic chair beside her. She brushed her hands through her hair, losing the battle with looking more presentable. "They took her into surgery about an hour ago. And yes, I called her mother." The sour look on her face expressed more than words ever could.

Maddy patted her on the knee. "Ida was less than helpful, huh?"

"She acted like she didn't care. She was more interested in baking for some Scout troop than her daughter's health. How is that possible?"

"Gibsy's family is an acquired taste," Maddy admitted. "When we were in school, I think she spent more time at my house than at her own."

Delaney shook her head. "I can't even imagine growing up with a mother like that. How did she turn out the way she did?"

"Pure stubbornness. The crazy thing is I know her parents love her. But I don't think they were very good at showing it. And they never talk about things. It's the strangest family dynamic I've ever seen."

"I'd go insane living like that," Delaney admitted.

Maddy sighed. "Me, too. It took me years to get her to talk about them, though. She's never been big on sharing."

"Are we talking about the same person? Because the Gib I know not only shares everything, but has taught me a lot about it, too."

Both of them looked up as the door opened. A handsome, dark haired man stepped into the waiting room. Maddy held out her hand and he sat next to her.

"How's your friend?" he asked Maddy.

Maddy squeezed his hand. "She's still in surgery." She turned to Delaney. "This is Gib's girlfriend, Delaney."

He stood and offered his reclaimed hand to the redhead. "Hi, Delaney. I'm Rob."

"Hello, Rob. Thanks for coming. Are you a friend of Gib's?"

Delaney asked as she returned to her chair.

Rob sat beside Maddy and put his arm across the back of her chair. "We've only met once. But I'm hoping to get to know her a lot better. And you too, if you don't mind."

"I can always use new friends." Delaney smiled for the first time all morning. She couldn't help but notice how Maddy glowed with happiness. "You make a good-looking couple," she whispered to the dark-haired woman.

Maddy blushed. "Thanks. Um, could you tell me a little more about Gib's injury? It was hard to hear on the voice message you left."

"Sorry. I was in the phone area downstairs, and it was hard to keep a signal. According to Gloria, Gib stepped into an old-fashioned bear trap. The ER doctor said that because of the way she stepped, the majority of the damage was put on the front of her leg, just above her ankle." Delaney paused and took a deep breath. "She has some nasty gashes on the back of her leg, too. But they were able to stitch those up."

"Good god. Do they think she'll be able to make a full recovery?" Maddy asked softly.

Delaney shrugged her shoulders. "The surgeon wasn't too sure until he saw the damage first hand. I'm still trying to figure out how she was able to walk on that leg."

"Well, Gibsy's always been hard-headed. And knowing her, she didn't want to appear weak in front of the bad guys."

"Stubborn, mule-headed," Delaney growled. "I don't know what I'm going to do with her."

Maddy laughed and patted her leg. "Just keep loving her. I've never seen Gib so happy."

Finally allowing her tears to flow, Delaney sobbed, "I'll never stop. But she scared me about half to death."

DRESSED IN HER Park Ranger's uniform, Gloria walked into the police station with a manila folder tucked beneath one arm. She stopped at the front desk where an older woman was sorting through papers. "I'm Ranger Hoover. I'm supposed to meet with a detective about the poachers we apprehended earlier this morning?"

The police admin nodded. "Detective Watkins is expecting you. Go through that door," she pointed to the other side of the room. "His desk is the third on the left."

"Thank you." Gloria stood at the door and waited to be buzzed through. Once inside the open space, she stopped and glanced around the room. People in street clothes and uniforms wandered from place to place, while a steady din of noise permeated the air. Gloria straightened her posture and headed for the desk of Detective Watkins.

Cluttered with paperwork and empty Styrofoam cups, the detective's desk looked much like the others. Behind it sat a middle-aged, heavyset man. His gray hair was thin on top, and the dark framed glasses he wore gave him a bug-like appearance. He glanced up when Gloria stopped at his desk. "You Hoover?"

She nodded. "That's right. Are you Watkins?" she asked just as brusquely.

His laughter was hoarse and phlegmy. "Have a seat, Ranger. Would you like some coffee?"

"No, thank you." She looked at the ancient folding chair he pointed out. "Is this thing safe?"

"Safer than my desk chair."

Gloria cautiously perched on the visitor's seat. "Have you had a chance to interrogate the men we captured?"

"Yup. The big guy had no qualms about ratting out his cousin. I understand you know the smaller fellow."

"Yeah. I haven't been with this park for very long, but I've worked with Dan Conroy."

The detective eyeballed her through his thick glasses. "What's your take on him?"

She considered the question seriously. "Spoiled whiner. And he hates women with authority. Especially Officer Proctor. I'm not sure why, though."

"I got an earful from him, that's for sure. Once he started talking, I thought he'd never shut up."

Gloria frowned. "Isn't that a good thing during an interrogation?"

"It would be, if it was pertinent to the investigation. But all he wanted to do was bitch and moan about Proctor, and how he's superior to everyone else." Watkins sighed. "Got to be a broken record. So I sat in on the interrogation with Martin for a while."

She nodded. "The big guy. He seemed all right to me. Even helped get Proctor out."

"Right. I think he was just going along for the fun of it. His cousin had promised he could bow hunt, which I understand is a favorite pastime of his. But when they weren't getting enough meat, Dan decided to use some old traps he'd come across at another park."

"I was wondering where he'd gotten them. The one Proctor stepped on looked almost antique." Gloria tapped her fingers on the folder she had on her knee. "Did you find out why Dan had it in for Proctor?"

Watkins took a toothpick from his desk drawer and stuck it in his mouth. He wriggled it with his tongue. "According to Martin Conroy," he checked his notes, "Dan's father left the family when Dan was a little boy. And his mother still harps about it. She evidently is a religious nut that rode him hard his whole life. Which gives him a pretty good reason to hate women, I suppose."

"Wonderful." Satisfied that the chair was indeed safe, Gloria leaned back. "Why was he poaching? Didn't he realize that sooner or later he'd get caught?"

"Nah. He figured that being with the park made it easy for him to keep it a secret and throw the investigation off course. And he wanted to, and I quote, 'make those fucking bitches look stupid.' His ultimate plan was to be the one to find the clearing where the poachers dressed their kills. He thought it would get him a promotion. But your Park Officer ruined that for him."

Gloria let out a derisive snort. "Didn't do her a lot of good, either. Did they tell you how many more traps are out there?"

"Did better than that. Martin said they had a marked map in their truck." He took a piece of paper from the folder and handed it across the desk. "Here's a copy, since we have the truck in our impound lot."

"Thank you." Gloria looked at the crude rendering. It had ten x's scrawled on it. "Good grief. It's going to take days to find all of these damned things."

He grinned. "Better you than me. Do you want to talk to either of them?"

"Not really." She took several sheets of paper out of her folder and handed them to him. "Here's my statement. I typed it up as soon as I got home."

Watkins glanced at the neatly typed paper and nodded. "Nice work. Now all I need is Officer Proctor's statement. I'll give you a call if we need anything else. Thanks for stopping by so soon."

She got to her feet. "It might be a few days before Proctor's up to a statement. My boss told me she went into surgery this morning to repair the damage on her leg. Let me know if I can be of any assistance down the road." Gloria shook the detective's hand before she walked away from the desk. Although she was expected back at work, there was somewhere else she wanted to be.

THE DAY PASSED slowly for Jessica since she had been stuck patrolling the park. Now that she was in her car with the air conditioner blowing, she was thrilled to be off-duty. On her way to her apartment, she decided to stop by the grocery store and pick up a frozen pizza.

Once inside, she took a cart and began to cruise through the store. "Might as well get some extra shopping done while I'm here." Cans of soup, a loaf of bread and a jar of instant coffee were carelessly dropped into the cart. She cruised along the cereal aisle when a voice from her past spoke out behind her.

"Is that little Jessie I see?" the woman loudly asked.

Jessica cringed and thought about ignoring her.

"Little Jessie Middleton?"

"Fuck." Jessica plastered a smile on her face and turned around. "Darla?"

Darla Greening had dark blue eyes, a perfect body and short, dark hair. She was wearing navy dress slacks and a light blue button-down shirt. One ear had four earrings, the other six. She joined Jessica next to the cart. "Hello there, cutie." She fingered the sleeve of Jessica's shirt. "I've always been partial to uniforms."

"Uh, what?" Jessica felt as if her head would explode. Here was her high school head cheerleader and secret crush talking to her as if she truly existed. It was something much different from when they went to school together. Jessica was never popular, yet adored the other girl from afar.

"Oh, my. I haven't misread you, have I?" Darla took a step back. "I thought you were family."

Jessica frowned. "Family? We're not related."

Darla's laugh was loud and hearty. "Oh, hon, you're priceless." She moved closer and lowered her voice. "I'm a lesbian. I thought you were, too. That's the family I'm talking about."

Although her face was beet-red, Jessica nodded. "Yeah, I'm," she looked around to see if anyone else was paying attention to them and whispered, "gay, too."

"Wonderful!" Darla swatted her on the back. "Are you seeing anyone?"

"Umm, well, not exactly." Jessica looked at the contents of her basket. "I'm kind of new at this."

Darla put her arm around the smaller woman. "A virgin, are you? Well, we'll have to see what we can do about that."

"Ssssh!" Jessica covered Darla's mouth with her hand. She jumped back as if she were burned when she felt a warm tongue lick her palm. "Oh, god!"

"I've been called lots of things, but never that," Darla teased. "Hey, are you busy tonight? I'd love to get a chance to catch up with you."

Anything was better than carrying on this conversation in the middle of the grocery store. Jessica wiped her hand on her pants. "Want to follow me over to my apartment? It's not far from here."

"That sounds wonderful. I'll even buy a pizza." Darla gave her a quick hug. "Meet you out front."

BY FRIDAY EVENING, Gib was resting comfortably in a private room. She had trouble staying awake, but Delaney didn't mind. Delaney sat in a chair beside the bed, unwilling to be far from her lover. The soft tap on the closed door caused her to stand and hurry to see who was there.

The door opened and revealed a curious Gloria. "How is she?" she asked quietly.

"Sleeping off and on. Come on in." Delaney held the door and gestured to the chair. "Would you like to sit down?"

"No, that's okay. I just stopped by on my way home from work." Gloria moved closer to the bed and looked at Gib's splinted leg. It was swollen and discolored all the way up to her knee. "Good god. What did they do?"

Delaney joined her. "According to the surgeon, Dr. Madding, it looks a lot worse than it actually is. He was able to realign the bone and stabilize it with a rod and plate. Now all he's worried about is infection from the wounds." Her hand drifted to Gib's head and began to lightly brush through her hair.

Gib's eyes slowly opened and she blinked several times. "Dee?"

"Hi, honey." Delaney smiled and caressed her lover's face. "How are you feeling?"

"Woozy." Gib noticed Gloria standing behind Delaney. "Hey, Glor."

Gloria touched Gib's uninjured leg. "You'll probably be getting a visit from a Detective Watkins in the next day or so. He wants to get your statement."

"Statement?"

"Yeah. I turned mine in earlier today. Dan's cousin rolled on him, so I don't think anything we say really matters."

Gib broke into a yawn. "Sorry."

"Not a problem. I only wanted to give you a heads up." Gloria patted her good leg and backed away from the bed. "Don't give the nurses too much grief, Gibson. I'll drop by again tomorrow to see you."

"'kay." Gib closed her eyes and her breathing evened out immediately.

Delaney continued to play with her lover's hair. "She's been doing this since she got out of recovery." Reluctantly, she stopped what she was doing and followed Gloria to the door. "Thanks for coming to see her."

"It was on my way home." The statuesque woman leaned against the wall beside the door. "How are you doing, Red? This had to be pretty rough on you, too."

"I'm all right. My mother was here with me until about an hour ago, and Gib's friend Maddy is supposed to be back soon." Delaney crossed her arms beneath her breasts. "Can I ask you something?"

Gloria nodded. "I won't guarantee I'll answer, but sure."

With a look over her shoulder to see if Gib was still asleep, Delaney softened her voice. "Do you still love her?"

"I thought I did," Gloria admitted just as quietly. "But she's still the same person I couldn't see myself with in Austin. Nothing's changed." She shrugged. "I'll always care for her, but no. I don't love her. Don't tell Gibson, but I'm not sure I ever did."

"How could," Delaney's voice broke. "How could you not love her?" She turned so that her full attention was on the woman lying in bed.

Gloria put a hand on the redhead's shoulder. "She's got a good heart, I know. But we were just too different. She likes to fish and I'd rather be at a concert or the theater." One final squeeze and she dropped her hand. "To tell you the truth, you're more my type than Gibson."

Delaney spun around. "What?"

"Come on, Red. You're smart and beautiful. Just the way I like 'em." Gloria chucked her under the chin and smirked. "But don't worry. I'm not going to try and take you away from her. Just stating a fact."

"Good lord, you're full of yourself." Delaney laughed. "But you don't fool me. Underneath all your bravado, I think you're a caring woman. People are going to figure out that you're nice."

Gloria shook her head. "Not going to happen, Red." She winked and turned for the door. "If you need someone else to sit with her, give me a call. My motel isn't far from here." She strutted out of the room.

Delaney returned to her chair. "How on earth did you two ever hook up?" she asked her sleeping lover. "I mean, she's gorgeous, but still. A person could only handle so much of her arrogance before losing it." She put her hand on Gib's and held it loosely. "Although, you did fall in love with me. You must be a glutton for punishment."

"Nah," Gib muttered. "One look at you and I fell hopelessly in love." She opened her eyes and turned her head toward Delaney. For the first time all day, her eyes were clear and alert. "When I met her I was lonely. But the moment you came along, I was lost."

"Listen to you," Delaney said, with tears in her eyes. "Lying in a hospital bed and sweet talking me."

Gib gave her a lopsided grin. "I can't help it. You bring it out in me." She tugged on their joined hands. "Come here and give me a kiss."

Doing as she was told, Delaney leaned over the bed and gave her a long, gentle kiss. "How's that?"

"Nice." Gib raised her other hand and touched Delaney's cheek. "Why don't you go home and get some rest?"

"Is that a polite way to say I look like hell?"

"I'll never tell." Gib yawned. "Sorry." Her hand dropped to the bed. "I can't believe I'm so damned tired."

Delaney kissed her on the forehead. "Your body's been through a lot. And I'm sure you're still fighting the effects of the anesthesia. Rest."

"I will, if you promise to go home and do the same." Gib blinked and failed in her struggle to keep her eyes open. "Please?"

"You fight dirty, officer." The redhead played with Gib's hair. "But okay. I promise. Maddy's supposed to be back soon, anyway."

One of Gib's eyes opened. "Yeah?"

"Uh-huh. Don't worry, honey. We won't leave you alone in here."

"Not worried," Gib mumbled. "Love you."

Delaney fondly smiled as her lover dozed off. "I love you, tough stuff." She looked up as the door opened and Maddy stepped inside. "Hi."

"Hi." Carrying a paper bag in her arms, Maddy crossed the room.

"How's she doing?" She set the bag on a nearby table.

"Pretty good. She was actually coherent for a few minutes. What's in the bag?"

"A few essentials for her. Toothbrush, toothpaste, that sort of thing." Maddy gave her a one-armed hug. "How are you holding up?"

Delaney leaned her head on Maddy's shoulder and ruefully chuckled. "Do I look that bad? You're the second person to ask me that."

"I wouldn't say bad." Maddy guided her into the chair. "More like worn out. Have you had any kind of break?"

"No, but—"

"Then I think you need to go home. I can handle things here for the night."

The redhead stood and put her hands on her hips. Although she had planned on leaving, she didn't like being told to by someone else. "Now, look. I'm perfectly capable—"

"Of doing as you're told," Maddy finished for her. She gentled her tone. "How are you handling it, really?"

A huge breath of air escaped through Delaney's lips as she dropped into the chair. "Like hell." She looked at the still form on the bed. "Is this what being a police officer's wife is like? Because I don't know if I can go through this again."

Maddy knelt beside her and placed her hand on Delaney's thigh. "I can't answer that. But being a Park Officer is a lot different from being a regular cop. Would you feel better if Gib gave up her job? Is that what you want?"

"No, of course not." Delaney covered Maddy's hand with hers. "Part of what I love about her is how she carries herself at work. It's who she is. I'm just being silly."

"It's not silly, hon, but if you have worries, don't shut Gibsy out. Talk to her."

"Don't worry, Maddy. I'm just feeling a little overwhelmed." She gazed at the peacefully sleeping Gib. "I'm not going anywhere."

With a sigh of relief, Maddy stood and tugged Delaney to her feet. "Good." She took a paperback out of the bag. "Now, go home. I've got a chance to catch up on some reading."

Delaney gave her a hug. "Yes, ma'am." She leaned over and kissed Gib on the cheek. "Be good. I love you." When she straightened up, there were tears in her eyes. "Call me if anything happens?"

"You know I will." Maddy made a shooing motion with her hands. "Go on, now. I've got your number on speed dial."

"Are you always this bossy?" Delaney teased as she headed for the door.

Maddy wriggled her eyebrows. "Of course. How do you think my restaurant runs so smoothly? Now get."

With a backwards glance toward the bed, Delaney slipped out the room.

THE DIGITAL READOUT on her dash read nine-thirty. As Delaney parked in her parent's driveway she considered the wisdom of her decision. When the front porch light flickered on, she rolled her eyes and turned off the engine.

Dressed in a long, midnight blue housecoat, Maureen stepped out on the front porch and crossed her arms over her chest. She remained silent until Delaney was within a few feet of her. "I wasn't expecting you tonight, honey. How's Gib?"

"She's resting. Her friend Maddy ran me off." She gave her mother a hug. "I didn't feel like going home. Do you mind if I crash here?"

"Of course not. I think I can find something for you to sleep in." Maureen led her inside and closed the door behind them. While they walked through the foyer, she took a moment to look at her daughter. "Are you hungry? Maybe a nice warm bath."

Delaney chuckled at her mother's fussing. "Mom, I'm fine. I think a bath sounds good, though." She couldn't help but groan as they moved up the staircase. "I'm so glad this day is over."

"I can just imagine," Maureen commiserated. "Why don't you go start your bath water and I'll bring you something to sleep in?"

"Thanks, Mom." After another quick hug, they went their separate ways. The guest bathroom was the one Delaney had shared with her brothers while growing up. It had been remodeled in recent years, the regular tub replaced with a deep jet tub. She sat on the edge and turned on the water, adding a small amount of bath salts.

Maureen tapped on the open door. "I know they'll be big, but how about a pair of your father's pajamas? You used to love wearing them when you were younger. And I've turned down the bed in the room across the hall."

"Sounds perfect. Thanks." When her mother turned to leave, she asked, "Mom? Can I ask you something?"

"Of course." Maureen joined her on the edge of the tub and put her arm around Delaney. "What is it?"

With her head on her mother's shoulder, Delaney felt her reserves weaken and she began to cry. The comforting embrace she was pulled into only made her tears come harder.

Maureen held her close and brushed her hand over Delaney's hair, much like she did when her daughter was younger. She whispered nonsensical words of comfort, until Delaney quieted and sat up. "Feel better?"

"Yes," the redhead sniffled, wiping her cheeks with the back of her hand. "Thanks."

"We all need a good cry every now and then." Maureen picked up a clean washcloth and handed it to her. "What did you want to ask me?"

Delaney dipped the washcloth into the tub and cleaned her face. "Do you think I rushed into things with Gib? I mean, I really didn't have any idea what her job entailed until this happened."

"Are you having second thoughts?"

"No, not really. I'm just trying to work some things out in my head." With the tub filled, Delaney turned off the water. She took off her shoes and socks. "What do you think of her?"

Cocking her head to one side, Maureen frowned. "Why? What does it matter what I think?"

"Because I value your opinion," Delaney stated as she unbuttoned her shirt.

Maureen laughed. "Since when?"

"Mom!"

"Oh, come on. Quit being so damned serious." She splashed her daughter with a handful of water.

"Hey!" Delaney splashed back.

Water flew back and forth, and soon both women were drenched. Their giggles turned to laughter until there was a knock on the door.

"What's going on in there?" Colin asked. "Is everything all right?"

Delaney covered her mouth with her hand, her eyes wide.

"We're fine, dear," Maureen answered. "Just some girl talk."

He grumbled something. "Well, try to talk a little quieter. I could barely hear the television."

"Sorry, Dad," Delaney called.

"Yeah, yeah," he muttered as he walked away.

The two women looked at each other and broke into giggles again.

Maureen gathered Delaney's clothes while her daughter climbed into the tub. "For the record, I think your Gib is a wonderful person, honey. And I'm sure her job isn't usually so dangerous. One of your father's friends has been on the police force for over twenty years, and he's never had to draw his weapon. So don't let her job ruin what you two have."

"It won't. I love her too much for that."

"Good to hear." Maureen stood at the door. "After you're finished, go downstairs. There's some leftover chicken in the refrigerator."

Delaney fought the urge to roll her eyes at Maureen's maternal clucking. The last time she did it in her mother's presence she got a swat across the head. "Yes, ma'am."

"And don't even think about rolling those eyes at me, young lady."

Biting her lip to keep from giggling, Delaney nodded.

"Good." Maureen blew her a kiss. "Get some rest, and I'll see you in the morning." She closed the door behind her, yelling, "No eye rolling!"

Losing the battle, the redhead dissolved into giggles and sank beneath the water.

Chapter Twenty

GIB POKED AT the food in front of her. "I think I figured out why they feed people this stuff," she grumbled to Maddy.

"You have, have you?" Maddy stood and stretched. She dozed throughout the night, only waking when Gib's breakfast was delivered. "Please, enlighten me."

"Job security." The congealed mess that was supposed to be oatmeal took hold of Gib's plastic spoon and wouldn't let go. "They feed you this crap and you never get better, so they keep all the beds full."

Maddy laughed. "Wake up on the wrong side of the bed this morning, Gibsy?"

Gib glared at her. "Do *you* want this?" She raised the spoon, lifting the bowl off the table. "Gross."

A man's voice chimed in. "Officer Proctor, I know I told you to come see me sometime, but I think this was a bit extreme," Dr. Madding teased. He looked at her chart. "Other than our cuisine, how are you feeling this morning?"

"I'll live." Gib pushed the rolling table away from her. "As long as I stay away from your oatmeal."

"I have to agree, at least with your diagnosis." He studied her leg for several minutes. "Not bad work, if I do say so myself." He patted her good leg. "Here's the good news. Nice, clean break. But because of where it was, I had to add a plate and rods to stabilize the bone. Bad news? You'll have to use a wheelchair for a while, but I should be able to get you into a walking splint in a month or two."

The older couple standing in the doorway overhead him. "Wheelchair?" the woman exclaimed. "For how long?"

Dr. Madding turned to face the couple. "I'm sorry?"

"It's all right, Doc. These are my parents, Ida and Eric Proctor. Hi, guys."

Ida stood beside the bed and smiled at Maddy. "Hi, Madina. Have you been here long?"

"All night. It's good to see you, Ida." Maddy made no move to leave the room, but she kept her position by the window. "Mr. Proctor."

Eric gave her a deferential nod. "Madina." He gave the doctor a firm handshake. "How long will she be off work?"

"It's hard to say. Most of it depends on complications and healing time. If all goes well, she should be on her feet again in a few months."

"That figures," Eric grumbled. "I suppose you'll want to stay with us, so your mother can wait on you?" he asked his daughter.

Gib shook her head. "I can do fine on my own."

"We'll probably end up supporting you," Eric countered.

"You haven't supported me since I was in high school. And even then, I worked to pay for my own things."

Eric looked as if he were about to explode. "What? How dare you!"

Maddy tried to intervene before things got completely out of control. "Doctor, how long will Gib be here?"

He appeared relieved at the question. "A few more days until we can make certain there are no complications from the surgery." He shook Gib's hand. "I'll be back in to see you tomorrow. Try to get some rest."

"Gibson, you know that you're going to need some help for a while." Ida adjusted the blanket covering her daughter. "And if you're at home—"

"My home is on the lake. I'm an adult and I'm perfectly capable of taking care of myself. As I've proven most of my life."

Maddy had heard enough. "She can stay with me."

"I don't think so," Gib retorted. "No way. I'm going home."

With a sigh, Maddy shook her head and turned her back on the threesome. She took her cell phone off of her belt and dialed the most recently added number.

STILL GROGGY FROM oversleeping, Delaney was on her way to the hospital when her cell phone rang. She fumbled around in her purse in a panic. "Hello?"

"Delaney? This is Maddy."

"I'm on my way to the hospital. Is something wrong?"

Maddy's chuckle echoed through the line. "Not really. Unless you consider Gibsy acting like a complete ass this morning as wrong, everything's just peachy."

"Good lord, don't scare me like that." Delaney took a deep breath and released it slowly. "I'm sorry I'm running late, but my mother didn't bother to wake me this morning." She was still fuming over it. Maureen had taken it upon herself to sneak into her bedroom and take her phone. Delaney hadn't realized it was missing until she woke a few minutes after nine.

"It's not a problem." Maddy lowered her voice. "As a matter of fact, if you get here soon, you'll get the pleasure of seeing both of Gibsy's parents."

Delaney snorted. "They actually showed up? What's the matter? No grandchildren to spoil today?"

"Oooh. Mee-oow," Maddy teased. "Would you like a saucer of milk with that?" The growl she received caused her to laugh. "Sorry. I thought you could use a little levity."

The hospital parking lot wasn't very full and Delaney was able to find a space near the entrance. "No, I'm sorry. I'm still not awake, I guess."

"That's all right. No harm done."

"What exactly is Gib doing? I can't see her being rude." Delaney got out of the Lexus and locked it with the remote as she walked toward the hospital. The sound of loud voices in the background caused her to quicken her steps. "Maddy?"

"Please tell me you're almost here."

Delaney grinned as she crossed the threshold. "I'm almost here."

"Ugh. You're just as big a smartass as Gibsy, aren't you?"

"Probably more."

Maddy groaned. "God help me," she muttered. "No, Mr. Proctor. I'm speaking to Delaney."

The elevator moved slowly and the noise made it nearly impossible to hear what else Maddy said. "I'm hanging up," Delaney told her as the doors opened. She nodded politely to the nurse at the station as she passed.

Loud voices were coming from Gib's room, and a nurse stood at the door with a disapproving look on her face. She turned when Delaney approached.

"Hi. Is there a problem?" Delaney asked her.

The nurse, older and heavier than Delaney, wrinkled her nose. "They're going to have to leave if they keep upsetting my patient," she scolded.

Delaney gave her a reassuring smile. "I'll take care of it." She edged around the nurse and moved into the room.

Gib was seated upright on the bed with her arms crossed over her chest. Maddy stood beside her, facing off against the other two people in the room. One was Ida, dressed in a powder-blue, glittery sweat suit. The other was a tall, grizzled and slightly overweight man wearing a security uniform.

Squeezing past the older pair, Delaney crossed the room and gave her lover a kiss on the cheek. "Hi, honey. I'm sorry I'm so late this morning."

"You're fine." Gib held onto Delaney's hand as if her life depended on it.

The man couldn't quite hide his discomfort at their familiarity. He cleared his throat. "Gibson?"

Gib squeezed Delaney's hand. "Honey, this is my father, Eric Proctor. Dad, this is my, um—" Nothing she could think of could describe how important the redhead was to her.

"Partner," Delaney supplied helpfully. "Delaney Kavanagh, Mr. Proctor. It's a pleasure to meet you." She held out her free hand.

He stood still for a moment before moving forward and taking her hand. "Delaney." After a perfunctory shake he returned to his place beside Ida.

Delaney kept her smile as friendly as possible. "Ida, it's nice to see you again."

"Nice to see you, too." Ida glared at Gib.

"What am I missing here?" Delaney asked.

Gib blew out a frustrated breath. "The doctor said if everything looks okay, I can go home in a couple of days."

"That's good news, isn't it?" the redhead asked.

Maddy finally piped up. "It would be, but there's no way to get the wheelchair into the cabin. Ms. Stubborn refuses to go home with me."

"Your place isn't big enough for you, much less both of us," Gib reminded her. "And as much as I like Rob, I really don't want to see—" her mouth was covered by Maddy's hand.

"Sssh." Maddy tipped her head toward Gib's parents.

Ida frowned. "I've already said that Gibson would stay with us. There's a perfectly good futon in my sewing room. I'll be watching Morgan's cat, Mr. Spunky, while they go to Six Flags for vacation and could use her help. He has to have his medicine three times a day, and it's hard for one person to hold him and give him the pills."

Gib moved Maddy's hand away from her mouth. "Mom, I—"

Maddy squeezed her shoulders. "Isn't Gib allergic to cats?"

"So she says," Eric butted in. "I don't see how she ever figured that out since we've never had a cat. But it won't kill her to help out. We're not running a boarding house."

"That's not necessary." Delaney sat on the bed beside Gib. "Since I work from home most of the time, why don't you stay with me, honey? I'd love to have the company."

Looking into the sincere blue eyes of her love, Gib could only nod.

"Good. That's settled, then." When Eric jingled the change in his pocket and looked as if he was going to argue, Delaney thought it was time to clear the air. "Mr. Proctor, can I speak to you outside?"

"I don't think that's necessary," Eric argued. "We're her family, and she belongs with us. I work all day, so having Gibson at home will help Ida, and she can make herself useful. I don't even know you. Why should she stay with you?"

"Dad, don't," Gib pleaded.

Delaney stood. "It's okay, honey. I'll be right back. Mr. Proctor, please?" She kissed Gib lightly on the lips and motioned for Eric to precede her from of the room.

Once they were in the hall, Eric gestured to the elevators. "All right. If you really want to talk, let's go outside. I need a smoke."

"Sounds good to me."

They were silent until they reached the smoking area outside. Eric fished in his uniform breast pocket for a smashed pack of cigarettes. He lit one and inhaled deeply. "That's better." His eyes, the same shade of brown as Gib's, stared intently at the redhead. "So, Ida tells me you're in construction. Or something like that?"

"Something like that, yes." Delaney stared right back at him. "I have a nice apartment that's one level, so Gib will have no trouble navigating a wheelchair around. As I mentioned before, I can work from home on my laptop so that she's well-cared for. Gib means a lot to me, so if you're worried about her well-being—"

He shook his head. "Nah, not really. But I do want to warn you. Gibson's a pretty decent girl, but she can be lazy. After all, look at what she does for a living. She could have been a lawyer but she gave up. Less than a year left in law school and she turns around and becomes some kind of park ranger."

"She's a Park Police Officer," Delaney automatically corrected. "And you must mean someone else because the Gib I know is the least lazy person I've ever met." She moved a step closer to him. "I don't care if you're her father, I won't have you speak about Gib that way. She's a kind, hard-working woman who cares more about the people around her than herself."

"Now, listen here—"

"No, you listen." Delaney pointed a finger at him. "I know you don't approve of our relationship. I can see it in your eyes. But don't you dare say another derogatory word about the woman I love. I won't stand for it."

Eric frowned around the cigarette in his mouth. "I think I know my daughter better than you do. How long have you known each other? A week? A month?"

"It doesn't matter how long we've been together, Mr. Proctor. The fact is I learned more about her in a few days than you probably have in years."

"And how did you do that?"

Delaney lowered her voice. "By listening to her. Have you ever just sat down with Gib and talked? Or do you do most of the talking?"

"How we are isn't any of your business." He rubbed the stubble on his cheek. "Our relationship is what it is. Don't try to make more or less out of it." He took another drag from the cigarette before crushing it beneath his shiny black shoe. He picked up the butt and carried it to the trashcan by the door.

Frozen like a deer in the headlights, Delaney could only watch him leave. "What the hell just happened here?" She continued to stare at the door Eric had disappeared through. As much as she wanted to check on her lover, Delaney decided to take a walk and cool off. "I don't know who he thinks he is," she muttered. The grass was soft beneath her shoes and the fresh air helped to calm her down. "Okay. So her dad's a jackass. It's not like I haven't put up with one of those before."

Before she knew it, Delaney found herself in the parking lot. "Well, crap. Guess I'd better head back." She thrust her hands into the pockets of her jeans and stomped toward the doors. "Hopefully I can keep my mouth shut and not slap the shit out of the old bastard." She headed for the elevators. "If he says anything to hurt Gib, I'll kick his ass, father or not." Satisfied with her plan of attack, she stood in the elevator and exhaled slowly in an attempt to relax.

BACK IN THE room, Ida watched her husband follow the redhead outside. "She certainly seems forceful."

"She loves me," Gib explained. "And I love her. Is that a problem, Mom?"

Ida turned to face her. "No, of course not. I mean, you've always said you were," she waved her hands in a dismissive gesture, "that way, but I never thought you'd throw it in our faces."

"Are you serious?" Maddy exclaimed.

"Madina, how you can just stand there and listen to this? I thought you and Gibson—"

"Mom!"

Maddy put her hand on Gib's shoulder. "I should be so lucky, Ida. Unfortunately, Gib doesn't have the right physiology for me, but I love her like a sister."

"Really?" Ida frowned. "Well, I always thought if she found the right man," she looked at her daughter. "Or maybe it was my fault, for letting you wear jeans all the time as a girl. I tried to get you to be more ladylike, but you were always so stubborn."

"Damn it, Mom. We've been over and over this. How I dressed as a kid has nothing to do with the fact that I'm a lesbian."

Ida cringed. "Do you have to say that so loud?"

Maddy shook her head. "Ida, you've got some really warped ideas about things, but this takes the cake." She could see the lines of tension on her friend's face, as Gib tried to hide the pain she was in. "Please, just drop this."

They all quieted when an older man appeared with a wheelchair. "Good morning, Ms. Proctor. I'm here to chauffeur you to a few rounds of tests."

"Saved by the bell," Gib muttered. "All right." She whipped the sheet away from her body as he came forward to help. "Thank you."

When she returned to the room, Delaney noticed that Maddy was sitting alone on the bed. "Where did everyone go?"

"Gib was taken for some tests, and her father had to get to work. Ida, of course, followed like a good little Stepford wife."

Delaney sat beside her. "I take it you don't get along well with her parents?"

"Caught that, did you?" Maddy wriggled her feet like a child. "Ida's a little out there, especially with her old-fashioned ideas. Did you notice that Gib's father never offered his first name?"

"I heard you call him Mr. Proctor. How long have you known him?"

Maddy snorted. "Almost my entire life. He still sees me and Gib as children. After we got into high school, Ida told me to call her by her first name. But her dad? Nope."

"Wow. That's unbelievable."

"Yeah. Although I think a lot of it is because I'm a Mexican. He's a good old-fashioned redneck. Gib doesn't know this, but when we were around twelve, I overheard him griping to Ida about her spending so much time with 'those wetbacks.'"

Delaney was shocked. "That's horrible. But you were just children!"

"Hon, a lot of people feel that way. The funny part is my family was in Texas before it was a state. So I'm a hell of a lot more native than ol' Eric will ever be." Maddy bumped shoulders with Delaney as they shared a laugh.

Gib was wheeled in by a hospital volunteer. "What's so funny, you two?"

"The usual," Maddy deferred.

The volunteer, an older man, patted Gib on the arm. "Do you need any help getting back into bed?"

"No, sir. I'm sure my friends will help." Gib shook his hand. "Thanks for being the driver. I would have probably gotten lost."

He chuckled. "That's what we're here for, young lady." He waved to the women on the bed on his way out of the room.

Delaney hopped down. "Are you ready to get back in bed?"

"Not yet." Gib carefully wheeled herself over to the window and looked outside. "Damn."

After sharing a look with Delaney, Maddy slid off the bed. "I think I'll head home and get some sleep." She crossed the room to give Gib a kiss on the cheek. "No chasing the nurses, Gibsy. If you behave, I'll bring you some fajitas for dinner tonight."

"You don't have to do that. I'm sure the dinner will be better than the breakfast."

Maddy shook her head. "You're sweet, but delusional." She tugged on Gib's ear. "Do as I say, woman."

"Yes'm." Gib saluted and pinched her on the rear when Maddy turned to leave.

"Ow!" Maddy spun and swatted Gib on the arm. "Just for that, I won't bring you any jammies."

Delaney put her hands on Gib's shoulders. "That's okay. She won't need them at my place."

"Dee!" Gib flushed a bright red.

"And on that note, I'm out of here." Maddy blew them a kiss and strolled out, humming softly to herself.

Once they were alone, Gib turned away from the window. "Were you serious?" she asked in a vulnerable voice.

"About not needing pajamas? You betcha." Delaney perched on the wheelchair's arm.

Gib hooked her arm around the redhead to help her balance. "No, about me staying with you. I'm sure I can manage all right at the cabin, once someone helps me get inside."

"I'm sure you can, too." Delaney lowered her head so she could look Gib directly in the eyes. "I know we haven't been together that long, but there's something you should know about me."

"What?"

"If I ask you a question, I honestly want to hear your answer. And, if I tell you something, I really mean it." She touched the tip of Gib's nose with her index finger. "So, when I ask you if you'd like to stay with me until you get back on your feet, then I truly want you there. Got it?"

Grinning bashfully, Gib leaned forward and kissed her. "Got it."

"Good." Something had been weighing on Delaney's mind since she met Gib's father. "Honey?"

"Yeah?"

"Earlier today, when you introducing me to your dad—"

Gib squeezed her. "You caught that, did you?"

Delaney nodded.

"I wasn't sure what to call you," Gib admitted. "I mean, 'friend' certainly doesn't cut it. 'Girlfriend' is a little too high school. I liked what you came up with, though."

"Thanks." Delaney played with the blonde's hair. "Are you ashamed of us?"

"Not at all." Gib caught her hand and kissed the palm. "I wanted my father to know that you're the most important person in my life, and I won't stand for him cutting you down with his smartass remarks. He's real good at that."

Delaney leaned her head against Gib's and closed her eyes. "I love you."

"I love you, too."

The redhead sat up. "I think I can handle your dad, honey. Remember, I grew up in a house full of boys. His little digs won't hurt me."

"I figured that. It's just that he'll disguise them as jokes. My brother is the same way. They hide their bigotry and nastiness in snarky comments. I've learned to let them slide off, but it can get to you after a while."

Hearing the hurt in her lover's voice, Delaney put both arms around Gib's neck. "I won't let them hurt you anymore, honey. I swear it."

Gib threaded her free hand into Delaney's hair and brought her close. "And I won't let anyone hurt you, either," she promised, right before their lips met.

WITH HER VISITORS gone for the evening, Gib stared at the ceiling in disgust. She hated being confined indoors. The pain in her leg had gotten worse, yet she refused to push the button that would place the drops of liquid relief in her IV bag. As the shadows deepened in the room she cursed herself for insisting that Delaney go home for the night. Bored and wide awake she turned her head toward the open door in time to see a woman dressed in a park ranger's uniform.

"Hi, Gib." Kennie, holding a small vase with flowers, looked around before stepping into the room. She set it on a table by the window. "Sorry it took me so long to come by."

"Don't apologize. It's great to see you." Gib shifted and grimaced as she accidentally moved her leg. "Damn."

Kennie hurried toward the bed. "Do you need me to call a nurse?"

"No," Gib exhaled slowly. "I've got to remember not to do that," she grumbled.

"Aren't they giving you anything for the pain?"

Gib nodded. "I hate taking it, though. Makes me sleepy."

Kennie sat on the chair beside the bed. "That's the whole point, goofy. Rest is the best thing for healing."

"Why are you in uniform?" Gib asked in an attempt to change the subject.

"I was cleared to work. Well, part time, anyway. Besides, the park was running shorthanded. I still can't believe Dan would do something like that."

Gib's eyes narrowed as she struggled against the pain. "Yeah. He was a jerk, but I never thought someone who worked in the Parks system would stoop to poaching." She grimaced as another wave of pain hit.

"I swear. You're impossible." Kennie pushed the button and looked extremely proud of herself. "There. Now maybe you won't be so miserable."

"I would have done it after you left."

Kennie grinned. "Now you won't have to. I heard that Dan's family won't have anything to do with him, and he can't raise bail money. Isn't that sad?"

"No. What's sad is the amount of animals that bastard killed. I hope he rots in jail." Gib blinked a few times as she felt herself become more lethargic. "That's some powerful stuff."

"You need it." Kennie stood and squeezed Gib's hand. "Behave yourself and take your meds."

Gib tried to glare at her, but the effects of the pain medication turned it into a bleary stare. "Don't overdo it at work."

"Like anyone will let me. I'm either goofing off in the office or riding with Gloria."

"Gloria? You watch out for her, she's," Gib's eyes closed. She reopened one of them and tried to point a finger at her visitor but her hand wouldn't quite cooperate. Instead, she made an awkward peace sign. "Bad news."

Kennie took Gib's hand and gently placed it on the bed. "I'm a big girl. Don't get all protective on me. Now close your eyes and get some rest."

"She's trouble," Gib slurred as her eye closed.

"I know Mama Bear. See you later." Kennie kissed the top of Gib's head before she left.

THE MUSIC IN Little Sisters was loud, but not annoyingly so. Gloria sipped her drink. The caramel-colored liquid brought a warm burn to her empty stomach. Being the most experienced Ranger at the park, her work week had been hectic with Gib in the hospital. She sat with her back to the bar, her eyes scanning the raucous crowd. She had turned away several women already, not finding anyone up to her standards. Even though her ex-lover wasn't her usual type, it irked her that Gib had refused her overtures.

Bored after the first hour, Gloria finished her drink with the idea to go to her motel and watch television. She didn't bother to turn when she sensed someone sit beside her.

"Can I buy you a drink?" the woman asked.

Gloria turned to see Jessica Middleton giving her a shy smile. The young woman was dressed casually in black jeans and a white tank top, and her dark hair curled gently against her shoulders. "Only if you'll let me get the next round." She waved the bartender over.

"Another rum and coke?" Lisa asked.

"Yeah. My friend here is buying."

Lisa looked from one woman to the other. While the blonde seemed in her element, the little brunette appeared about halfway frightened. "Is that right?" she asked Jessica.

"Uh, yeah." Jessica took a leather wallet from her back pocket and dug out a twenty dollar bill. "Could I have a beer?"

"I'll need to see your ID."

Jessica blushed but handed over her license.

After verifying that Jessica was over twenty-one, if only by a year, Lisa handed the plastic card back to her. "Any particular beer?"

"Um, what do you have?"

Gloria could tell the question irritated the bartender. "Just bring her whatever you have on draft."

Lisa nodded and went to fetch their order.

"So, what brings you here?" Gloria asked. "I don't think you're a regular."

Jessica shrugged. "I heard about this place from a friend and thought I'd check it out. I was surprised to see you here."

Gloria laughed. "You mean I don't look like a dyke?"

"No. I mean, I had no idea that you were, um," Jessica continued to stammer for a moment before closing her mouth.

Gloria lightly patted the younger woman's thigh. Her boring evening was beginning to look up. "I was only kidding." When Lisa placed their drinks in front of them, she picked up hers. "Why don't we go find a table where we can chat?"

"Okay." Jessica took her beer mug and left a five dollar bill on the counter. "Thanks."

Lisa grinned and shook her head as the pair headed for a quiet corner. "Good luck, kid," she muttered after the pair.

Once they were seated, Jessica felt her heartbeat pick up when Gloria scooted her chair close enough that their thighs touched. "So, do you come here often?" Jessica asked. She cringed when she realized how it sounded.

"God, you're too cute," Gloria chuckled. "And no, I don't. But I didn't feel like going back to my motel room." She wondered if the younger woman would be interested in joining her for the night.

"You're still in a motel? Why?"

Gloria raised her glass and took a drink. "I haven't been told how long I'll be here. Although, since we busted Dumbass Dan, I may be asked to stay permanently."

"That would be okay, wouldn't it?" With a shaky hand, Jessica picked up her glass of beer and had two or three swallows before she returned it to the table.

"I've been in worse places," Gloria admitted. "Although I don't know if I can stand seeing Gibson every day."

Jessica's head jerked up. "Gibson? Oh, you mean Proctor? She's not so bad, once you get to know her." She was unable to keep from blushing at the thought of the park officer.

"No, really?" Gloria was openly grinning. "She's cute, isn't she?"

"Oh, yeah," Jessica sighed. Her eyes widened. "I mean, um, oh, damn." She covered her face with her hands. "I'm such a dork." Mortally embarrassed, she pushed her chair away from the table. Only the blonde's hand on her shoulder kept her from fleeing.

"Chill out, hon. There are worse people to be attracted to. Hell, I should know." Gloria put her arm around Jessica's shoulder and leaned closer to speak into her ear. "Would you like to have a little party with me tonight?"

The silky voice brought chills down her spine. Jessica struggled to speak, but her mouth had gone dry. "I, uh—"

"It's all right, hon. Calm down. You're among friends." Gloria kissed the edge of Jessica's ear. She decided on a different tactic. "Would you like to dance?"

Her brain still short circuited, Jessica could only nod.

"Come on. Let's have some fun." Gloria helped her up and led her across the room.

The song ended when they made it to the dance floor, but a slower tempo soon began. Jessica wiped her sweaty palms on her jeans and stood uncertain. She held out her hands and was surprised when Gloria grabbed her hips and tugged her close. The feel of the older woman's hands on her butt caused Jessica to stiffen.

"Relax," Gloria said into her ear. "Just enjoy the music." She shuffled them slowly around the floor.

Jessica closed her eyes and put her head on Gloria's shoulder. One of the hands on her butt slid upward and caressed her back. The blonde's musky perfume warmed her senses and her body relaxed into Gloria's embrace.

They stayed on the floor for three more songs. When a fast beat started, Gloria led them back to their table. "Are you having a good time?" she asked, as she sipped on her watery drink. She could see how nervous Jessica was in the club, and wanted to find a way to get her to loosen up.

"Yeah." Jessica drained her glass and set it shakily on the table.

Maybe a few drinks will help. Gloria waved to a waitress. "Want to try some shots?"

"I've never done shots. Are they terribly strong?" Jessica asked, having to lean closer to hear Gloria's answer.

"Nah. Piece of cake." Gloria winked at the waitress. "Bring us a couple of Jagermeister shots, please. Oh, and refill my friend's beer."

The waitress looked from one to the other and shrugged. "All righty. Be back in a jiff."

After the drinks were placed on the table, Jessica picked up her shot glass and sniffed. "Oh, wow. That's strong."

"But really good," Gloria assured her. "Go on, try it. Just toss it back."

Jessica watched as Gloria did just that, swallowing the liquid and slamming the glass on the table. "Okay." She raised it to her lips and mimicked the blonde's actions. Coughing and sputtering, she placed the empty shot glass in front of her. "Ugh." She shivered as the alcohol hit her stomach.

"How 'bout another one?"

Jessica shook her head.

"All right. But I'm going to have another." Gloria signaled to the waitress.

"I don't know." Jessica sipped on the beer to get the taste of the shot out of her mouth. "How can you drink that stuff?"

Gloria shrugged. "It's an acquired taste. Maybe you're too young to appreciate it."

"No I'm not." Jessica turned and waved to the waitress, who was already on her way with two more shots.

"Another round, ladies?" the waitress asked.

Jessica took her wallet out. "I'm paying for this round." She gave the woman some bills. "Keep the change."

"Thanks. Enjoy your drinks."

Once the woman had left, Jessica raised her shot. "Cheers."

Gloria laughed and raised hers as well. "Cheers."

The burn wasn't as bad this time around, although Jessica could swear the chair she was on seemed to be rocking. She blinked and grinned stupidly at Gloria. "See? I'm not a kid."

"No, you're all grown up." Gloria leaned forward and pressed her lips against Jessica's.

Surprised, Jessica opened her mouth to say something, but was stopped when Gloria's tongue darted inside. The burning in her stomach flared to a fire and she hooked her arms around the blonde's neck and moaned as the soft tongue explored her mouth.

The signal was all she needed. Gloria placed several short pecks on Jessica's lips. "Come back to my motel with me," she asked breathlessly, lowering her mouth to the younger woman's throat.

"Mmm." Jessica squirmed under the attention. Her head was spinning, not only from the alcohol but the attention. When Gloria caressed her breasts, she thought she was going to melt. "Yes."

Gloria stood and pulled Jessica up with her. Although she had a slight buzz, she was still able to navigate well enough to get them through the club. She kept her arm around the young woman's waist. They were almost to the door when a slender, dark-haired woman put her hand on Jessica's arm.

"Hey, Jessie! I'm glad to see you here," Darla shouted over the music. "Who's your friend?" she asked, eyeballing the sexy blonde.

Jessica grinned broadly. "Hi, Darla!" She looked up at Gloria. "This is my friend, Darla. We went to school together." She leaned her head against Gloria's arm. "Gloria and I work together, don't we?"

"We sure do." Gloria held out her hand. "Nice to meet you, Darla. Are you the friend that told Jess about this place?"

"I did. But y'all aren't leaving so early, are you? I'd love to buy you a drink."

Gloria smirked. "We've got better things to do."

"Are you sure that's a good idea, Jessie? I mean, this is your *first* time here," Darla stressed. The evening she had spent at Jessica's apartment was a revelation for them both, and she knew how sheltered the other woman had been. They ended the night as friends, but Darla wanted more.

Jessica looked from one woman to another. "Well, maybe we could have just one teensy little drink. What do you say, Gloria?"

It took her a moment, but Gloria finally understood Darla's problem. *Jealous, much?* She tightened her grip on Jessica. "It's up to you, hon."

"Whoo! Let's par-tay!" Jessica yelled, linking arms with both women. "Barkeep, set up some shots," she hollered, waving toward the bar. "And keep 'em comin'!"

Chapter Twenty-one

THE EARLY MORNING sun was warm against her neck, but the passing scenery was lost on Gib. Her injured leg was stretched out along the backseat of the Lexus and she stared out the window across from her. Although she was happy to be out of the hospital, she hated knowing she'd be dependent on Delaney for an extended period of time. The week-long hospital stay had depressed her and not even her lover could bring her out of her dark mood. Gib's heavy sigh didn't go unnoticed.

"Honey? Is everything all right?" Delaney asked with a quick glance in the rearview mirror.

"Yeah, I'm fine." Gib forced a smile onto her face. "Thanks for bringing me to the cabin. I know I can't go in, but I really appreciate you getting some of my things together."

"It's no trouble at all. As a matter of fact, with you along, I won't be able to forget anything."

Gib smile turned genuine. "I doubt that. The drugs they have me on make my brain fuzzy. I'm lucky I can even talk."

"Aww." Delaney blew her a kiss and turned her attentions back to the road. She turned onto the entrance to the park and parked next to Gib's vehicle. "I'm surprised they kept your truck here instead of the cabin."

"Clint talked me out of it," Gib explained. "He wanted it at the office so they could keep an eye on it. He also promised to start it at least once a week."

Delaney left the engine running and opened her door. "That's nice of him." She climbed out and poked her head back into the SUV. "I'll be right back."

Gib had to chuckle. "I'm not going anywhere."

"Oh, yeah. Sorry." Delaney closed the door softly and headed toward the office.

As muddled as her head was, Gib still enjoyed watching her lover walk away. "She's got a nice...damn." Her pleasure was rudely interrupted by Clint stepping outside.

Clint used his hand to block the sun and looked toward the Lexus. He grinned and waved.

Gib sighed and wriggled her fingers. "Don't come over, don't come over, don't come over," she whispered. "Shit."

Waving Gib's keys in front of him, Clint sauntered to the SUV. He opened the front passenger door and stuck his head in. "How are you doing?"

"I'm all right. How are things here?"

He shrugged his shoulders. "About the same. I heard that Conroy made a deal and got a probated sentence."

Walking up behind Clint, Delaney overheard his last sentence. "Are you expecting any trouble from him?"

"Nah. He's a cowardly little pissant." When Gib glowered at him, Clint turned to Delaney. "Pardon my language, Ms. Kavanagh. I meant no disrespect."

She laughed. "That's quite all right, Mr. Wright. I think I've heard the word before."

"Please, call me Clint." He held out his hand, blushing when she took it.

"As long as you call me Delaney." She pulled away, holding Gib's keys.

"How did—"

Gib laughed at the confused look on his face. "Better check for your wallet, Clint. She's quick."

He patted his back pocket. "Still there."

The office door opened and Kennie bounded outside. She joined the others by the vehicle. "Hey, Gib. Nice to see you out and about."

"It's good to see you, too. How are you feeling? You're not doing too much, are you?"

"No, Mama Bear. I'm being good." She climbed onto the front passenger seat and carefully patted Gib's thigh. "You're not giving your lady a hard time, are you?"

Gib opened her mouth, but Delaney's laughter stopped her from answering.

"Mama Bear? That's perfect," the redhead giggled. "She's got you pegged, honey."

She considered growling for effect, but Gib shook her head and grinned. "I'll have to come up with a suitable nickname for you, Kennie. Clint, don't you have something for her to do?"

"Not at the moment."

Delaney rattled the keys. "We need to get going. We're supposed to meet someone at my place in less than an hour. But you're both welcome to stop by the apartment anytime. Right, Gib?"

"Uh, yeah. Sure. As long as it's okay with you." Unable to stop it, Gib yawned. "Sorry, guys."

Kennie gave her one last pat and backed out of the Lexus. "You take care of yourself."

"I will."

Clint nodded. "Don't worry about a thing. George has been itching to get out in the field, and Hoover's going to make sure he's trained right."

"Speaking of Gloria, where is she?" Gib asked.

"She's scheduled to be in at noon. I'm sure she'll be upset that she missed you."

Delaney snorted. "I'm sure she will." She gave Kennie a hug. They had become well acquainted during Gib's hospital stay, and she had a soft spot for the younger woman. "Don't be a stranger."

"Not a chance," Kennie assured her. "Take care of Mama Bear. She's pretty special," Kennie whispered.

"I will." In a louder voice, Delaney said, "Ready to go, honey?"

Fighting off a wave of lethargy, Gib nodded. As glad as she was to be out of the hospital, she couldn't wait to get to Delaney's and lie down. "Yeah. Maddy will be at your place soon. We'd better get a move on." She grimaced as Clint slammed the door.

After a few more goodbyes, Delaney climbed into the Lexus and carefully closed her door. "Is he for real?"

"Who, Clint?"

"Yeah. I don't think I've ever met a guy so old-fashioned."

From the backseat, Gib chuckled. "He's a great guy, though. And you should see how he treats his wife. She brought him lunch one day, and he walked all the way out to her car and opened the door for her. Probably one of the last gentlemen on the planet." After the SUV hit a rough patch of road, she bit her lip.

Delaney could see the pain on her lover's face. "Are you going to make it?"

Gib took a cleansing breath. "Yeah. But I'll be glad to get settled at your apartment."

"Me, too." Delaney slowed as they turned onto the lake road. "I'm glad we repaired this road," she muttered to herself.

"So am I," Gib answered. "It made getting to work a hell of a lot easier." She frowned. "Although I guess that's not going to be a problem for a while."

Delaney slowed the SUV to a crawl. She watched the road carefully in an attempt to miss any bumps or potholes. "You can always think of it as a vacation."

"I don't need a vacation," Gib grumbled.

"Well, then think of it as a chance to spend some time with me." Delaney parked in front of the cabin. "Do you have a suitcase?"

"Yeah. It's under my bed." Gib looked down at her leg and started picking at the splint. "I, uh, don't have a lot of casual clothes. I was going to buy some new stuff once I got settled, but never got around to it. What little I have should be in my dresser."

The redhead rolled down the window Gib faced. "Don't worry about it. If you need more things, I'll be glad to pick them up for you." She got out of the SUV. "Give me a few minutes to play in your underwear drawer, and I'll be right back."

Gib laughed at the silly look her lover sported. "Only you would have fun doing that."

"Well, I'd rather play with what goes in the underwear, but," Delaney winked, "I'll be patient." She jogged up the steps while Gib laughed, wriggling her rear for good measure.

SLOWLY RISING TO consciousness, Jessica didn't know which was worse: her excruciating headache or the rampaging nausea. She blinked her crusty eyes open, confused when she didn't recognize the room.

"Good morning," a much too perky voice greeted.

Jessica rolled onto her back and carefully sat up. "Where," she croaked. After clearing her throat, she tried again. "Where am I?" With a gasp, she realized she was naked. She jerked the sheet up over her chest and frowned.

Gloria, dressed in her uniform, brushed the younger woman's cheek with the back of her knuckles. "You don't remember last night?"

"What did, I mean, how," Jessica stammered. "Oh, god. Did we?"

"I should be upset." Gloria watched her face for a reaction. "Especially since you were all over me at the bar."

Jessica shook her head, then winced and cradled her head in her hands. "Fuck."

"Hey, now. It's all right. You don't think I'd take advantage of a woman who was drunk, do you?" Gloria walked across the room to the sink area, where a coffee pot gurgled. She poured two cups and carried them to the bed. After handing one to Jessica, she sat next to her.

"If we didn't, um," Jessica took the coffee, "*you know,* then why don't I have any clothes on?" She took a cautious sip of the dark brew and made a face. "Ugh."

Gloria also sipped her coffee, but didn't seem to mind its strength. "You really don't know, do you?"

"No."

"What's the last thing you remember?"

Jessica closed her eyes against the vertigo and swallowed the urge to vomit. "I'm not sure." The gentle touch on her arm made her open her eyes. "Dancing."

"Ah. Yes. That was fun, wasn't it? You were so tense, I thought a couple of drinks would help you relax. So we drank, we danced and then I asked you to come back to my room with me. Which you happily agreed to, by the way." At Jessica's horrified look, Gloria couldn't help but laugh. "Wait, it gets better." She drank more of her coffee, watching Jessica over the brim of the cup. "As we were leaving, a woman stopped us."

"Oh, yeah. Darla. She's the friend who told me about Little Sisters. We went to high school together. I kind of remember seeing her." The bitter coffee, mixed with the acid in her stomach, was more than she could bear. "I gotta—" She jumped from the bed and raced to the bathroom, barely making it before the coffee returned with a vengeance.

Gloria placed her coffee on the nightstand and followed Jessica. She wet a washcloth with cool water and stood by the tub. While Jessica continued to retch, Gloria placed the cloth against the back of her neck. "Easy, now."

"God, just kill me now," Jessica moaned. She gagged and spit into the toilet. "Ugh."

"Sssh. It'll be okay." Gloria took the towel she had draped over the curtain rod and covered Jessica's shoulders. "Let's get you back to bed."

Jessica shivered and leaned into the strong body. "I'm such an idiot."

"Nah." Gloria waited while she rinsed her mouth at the sink. "Are you scheduled to work today?"

"At three. Why? What time is it?"

Gloria led her to the bed and tucked her in. "Eight-thirty. Think you'll be able to make it?"

"Yeah." Jessica closed her eyes and sunk back into the pillow. Her eyes popped open again. "What happened after we saw Darla?"

"Well, this is where it gets kind of interesting," Gloria sat on the edge of the bed. "She started teasing you about roaring out of the closet. Then she challenged you to a drinking contest."

Jessica covered her eyes with her arm. "I didn't."

"Oh, yeah. I tried to talk you out of it, but you were pretty insistent. After each round, you kissed me." When Jessica groaned, Gloria laughed. "Very well, I might add."

"Argh." Jessica started to cough, then grabbed her head. "Ow."

Gloria retrieved a glass of water. "Here. You're dehydrated." She helped Jessica sit up and held her as she sipped. "Slowly."

After she had her fill, Jessica closed her eyes as Gloria lowered her to the pillow. "Thank you."

"You're welcome."

"Tell me more, please?"

"Are you sure?"

Jessica nodded.

"After a few more shots, you stood up, thanked the bar and announced you were going to get laid."

"Was I loud?"

The older woman laughed. "Oh, yeah. Everyone was cheering us as we left. When we got outside, you tried to get me to dance with you. Then you threw up."

Mortified, Jessica pulled the sheet over her head. "Oh, my god."

"You were so wasted that I didn't want to leave you alone. So I brought you here and cleaned you up."

The sheet was lowered just enough so that Jessica's eyes were visible. "You did that for me?"

"Yeah." Gloria shrugged and looked away. "Even a bitch like me can be nice every once in a while." She appeared embarrassed. "I'm going to run and get some breakfast, okay?" She stood and brushed the wrinkles from her pants. "Get some rest and I'll bring you something back."

"All right." Jessica lowered the sheet to right above her breasts. Before Gloria could open the door, she called out to her. "Gloria?"

The older woman turned around. "Yes?"

"Thanks."

"Don't mention it, kid."

Jessica was too miserable to argue the kid comment. Instead, once the door closed, she covered her face again and tried to keep from throwing up.

ON THE SIDEWALK of Delaney's apartment complex, Gib and Maddy were arguing. "Maddy, stop." Gib slapped at her friend, who dodged out of the way. "I can do this by myself."

"I told you I was sorry." Maddy apologized. "If you hadn't spun around so fast I wouldn't have hit your leg with the suitcase."

"I know. And I told you it was okay." The pain in her leg was making Gib short-tempered. "But I need to be able to get myself around without any help."

The door opened and Delaney stepped out. "What's the problem? I've got everything else upstairs."

"Nothing," Gib muttered. "Could you hold the door for me, please?"

Delaney opened it wide. "Here you go."

"Thanks." Gib wheeled herself through, ignoring Maddy's sputtering.

Once the injured woman was out of earshot, Maddy whispered, "I feel sorry for you."

"Why?" Delaney motioned for Maddy to precede her through the door.

"Because you have to put up with Ms. Grumpy Ass. I hope the doctor gave you some good tranquilizers. You're going to need them."

"I heard that," Gib said, her voice carrying across the marbled foyer.

Maddy stuck her tongue out at her friend. "I stand by my statement."

"Ladies, please." Delaney pushed the button for the elevator. "Every time you two get together, I feel like a referee."

"She started it," Maddy muttered.

"Did not," Gib countered.

"Did too."

Delaney held the door open for Gib. "That's enough, children." She giggled as the two women poked at each other and laughed.

"I'm sorry, Maddy. You're right. I've been grumpy." Gib held her hand out toward her friend. "Forgive me?"

"Of course, you big goof." Maddy kissed the top of Gib's head. She stood behind the wheelchair. "Now, enjoy the help while you have it."

When the door opened, she handed the suitcase to Delaney and pushed Gib forward. "Do you think you can handle her, Delaney?"

The redhead opened her apartment door and held it open for them. "I believe I can manage. But I have your number on speed dial, just in case."

"You're both *sooo* funny," Gib crossed her arms as she was wheeled inside.

Maddy thumped her on the head. "Behave." She stopped in the living room. "Where do you want her?"

"'Her' is capable of answering for herself," Gib answered. She rubbed her head where she had received a second thump. "Ow. Stop that."

"Quit your whining, Gibsy."

Delaney could see the exhaustion that Gib was trying so hard to hide. "Honey? How about getting settled in the bedroom?"

"Sounds good." Gib snapped her fingers and pointed. "Well? Onward, woman."

After they had Gib tucked into bed and medicated, Maddy followed Delaney to the kitchen. "I meant what I said on the phone this morning. If you need someone to stay with Gib, let me know. I can have my brother take care of the restaurant and be here in ten minutes." She sat at one of the bar stools while the redhead opened a cabinet.

"Thanks. I appreciate it. But I think we'll be fine." Delaney fiddled with her coffeemaker and stood nearby as it began to percolate. "I don't have any new projects at the moment, so having her here is a blessing."

"Well, the offer's open. Do you think it's a good idea to spend so much time together? I've known happily married couples who cracked under too much togetherness."

Delaney poured them each a cup of coffee. "How do you take it?"

"Black, thanks."

"Let's go to the living room where it's more comfortable." Delaney led the way and they were soon seated on opposite ends of the sofa. "I appreciate your concern, Maddy. But I think we'll be okay."

Maddy leaned back and crossed her legs. "I know you say that now. And I swear I'm not trying to butt into your relationship. I've never seen Gibsy so happy. It would break my heart to see anything mess that up."

The smile on Delaney's face widened. "Can I tell you a secret?"

"Sure."

Delaney turned and tucked one foot beneath her so that she was facing Maddy. "We've spent days at a time together, and it's never seemed like enough. If this hadn't happened, I was on the verge of asking her if we could move in together."

"Really?"

"Yeah. Crazy thing is I've always valued my space. I never even liked sleeping overnight with someone. But with Gib," she sighed. "I don't know what it is about her. She makes me a better person. And I've laughed more since we've been together than I have my entire life."

Maddy touched her knee. "I'm glad you two have such a good time. But, forgive me for asking this, is that enough? I would hate to see either one of you hurt."

"If it was just the fun, no. It probably wouldn't be enough. But there's a deeper connection, Maddy. One that I never thought was possible." Delaney's voice softened. "I love her with everything I am. I don't think there are words to describe it."

"You just did," Maddy assured her. "And it was beautiful."She checked her watch. "Unfortunately, I've got to run. Our lunch rush should start pretty soon."

Once Maddy left, Delaney stood in the doorway of the bedroom and watched her lover sleep. Even with the dark circles of stress beneath her eyes, Gib had never been more appealing to her.

As if feeling the scrutiny, Gib murmured and stretched her arm out across the bed until her hand was on Delaney's pillow.

Unable to resist the temptation, Delaney walked across the room, removing her clothes as she went. By the time she was beside the bed, all she had left on were her socks. She sat on the edge of the bed and soon lost those as well. She scooted beneath the covers and snuggled against Gib.

"Mmm." Gib's arm automatically encircled Delaney. Her eyes slowly opened when she realized the body beside her wasn't a dream. "Dee?"

"Hi, love." Delaney kissed Gib's shoulder. "I'm sorry to disturb you, but I lasted as long as I could."

Gib wearily chuckled. "Don't ever apologize for that, sweetheart. I'm glad you're here. I'm guessing Maddy's gone?"

"About five minutes ago."

"You lasted longer than I would have," Gib teased. She kissed her lover's head. "If I haven't mentioned it, I really appreciate you allowing me to crash here. I promise I'll be out of your hair as soon as I can."

Delaney traced her finger along Gib's chest. The ancient, gray tee shirt she wore was soft as butter. "You know, Maddy offered to give me a 'break' whenever I needed it."

"Um, okay. That's nice of her."

"I thought so, too. There's only one problem."

Gib smiled when Delaney looked into her eyes. "Yeah?"

"Uh-huh." The redhead raised herself to lean over Gib. "If it were up to me, you'd never leave." She lowered her head and kissed Gib tenderly. The feel of her lover's hand in her hair spurred her on, and soon they were both panting. Delaney reluctantly pulled away. "We need to slow down."

"Why?" Gib asked, tugging her forward again.

"Your leg." After being kissed senseless, Delaney gasped and pressed her forehead to Gib's chest. "You're going to kill me."

"Yeah, but what a way to go. Come here."

Chapter Twenty-two

GLORIA SIGNED HER name to the log sheet and gave George a nod. "How's it been this morning?"

He shrugged his shoulders. "About the same. Things won't heat up until after the Fourth of July. Then we get truckloads of people." He motioned with his head for her to come closer. "Um, listen. It's none of my business, but maybe you should be careful."

"About what?" She leaned on the counter and propped her chin in her hand.

"I overheard Jessica on the phone to someone earlier, and she's, uh," his voice lowered, "she was going on and on about you."

Gloria straightened up and frowned. "You're right. It's none of your business."

"Look, she's just a kid. A young, impressionable kid. And you're—"

"Old enough to know what I'm doing," she finished for him. "She's an adult and can make her own decisions. So back off."

George held up his hands. "All right. I just thought you should know, before she moves in with you."

"What?"

"Apparently she's in love. At least that's what she told her friend on the phone."

The blonde's face turned a sickly shade of white. "Love? But we didn't, we haven't, uh, shit."

"Well, whatever you've done, be careful. Up until now she was mooning over Gib. But more like a crush. I think she's serious with you."

"Fuck." Gloria flipped her hair over her shoulder. "That's what I get for being nice." It had been a week since that night at the bar, and she had purposely avoided the younger woman.

"Gloria?" Clint called from his office door. "Could you come in here, please?"

She turned and fought the urge to curse again. "Sure. Be right there." After Clint disappeared into his office, Gloria tapped the counter. "Thanks for the warning, George."

He nodded. "Good luck."

Like a woman headed for the gallows, Gloria walked slowly to Clint's office. She stood at the door. "What's up?"

"Could you come in and close the door, please?" Clint asked from behind the desk.

Gloria did as he requested and sat in the chair across from him. "Is there a problem?"

"No, not at all. I got a memo from Austin. With Gib out for months and Dan no longer with us, you've been assigned here indefinitely."

"What about my request? I was promised a post closer to a big city if I took this temporary assignment. And I'm tired of living in a motel room. Don't they understand what an inconvenience this is for me?"

Clint nodded. "I'm sure they do. It's not permanent. But we had no way of knowing that Gib would be laid up for months. If you're just patient—"

"Patient? I'm bored out of my mind! Nothing against you or the park, but Benton isn't even a blip on the radar. I have to go across the county line just to buy a bottle of wine. There are only four bars and at least two dozen churches. How screwed up is that?"

"Hey, I totally understand. I thought the same thing when I was first assigned here. But after a few years, Benton's grown on me. Maybe it will grow on you, too."

She shook her head. "Not likely. I need more stimulation than a rodeo or garden club can give. In Austin, there was always an art show or theater to go to. Here, it's big news when the high school has a play." She slapped her hands on the chair arms. "I can't stay here, Clint. I'll go crazy."

"All right. Let me see what I can do. Would you be okay with the assignment until Gib returns? We really need a senior Ranger or Officer around. George has another year of classes before he's qualified."

"Damn." Gloria lowered her head into her hands. "I don't have much choice, do I?"

"Not really. I'm sorry." Clint shuffled through the papers on his desk. "We have another rental cabin by the lake that will be available in a month. Can you hold out at your motel until then?"

She raised her head. "A month? I suppose so. I haven't been able to find a furnished apartment that allows for month-to-month rent, so I guess I'm stuck."

"Maybe something will turn up sooner," Clint offered helpfully. "Have you talked to Gib? Since she's staying in town, maybe you can use her place."

Gloria chuckled. "Oh, yeah. I'm sure that would go over *real* well. Especially with Red."

"Red?"

"Her girlfriend."

Clint's mouth formed a small o. "I hadn't thought of that. But why would it bother her?"

"You don't listen to the office gossip, do you?"

He shook his head. "I wasn't aware there was any office gossip."

"Gibson and I dated when we were both posted near Austin." She eyeballed him. "You really had no clue?"

"No. Why should I? As long as it doesn't affect your work, it's really none of my business."

Her laugh surprised him. "Clint, you're an unusual guy. Nice, but unusual." Gloria stood and adjusted her duty belt. "Is that all?"

"Uh, yeah." He scratched his head as she left, still laughing.

"ARE YOU SURE you want me there?" Delaney asked. They were on their way to the Proctor's house. Ida had called and requested Gib's appearance for dinner. It was Roger's birthday and she wanted everyone present. "I can always drop you off and come back when you're ready."

Gib played with the edge of her jeans. Since she didn't want to show up to her parent's house dressed as a slob she had asked her lover to cut off one leg of her jeans. To keep from being teased on her non-working status, she also wore a nice polo shirt. "If you've got something else to do, that's okay."

"What do *you* want?"

"To spend the evening with you instead of them."

Delaney gave her a sympathetic look. "We can go wherever you want. I was surprised when you agreed to go over there."

"My mother would hold it over my head for months if I don't at least make an appearance."

"Do they always have gatherings for birthdays?"

Gib shook her head. "Not always. Mine passed without any fanfare, so I assumed she had stopped doing it. But in my mother's defense, I haven't been home long enough for her to remember."

"When was your birthday?"

"March twenty-sixth. When's yours?"

Delaney flipped her hair over her shoulder. "A lady really shouldn't tell," she teased, trying to get her lover to smile. When they had to stop for a red light, she felt a finger hit her ribs, making her squeal. "Hey!"

"Deeeee." Gib wriggled her fingers at her. "Give it up, or I'll tickle the information out of you."

"November fifteenth," Delaney quickly divulged.

Gib, inordinately pleased with herself, leaned back and grinned. "You know, you're a pretty awesome lady."

The compliment was unexpected and Delaney turned to look at Gib. "I am?"

"Most definitely. Here I was, feeling sorry for myself for having to see my family, and you bring me out of it with one of your beautiful smiles." Gib was rewarded with an even bigger smile. "You're beautiful, too. Inside and out."

When the car behind them honked, Delaney faced the front and hurried through the green light. "I don't think anyone has ever told me my insides were beautiful."

"Then you haven't been around the right people." Gib rested one hand on her partner's shoulder. "I'd really appreciate it if you'd stay. If you don't mind."

Delaney parked across the street from the Proctor's house, since the two cars in the driveway weren't pulled up enough to park behind. Another car was on the street in front of the house. "They know we're coming, don't they?"

"Yes. Why?"

"It would have been nice if they'd left room for us in the driveway, since you're in a wheelchair." Delaney got out of the Lexus and removed the chair from the back. After she helped Gib out, she got behind the chair and pushed it up the steep driveway.

Gib used her good upper body strength to aid Delaney. Once they were on level ground, they stopped to catch their breath. "My family's motto is 'look out for number one.' No one's going to go out of their way for someone else."

Delaney used her fingers to comb Gib's hair. "I'm beginning to see that. Will you do something for me?"

"Sure."

"The moment you've had enough, let me know. We'll leave as soon as you're ready." Delaney leaned over and kissed Gib softly.

"Do you have to do that out here?" Eric asked.

Gib looked over Delaney's shoulder. "Hi, Dad. Nice to see you, too. Could you hold the door open for me, please?" She had long ago learned not to let his comments get to her. The best way to handle Eric was to ignore him and move on.

Delaney moved behind Gib and tightly gripped the chair's handles. "Mr. Proctor. It's nice to see you again."

"Delaney. Thank you for bringing my daughter over."

"I've invited Dee to stay, Dad. Mom already knows," Gib called from the hallway. She wheeled into the living room, Delaney not far behind her. Roger was stretched out on one sofa, sound asleep. His children were scattered around the room. Chase was asleep on a quilt on the floor, while Morgan played with several dolls near a pink dollhouse. Trevor was draped across the loveseat, his eyes glued to the baseball game on the television.

Eric closed the door and grumbled something under his breath as he followed the pair. "The women are in the kitchen." He walked over to an expensive, black leather recliner and dropped gracelessly into it.

Gib stopped and turned the chair to face him. "Where would you like to be, sweetheart?"

"With you," Delaney admitted.

Roger snorted and awakened. He sat up and scratched at his belly. "Is dinner ready?"

"Not yet," Eric answered, before returning his attention to the game.

"Well, hello," Roger crooned to Delaney. "I'm surprised to see you."

Delaney sent him an insincere smile. "You'd better get used to seeing me, since Gib and I are together."

"Sure." Roger stood and stretched his arms over his head, moaning loudly. "Damn, that felt good. How's the leg, Gib?"

"Better every day." Gib moved the wheelchair near the raised hearth of the fireplace, which had a long, red cushion across it. "Why don't you sit over here, Dee? Unless you would rather go to the kitchen."

Delaney seated herself on the cushion, as close to Gib as possible. "This is fine. Thank you."

Roger looked at his kids, who hadn't bothered to greet the newcomers. His sly grin should have been a warning. "So, Dee. Is your hair color natural?"

"Roger," Gib warned.

"Hey, just making conversation," he defended. When Delaney hadn't answered, he rephrased his query. "Does the carpet match the drapes?"

Gib slapped the arms of her wheelchair and started across the room after him. "That's enough! I won't sit here and let you talk to her like that."

Delaney grabbed the handles. "Honey, no."

"Come on, Gib," Roger taunted. He made sure his father wasn't paying any attention. But Eric was completely enthralled by the baseball game. He never had a problem tuning out his kids, no matter what their age. Roger waved his hands toward himself. "What are you going to do, ram my knees?"

"I'll take you down," Gib promised with a growl. She turned to Delaney, who still held the chair. "Let me go."

Delaney shook her head. "No. He's not worth hurting your leg."

When Gib exhaled heavily but didn't argue, Roger quietly laughed. "Oh, I get it. She's the top."

"That's it." Delaney stalked around her lover and stood in front of him. "If you don't want me to embarrass you in front of your children, I'd advise you to shut up."

He shrugged and snorted. "Like I'm scared of you."

"You should be." Delaney grabbed the front of his shirt and caught a few chest hairs as she twisted it.

"Ow!"

She lowered her voice. "I grew up in a house full of boys, so believe me when I tell you that I know *all* the best tricks."

"Okay, okay!" Roger rubbed his chest after she released his shirt. "You're lucky I was raised not to hit women."

Delaney laughed at him. "And you're lucky I'm on my best behavior, or I would have taken you out. Like I have my older brothers." She poked him in the chest. "*Many* times."

"Gib, Delaney. How nice to see you both," Ida called from the kitchen doorway. "Eric, why didn't you tell me they were here?"

Eric grumbled something but didn't take his eyes off the game.

"I swear, if the TV is on, that man will watch." She walked around the sofa. "Roger, Ann isn't feeling well. She asked if you'd get her purse out of the bedroom."

He rolled his eyes. "It's not even Saturday." But he headed out of the room to do as he was asked.

Ida patted Gib on the arm. "You look a little pale. Are you feeling all right?"

"Honestly? No. My leg is really starting to hurt." Gib looked at Delaney. "Would you mind taking me home, sweetheart?"

Delaney nodded. "Certainly." She turned to Ida. "I'm sorry. Please give our apologies to everyone, but I think it's best if I get her home so she can take her medication." She stood in front of the television and waved to Eric. "Mr. Proctor, have a nice evening. Gib's not feeling well, so I'm taking her home."

"Right." He pursed his lips. "Call us when you get tired of taking care of her."

"Don't hold your breath, waiting for my call. Sir." Delaney gave him her most polite smile. "Good night." She pushed Gib's chair. "We'll have to get together again sometime, Ida."

"Of course." Ida followed them to the door. "I'm sure Roger will be disappointed, but I understand."

Gib bit off the retort on the tip of her tongue. "I'll call you tomorrow, Mom."

"All right." Ida held the door open for them and waved as they left.

Once they were safely inside the Lexus, Delaney turned in her seat to face her lover. "Are you in a lot of pain?"

"Not really. I just didn't want to spend the evening looking at my brother's face across the table." Gib held out her hand, which Delaney quickly took. "I'm sorry. I know you were looking forward to my mother's overcooked chicken and rubbery dumplings."

Delaney laughed. "I'll try to get over it, somehow." She kissed Gib's hand before letting it go. "What are you in the mood for?" At her lover's smirk, she shook her head. "Besides that."

"Italian?"

"Tony's it is." The redhead turned and buckled her seatbelt, still laughing.

A FEW DAYS after the fiasco at the Proctor's, Delaney spent the morning working in her home office. She put the finishing touches on an email before standing and stretching. She glanced at her watch. "Damn. I've been in here for hours and it's past lunchtime. Poor Gib's probably starving by now." She shut down her laptop and headed for the kitchen. "Gib?" Not hearing an answer, she stepped into the living room. "Honey?"

She caught a motion out of the corner of her eye and turned toward the sliding glass doors to the patio. "Ah-ha. There you are." She made her way over and opened the doors. "Hi."

Gib turned her head and smiled. "Hey there, beautiful. How's it going?"

"I was going to ask you the same thing." Delaney edged around the wheelchair. She sat in the plastic lawn chair she had recently bought so they could sit outside together in the evenings. "Are you okay?"

"Sure." Gib held up a book that was in her lap. "Been doing a little reading. There's a nice breeze today." The week out of the hospital had returned her normal, tanned coloring and erased the lines of pain around her eyes and mouth. Her light-brown eyes held a sparkle as she grinned at her lover. "Did you get caught up?"

Delaney returned the grin. "Mostly. Are you hungry?"

"I could eat," Gib remarked, as her stomach grumbled its displeasure. "What time is it?"

"Around two. I totally lost track of time. I'm sorry."

Gib maneuvered the chair so that she could see Delaney without twisting. "No worries. I was enjoying the day and didn't think about it. Need some help in the kitchen?"

Delaney stood. "Are you up to a field trip? We could always go surprise Maddy."

"That could be fun." Gib wheeled through the door that Delaney opened. "Thanks." She followed her into the living room. "I'll buy, since you bought dinner the other night."

After gathering her purse and keys, Delaney held open the front door. "Sounds fair to me. But I'm warning you, officer. I'm going to order dessert."

"Mmm. Flan," Gib moaned. She grabbed her wallet from the table near the door. "Would you mind carrying this in your purse for me? I don't seem to have any pockets." She was wearing a pair of sweats with one leg cut off and a navy blue law enforcement tee shirt.

"Sure." Delaney took the black leather wallet. "You trust me with your credit cards?"

Gib laughed as she headed toward the elevator. "I don't have any. Just a debit card. So you're out of luck." Once they were inside the elevator, she took Delaney's hand. "But if I did, yes. I'd trust you completely."

After the doors opened, Delaney pushed Gib into the foyer. She waved at the older woman sitting behind the desk. "Good afternoon, Theresa."

"Good afternoon, Ms. Kavanagh, Ms. Proctor." The concierge met Gib earlier in the week, when the officer had wheeled downstairs to get Delaney's mail. "We've got a good chance for thunderstorms this afternoon, just so's you know."

Gib nodded. "I saw that on the news this morning. Do you think the weatherman got it right this time?"

"I sure hope so. My garden needs it," Theresa lamented. "You two have a nice afternoon."

Delaney held the outside door open for her lover. "You too, Theresa." Once they were on the sidewalk, she patted Gib's shoulder. "Why don't you wait here for me? It'll be easier to get you into the car."

"All right." Gib watched her lover's backside as Delaney walked away. "Shake it like you mean it," she hollered, getting a one-fingered salute in retaliation. The cell phone clipped to the waistband of her sweatpants rang, and she was still laughing when she answered. "Proctor."

"Hey, Gib. How's it hanging?" Roger asked. He was making loud chewing noises, obviously eating.

She rolled her eyes. In her heart, she knew that this call was Roger's way of apologizing for his behavior the other night. "I'm doing pretty well, thanks." The Lexus parked next to the curb and she waved to Delaney.

"Good, good. Hey, I heard a good one in the break room today." He related an extremely nasty joke with two lesbian protagonists. "Get it? In the garden?"

"Roger, I've asked you not to tell me that kind of crap. I don't think it's funny."

"You're a prude, Gib. The coaches who told it thought it was funny. And I know one of them's got to be a dyke. Why don't you tell your girlfriend? I bet she'd appreciate it." Roger smacked as he continued to eat his lunch. "I didn't get to tell you the other night, but you missed a good time at Six Flags. Saw some pretty hot babes in tank tops. Just your speed."

Gib waited while Delaney opened the back door for her. "You know, Roger, just because you're a dog in heat, doesn't mean everyone else is. I've got to go. Bye." She turned her phone off, in case he decided to call back.

"Who was that?" Delaney asked, seeing Gib upset. "Is everything okay?"

"Yeah. Let me get inside and I'll tell you." Gib wheeled to the SUV and flicked on the chair brakes. With Delaney's help, she rose to stand on her good leg and turned to sit on the seat. Using her arms, she pulled herself across the seat until she was sitting behind the driver, with her injured leg stretched out. "Whew. That was a workout."

Delaney loaded the wheelchair into the back and got behind the steering wheel shortly after Gib was settled. "Maybe I should rent a van."

"Nah. How would I get my exercise?" Gib joked. "Don't worry about it. If things go well, maybe I can get a walking cast in a few more weeks. Then I can sit up there with you like a grownup."

"Does that mean you'd have to act like one?"

Gib stuck her tongue out at her lover, who watched her in the rearview mirror.

"You just proved my point," the redhead crowed. As she pulled out of the parking lot, she asked, "Who was it on the phone that upset you?"

"Roger. Usually he only calls me when he wants something, but today he had a dirty lesbian joke he decided to share."

Delaney stopped at a red light and turned her head. "Jackass. I'll show him what a lesbian is capable of. Does he do that often?"

"Not as much as he used to. I asked him to stop, but he thinks he's funny. It's not a big deal." Gib tapped on the headrest. "Green light."

"Thanks." Something had been bothering Delaney since she met the Proctors. "Honey? Can I ask you a question?"

Gib nodded. "Sure."

"Well, after seeing everyone, I couldn't help but wonder. You don't have much in common with anyone in your family, do you?"

"No, not really. Mom doted on Roger constantly, and now lives for his kids. My dad always had these certain expectations for me. I think I disappointed him when I didn't go to law school. He's always told me that I haven't lived up to my potential." Gib looked out the window. "Maybe he's right."

Delaney frowned. "You don't really believe that, do you?"

"Sometimes," was the quiet answer.

"Well, I think he's full of shit."

Gib couldn't help but grin at her lover's anger. "Now you see where my brother gets it."

"Isn't that the damned truth," Delaney muttered. "Do you like what you do?"

"Yeah. I enjoy being outdoors, and I've always wanted to be in law enforcement. I thought it was the best of both worlds."

Delaney pulled into the parking lot of Rodrigo's. "Then don't let a bitter old man ruin it for you."

"Don't worry, I won't."

"Good." Delaney got out of the Lexus, took the wheelchair from the back and helped Gib out. "Let's go pig out. I'm starving." She glanced around. Seeing they were the only ones outside, she leaned down and kissed Gib lightly on the lips. "I love you, Officer Proctor."

Gib brushed her fingers across Delaney's cheek. "I love you, too. Come on, I hear fajitas and flan calling us."

AFTER A LONG, hot day at the park, Gloria had been in the motel room for less than fifteen minutes when there was a knock on the door. Barefoot and with her uniform shirt unbuttoned, she looked through the peep hole. "Damn it."

Another knock. "Gloria?"

"Fuck." Gloria slid the chain off the door and opened it. "Jessica. What do you want?"

"Can I come in?"

Gloria backed away and motioned for her to enter. "What are you doing here?"

"I haven't seen you all week." Still in uniform as well, Jessica stood close to Gloria and ran her fingers down the older woman's bare stomach. "I've missed you." Her hands were grabbed and she frowned. "We never got to finish what we started."

"Jess, no."

Jessica jerked her hands free and stepped away. "But, I thought you liked me."

"I do, Jess. That's why we can't do this." Gloria buttoned her shirt, but didn't tuck it in. "Why don't you sit down?"

With a sultry smile, Jessica stretched out across the bed. She raised her arms over her head. "How's this?"

Gloria closed her eyes and silently prayed for strength. Although her ego was flattered by the attention, her seldom heard from conscience overruled. "That's not exactly what I had in mind." She took a seat in the chair across the room. "What happened last week was a mistake, Jess. We have to see each other every day at work. I don't think getting into a relationship is a good idea."

"But, at the bar," Jessica sniffled, as she rolled to an upright position. "You danced with me." She wrapped her arms around her knees. "You *kissed* me."

"Yeah, I know." Gloria lowered her head. "I wasn't thinking very clearly. We'd both had a lot to drink, and the music, the lights. Well, you know." She sighed and covered her face with her hands.

Jessica got off the bed. "So, you don't love me?"

The blonde's head snapped up. "Love? What the hell gave you that idea?"

"Well, the way you treated me." Jessica sat on the bed. "I talked to Darla, and she said that since you didn't sleep with me, it meant you must love me too much to take advantage of me."

Gloria felt like tearing her hair out. Instead, she moved to sit beside Jessica. "Jess, I do care for you." She put her arm around the younger woman's shoulders. "But as a friend." She softened her voice. "I'm sorry."

Jessica began to cry in earnest as she rested her head on Gloria's upper arm. "You must think I'm the biggest idiot in the world."

"No, not at all." Gloria pulled her into her lap. She stroked the dark head while Jessica continued to sob. "Sssh. It's going to be okay," she murmured.

"But I love you," Jessica bawled, clutching Gloria's shirt. "I love you so much."

Although she felt as if she had been kicked in the stomach, Gloria kept her composure. "No, hon. You don't. All we had was a night of dancing in a dark, smoky bar. That's not enough to fall in love, trust me."

Jessica raised her head and looked at her tearfully. "But I do."

Gloria wiped the younger woman's face with her fingertips. "Can I ask you a question?"

"Uh-huh."

"You said before that you'd never been with a woman. Have you been with a man?" The flush on Jessica's face was all the answer she needed. "That's nothing to be ashamed of."

Jessica lowered her face. "I don't want to be a virgin for the rest of my life."

"You won't," Gloria assured her. "But don't let it be someone you picked up in a bar. Wait for someone special. Preferably closer to your own age." She kissed the top of Jessica's head. "I'd like to be your friend, if that's possible."

"Really?" Jessica sat up and wiped her face with the palms of her hands. "Even with me being a stupid kid?"

Gloria laughed. "I'll give you the kid part. But you're far from stupid." She brushed the hair away from Jessica's eyes. "Would you like to go get something to eat?"

"No, I don't think so." Jessica stood. "I need some time to myself, if that's okay."

"Sure." Gloria watched her walk to the door. "Jess?"

Jessica turned around. "Yeah?"

"It'll get better, I promise."

"I hope so." Jessica lowered her head as she closed the door behind her.

SINCE SHE COULDN'T get her leg wet, Gib sat in the living room watching the news while Delaney took a shower. When the intercom buzzed, she wheeled over and answered. "Hello?"

"Hi, this is the concierge. We have someone down here that's requesting access."

"Who is it?" Gib asked.

The concierge, a young man by the name of Alan, cleared his throat. "Um, she said, 'just tell Laney to let me come up.' I'm sorry, ma'am. She won't give her name."

Gib had a pretty good idea who it was. "I'll be right down. Thanks, Alan." She rolled to the living room and picked up Delaney's keys. It wasn't easy, but she was able to get through the door and to the elevator.

When the elevator door opened into the foyer, Gib's notion was confirmed. Standing next to the concierge desk was a slender, dark-haired woman, who turned toward the elevator. Gib slowly wheeled herself into the foyer. "Thank you for contacting us, Alan."

"Sure, Ms. Proctor. Let me know if I can do anything else." He pointed to the phone and mouthed the word 'police.' He looked concerned when she shook her head.

Chris glared at Gib. "What the hell are you doing here?"

"I think it's obvious," Gib replied. She pointed to a waiting area to their left. "Why don't we sit over there where it's quiet?"

"I want to talk to Laney." Chris followed the wheelchair and plopped onto a black leather loveseat. "I know she's home because I saw her SUV in the parking lot."

Gib rolled closer, but kept her injured leg out of Chris' reach. She locked the brakes out of habit. "I understand you're upset. But you need to move on."

"Upset? Did you know that because of you, I have to do twenty hours of community service? I've been getting up at dawn and picking up garbage beside the road. Fucking garbage!" Chris stood over Gib. "Laney's mine!"

"She's her own person, Chris. And you were given community service because you attacked me. You're lucky they didn't put you in the county jail." Gib sat up taller in the wheelchair, unafraid of the woman who stood over her with her fists clenched. "And just in case you've forgotten, I'll tell you again. I'm a licensed peace officer for the state of Texas. You could have been imprisoned for years in the state penitentiary for your assault on me."

Chris looked as if she was about to explode. "Fuck that!" She grabbed the armrests of the wheelchair and got into Gib's face. "You stole my girlfriend, bitch!"

Gib smiled and took hold of one of Chris' thumbs. She bent it at an unnatural angle, causing the younger woman to howl and drop to her knees beside the wheelchair. "I think I've been pretty nice to you so far, Chris. But if you ever bother Delaney again, I'll make you sorry you were ever born."

"Aaah! Let go of me!" Chris cried.

"I want you to promise to leave us alone. Can you do that?"

Chris slapped at the wheelchair with her free hand. "Stop! Please!" Her head went closer to the ground when Gib put more pressure on her thumb. "Okay! Okay! I promise!"

With a rough shove, Gib released the hold she had on Chris' thumb. She unlocked her brakes and kept on her guard, in case Chris tried anything. "I think you need to leave."

Chris stayed on her knees and cradled her hand to her chest. "What do you think Laney's going to say when she finds out what you did to me?"

"I'd say, 'You'd better be glad it was her, and not me, or you'd be needing a doctor,'" Delaney called out from where she had stepped from the elevator. Dressed in sandals, shorts and a tee shirt, her hair was wet from her shower. She moved to stand behind Gib's chair, where she put her hands on her lover's shoulders. "Are you all right, honey?"

"Yeah. Chris was just leaving. Weren't you?" Gib said, moving the wheelchair closer to the woman on the floor.

Still cradling her hand, Chris got to her feet and backed away from Gib. "I loved you, Laney."

"No, Chris. You wanted to own me. That's not love." Delaney squeezed Gib's shoulders. "I know what love is, *now*. Please go."

Chris looked at the two women for a long moment. She lowered her eyes, and with a slight nod, turned and walked away.

Once Chris had gone, Delaney moved to kneel beside Gib's chair. "When I noticed you had left, I came down to see what was going on. I'm glad I did." She caressed her lover's face. "Are you all right?"

Gib caught her hand and lovingly kissed the palm. "More than all right." At the sound of Alan clearing his throat, she laughed.

Delaney stood and pushed Gib toward the elevators. "Do me a favor, Alan?"

"Sure."

"If that woman comes in again, call the police and report her as a trespasser. Her name is Christine Fannin, and she has no business with us."

He nodded and wrote it down. "I'll pass it along, Ms. Kavanagh. But I think she's learned her lesson. Nice move, Ms. Proctor." He pulled a wooden baseball bat out from under the counter. "I was about to help when you took her down. That was awesome."

Gib chuckled. "Thanks. Glad to know you had my back." She waved as Delaney pushed her into the elevator. "Have a good night, Alan."

"You too."

As they rode the elevator up, Delaney released a heavy sigh.

"Are you okay?" Gib asked. She tried to turn in the chair to see her lover's face.

Delaney patted her shoulder. "I'm disgusted with myself for ever hooking up with her." The elevator door opened and she pushed Gib's chair.

Once they were in the apartment, Gib followed her into the bedroom. "She had to have had some redeeming qualities, at least at one point."

"I thought so, at first." Delaney sat on the bed and took off her sandals. "She was a nice change of pace from my previous girlfriend."

Gib moved closer until she was aligned sideways next to the redhead. She took Delaney's hand and held it gently. "I'm sorry."

Delaney kissed Gib's hand. "Thank you." She looked away. "It's not Chris' fault that I strung her along. I'm such a self-absorbed bitch. I don't know how you can stand to be in the same room with me."

"Dee," Gib tugged on her hand, "look at me." She waited until she had her lover's full attention. "I love you. All of you. And I completely understand staying in a relationship like that. I stuck with Gloria longer than I should, hoping that she'd change. But she didn't. She wanted me to change to fit her ideal, and that wasn't going to happen, either. So we're all guilty of holding on too long. It's not the worst thing in the world. And we all survived. Chris will, too."

"How did you get so smart?" Delaney tearfully asked.

Gib grinned. "I hooked up with a pretty redhead. She seems to bring out the best in me." We she saw the tears trail down her lover's face, she held out her arms. "Come here, sweetheart."

Delaney carefully crawled onto Gib's lap and tucked her head against her shoulder. "I love you so much, Gib. Please don't ever let me hurt you like that."

"As long as we keep talking to each other, that's not going to happen, Dee." Gib kissed her on the forehead. "All you have to do is tell me when you're tired of me."

The laugh that escaped her lips turned into a half-sob. "Oh, god. That will never happen. But I don't think I'd survive if you quit loving me."

Gib used her finger under Delaney's chin to raise her face. Once they were looking into each other's eyes, she said, "You have nothing to worry about, sweetheart. I love you with everything that I am, and that's never going to change." She wiped the tears from the redhead's face. "Do you believe me?"

Delaney stared into those warm, brown eyes and could feel her heart almost burst from the love she received. "I do." She hooked her hand behind Gib's head and pulled it forward, putting everything she had into the kiss. "I love you, too. And I always will."

Other Carrie Carr titles published by Yellow Rose Books

LEX AND AMANDA SERIES

Destiny's Bridge - Rancher Lexington (Lex) Walters pulls young Amanda Cauble from a raging creek and the two women quickly develop a strong bond of friendship. Overcoming severe weather, cattle thieves, and their own fears, their friendship deepens into a strong and lasting love. ISBN: 1-932300-11-2

Faith's Crossing - Lexington Walters and Amanda Cauble withstood raging floods, cattle rustlers and other obstacles to be together...but can they handle Amanda's parents? When Amanda decides to move to Texas for good, she goes back to her parents' home in California to get the rest of her things, taking the rancher with her. ISBN: 1-932300-12-0

Hope's Path - Someone is determined to ruin Lex. Efforts to destroy her ranch lead to attempts on her life. Lex and Amanda desperately try to find out who hates Lex so much that they are willing to ruin the lives of everyone in their path. Can they survive long enough to find out who's responsible? And will their love survive when they find out who it is? ISBN: 1-932300-40-6

Love's Journey - Lex and Amanda embark on a new journey as Lexington rediscovers the love her mother's family has for her, and Amanda begins to build her relationship with her father. Meanwhile, attacks on the two young women grow more violent and deadly as someone tries to tear apart the love they share. ISBN: 978-1-932300-65-9

Strength of the Heart - Lex and Amanda are caught up in the planning of their upcoming nuptials while trying to get the ranch house rebuilt. But an arrest, a brushfire, and the death of someone close to her forces Lex to try and work through feelings of guilt and anger. Is Amanda's love strong enough to help her, or will Lex's own personal demons tear them apart? ISBN: 978-1-932300-81-9

The Way Things Should Be - In this, the sixth novel, Amanda begins to feel her own biological clock ticking while her sister prepares for the birth of her first child. Lex is busy with trying to keep her hands on some newly acquired land, as well trying to get along with a new member of her family. Everything comes to a head, and a tragedy brings pain—and hope—to them all. ISBN: 1-932300-39-2

To Hold Forever - Three years have passed since Lex and Amanda took over the care of Lorrie, their rambunctious niece. Amanda's sister, Jeannie, has fully recovered from her debilitating stroke and returns with her fiancé, ready to start their own family. Attempts to become pregnant have been unsuccessful for Amanda. Meanwhile, a hostile new relative who resents everything about Lex shows up. Add in Lex's brother Hubert getting paroled and an old adversary returning with more than a simple reunion in mind and Lex begins to have doubts about continuing to run the ranch she's worked so hard to build. ISBN: 978-1-932300-21-5

Trust Our Tomorrows - Set six years after To Hold Forever, life at the Rocking W ranch is constantly changing. Lex and Amanda are back, struggling through a drought and trying to raise their two daughters as best they can. Lorrie is now ten and gets into as much trouble as Lex ever did, while six-year old Melanie is content to follow along. When someone from the past returns and asks for an unusual favor, will Lex and Amanda agree? And, considering the favor, can they refuse? ISBN: 978-1-61929-011-2

Piperton

Sam Hendrickson has been traveling around the Southwest for ten years, never staying in one place long enough to call it home. Doing odd jobs to pay for her food and gas, she thinks her life is fine, until fate intervenes. On her way to Dallas to find work for the upcoming winter, her car breaks down in the small town of Piperton. Sam's never concerned herself over what other people think, but the small minds of a West Texas town may be more than she bargained for—especially when she meets Janie Clarke. Janie's always done what's expected of her. But when she becomes acquainted with Sam, she's finally got a reason to rebel.

ISBN 978-1-935053-20-0

Diving Into The Turn

Diving Into the Turn is set in the fast-paced Texas rodeo world. Riding bulls in the rodeo is the only life Shelby Fisher has ever known. She thinks she's happy drifting from place to place in her tiny trailer, engaging in one night stands, and living from one rodeo paycheck to another - until the day she meets barrel racer Rebecca Starrett. Rebecca comes from a solid, middle-class background and owns her horse. She's had money and support that Shelby has never had. Shelby and Rebecca take an instant dislike to each other, but there's something about Rebecca that draws the silent and angry bull rider to her. Suddenly, Shelby's life feels emptier, and she can't figure out why. Gradually, Rebecca attempts to win Shelby over, and a shaky friendship starts to grow into something more.

Against a backdrop of mysterious accidents that happen at the rodeo grounds, their attraction to one another is tested. When Shelby is implicated as the culprit to what's been happening will Rebecca stand by her side?

ISBN 978-1-932300-54-3

Something To Be Thankful For

Randi Meyers is at a crossroads in her life. She's got no girlfriend, bad knees, and her fill of loneliness. The one thing she does have in her favor is a veterinarian job in Fort Worth, Texas, but even that isn't going as well as she hoped. Her supervisor is cold-hearted and dumps long hours of work on her. Even if she did want a girlfriend, she has little time to look.

When a distant uncle dies, Randi returns to her hometown of Woodbridge, Texas, to attend the funeral. During the graveside services, she wanders away from the crowd and is beseeched by a young boy to follow him into the woods to help his injured sister. After coming upon an unconscious woman, the boy disappears. Randi brings the woman to the hospital and finds out that her name is Kay Newcombe.

Randi is intrigued by Kay. Who is this unusual woman? Where did her little brother disappear to? And why does Randi feel compelled to help her? Despite living in different cities, a tentative friendship forms, but Randi is hesitant. Can she trust her newfound friend? How much of her life and feelings can Randi reveal? And what secrets is Kay keeping from her? Together, Randi and Kay must unravel these questions, trust one another, and find the answers in order to protect themselves from outside threats—and discover what they mean to one another.

ISBN 978-1-932300-04-8

Other Yellow Rose Titles You Might Enjoy:

Casa Parisi
by Janet Albert

Lucia Parisi holds the world within her grasp until one tragic afternoon when everything slips through her fingers. In an attempt to re-build her shattered life she moves back home to the Finger Lakes region of central New York State where she opens a winery. On the surface the pieces of her new life are falling into place except for one vital thing...Lucia can't find a way to heal her heart.

French Canadian winemaker, Juliet Renard, is rapidly gaining a reputation as a rising young talent among local winery owners. She's paid her dues and now it is time to leave her current job as an assistant in the hopes of finding a position as a head winemaker.

When Lucia asks a friend if she knows any available winemakers, her friend encourages her to bring Juliet in for an interview. For both women, their meeting marks a major turning point, but for vastly different reasons. Lucia is forced to take a look at what tragedy has done to her and Juliet discovers something about herself that changes her life forever.

ISBN 978-1-61929-015-0

Callie's Dilemma
by Vicki Stevenson

While attending a convention for authors and fans of chick lit, Callie Delaney, closeted reigning queen of mainstream romance, meets Dale Kirby, irresistible fitness instructor for the health club at the hotel that's hosting the event. She also inadvertently walks into the prelude to a murder. Although Callie is unaware of the significance of what she sees, the killer is not, and he embarks on a relentless campaign to eliminate the only witness to his crime.

With help from Dale's LGBT family, the women set out to uncover the motivation for the threats against Callie, identify her mysterious stalker, and ultimately prove him guilty of murder. As a fragile relationship develops between Dale and Callie, they are forced to confront escalating danger and the irresolvable conflict between the demands of Callie's public image and the reality of her personal desire.

ISBN 978-1-61929-003-7

OTHER YELLOW ROSE PUBLICATIONS

Brenda Adcock	Soiled Dove	978-1-935053-35-4
Brenda Adcock	The Sea Hawk	978-1-935053-10-1
Brenda Adcock	The Other Mrs. Champion	978-1-935053-46-0
Janet Albert	Twenty-four Days	978-1-935053-16-3
Janet Albert	A Table for Two	978-1-935053-27-9
Janet Albert	Casa Parisi	978-1-61929-015-0
Georgia Beers	Thy Neighbor's Wife	1-932300-15-5
Georgia Beers	Turning the Page	978-1-932300-71-0
Carrie Brennan	Curve	978-1-932300-41-3
Carrie Carr	Destiny's Bridge	1-932300-11-2
Carrie Carr	Faith's Crossing	1-932300-12-0
Carrie Carr	Hope's Path	1-932300-40-6
Carrie Carr	Love's Journey	978-1-932300-65-9
Carrie Carr	Strength of the Heart	978-1-932300-81-9
Carrie Carr	The Way Things Should Be	978-1-932300-39-0
Carrie Carr	To Hold Forever	978-1-932300-21-5
Carrie Carr	Trust Our Tomorrows	978-1-61929-011-2
Carrie Carr	Piperton	978-1-935053-20-0
Carrie Carr	Something to Be Thankful For	1-932300-04-X
Carrie Carr	Diving Into the Turn	978-1-932300-54-3
Carrie Carr	Heart's Resolve	978-1-61929-051-8
Cronin and Foster	Blue Collar Lesbian Erotica	978-1-935053-01-9
Cronin and Foster	Women in Uniform	978-1-935053-31-6
Pat Cronin	Souls' Rescue	978-1-935053-30-9
Anna Furtado	The Heart's Desire	1-932300-32-5
Anna Furtado	The Heart's Strength	978-1-932300-93-2
Anna Furtado	The Heart's Longing	978-1-935053-26-2
Melissa Good	Eye of the Storm	1-932300-13-9
Melissa Good	Hurricane Watch	978-1-935053-00-2
Melissa Good	Red Sky At Morning	978-1-932300-80-2
Melissa Good	Storm Surge: Book One	978-1-935053-28-6
Melissa Good	Storm Surge: Book Two	978-1-935053-39-2
Melissa Good	Thicker Than Water	1-932300-24-4
Melissa Good	Terrors of the High Seas	1-932300-45-7
Melissa Good	Tropical Storm	978-1-932300-60-4
Melissa Good	Tropical Convergence	978-1-935053-18-7
Regina A. Hanel	Love Another Day	978-1-935053-44-6
Maya Indigal	Until Soon	978-1-932300-31-4
Lori L. Lake	Different Dress	1-932300-08-2
Lori L. Lake	Ricochet In Time	1-932300-17-1
Lori L. Lake	Like Lovers Do	978-1-935053-66-8
K. E. Lane	And, Playing the Role of Herself	978-1-932300-72-7
Helen Macpherson	Love's Redemption	978-1-935053-04-0
J. Y Morgan	Learning To Trust	978-1-932300-59-8
J. Y. Morgan	Download	978-1-932300-88-8
A. K. Naten	Turning Tides	978-1-932300-47-5
Lynne Norris	One Promise	978-1-932300-92-5
Linda S. North	The Dreamer, Her Angel, and the Stars	978-1-935053-45-3
Paula Offutt	Butch Girls Can Fix Anything	978-1-932300-74-1

Surtees and Dunne	True Colours	978-1-932300-529
Surtees and Dunne	Many Roads to Travel	978-1-932300-55-0
Vicki Stevenson	Family Affairs	978-1-932300-97-0
Vicki Stevenson	Family Values	978-1-932300-89-5
Vicki Stevenson	Family Ties	978-1-935053-03-3
Vicki Stevenson	Certain Personal Matters	978-1-935053-06-4
Cate Swannell	Heart's Passage	978-1-932300-09-3
Cate Swannell	No Ocean Deep	978-1-932300-36-9

About the Author

Carrie calls herself a "true Texan." She was born in the Lone Star State in the early sixties and has never lived outside of it. Currently a resident of the Dallas-Fort Worth Metroplex, she lives with her partner of 10+ years whom she legally married in Toronto in September 2003. As a technical school graduate and a quiet introvert, publishing her fiction—lesbian-based books—was something she never expected. She says, "Living on a farm probably influenced me the most because I had to use my imagination for recreation. I made up stories for myself, and my only regret is that I didn't save the ones I had written down and hidden away when I was growing up." Her writing also brought Carrie her greatest joy—her wife, Jan, who wrote her when she posted *Destiny's Bridge* online. They've been together since 1999. She has written eight books in the Lex & Amanda series. Carrie has also published four stand-alone romances. She is currently working on several projects—updates can be found on her website. Carrie's website is: www.CarrieLCarr.com.

VISIT US ONLINE AT
www.regalcrest.biz

At the Regal Crest Website You'll Find

- The latest news about forthcoming titles and new releases
- Our complete backlist of romance, mystery, thriller, adventure, drama, young adult and non-fiction titles
- Information about your favorite authors
- Current bestsellers
- Media tearsheets to print and take with you when you shop
- Which books are also available as eBooks.

Regal Crest print titles are available from all progressive booksellers including numerous sources online. Our distributors are Bella Distribution and Ingram.